I can get throug

weeks without m

myself,

Cassie told herself as s... ...up at the imposing facade of the house.

Suddenly the door flung open and the man who had invaded her thoughts—and her dreams—appeared.

"Thank God," he said, hurrying toward her. "I didn't think you'd ever get here."

"I'm on time," she said.

"It's not that. We're not having a good morning."

Cassie gave the heartstoppingly handsome, harried man a quick once-over. There was a juice stain on his shirt, one of his athletic shoes had come untied. He'd cut himself shaving and his hair was mussed. All this and it was still relatively early in the day.

"A problem with Sasha?" she asked sympathetically, knowing the toddler was thirty-plus pounds of pure energy and motion.

"The worst. She's been crying."

Ryan's emotional distress now added fuel to the fire that was her infatuation. Now he was more than a gorgeous face—he also needed her.

How was she supposed to resist that?

Dear Reader,

This month, Silhouette Special Edition presents an exciting selection of stories about forever love, fanciful weddings—and the warm bonds of family.

Longtime author Gina Wilkins returns to Special Edition with *Her Very Own Family,* which is part of her FAMILY FOUND: SONS & DAUGHTERS series. The Walker and D'Alessandro clans first captivated readers when they were introduced in the author's original Special Edition series, FAMILY FOUND. In this new story, THAT SPECIAL WOMAN! Brynn Larkin's life is about to change when she finds herself being wooed by a drop-dead gorgeous surgeon....

The heroines in these next three books are destined for happiness—or are they? First, Susan Mallery concludes her enchanting series duet, BRIDES OF BRADLEY HOUSE, with a story about a hometown nanny who becomes infatuated with her very own *Dream Groom.* Then the rocky road to love continues with *The Long Way Home* by RITA Award-winning author Cheryl Reavis—a poignant tale about a street-smart gal who finds acceptance where she least expects it. And you won't want to miss the passionate reunion romance in *If I Only Had a... Husband* by Andrea Edwards. This book launches the fun-filled new series, THE BRIDAL CIRCLE, about four long-term friends who discover there's no place like home—to find romance!

Rounding off the month, we have *Accidental Parents* by Jane Toombs—an emotional story about an orphan who draws his new parents together. And a no-strings-attached arrangement goes awry when a newlywed couple becomes truly smitten in *Their Marriage Contract* by Val Daniels.

I hope you enjoy all our selections this month!

Sincerely,

Karen Taylor Richman
Senior Editor

SUSAN MALLERY

DREAM GROOM

Published by Silhouette Books

America's Publisher of Contemporary Romance

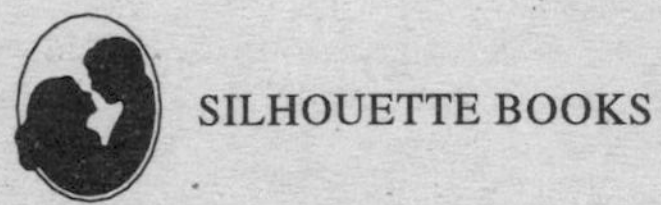

ISBN 0-373-24244-1

DREAM GROOM

This edition published by arrangement with Harlequin Books S.A.

Look us up on-line at: http://www.romance.net

Printed in U.S.A.

Books by Susan Mallery

Silhouette Special Edition

Tender Loving Care #717
More Than Friends #802
A Dad for Billie #834
Cowboy Daddy #898
**The Best Bride* #933
**Marriage on Demand* #939
**Father in Training* #969
The Bodyguard & Ms. Jones #1008
**Part-Time Wife* #1027
Full-Time Father #1042
**Holly and Mistletoe* #1071
**Husband by the Hour* #1099
†*The Girl of His Dreams* #1118
†*The Secret Wife* #1123
†*The Mysterious Stranger* #1130
The Wedding Ring Promise #1190
Prince Charming, M.D. #1209
The Millionaire Bachelor #1220
§*Dream Bride* #1231
§*Dream Groom* #1244

Harlequin Historicals

Justin's Bride #270
‡*Wild West Wife* #419

Silhouette Intimate Moments

Tempting Faith #554
The Only Way Out #646
Surrender in Silk #770

Silhouette Books

36 Hours
The Rancher and the Runaway Bride

‡*Montana Mavericks Weddings*
"Cowgirl Bride"

*Hometown Heartbreakers
†Triple Trouble
§Brides of Bradley House
‡Montana Mavericks: Return to Whitehorn

SUSAN MALLERY

lives in sunny Southern California, where the eccentricities of a writer are considered fairly normal. Her books are both reader favorites and bestsellers, with recent titles appearing on the Waldenbooks bestseller list and the *USA Today* bestseller list. Her 1995 Special Edition novel, *Marriage on Demand,* was awarded Best Special Edition by *Romantic Times Magazine*.

Long ago, on a dark night in a darker forest, angry men chased an old woman through the woods. Some said she was a healer, others called her a witch. They whispered she was blessed…and cursed. The old woman knew each was correct.

When the men were upon her, fists poised to strike, the old woman cried out her fear. Only one in the gathering crowd faced them fearlessly. Only Clarinda Bradley ignored the blows and offered a safe haven.

In return, the old woman thanked her with a legacy. A promise of love, faithful enough to last a lifetime.

She gave Clarinda a special nightgown that, if worn on the night of her twenty-fifth birthday, would reveal to her the face of her one true love. If Clarinda followed the prophecy and married the man, she would know great joy all the rest of her days. If her heirs did likewise, they, too, would be blessed.

Two months later, on the night of her twenty-fifth birthday, Clarinda donned the nightgown and dreamed of a handsome stranger. The next morning he rode into the village. Clarinda married him and, as foretold, knew great joy all of her days. So began the legacy of the Bradley women….

Chapter One

"He hungry," said twenty-six-month-old Sasha solemnly, her large blue eyes darkening with the first hint of worry. "He want peanny butter."

Ryan Lawford glanced from his niece to the "he" in question. Unfortunately the hungry creature wasn't a baby brother or even a pet. It was, instead, a beeping fax machine. Crumpled paper jammed the feed, gooey peanut butter covered the keys, while a sticky spoon sat where the receiver should be. His fingers tightened around the ten-page report that he was supposed to be faxing to Japan in less than twenty minutes.

"Me hungry, too," Sasha announced. "Me want esghetti."

"Sure," Ryan said, his teeth clenched, his blood pressure climbing toward quadruple digits.

Spaghetti—why not? He could just whip some up, maybe a nice salad and some garlic bread. Red wine for himself, milk for his niece. There were only two things standing in his way. Make that three things. First, unless the meal came in a little plastic dish with instructions on how long to heat it in the microwave, he wasn't going to be much help in the kitchen. Second, last time he'd checked, the only food in the refrigerator had been a half-empty jar of peanut butter that the fax machine had just consumed. Third, what the hell was he doing here? Children and their needs were beyond him. Helen and John had been crazy to make him Sasha's guardian.

He spun on his heel. "I'll be right back," he said, in an effort to keep Sasha from following him. Ever since he'd arrived at the end of last week to help with the funeral arrangements for his brother and sister-in-law, the kid had been dogging his every footstep.

Sasha wasn't deterred. Still clutching the jar of peanut butter to her chest, she trailed after him. "Unk Ryan? Go see Mommy?"

The phone in his makeshift office began to ring. He headed toward the back of the house. Sasha hurried to keep up.

"Unk Ryan? Me want M-Mommy."

Her tiny voice cracked. He didn't have to look at her to know that tears had started down her face. In the background the fax machine continued to beep. His phone rang again. As he reached for it, he eyed his computer and figured he would scan the pages and send them out using the modem.

He picked up a receiver and barked "Hello?" into it.

The jar of peanut butter dropped to the floor. Mercifully it didn't break, but now Sasha's tears began in earnest.

"Mommy," she sobbed as if her baby heart were breaking. Ryan grimaced. It probably was. Her chin wobbled, soft dark curls clung to her forehead and her tiny hands twisted together.

One of his staff members began discussing a difficult problem. Ryan couldn't concentrate. "Hold on," he said, set down the receiver and started toward Sasha. Before he could reach her, the doorbell rang.

He clamped his lips down on the curse waiting to slip out. What else could go wrong today? he wondered, then mentally banished the question. He didn't need to tempt fate to try harder to mess things up. Life was complicated enough.

He picked up the phone. "I'll call you back," he said and hung up before hearing a reply, then turned to Sasha. "We'll talk about your problem in a minute. I have to get the door."

The little girl sniffed. "Mommy," she whispered.

Ryan swallowed another oath. How was he supposed to tell a toddler that neither her mother nor her father was going to come home? For the thousandth time in less than a week, he cursed his brother for making him the sole guardian of his only child.

He crossed the wood floor of the foyer and jerked open the front door. "What?" he demanded.

A young woman stood on the porch and smiled at him. "Hi, Mr. Lawford, I'm Cassie Wright. We met after the funeral, but I don't expect you to remember me."

She carried two bags of groceries in her arms, one of which she thrust at him. He had a brief impression of average if pleasant features, chin-length thick, dark hair and big eyes.

"It's been nearly a week," she said as she stepped past him into the house. "I figured you would probably be pretty frustrated about now. Sasha's a sweet kid, but the terrible twos are called that for a reason. I knew you didn't have any kids of your own. Your brother's wife talked about you some when she was at the school. So here I am."

She'd kept moving during her speech, and by the end she was standing in the center of the kitchen, surveying the disaster that had once been a pleasantly decorated room. Dishes and microwave-safe containers filled the sink, along with every inch of counter space. There were spills on the floor from his attempts to feed Sasha at the table, before he'd figured out that she was too small and, despite her claims to the contrary, really *did* need her high chair.

Cassie Wright turned in a slow circle, then faced him. "I brought food, but a cleaning crew would have been a better idea."

Ryan didn't like feeling inadequate, but he was not equipped to take care of a child. "It's been a difficult few days."

"I'm sure." Cassie's friendly expression softened into sympathy. She set her bag of groceries on a chair, which, except for the floor, was about the only free space.

He looked at her, then at the bag in his arms, then back at her. "Who are you and why are you here?"

Before she could answer, he heard a soft shriek from the hallway, followed by the sound of small feet racing toward the kitchen. "Cassie!" Sasha called in obvious pleasure. The toddler barreled into the room as fast as her short legs would allow. She threw herself at the strange woman.

"Hey, Munchkin," Cassie said, crouching down to collect the child in her arms. She straightened and hugged Sasha close to her chest. "I've missed you. How are you doing?"

Sasha gave her a fierce hug, then rested her arm around Cassie's neck and gave her a wide grin. "Me help Unk Ryan."

Cassie looked at him. "Uh-oh. Sasha's heart is in the right place, but her helping tends to create disasters. You have my sympathy."

"The fax machine needs it more. She tried to feed it peanut butter."

Cassie winced. "Did you do that?" she asked Sasha as

she wiped drying tears from her face. "Did you give the fax machine dinner?"

Sasha nodded vigorously. Her dark curls danced with her every movement. "He hungry. Me help."

Ryan stared at the young woman in front of him. She was comfortable with Sasha, and the kid obviously knew her. So he was the only one out of the loop. "Who *are* you?" he asked.

Cassie set Sasha on the floor, then smoothed her palms against her skirt. She took two steps closer to him and held out her right hand. "Sorry. I should have been more clear. I'm Cassie Wright. I'm a teacher at Sasha's preschool. I've known her for about a year, and she's been in my class for the past six months." She met his eyes and her voice softened. "I'm so sorry about your recent loss. I thought you might be having some trouble adjusting to life with a two-year-old, so I came by to see what I could do to help."

The feeling of relief was instant. He gripped her hand as if it were the winning lottery ticket, and he smiled at her. "This is great," he told her. "You're right. I don't have any kids, and I don't have any experience with them. I've been trying to do work, but Sasha follows me everywhere. It's nearly impossible to get anything done."

He released her hand and glanced at his watch. "I need to fax something to Japan. It's already late and I have to scan it into the computer before I can send it. Would you watch her? Just for a couple of minutes. I'll be right back."

He edged out the door as he spoke, then disappeared into the hall before she could refuse him.

His prayers had been answered, he thought as he saved the scanned documents into a file, then prepared to send them via modem. If Cassie whatever-her-last-name-was knew Sasha, she could be a great resource. He hadn't yet figured out what he was going to do about his niece. While he wanted to get back to San Jose as fast as he could, he didn't think that was going to be possible for a while. As if his own company didn't keep him busy enough, he had John and Helen's affairs to settle. He had to decide what to do about the big Victorian house his brother and sister-in-law had recently purchased. There were a thousand details he had neither the time nor the inclination to take care of. Unfortunately, there wasn't anyone else.

Cassie could help him with Sasha. Maybe she could babysit, or recommend someone who could move in full-time. That was what he needed, he decided. A nanny. Like Mary Poppins.

Thirty minutes later, Ryan made his way back to the kitchen. He wasn't ready to face Sasha again, but he knew he couldn't leave her alone with Cassie forever, despite the temptation to do just that.

Sasha sat at her high chair. As she was literally up to her elbows in a red sauce, she'd obviously just finished eating an early dinner. Cassie stood with her back to him as she bent over to fill the dishwasher.

He froze in the doorway. While he'd seen this exact domestic scene a thousand times on television or at the movies, he'd never experienced it in real life. There was something vaguely unsettling about having a woman and a child in his house, he thought. Of course this wasn't his house. If anyone was out of place in this scenario, it was he.

Cassie glanced up and saw him. "Did you get your papers sent?"

"Yeah. Thanks for looking after her."

As he glanced at Sasha, she gave him a big smile, then picked up her plastic-covered cup in both hands and carefully brought it to her lips. She managed to drink without pouring more than a couple of teaspoons. He winced quietly as he remembered the first time he'd given her a glass of milk...in a real glass...about ten ounces. The cold liquid had ended up down the front of her pajamas, over and in his shoes, not to mention coating the kitchen floor. He'd cleaned up as best he could, but his shoes still smelled funny.

Sasha set her cup back on her high chair tray and wiggled in her seat. "Down," she announced.

"Okay, but let's get you cleaned up first," Cassie told her. She dampened a paper towel and wiped off Sasha's face and hands. Then she untied the bib and set the little girl on her feet.

Sasha dashed over to him and wrapped her arms around his right leg and stared up at him. "Esghetti."

"For dinner?" he asked. When she nodded he glanced at Cassie. "I'm amazed. That was her request."

Cassie grinned. "Don't be too impressed. I feed her lunch nearly every day, so I know what she likes. It was just a matter of picking it up at the store."

"I see." He untangled himself from Sasha and walked to the kitchen table. Cassie had cleared off the chairs. He took the closest one and indicated that she should take the one across from his.

She crossed the floor toward the seat, pausing long enough to collect Sasha in her arms and bring her along, too. When Cassie sat down, she settled the toddler in her lap.

There was a moment of silence as he tried to figure out where he should begin. "This has been very difficult," he started, then paused as he wondered if she would think he was talking about his dealings with Sasha or the death of his brother.

"I'm sure it has been," Cassie said, before he could explain himself. "Everything was so sudden. The police came to the school to tell us. I took Sasha home with me those first couple of nights, until you could get here.''

He blinked at her. He'd never given it a thought, he realized. When he'd received the phone call informing him that his brother and sister-in-law had been killed, he'd had to wrap up as much work as possible, then drive over to Bradley. Sasha hadn't been at the house when he'd arrived. Until she'd been placed in his arms, he'd nearly forgotten about her existence.

''The woman who returned her to me was...'' His voice trailed off.

''My aunt Charity,'' Cassie said. ''I was working that day.'' Her gaze settled on his face. ''You didn't visit your brother and his family much.''

He couldn't tell if she was stating a fact or issuing a judgment. ''I run a large company in San Jose,'' he told her, even as he wondered why he cared what a nursery school teacher thought of him. ''I have a lot of responsibilities.''

She wrapped her arms around Sasha and kissed the top of the girl's head. ''This pretty girl looks small on the outside, but she's going to be one of your biggest.''

He didn't want to think about that. A child. ''I'm not parent material,'' he said. ''I don't know what John was thinking.''

''You're family,'' Cassie reminded him, as if that explained everything. ''Who else would he trust with his only daughter?''

''Someone who knew what he was doing. Someone in a position to take care of his child.'' Anyone but him. He didn't want the responsibility. Worse, he didn't know how to handle it. Work was his life and he preferred it that way. If only John had left a dog instead of a kid, things would have been a whole lot easier.

''You'll struggle at first,'' Cassie said, ''but that won't

last long. They look really breakable, but actually children are tough. All they need are attention and love.'' Her mouth curved up in a smile. ''The occasional meal helps, too.''

''What this child needs is a nanny.'' He looked at her. ''Would your aunt be interested in taking on the job for a couple of months? I'll be in Bradley about that long. I have to straighten out John and Helen's affairs while I'm figuring out what to do with her.'' He nodded at Sasha, who was happily playing with a spoon she'd discovered on the table.

''Aunt Charity isn't the nanny type.'' Cassie studied him for several seconds. ''If you're only talking about a couple of months, I could do it.''

His luck wasn't usually that good, he thought. A young woman who worked in a preschool and was familiar with Sasha. What could be better? ''You already have a job,'' he reminded her.

''I know, but because the school year has just started, my boss won't have any trouble getting replacements for me.'' She smiled at what he guessed was his look of confusion. ''The university has a large child development department, and all the students are required to work several hours a week with young children. The preschool always gets many more applicants than we have openings. The students work part-time so it takes two or three of them to make up for one full-time employee, but with the semester just beginning, that isn't a problem.''

Perfect, he thought. ''When can you start?''

She raised her eyebrows. ''You'll want to check my references, first. I don't have a formal résumé with me, but I can leave names and phone numbers with you.''

''Yes, of course.''

Ryan knew he was going about this all wrong. He knew he had to check on Cassie Wright and make sure she would take good care of Sasha. He just didn't have any experience in this sort of thing. "Assuming everything checks out, can you begin in the morning?"

She thought for a moment. "I'll have to make some arrangements with the preschool, but I believe that would be fine. Do you want me to live in, or just work days?"

"Live in. The house is huge and there are several guest rooms. You can have your pick and—"

Sasha threw back her hands and released her spoon. The piece of flatware sailed straight into the air. Cassie reached up and grabbed it. As she did so, he caught a glint of light from her left hand. A ring. He should have known. Of course it wasn't going to be this easy to solve his child-care problems.

"I doubt your husband will appreciate you staying in the house," he said, trying not to sound like a kid who just had his bike stolen. "Perhaps you can fill in during the day until I can find someone to live in."

Sasha wiggled to get down and Cassie helped her to her feet, then smoothed her skirt back in place. She frowned. "I'm not married."

He pointed to her left hand. "You're wearing a ring."

She glanced down, then extended her fingers toward him. "It's not a wedding band, it's a promise ring. I'm engaged to be engaged. Joel and I have been dating for years."

As she looked to be in her early twenties, he doubted it had really been years. A promise ring. He'd never heard of that. He leaned forward to study the slender band. There was a mark in the gold. "It's scratched," he said, pointing to the indentation. "Did you hit it?"

"It's not a scratch, it's a diamond." She sighed. "Well, a diamond chip, rather than a real stone."

He leaned a little closer, then took her hand in his so he could study the diamond chip. It looked like a speck of lint, but if he turned her hand back and forth it *almost* caught the light. Looked like Joel was not much of a spender.

"It's very nice," he told her.

"Thank you."

He released her hand and straightened in his chair. "If you'll leave me the phone number of your employer, I'll call and check the reference. Then I can phone you later and confirm our arrangements for tomorrow."

He sounded so formal, Cassie thought as she resisted the urge to smooth her hands against her thighs. Her fingers were still tingling from where he'd touched her. She didn't want Ryan to guess that she was nervous. Fortunately he couldn't hear the jackhammer pounding of her heart or know that her knees were practically bouncing together like bowling balls.

She'd never seen a man like him before. Of course she wasn't around that many men in the course of her day. Harried fathers picked up their children from the preschool. There was the UPS driver, although the new one was a woman. All in all, except for her sister's husband and Joel, she lived in a world of women.

Ryan was talking about the terms of her employment. He'd named a generous salary that far exceeded what she earned at the preschool, and was explaining that because her employment was for only two months there wouldn't be a benefit package, although he would be happy to reimburse her for her medical coverage during that time.

She nodded her agreement because it was a little hard to talk, what with her throat closing up and all. He was so incredibly sophisticated and worldly. Helen, his sister-in-law, had often talked about Ryan's business, his early success, how driven he was. He'd always been too busy to visit, even after Sasha was born. He was the younger of the two brothers, but older than Cassie, probably by eight or nine years. At least she'd thought ahead enough to wear her best summer dress, even if it was doubtful he'd noticed anything about her other than her ability to care for Sasha.

"I believe that's everything," he said. "If you can write down the phone numbers."

She did as he requested, all the while telling herself not to stare. She didn't usually have problems around people she didn't know, but Ryan was different. Part of the reason was he was so good-looking. He had a strong-jawed face with perfectly chiseled features. She could barely bring herself to glance away from his dark green eyes. It had been hard enough to maintain her equilibrium when they'd met at the memorial service, but at least there she'd had lots of other people to distract her. But here there was only Sasha, and the two-year-old was no match for her dreamboat uncle.

Cassie finished writing out her phone number and handed the paper to Ryan. She knew she was behaving like a schoolgirl with her first crush, maybe because he *was* her first crush. After all, the only boy she'd really noticed was Joel and they'd been dating forever.

"I'll call you this evening," he said in his well-modulated voice.

She had to fight back a sigh. Between his handsome face and his smooth-as-Godiva chocolate voice, he could be on television or in the movies. But instead he was in Bradley and she was going to work for him.

Sasha had wandered into the living room and was watching a video. "I'll just slip out," Cassie said quietly, as they passed in front of the open door. "I don't want to upset her by saying goodbye."

Ryan looked relieved. "The tears are the worst part."

"They pass quickly and then there are lots of smiles."

He didn't look convinced.

When they reached the front door, she thought about risking a second handshake, but the first one had about made her swoon, so instead, she waved. "I'll talk to you soon," she told him and walked quickly down the front stairs.

Fifteen minutes later she let herself in through the back door of her house, an equally large Victorian mansion in the small town of Bradley, California. Unlike the house Ryan's brother had bought three years before, this one had been in the family since it was built in the late 1800s.

Cassie made her way up to her room without encountering her aunt. Normally she loved to talk with Aunt Charity, but for once, she needed to be alone.

When she reached her bedroom, she moved to the window seat and sat down on the thick cushion. It was too dark to see the well-manicured backyard, but she wasn't staring out the window for the view. She didn't see the lace curtains that matched her bedspread, or her own reflection in the glass. Instead she saw Ryan Lawford, tall, broad, handsome. The perfect hero.

She drew in a deep breath, then released it as a sigh. If only someone like him could be interested in someone like her. The thought made her smile. She might be the romantic dreamer in the family, but she wasn't a fool. She was too young, too unsophisticated, too ordinary. Men like him fell in love with fashion models, or at the very least with beautiful, charming women like her sister, Chloe. Besides, she had Joel. While it was fun to fantasize about Ryan, she knew it was just a game. She loved Joel as much today as she had on their first date, nine years before.

Enough daydreaming, she thought. She should really start packing. After all, she knew exactly what Ryan was going to hear when he checked her references. Actually what she needed to do was call her boss and tell her that she was taking a two-month leave of absence from her job. Mary, her boss, wouldn't be surprised. They'd discussed Ryan's situation several times since they'd heard the news about Sasha's parents' death. They'd known that a single man was going to need help learning to deal with a toddler. Mary had been the one to encourage Cassie to visit him in the first place.

Cassie made the call and laughed when Mary told her that Ryan had already checked her out. "I gave you a glowing report," Mary said. "He's never going to want to let you go."

"I doubt that," Cassie said.

They chatted for a few more minutes, then hung up. Cassie crossed to her closet and pulled out her suitcase. She would take a few things in the morning, then come back for more clothes as she needed them.

As she reached for her makeup bag on the closet shelf, her hand bumped against a flat box. She caught it before it could tumble to the ground, then carried it over to her bed.

She didn't have to open the box to know what was inside, but she lifted the lid anyway, then stared at the familiar ivory nightgown. It was beautiful and old-fashioned with long sleeves and a high neck. Lace edged the cuffs and collar. She rubbed her fingers against the soft, aged fabric. Six weeks, she thought. Six weeks until she knew if the legend would come true for her.

She placed the lid back on the box and forced away the twinge of longing that threatened to overcome her. All she'd ever wanted was to belong, to have a place in the family history. The town of Bradley had been established by Cassie's mother's family. Bradley was Cassie's middle name, but only by law. Not by birth.

She reminded herself that being adopted meant that she'd been chosen. They'd really wanted her. But the familiar words didn't help very much. Chloe was their child by blood—they'd made that clear when they'd left her the family house in their will. Cassie's inheritance had matched in money, but not in legacy.

"Maybe with the nightgown," she whispered to herself, wishing it could be true for her, but fearing she wanted the impossible.

Legend had it that a family ancestor had saved an old gypsy woman from being stoned to death several hundred years ago. In gratitude, the women of the Bradley family had been given a nightgown said to possess magic powers. If they wore it on the night of their twenty-fifth birthday, they would dream of the man they were going to marry. If they married him they were guaranteed great happiness for all their days.

Nearly five months before, Chloe had worn the nightgown and dreamed of a handsome stranger. She'd met him the next day and they'd fallen in love. Cassie desperately wanted the nightgown to be magic for her, too.

She twisted the promise ring on her finger. Her dreams weren't fair to Joel, but he swore he didn't mind. They'd talked about the nightgown several times. She'd told him that she didn't want to get engaged until after her twenty-fifth birthday, now just six weeks away. He always told her he wasn't in any hurry, that he knew she was going to dream about him and waiting was just fine.

Cassie told herself she should be grateful. Not many men would be so patient. But sometimes she got tired of his patience and his willingness to wait. She wanted to be swept away by passion. She wanted to be overwhelmed. She wanted to feel the magic.

"Not tonight," she told herself as she returned the nightgown to the closet. The good news was that in the morning she was going to move in with an incredibly handsome man who made her whole body tingle just by being in the same room with her. The fact that he barely knew she was alive was a small detail, something she would deal with another time.

Chapter Two

Cassie pulled into the driveway of the Lawford house at exactly 8:25 the next morning. She assumed that Ryan would expect promptness on her part and she'd promised to arrive by 8:30. After parking her car to the left of the garage, she popped the trunk and pulled out her suitcase, along with a bag of toys she'd borrowed from the preschool. She'd stopped by there on her way over to pick up a few of Sasha's favorites.

I can do this, she told herself as she stared up at the imposing facade of the house. I can get through the next several weeks without making a fool of myself.

Cassie smiled. Of course she *could* get through her period of temporary employment without doing something completely humiliating. The real question was *would* she? She started up the walkway. She didn't really have a choice in the matter. She'd said she would help and she would. The fact that Ryan made her want to hyperventilate when they were in the same room was something she was going to have to deal with on her own time.

She was still ten feet from the door when it was flung open and the man who had haunted her thoughts, and humiliatingly enough, her dreams for the past fourteen or so hours, appeared on the porch.

"Thank God," he said, hurrying toward her and taking her suitcase. "I didn't think you'd ever get here."

She glanced at her watch. "I'm on time."

"I know. It's not that." He hesitated before stepping back into the house, as if he were an escaped soul being forced to return to hell. "We're not having a good morning."

Cassie gave him a quick once-over to check out his appearance. The poor man did look a little harried. There was a juice stain on his light blue shirt, one of his athletic shoes had come untied. He'd cut himself shaving and his hair was mussed. All this and it was still relatively early in the day.

"A problem with Sasha?" she asked sympathetically, knowing the toddler was thirty-plus pounds of pure energy and motion.

He closed the door behind her and set down her suitcase. "The worst. She's been crying."

Cassie had to bite her lower lip to keep from laughing. While she was sorry that Sasha was having a tough start to her day, Ryan had uttered the statement with all the solemnity and worry of a man talking about flood, famine and pestilence.

"It happens," Cassie said, working hard to keep her expression serious.

"But how do you make it stop?" He ran his hand through his hair and shook his head. "I'm completely at a loss. She looks at me with those big tears rolling down her face and I panic. I've told her I'll give her anything she wants if she just stops crying."

"You might want to rethink that philosophy," Cassie said. "It could get expensive in years to come. Plus it's never a good idea to give away power in the parent/child relationship. They're going to learn fifty different ways to play you as it is. Trust me on this."

His green eyes darkened. "She's asking for her mother."

Cassie's good humor faded. "I'm not surprised. This is a difficult time for both of you."

The previous day she'd seen Ryan as a cool, sophisticated businessman, but now, standing in the foyer of his late brother's house, he just looked confused. "What am I supposed to say?" he asked. "How do I tell her that her mother isn't coming home and I'm all she's got?" His mouth twisted. "They screwed up big time leaving that kid to me."

"No, they didn't. If leaving her to you had been a mistake, you wouldn't be worried about her feelings. You'd just be going on about your day and not giving her another thought."

His gaze locked with hers. "Then I'm the biggest bastard in town because that's exactly what I want to do."

She read the pain in his face, the questions. Having kids around could be difficult under the best of circumstances, but Ryan didn't even have the advantage of experience. He and Sasha were strangers.

"It doesn't matter what you *want* to do," she said quietly. "We all have thoughts we're not proud of. Fortunately we're judged on our actions, not our fantasies."

He didn't look convinced. "Will she get over losing her parents?"

Interesting question, Cassie thought. "Yes, but not in the way you think. She'll eventually stop asking for them. We can try to explain what happened in simple terms and she'll accept it. But she'll always carry an empty space around inside of her. She'll always wonder how it would have been different if her parents had lived."

"You sound like you know what you're talking about."

"I do. I'm adopted. It comes with the territory." She forced a lightness into her voice. "Everything will be fine. You'll see. Look at how great I turned out."

His gaze lingered on her face. "Thanks for listening. I don't usually dump on relative strangers."

She had a feeling he didn't talk about his emotions with anyone, but she didn't say that. "No problem. The advice is worth about what you paid for it."

"No, it's worth a lot more than that." He motioned to the family room off to the right. "She's watching a video. What did parents do before VCRs?"

"I have no idea."

"Thank God for technology." He picked up her suitcase. "I'll take this up to your room. I've put you across the hall from Sasha. I hope that's all right. The room is pretty big and it has its own bathroom. Everything is clean. From what I can figure out, a cleaning service comes through about once a week."

"I'm sure the room is fine," she said, as he headed for the family room. She wished there was a way to prolong their conversation. Ryan's confession of his feelings had only added fuel to the fire that was her infatuation. After all, now he was more than a pretty face—he was also emotionally tortured. How was she supposed to resist that? It was just like a scene out of *Pride and Prejudice,* she thought dreamily as she walked into the family room. Ryan was Darcy, proud and standoffish. She was plucky Elizabeth. In time he would realize that she was the—

"Cassie!" Sasha shrieked in delight when she saw her. The toddler grinned, then pointed at the television. "Toons."

"I know. Are they fun?"

Sasha nodded, her short curls flying up and down with the movement of her head. Cassie could see the lingering trace of tears on the child's face and resisted the urge to pull her close and hug her. There was no point in upsetting the little girl's happy mood. There would be plenty of tears later for her to cuddle away.

She settled on the floor next to Sasha and listened to her chatter about the video. While the fact that Ryan was handsome and sophisticated added a little spark to her temporary job, she knew she would have taken it even if he'd been an old man, or even a woman. Because no matter how she daydreamed about her boss, the reality was she'd committed herself to Joel. Even more important than that, Sasha needed her to help her through this difficult adjustment. Cassie had a big heart and there was more than enough room for one little girl to slip inside.

Ryan had gotten so used to the noise drifting in from different parts of the house that he wasn't sure at first what had broken his concentration. Then he realized it was the silence. He leaned back in his chair and turned to stare out the window at the well-manicured grounds around the Victorian house.

"Peace and quiet," he breathed with something close to awe. It was a sound he hadn't heard much of since Sasha had returned home after the funeral last week, especially not during the day. This was something else he had to thank Cassie for.

He'd gotten more work done in the past—he glanced at his watch—five hours, than in the previous five days. He didn't mind the sound of running feet or the bursts of laughter, the slamming doors or the clatter of toys falling somewhere in the house. None of that bothered him, mostly because his office door was closed and he knew that as long as Cassie was around, no pip-squeak with big eyes was going to come interrupt him. Until this moment, he'd never really appreciated the sound of silence.

He drew in a deep breath, reveling in the freedom of not being completely responsible for Sasha. Someone else would take care of feeding her and dealing with her tantrums and her tears. If he could keep full-time help around, the kid might not be so bad.

There was a light knock at his door. For a second he panicked, then he realized that Sasha was not one to ask politely for entrance. Instead she seemed to feel that the entire world existed for her pleasure.

"Come in," he called.

Cassie opened the door and stepped into his office. "Hi, do you have a minute? I need to talk to you about a couple of things."

"Sure. Please, have a seat."

He motioned her to the chair that sat on the opposite side of his desk. As she crossed the room, he took in her appearance. Yesterday he vaguely recalled that she'd worn a dress when she brought over the food. Today she was in jeans and a long-sleeved green T-shirt. She was of average height, maybe five-five or five-six, with short dark hair and a pleasant face. If he'd seen her on the street, he wouldn't have bothered looking at her a second time, but here in his brother's house, taking care of his brother's child, Ryan thought she was an angel.

"Is everything all right?" he asked, suddenly nervous that she was having second thoughts about the job. "If you need any supplies or want me to buy anything, I'll be happy to take care of it. Just say the word."

She smiled and held up a hand to stop him. "It's okay,

Ryan, you don't have to offer me the world. I promise not to cry, or quit.''

''Good.'' He rested his hands on his desk. ''Then what can I do for you?''

''I have a couple of questions. I just put Sasha down for her nap. She resisted me a little, but fell right asleep as soon as I got her quiet. Has she been sleeping okay?''

He stared at her blankly. ''Nap? The kid is supposed to take naps?'' He thought about the long afternoons when his niece had gotten more and more cranky. ''No wonder she was difficult,'' he muttered more to himself than Cassie. ''Shouldn't children come with instructions or something? How are people supposed to know this sort of thing?''

''They learn by doing,'' Cassie said with a straight face, although he caught the slight quivering at the corner of her mouth.

''You're laughing at me. You work in a preschool, you're around children all the time. I've never been around them. Not since I was one.''

He thought about his childhood, how his mother had been always pushing him to make the most of his time. He'd been the younger of the two brothers and there hadn't been many other children in their neighborhood. Now that he thought about it, except for school and his brother, he'd never been around kids.

''I swear I'm not laughing,'' Cassie said. ''You're right, I do have more experience. I have a degree in child development. I'm sure if you put me into your world of business and computers, I would be just as uncomfortable. And to answer your question, yes, Sasha still needs a nap. At the school all the children have to rest for at least half an hour every afternoon.'' Noticing his blank look, she continued her explanation. ''The littler ones like her have a separate room and they generally sleep for at least an hour. She'll still need a good night's sleep, but the nap will make her easier to deal with in the late afternoon and early evening.''

He grabbed a notepad and scrawled the word *nap*. He couldn't imagine how many other things he'd been doing wrong. ''What else?'' he asked.

Cassie wrinkled her nose. ''I know that Sasha's your niece and that you need to spend time getting to know each other. However, I wondered how you would feel about her going to the preschool a few mornings a week.''

He didn't say anything because all he could focus on was the sense of relief, followed by a flash of guilt. He knew it was wrong not to want to take responsibility for Sasha. He supposed he must have a defect in his character or something because a normal, caring uncle would be thrilled to take charge of his family. But Ryan just wanted to pack up and head back to San Jose. He wasn't proud to admit it but, given his choice, he would dump Sasha with Cassie indefinitely. However, no one was offering him that as an option.

''I know what you're thinking,'' Cassie said quickly, as if she was afraid he was going to protest. ''It seems a little soon.''

''Actually, that wasn't what I was thinking,'' he admitted.

''Good. I believe that what will help Sasha the most is to get back into her old routine. She needs her life to return to normal as much as it can. She has friends at the preschool, other teachers whom she really likes. I think a couple of hours three or four days a week will make her feel more secure.''

''That sounds fine,'' he told her. ''You're the expert.''

''You're her family. I don't want to interfere.''

He leaned forward. ''Cassie, until last week, I'd never seen her. I don't know anything about raising a child. To be honest, this was not part of my game plan, but Helen didn't have any family and John only had me, so the buck stops here. I would appreciate any suggestions or thoughts you might have on the best way to handle any situation with Sasha.''

''All right. Thank you for your candor.''

Dark eyes regarded him appraisingly. He wondered what she was thinking about him. No doubt she found him highly lacking in paternal skills and feelings.

''How has she been eating?'' Cassie asked. ''I didn't notice a problem at dinner last night, or at lunch today.''

She might as well have asked his opinion on the viability of a Mars colony in the next twenty years. ''I have no idea how she's eating,'' he said wryly. ''Sometimes she gets the food in her mouth, and sometimes she's more interested in getting it on me and everything around her.''

''Oh.'' Cassie smiled. ''You're right. You wouldn't know what is normal and what isn't. I'll watch things and let you know.'' She paused. ''What about at night? Has she been having nightmares?''

He thought about the past few nights. ''I think so,'' he told her. ''Sometimes she cries out. I've had to go in and rock her a couple of times. She just curls up in my arms and cries.''

He pushed those memories away. He didn't want to have to think about that.

''Are you surprised?'' Cassie asked.

''No. I guess not. I wish this hadn't happened.''

''Give her time,'' she said. ''The same time you're going to need. I suspect her pain will come in waves, then disappear for a while. She'll probably make up stories about her parents to comfort herself. A lot of children do that when they've suffered this kind of loss.''

''Is that what you did?'' he asked, then wondered if the question was inappropriate. But, he reminded himself, she'd been the one who had told him she was adopted.

"I didn't make up stories because I didn't have anything to remind me of my birth parents. Sasha will have photos, and you'll talk about them. I don't think she's going to have memories, though. She's pretty young." She shifted in her chair and tucked her hair behind her ears. "I grew up knowing I'd been adopted, just as Sasha is going to know she lost her parents. I was always grateful that the Wright family had wanted me in their life. Sasha is going to be pleased to have her uncle Ryan to look after her."

He didn't know about the latter, but he nodded as if he did.

"You don't believe me," she said.

Her perception startled him. "I didn't know you were a mind reader as well as being a genius when it came to kids."

"I'm not, but it's obvious you're uncomfortable with Sasha. You're feeling out of place, so the rest of it makes sense. It's going to be okay, Ryan. In time you'll be as thrilled to have her around as she is to have you around. Sometimes the family we have to earn can mean more than the family we're given." A warm glow filled her eyes. "My sister and my aunt are all I have left of my family and both are precious to me. Chloe, my sister, has always been there, but Aunt Charity is a relatively new addition. I treasure her all the more for being an unexpected bonus in my life." She flashed him another smile. "You're going to have to trust me on this."

"I guess you're right."

Her gaze dropped from him to his desk. "I see you have a lot of work to do, so I'll leave you to it. Thanks for taking the time to talk with me."

"You're welcome."

She rose to her feet and quickly walked out of the room. Ryan stared after her until the door closed and he was again alone, then he turned his chair and stared out at the unfamiliar view of manicured lawn and trimmed hedges.

He'd never met anyone like Cassie. There were some who would say that her views of family were old-fashioned. Actually, he would be one of the first people in line to say that, but he was starting to wonder if maybe he was the one out of step. Just because everyone he knew, including himself, was driven by career rather than a personal life didn't mean it was right.

He grimaced. "Who are you trying to kid?" he asked aloud. Yeah, family had its place, but everyone knew that getting ahead was the most important thing in the world. His own mother had spent her life dedicated to that philosophy.

He remembered all the times after he'd finally found success, when he'd wanted to give his mother something nice. Even though both of her sons had been secure in their careers and anxious for her to take it easy, she'd insisted on working two jobs, taking cash from her employers instead of vacation time. She'd always turned down their offers of nice clothes or a better house, urging them instead to invest the money. She'd been poor and hard-working for too long to believe it was okay to accept a "freebie" from anyone…even her children.

Now, when he thought about those years, he felt sad. She'd died without ever once taking time for herself, or time to enjoy all she'd earned. Her entire life had been a quest to have enough, and once she had enough, to have more.

Somewhere between her world and Cassie's lay what was normal. At least in his opinion. But for now, he was weeks behind on his work and with full-time help to take care of Sasha, his days could finally return to something close to productive.

Callie and Jake moved closer to the crib. "What do you think is in there?" Callie asked, her little pink nose all wrin-

kled and her white whiskers quivering.

"I don't know," Jake answered as he put first one paw up on the edge of the mattress, then the other as he tried to see. "It makes a lot of noise and it smells funny. I'm scared."

The calico cat and the marmalade cat looked at each other. Something strange was going on in their house and they weren't sure they liked it.

Cassie stopped reading out loud and pointed to the pictures in the children's storybook. "Can you see the kitties?" she asked Sasha.

The toddler cuddled against her as they moved back and forth in the rocking chair in Sasha's room.

"Cat!" Sasha announced proudly as she pointed to the color drawing of the two cats cautiously investigating the new crib in their home.

"That's right. Two cats. The calico one is Callie. She's a girl cat. The orange cat is Jake. He's her brother."

"Cat!" Sasha said again.

"Two cats. Can you say two?"

"Two!"

"Very good."

Cassie kissed the top of the little girl's head and inhaled the baby talc scent of her. After dinner she'd given Sasha a bath, and now they were reading a story before bedtime. As far as first days went, it had been successful. At least in her eyes.

Sasha stretched and yawned, then pointed at the book. "Read," she ordered. "Read cat story."

So Cassie read about the two kitties who were scared of the stranger in their house. How they didn't like the noises or the smells, but when they saw the baby for the first time, they got a warm feeling in their chest that made them purr.

And how when the neighbor's dog got inside by accident, they both stood up to the larger creature and protected the baby. The last picture showed the infant on its mother's lap with both cats curled up next to her, ever watchful over their new charge.

"The end," she said, and closed the book. "Time for bed."

"Gen…read story gen."

Cassie put the book down and carried Sasha to her crib. "Not *again.* Not tonight. You have to sleep." She set her on the mattress, then pulled up the blanket and kissed her cheek. "Night, muffin. Sleep well. I'll see you in the morning."

Heavy-lidded blue eyes blinked slowly. "Read peas. Not tired."

Cassie chuckled. "Liar. You're exhausted. You're going to be asleep in less than two minutes."

The sound of murmured conversation carried to Ryan as he stood in the shadowy darkness of the hall. He told himself he should go in and say good-night to his niece. Maybe pat her shoulder or something. But the thought made him nervous. He wasn't good at all the parenting stuff. Cassie was obviously a capable woman and Sasha was better off in her care.

So instead of joining them, he walked to his office and closed the door. But for once the silence and solitude didn't invigorate him, and the thought of working didn't inspire him. For the first time in a long time, he wanted something more than his computer and some time in which to concentrate.

It was that damn kid, he thought resentfully. She was going to change everything and he didn't like it. No wonder he felt unsettled.

He sure could relate to those cats in that dumb story. He

didn't like the smells and the noise either. But when he looked at Sasha *he* didn't want to purr…he wanted to run.

He wasn't very proud of himself these days, but he didn't know how to change. Worse, he wasn't sure he wanted to change.

He turned and looked at the portrait hanging over the fireplace in the makeshift office. It showed a laughing couple holding their baby daughter close. It had been done about a year before, when Sasha had been about a year old.

Ryan took in the man's features, which were so similar to his own. His throat tightened. "Dammit, John, what do you want from me?"

Of course there wasn't any answer. He hadn't been expecting one.

"I wish…" he started, then his voice trailed off. He coughed to clear his throat. "I wish you hadn't died. I miss you."

Then, because he was a busy man who didn't have time for all the emotional nonsense in his life, he turned his back on the portrait and settled down in front of his computer.

Chapter Three

"Me help," Sasha informed Cassie as she banged the wooden spoon on the inside of the pot.

"I know," Cassie said and smiled down at the toddler sitting by the kitchen table. "You're a big girl and you help me a lot."

The praise earned her a big grin. Sasha was such a sweet child, she thought as she turned back to the stove and checked on the meat loaf. A glance at the timer told her the main course still had about forty minutes to cook. Time for her to get started on the potatoes.

She collected a half dozen and began peeling them. Sasha sang tunelessly in an effort to accompany herself on her pot banging. Cassie wondered how far the noise would travel in the big house and if Ryan was having trouble concentrating.

This was her third day working for him, taking care of his niece. They'd all settled into a routine fairly quickly. She took care of Sasha while Ryan hid out in his office. He made occasional appearances, but most of them occurred after the toddler was in bed. Still, despite his lack of participation in the day-to-day events, Cassie knew he was in the house with her. There was something oddly domestic about the arrangement. While she liked it, the situation also made her a little nervous.

On occasion, she allowed herself to imagine everything was real. That this was her home, Sasha her child. By default, of course, Ryan was the adoring husband and father. It was like being a kid again and playing house, she thought. Only this time she couldn't walk away if she got tired or wanted to play something else. There was also the added twist of hormones. Hers were still deeply infatuated with Ryan.

The mental image of microscopic hormone-filled cells swaying in time with some love song from the fifties caused her to chuckle out loud.

''What's so funny?''

The unexpected male voice made her jump. Cassie spun and saw Ryan standing in the doorway to the kitchen. He propped one shoulder against the door frame and crossed his arms over his chest. As usual, he wore jeans and a long-sleeved shirt rolled up to the elbows. Today that shirt was blue.

There was something so incredibly masculine about him. While she knew in her head that Joel was also male, he seemed to have nothing in common with Ryan. It was as if the two men were two completely different species.

''I, um, was just thinking about some things,'' she said when he continued to look at her expectantly. She could feel a flush heating her cheeks and she hoped that if he noticed, he would assume it was from the oven or the exertion of cooking.

''I see.''

She couldn't tell if he was letting her off the hook because he was being polite or because he had figured out what had been on her mind and he didn't want to talk about it. Please God, let it be the former.

"Unk Ryan!" Sasha waved her wooden spoon in the air. "Me help."

"You're like the drum major for a marching band," he said. "I'm sure Cassie appreciates you setting the beat."

Sasha frowned in confusion, returned to her pot and began banging against the side and singing. Ryan winced at the noise, then moved into the kitchen.

"What are you cooking?" he asked, raising his voice slightly to be heard over the noise.

"There's a meat loaf in the oven. I'm going to make mashed potatoes and green beans." Cassie paused, then lowered her voice as Sasha got caught up in the play of light on the pot lid and stopped banging. "I never thought to ask what you liked to eat. I generally fix simple things like this or spaghetti. Roast chicken, that sort of stuff. But if you have a preference, I can see what I can do."

He tucked his hands into his jeans pockets and looked at her. "You're not here to cook for me. You're Sasha's nanny." He glanced around the kitchen. "I should have hired someone to take care of meals. I never thought about it."

"It's all right. I don't mind. In fact, I sort of like cooking."

His green-eyed gaze settled on her face. "Practice?"

His features were strong and so perfectly proportioned, she thought as she stared back. She'd never met a man with such gorgeous eyes before and she found that she really liked how they looked. He didn't smile much, but when he did she could feel it all the way down to her toes. And his voice. Smooth and low, his voice belonged on the radio, or maybe recording books on tape.

"Cassie?"

"Huh? Oh, um, practice." That had been the last thing he'd said, right? At least she thought so. "Practice for what?"

He pointed to her left hand. "When you get married. I was asking if you were seeing what all that would be like. This is a great simulation."

Yeah, she thought dreamily, except they weren't simulating the good parts.

"I hadn't thought of it that way," she forced herself to say, because he seemed to expect a response from her.

"You're a natural. Your boyfriend is a lucky guy." He smiled.

On cue, her toes curled, her stomach dove for her knees and her mouth went dry. The man had a smile that could change carbon into diamonds. Boyfriend, she thought vaguely. Oh, yeah, Joel.

Joel! Yikes, what was she doing? She was practically an engaged woman. Cassie stiffened her spine and forced away all warm and yummy thoughts about her employer. She was wasting her time daydreaming. He was not for her. The man was successful, probably rich and definitely older by at least seven or eight years. She didn't usually act like this. What was wrong with her? She forced her attention back to the potato she was supposed to be peeling.

"Thanks," she said and was proud when her voice came out sounding completely normal. "I'll tell him you said that the next time he and I are together."

"You do that."

"Unk Ryan, up!"

Sasha had abandoned her pots and spoon and now stood

in front of her uncle. She raised her arms toward him. "Up," she repeated.

"What does she want?" Ryan asked.

"Just what you think she does," Cassie answered, not sure how it was possible to misinterpret the toddler's request. "She wants you to pick her up and hold her."

"That's what I was afraid of."

He mumbled more than spoke the comment as he bent over and reached for his niece. Sasha smiled broadly as he picked her up and held her in front of him. But when he didn't move her close to his body, but instead kept her nearly at arm's length, her smile faded.

Cassie dropped the knife and potato onto the counter, then moved next to him. "You've got to hold her so she feels safe," she told him. "Sasha wants to snuggle. Rest her on your hip."

She put her hands on the toddler's waist and supported her while Ryan awkwardly shifted the child to his left. Only he didn't have the same naturally curved hips that women had, Cassie realized a half second later as Sasha started to slide down.

"Wrap one arm around her waist and pull her to your chest. She can put her arms around your neck."

She stepped back to give them room to maneuver, but it was too late. Sasha struggled to break free of him. "Down," she said forcefully.

Ryan set her on her feet and shifted awkwardly. "I'm not around kids much."

"It will get easier," Cassie assured him, hoping she was telling the truth.

Sasha stared at her uncle with a hurt look of betrayal on her face. Tears were only a couple of seconds away, Cassie realized and moved to the silverware drawer.

"Can you help me set the table?" she asked, then handed

the little girl three spoons. ‘‘Will you please put these on the table?’’

Sasha sniffed twice, then took the spoons and carried them over to the table. She pushed them up onto the wooden surface, then took one back and returned her attention to her uncle.

‘‘I’m not like you,’’ Ryan said, barely noticing the child. ‘‘I don’t have any natural ability in this arena.’’

Sasha carried the spoon over to her uncle. She thrust it toward him. He glanced down at her, then at Cassie. When she nodded encouragingly, he took the spoon and patted the top of Sasha’s head. She beamed.

It was sad, Cassie thought as she watched them. If only Ryan had spent a little time in his niece’s company, he wouldn’t be feeling so out of place now. But he hadn’t and they were both paying the price. Every situation seemed so forced between them. She wished there was a way to make it easier…for both of them. The only solution was for them to spend more time together, but Ryan didn’t seem willing to pursue that option. He passed through their day like a ship’s captain checking briefly on the passengers before returning to more important duties.

‘‘Be back,’’ Sasha said, then trotted out of the room.

‘‘Was that a request or information?’’ Ryan asked.

‘‘I think it was information.’’

Cassie finished peeling the potatoes. She sliced them, then dropped them into the pot and set it on the stove.

‘‘Do you want me to finish setting the table?’’ he asked. ‘‘You can probably trust me with the forks and knives.’’

‘‘Sure,’’ she told him. ‘‘Thanks.’’

While he pulled out napkins and place mats, she went to work on the green beans. After a couple of minutes of silence, she began trying to think of something clever to say. When she failed on witty, she went with the obvious.

"How are you adjusting to working here?" she asked.

"I'm doing better." He set out two place mats, then collected Sasha's high chair from the corner and brought it over to the table. "I can do nearly everything I need to via conference call or through the modem. I might have to take a couple of trips back to San Jose, but they would be pretty short."

Sasha raced into the kitchen and handed Ryan one of her dolls. He stared at it for a couple of seconds, then finally took it from her.

"Thank you," he said.

Sasha grinned and raced out again.

"What am I supposed to do with this?" he asked.

"Just hold it. She'll be back shortly and it will hurt her feelings if you've put it down."

"Great." He looked at the doll. "I'm not much into redheads."

"Maybe you should let her know," Cassie said. But what she'd wanted to ask instead was how he felt about brunettes. Ah, she had it bad, she thought with resignation. But at least she would probably get over him just as quickly. Crushes didn't usually last...at least she didn't think they did. She didn't have any personal experience with the subject. Maybe she should phone her sister and get some advice.

Sasha returned to the kitchen and skittered to a stop in front of Ryan. This time she held out a battered, flop-eared bunny.

"You are too kind," he said.

Sasha giggled, clapped her hands together and made another mad dash out of the room.

"Looks like she's going to empty her toy box just for your pleasure," Cassie said. "You might want to get comfortable."

The toddler returned with a book. This time, instead of

just thanking her, Ryan reached into his pocket and offered her a penny.

Her rosebud-shaped mouth fell open as her eyes widened. "Money," she said with all the reverence of clergy addressing God. She held it out to Cassie.

"Wow. Look at what you've got."

Sasha clutched it to her chest as she ran out of the room.

"You've made a friend now," Cassie told Ryan.

"I wasn't sure she would know what it was."

"I doubt she knows the value of a penny over a quarter, but she has a slight grasp of the concept. I don't think she would be as thrilled with bills as she is with coins, though."

"So she's a cheap date."

A rattling sound warned them of Sasha's approach. This time she carried her Mickey Mouse bank in her arms. When she stopped in front of Ryan, she set the bank on the floor, sat beside it and carefully placed the penny inside.

Cassie applauded. After a half-second delay, Ryan did the same. Then he reached into his pocket and pulled out another coin. Sasha took it and again slowly slid it inside. When it clinked against the other coins, she laughed.

They continued the game until Ryan held up his hands in mock dismay. "I don't have any more change, kid. Sorry."

"Kay," Sasha said in an attempt to reassure him.

Cassie checked on the dinner, then glanced at the picture uncle and niece made. Handsome, businesslike Ryan sat on a kitchen chair with a red-haired doll and a worn stuffed rabbit tucked into the crook of his arm. Sasha sat at his feet, leaning against him, currently mesmerized by the laces on his athletic shoes.

His hair was lighter than Sasha's curls; their eyes were different colors. But Cassie saw some family resemblance between them. She caught it in a glance, the curve of a smile. She suspected they would look more alike as Sasha grew from a toddler to a little girl and her features became more defined.

The oven timer buzzed. Sasha straightened. ''Food,'' she said.

''That's right. The meat loaf is done and the potatoes will be ready in about five minutes. It's time to wash up so we can eat.'' She pointed at the toys in Ryan's arms. ''Will you please take those back to your room for me?''

''I'll do it,'' Ryan told her as he stood. ''I'm heading back to my office anyway.''

Cassie tried to ignore the flash of disappointment that raced through her. He wasn't going to eat dinner with them? She wanted to pout like Sasha, thrusting out her lower lip and threatening tears if she didn't get her way. Instead she asked, ''Aren't you hungry?''

He looked down at his niece, then at the set table. ''Not right now. I'll grab something later.''

Then he was gone. Cassie stared after him and wondered what had happened to chase him away. Her gaze moved to Sasha who was looking down the hall with the most forlorn expression on her face.

''I know just how you feel,'' Cassie told her. ''I wanted him to stay, too. And not just for me, but also because you two need each other. Unfortunately I don't think your uncle has figured that out yet.''

''So tell me what to do,'' Cassie said as she leaned forward and rested her elbows on the kitchen table.

Aunt Charity poured coffee into her mug. ''I'm sure it's frustrating.''

''Exactly,'' Cassie said, relieved to finally have a chance to come home and talk with her sister and her aunt about Ryan Lawford. The old Victorian house was similar in size to Ryan's, but had a completely different floor plan. Here

Cassie knew every room, every picture. She was familiar with the sounds and smells. Who would have thought that just a week away would have left her homesick? She'd even been pleased to see Old Man Withers sitting on his power mower as he trimmed the lawn. Even though the old goat did little more than insult any woman who made the mistake of offering him a friendly greeting.

"Sasha and I see Ryan less now than we did when I first arrived."

Her aunt looked at her sister. They were, Cassie realized, a study in contrasts—these three women who had, for a time, lived in the same house. Her aunt was slender with dark hair pulled back in a neat chignon. Her tailored clothing emphasized the youthful shape of her body, despite the fact that she was well into her fifties. Chloe was beautiful, as always, but especially radiant at nearly six months pregnant. Her curly red hair tumbled down her back in loose disarray. If Cassie hadn't loved her sister so much, she could have easily hated her for being so darned attractive. As it was, she depended on her. Chloe was her best friend and had been so all of her life.

"I don't know what to do," Cassie continued as she settled her hands around her mug. She glanced at the clock over the stove. She only had a short time until she had to pick up Sasha at the preschool. "It's not that he's hostile. I don't think he dislikes her as much as he's uncomfortable being around her. A few days ago he came in the kitchen while I was fixing dinner. Sasha was bringing him toys. He seemed fine with that. He even gave her a penny, which sent her racing for her Mickey Mouse bank. They seemed to be having fun together, but then he just left."

She looked at the two women she cared about most in the world. "I'm completely at a loss."

"How is Sasha doing?" Chloe asked. She was drinking

a warm glass of milk instead of coffee, having given up caffeine for her pregnancy.

"Pretty well, considering everything she's been through. She has her spells when she wants her mother. I hold her when she cries and, after a time, it passes. We haven't really talked about her parents going to heaven and not coming back. I don't know how to do that." She drew in a breath. Despite her degree and her experience working at the preschool, at times she had no idea how she was supposed to help Sasha deal with her loss. Sometimes all she had to go on was what her gut told her to do.

"She's sleeping and eating?" Aunt Charity asked as she set out a plate of cookies, then took the seat opposite Cassie's.

"Yes. That's all fine. I'm sure being in her house with her room and her routine is helping her. Ryan said he didn't want to deal with the issue of moving her just yet and decided to stay for a few more weeks." She pressed her lips together. "It's not that he's mean or rude. I think he forgets that she's around."

"Hard to imagine a toddler being quiet enough for that to happen," Chloe said wryly.

Cassie smiled. "Okay, maybe forget is too strong a word. I think he has a fabulous ability to focus on his work and he can ignore her for long periods of time."

"If he's never been around children, I'm not surprised by any of this," Chloe told her. "You shouldn't be either. How many times have you gotten frantic calls from fathers left with their kids for the first time? If you don't know how to deal with kids, it can be traumatic."

Aunt Charity pushed the plate of cookies closer. "This withdrawal might be his way of dealing with the loss of his brother."

Cassie took a chocolate chip cookie and nibbled on it. "I

hadn't thought of that, but you could be right. The question is, what do I do about it?"

"You're going to have to remind him of his responsibilities," her aunt told her. "He's using you as a buffer and that's fine for now, but you're not always going to be there."

Cassie sighed. "I know," she said, even though she didn't want to agree. The thought of having that conversation with Ryan put a knot in her stomach. "He hadn't even met Sasha before the funeral," she said. "I don't understand families spending that much time apart."

Chloe touched her hand and smiled. "Not everyone is like us. Some siblings don't get along."

"What a waste." Cassie couldn't imagine living in a household like that. She returned her attention to the problem at hand. "I guess I'll say something to him. I'm just not surc what."

"How is Sasha acting around her uncle?" Chloe asked. "Is she frightened of him?"

"Not at all. She keeps including him in things. She often wants him to pick her up, but he doesn't know how to do it. He's too stiff, which scares her. It's never a positive experience for either of them. But Sasha is a sweetie and very forgiving. Ryan has a long way to go before he chases her off."

"That's something," Chloe pointed out. "She can be your ally in all this."

Cassie smiled at her aunt and her sister. "Thanks for the advice. That's why I came here. I knew you two would be able to steer me in the right direction."

Chloe sipped her milk, then smiled. "Our pleasure. And speaking of men who don't have a clue, what does Joel think about all this?"

"Don't insult Joel," Cassie said automatically, stalling for time, even though she knew what her sister was asking. She did *not* want to have this conversation with Chloe.

"Okay. What does Joel think about your new living arrangements?" her sister asked. "Is he concerned that you're staying alone in a house with a good-looking, older man? Someone sophisticated enough to sweep you off your feet?"

Chloe's words were close enough to Cassie's own fantasies that she was afraid she would blush. "Joel doesn't think anything about it. We've spoken on the phone several times. He knows what I'm doing and why, and he's very supportive. He's not the jealous type."

She made the last statement with a note of defiance in her voice, even though she wasn't feeling especially pleased with Joel's actions…or lack thereof. In truth she would have liked him to be a *little* concerned about her close proximity to another man. After all, Ryan was everything Chloe had said and then some. Ryan was handsome and brilliant, and while she didn't know him that well, she could easily imagine him to have other fine qualities, qualities that every woman looked for in a partner. What she did know was that he was smart and driven about his work. She wasn't so sure about his humanity, though. He wasn't an obviously warm person, although she'd caught glimpses of humor now and then.

"It's very nice that Joel is being understanding," Aunt Charity said, and shot Chloe a warning look.

Chloe ignored it. "Joel doesn't have the sense God gave a turnip. I can't believe he's just sitting back and letting you do this without protesting."

"That's not fair," Cassie told her sister. "If Joel had gotten all macho on me and insisted I not live there, or if he'd been otherwise concerned, you would have called him a bully. You're not going to let him win either way."

Chloe had the good grace to look a little uncomfortable

with her sister's words. "I would not," she said, but without much conviction.

Aunt Charity patted Cassie's hand. "You're going to be fine. I'm sure Joel feels a little jealousy. What man wouldn't? But he doesn't want to show it. As for Ryan and Sasha, it seems to me that you're on the right track. Be patient. It will all work out."

"I hope you're right," Cassie said.

The three women chatted for a little longer, then Cassie got up to leave. Chloe walked her to her car.

"You're glowing," Cassie said as they paused in the driveway. She had to speak up to be heard over the lawn mower. Old Man Withers was still out doing his weekly round over the grounds.

Chloe pressed her hand against her bulging tummy. "I don't know about glowing but I do know that I'm very happy." Her smile was tender. "Being in love will do that to a woman."

Cassie searched her face. "No regrets? It happened so fast. One minute he was a stranger, the next you were involved."

"I know. When I think about how quickly we found each other, I have trouble believing any of it is real." She smiled. "But the more we're together, the more I'm sure this is exactly right. Arizona isn't the perfect man, but he's perfect for me. We understand each other so well, it's almost scary. It must be the magic nightgown."

"Must be," Cassie agreed, trying not to be envious of her sister's happiness. Despite being a nonbeliever, Chloe had worn the Bradley nightgown when she'd turned twenty-five and she'd dreamed about Arizona Smith. They'd met the next morning and sparks had started to fly instantly. They'd had passion...they still did.

"You'll get your chance in a few weeks," Chloe reminded her. "Are you excited?"

Usually, she was, Cassie thought with surprise. But not today. "I'm not a real Bradley," she said. "Even if I was, there's Joel."

Chloe gave her a quick hug. "You're a Bradley in your heart and I'm sure that's all that matters. As for Joel..." Her voice trailed off. "I swear, Cassie, you make me insane with your devotion to that man. What do you see in him?"

For once Cassie couldn't answer the question. "We're going to have to agree to disagree on this one."

"I know. I'm sorry. You have enough going on in your life without me making trouble with this old argument. I'll be good."

"Thanks."

They said their goodbyes. Cassie got into her car and started driving toward the preschool to pick up Sasha. She had to wrestle with an unfamiliar emotion—guilt. She didn't want to envy her sister's happiness, but she did. She didn't want to feel unsettled about Joel, but she did.

It wasn't fair to him, she reminded herself. He hadn't changed. He was exactly the same man she'd fallen in love with nine years ago. He was kind and gentle and caring. Okay, maybe he wasn't flashy and he didn't have a high-powered career or a lot of ambition, but he was good and decent. Wasn't that more important?

"What about passion?" a little voice whispered.

Cassie tried to push it away. There was more to life than sex. She should know. She'd gone her whole life without once experiencing what it would be like to be with a man. She knew that in time, if things continued on their present course, she and Joel would marry. They would become lovers. She was sure that their physical intimacy would be as pleasant as the rest of their relationship.

"I don't want pleasant," she muttered rebelliously. "I want fire. I want to be swept away by needing someone. I want to feel alive."

She was being foolish, she told herself. Her priorities were messed up and the quicker she got them back in order, the happier she would be. But the traitorous thoughts wouldn't go away, and deep in her heart, she wasn't sure she wanted them to.

Chapter Four

"I'm gonna get you!"

Cassie's voice drifted down from upstairs, followed by Sasha's laughter. The sound of thundering tiny feet accompanied the giggles. Earlier Ryan had heard running water, then splashing, so he assumed that Cassie had given his niece a bath before getting her ready for bed.

Over the past week, his life had taken on some kind of order, the movement of the hours marked by Sasha and Cassie's comings and goings to preschool, followed by the excitement of lunch, early-afternoon reading time, the quiet of his niece's nap, the preparation for dinner, evening playtime, then bath and bed. Despite his attempts to distance himself from the child as much as possible, he was still aware of what went on in her day.

He'd assumed that as he got used to being in the house with her and as he developed a routine, he would find her easier to forget. He could go for long stretches of time without thinking about her, but then she appeared in his mind without warning. He would think about how she smiled at him as he passed her and Cassie in the hall, or the way she liked him to read her at least one story before dinner each evening. He didn't understand her need for him to be there, but he found himself showing up before he was asked and lingering in the room until Cassie had prepared dinner, even though he rarely ate with the two of them.

One of the things that startled him the most about Sasha was her blind trust. Not so much of him as of Cassie. The toddler simply expected Cassie to be there to take care of her. If she had a need, she expected it to be fulfilled. If she wanted a hug, she asked and expected to receive affection. He couldn't imagine trusting another person so completely.

It was a curious situation, he thought as he returned his attention to his computer and buried himself in his work.

Sometime later he noticed the silence in the house and knew that Sasha was asleep. Peace reigned again. But before he could focus on his work, there was a knock at his door.

''Come in,'' he called and gave Cassie a welcoming smile as she entered his office. Except for seeing her with Sasha a couple of times a day, they were rarely together. He didn't know anything about this young woman who took care of his niece and quietly brought him food on trays so he could continue working through the day.

She moved across the floor toward him, then paused in front of his desk. ''I have a couple of things I would like to talk to you about,'' she said. ''Is this a convenient time?''

''Sure. Have a seat.''

''Thanks.'' She settled in the chair across from his.

He leaned forward. ''Before you start, I want to tell you that you're doing a terrific job with Sasha. She seems very happy these days. You've got her on a schedule, the house is in order. I really appreciate that.''

"You're welcome." Cassie tucked a strand of dark hair behind her ear. "To be honest, it's easy duty. Your niece is a very happy little girl. She's intelligent and fun to be with." She paused and cleared her throat. "Although we talked about salary when I was first hired, we never discussed time off."

Ryan stared at her for a couple of seconds. He opened his mouth to respond, then closed it. "You're right," he said at last. "I'm sorry. I should have thought of that and I don't know why I didn't." He shrugged. "Evidence to the contrary, I'm not usually a slave driver when it comes to my employees. What seems fair to you?"

"I don't need that much," Cassie told him. "I have some time to myself when I drop her off at the preschool. They invited me to come back to work for those few hours each morning but I told them I had my hands full already. So I'm able to get any personal things done then. What about two evenings a week, and one full day every other week? Just to make it easy on you, I'll arrange day care for the full day. You should be fine on your own in the evening. Sasha sleeps soundly through the night."

He felt a faint whisper of panic at the thought of being left alone with his niece again. Their first few days together hadn't gone well. But, he reminded himself, Cassie was right. Sasha slept through until morning. As long as he wouldn't have to deal with her during waking hours, he would be all right.

"When did you want to start your nights off?" he asked.

"Tonight."

He heard the words as she spoke them but it took a little longer for the meaning to sink in. Great, he thought grimly. He was being thrown into the fire without warning. "That will be fine," he told her, careful to keep his voice and his expression neutral.

She continued to stay in her seat, but instead of sitting quietly, she fidgeted slightly. Obviously she had more on her mind.

"What else did you want to talk about?" he asked when it became clear she needed prompting. He could only hope it wasn't another bombshell about leaving him alone with Sasha.

She touched her right heart-shaped earring, then laced her fingers together. She was nervous about something, he thought as warning bells went off in his head.

"It's about Sasha," she started.

Despite the fact that he didn't want to hear anything negative she had to say on that topic, he told her to continue.

"She's your niece," Cassie continued.

"Surprisingly enough, I'm aware of that."

She gave him a brief smile. "I know it's hard for you to connect with her. You haven't been around children much. Your work is very demanding. Adding to the stress in your life is the fact that you recently lost your only brother and you've had to temporarily relocate to a new town."

Ryan wasn't sure where all this was going, but he knew he wasn't going to like it when they got there. "None of this is news to me."

She squared her shoulders and met his gaze. "You can't ignore Sasha forever. She's not going away. If it's difficult for you to deal with the loss of your family, imagine how she feels. She's too young to understand anything except that her parents—in essence her entire known family and her whole world—are gone. She's scared and alone and she's barely two years old. She needs you to be around more. She needs to know she can count on you."

Ryan wasn't ready for a child to count on him, nor was he any great prize in the family or responsibility department, but one look at Cassie's determined expression told him he wasn't going to get away with saying that to her.

"I'm not going anywhere," he said at last, when it became obvious Cassie was waiting for a response. He was stuck, even if he didn't want to be.

"I appreciate that, and I'm sure if Sasha was old enough to understand, she would appreciate hearing that, too. But right now actions are going to speak louder than words for her." Her eyes darkened with compassion. "I know this has been terrible for you. Losing your brother and Helen, taking responsibility for Sasha. While it might make sense for you to hide out until you feel as if you've started to heal, it would be so much better for Sasha if you could allow yourself to need her, at least a little. She needs *you* so very much."

He didn't need Sasha, he thought. He hadn't needed anyone since he was seven or eight years old. His mother hadn't only taught him the power of hard work, she'd also taught him self-reliance. But he couldn't tell that to Cassie; she wouldn't understand. Besides, there was an odd knot in his stomach when he thought about his niece and he had a feeling that if he examined the sensation too closely he would find it was fueled by guilt.

Cassie was right—he couldn't ignore Sasha forever. Even though a part of him wanted to. Even though he was the wrong person to raise her and he didn't know what the hell he was supposed to do with her. But his only brother had entrusted him with Sasha and he couldn't turn his back on that trust.

In truth he'd been hoping the problem would go away by itself. He wanted to remind Cassie that he'd relocated to Bradley, had moved into his brother's house, and wasn't that enough? Why should he have to do more?

"I see your point," he said quietly. "What do you want me to do?"

"Nothing that scary." She tilted her head and smiled. "Just get to know her. Pretend she's your new neighbor. How would you meet someone like that?"

"I wouldn't." At her look of surprise he found himself adding, "I'm not a very social person."

"Why would you choose to spend your life alone?"

No one had ever asked him that before, but he didn't have any trouble with the answer. "It's easier."

"Not getting involved?"

He nodded. "Things are a lot more tidy when people don't get involved."

Her dark brown eyes seemed to be staring into his soul. "Sounds lonely."

"Sometimes, but it's a small price to pay for autonomy." He drew in a breath. For some reason, Cassie's questions made him uncomfortable. He decided to shift the conversation back to something safer. "If I wanted to get to know my neighbor, I would say 'hi,' strike up a conversation in the elevator, that sort of thing."

"It's not so different with Sasha," Cassie told him. "You need to spend more time with her. Get to know her in her world."

"She's two."

"She still has a world of her own. It's a little different from yours but it's not so very foreign."

"You want me to play dolls with her?"

Cassie grinned. "I was thinking more of spending time with her at meals, maybe reading to her at bedtime, going for walks. Although if you like the idea of playing dolls, go ahead."

"Gee, thanks." He shifted in his seat. She made it sound so simple, but it wasn't. At least not for him. "I'm not dismissing your advice, but I feel awkward around her.

She's so small. I'm afraid I'm going to step on her or something. Worse, I don't understand half of what she's saying."

"Oh and I do?"

He stared at her. "You don't?"

"Of course not." Cassie leaned toward him. Her mouth curved up in a smile. "She's doing great on her verbal skills, but she's not ready for the debate team. Some of what she says is hard to interpret, but if you pay attention to her facial expressions and her body language, you can usually understand what she's asking for or telling you. Sometimes, though, you've just got to nod and act interested even if you don't have a clue."

"You make it sound simple."

"It is, Ryan. You're a smart man and this isn't going to be that hard for you. I'm not asking you to take over all her care." Her smile turned impish. "After all, that would mean I would lose my great job. But you need to be with her more each day. Start slowly. That's how everyone does it. Most parents get to begin in the baby stage, where they're caught up in crisis management all the time and there isn't so much communication involved. By the time their child is a toddler, they've grown to understand her. But I think you're more than capable of figuring this all out."

He gazed at her speculatively. "*I* think I'm being given a snow job."

"Excuse me?"

"All those compliments you're throwing my way—I think they have a purpose."

"Is that bad?"

There was a teasing quality to her voice. Something completely feminine and intriguing. As he stared at her, taking in the thick brown hair that moved with each movement of her head, her big eyes accentuated by light makeup and her generous smile, he realized he'd never seen her before. Oh, of course he'd physically noticed her presence in his house. But he'd never noticed she was a woman.

It just went to show what bad shape he was in, he thought as he stared at the faint color on her smooth cheeks and the generous curves of her breasts. Tonight she wore a long-sleeved cream-colored dress with high heels. Heart-shaped earrings dangled from her ears. He vaguely recalled that she'd worn a dress on their first meeting and jeans ever since. He'd catalogued her presence, the sound of her voice, her competence, but he'd never *seen* her. Dear Lord, there was an attractive young woman living in his house. She'd been there an entire week and he'd just got the message.

''Who are you?'' he asked without thinking. ''Where are you from?''

Her smile widened. ''Practicing your skills on me? The questions are a little complicated for your niece.''

Perhaps, he thought, but he wasn't interested in Sasha's answers. He alrcady knew those. He wanted to know about Cassie Wright. How old was she? She'd told him, he remembered that. Twenty-three, maybe? Twenty-four? How could he not have been paying attention? Maybe it was because she was so different from all the other women in his world. Those he worked with he acknowledged as female, but only in the most superficial way. Long ago he'd found life much easier if he viewed all his colleagues the same way. The women he dated were usually smooth, sophisticated career types who wanted the same things he did and clearly understood how it was all to be played. Cassie didn't even know there was a game in progress.

Her smiled faded. ''That was all I had to talk about,'' she said. ''I don't want to keep you from your work.''

She was going to leave. He stiffened as he realized he didn't want her to. He searched his mind for some excuse to keep her sitting in place. "Where are you off to tonight?" he asked.

"Joel and I are going to a movie."

Joel? Ah, the boyfriend. His gaze strayed to the slender band on her left hand. Joel of the diamond lint promise ring.

"Tell me about Joel."

"Joel is, well, Joel." She frowned slightly as if not sure what kind of information to share. "He works long hours. You two have that in common."

At least Joel dated, he thought grimly as he tried to remember the last time he'd been out with one of his female friends. It had been months. Lately he'd spent all his time at the office. Maybe because most of the women of his acquaintance had started to all sound the same.

"What does he do?"

"He's the assistant manager of Bradley Discount Store." She fingered the promise ring. "His is a very responsible position. He's going to be manager in a couple of years, and when that happens he'll be their youngest manager ever. He's worked there since he was sixteen."

"Sounds like they appreciate him," he said, wondering why he'd thought Cassie would be dating a lawyer or a doctor.

She nodded. "He's done well. He takes management classes at the community college. One day he'll be able to transfer to the university." She paused, then added, "He's very nice."

"I'm sure he is."

"He's nothing like you, of course." Her voice sounded defensive.

He raised his eyebrows. "Because I'm not nice?"

Cassie opened her mouth, then snapped it shut and closed her eyes. A bright flush swept up her cheeks. "I didn't mean that the way it came out," she mumbled.

He'd been interested before, but now he was intrigued. Not only by Cassie and her faux pas, but by the differences between himself and Joel. "So Joel and I don't have much in common?" he asked in an attempt to rescue her.

She shot him a look of gratitude. "Not really. He's lived in Bradley all his life. You're a lot more sophisticated. Then there's the age difference. He's only a year older than me. We're just the country mice here, while you've been all over."

He thought about telling her that the big world beyond Bradley wasn't as wonderful as she made it out to be, but doubted she would believe him. "How long have you two been dating?"

"Nine years."

He blinked…twice. "I'm sorry, did you say *nine* years?"

Some of the color had faded from her cheeks. It returned now, although she didn't turn from his incredulous gaze. "Yes. I started dating Joel when I was in high school."

"And you're not married?"

"No."

"You're not officially engaged?"

"No."

"But you've been dating for nine years?"

"Why is that so hard to understand?"

"I've never known anyone who has done that," he admitted. "I doubt I've dated anyone for nine months, let alone that long." He couldn't imagine any situation in which that made sense. Of course his personal life had never been all that important to him.

She shrugged. "We don't want to make a mistake. Getting married is a serious commitment and we want to be sure."

Ryan didn't think they could be any *more* sure, unless

they were planning to experience old age together first, to see what that was like.

He had several other questions he wanted to ask, but before he could, the doorbell rang. Cassie shot out of her chair.

"I'll get that," she said quickly and practically ran from the room.

Ryan followed. While he didn't really have the right to intrude on Cassie's private time, he couldn't help wanting to get a look at the young man who had dated Cassie for nine years without "being sure" of his commitment. He walked into the foyer just as Joel stepped in from the porch.

The two men stared at each other. Joel was a few inches shorter, maybe five nine or ten, with wavy light brown hair and glasses. He was slight, dressed in freshly pressed khakis and a blue, long-sleeved shirt.

Joel blinked first. He stepped forward, offering both his hand and an easy grin. "You must be Ryan Lawford," he said. "Cassie has told me a lot about you. She's really pleased to be able to help out. She's the best," he added, a note of pride in his voice. "Great with kids." His smile faded. "I was real sorry to hear about your brother and sister-in-law. It's a tragic loss."

Until that moment Ryan hadn't realized that he'd wanted to dislike Joel, or at least have the kid show up with hay in his hair, dressed like some hick out on the town for the first time in a year. Instead, Joel was exactly what Ryan should have expected. A nice, sincere young man with prospects.

"Thank you," Ryan said, shook Joel's hand, then stepped back.

Cassie moved to her boyfriend's side and gave him a quick hug. "Hi," she murmured.

They didn't kiss, or show any outward affection, but Ryan figured that was because he was there, cramping their style. No doubt they would be more intimate later, maybe going back to Joel's place and making love. There was a definite connection between them. He could see it in the shared glance, the way they stood so close together. He'd thought he would feel superior and a little worldly when compared with Joel and Cassie, but instead he felt inadequate and out of place.

"Enjoy yourselves," Ryan said as Joel held the front door open for Cassie. "You've got a key, right?"

She gave him a quick smile over her shoulder. "Yes, you gave me one last week. Don't worry, Ryan, I'll be back before midnight."

"You don't have to be."

Her dark eyes slipped away from his, as if she had something she was trying to hide. "I know, but it's a weeknight. Joel and I both have to be up early in the morning."

She gave him a quick wave, then they were gone and he was alone.

Ryan stood in the foyer until he'd heard Joel's car pull out of the drive and the silence settled around him. Silence and loneliness. He was in a strange place and the only person he knew in town had just left for the evening.

Maybe he could call a friend and talk, he thought, then dismissed the idea. He didn't have the kind of friends he could just call. Guys didn't just call; there had to be a reason. Except for his brother. He and John had talked on occasion. But his brother was gone...forever.

Ryan stiffened as he realized, perhaps for the first time since the funeral, that John was never going to be coming back. The last of his family had died.

Except for Sasha. His gaze turned toward the stairs. Toward the toy-filled room on the second floor. He remembered Cassie's comments that he had to take more time to get to know his niece, that they only had each other now. As she'd talked, he'd wanted to protest the additional responsibility, to tell her that he wasn't interested. But now, alone in the too-quiet house, he thought it might not be so bad. Tomorrow he would start getting to know his niece a little more.

For some reason the plan cheered him. He returned to his makeshift office and got back to work. As he did, he suddenly realized that the quiet didn't seem so lonely after all.

Chapter Five

Cassie sipped her soda and tried to think of something to say. Although it was nearly ten in the evening, the restaurant bustled with an after-movie crowd. As usual, Cassie and Joel's midweek date had consisted of going to a movie, then stopping for pie. Their other favorite date was to go out to dinner.

It was all just too exciting for words, Cassie thought sarcastically, then scolded herself for being critical. In the past she'd been very happy with her and Joel's dating routine. The sameness had made her feel safe. But not anymore, she realized. Now she just felt trapped.

"The new shipment was just as bad," Joel was saying. "Nearly all the lamps were broken. I called the distributor. I asked him what I was supposed to do with a hundred broken lamps. The very same lamps that are featured in the Sunday newspaper circular." Joel paused to chew another bite of chocolate cream pie. "I told him that if he couldn't get me a hundred perfect lamps by Saturday morning, I wouldn't be doing business with him again.''

''Do you think he'll deliver the lamps?'' Cassie asked.

''Sure. He doesn't want to lose the Bradley Discount Store account. It's one of his biggest.''

None of this was fair, Cassie thought sadly. It wasn't Joel's fault that he wasn't the most interesting guy on the planet. He started another story about yet another crisis with the delivery of merchandise. She tried to pay attention, but her mind wandered…about five miles east to the Lawford house on the other side of Bradley. What was Ryan doing now? Was he still working? Had he gone to bed?

Stop thinking about him! she told herself firmly. It was wrong to be on a date with one man and dwelling on another. If only things were different between her and Joel. If only there was more spark.

She studied her boyfriend's face, the light brown eyes, the wire-rimmed glasses, the freshly shaved jaw. He was a good man; nice-looking and kind. There was a time when she'd thought they would spend the rest of their lives together. What had changed?

She wanted to blame it all on her blossoming feelings for Ryan, but she knew it wasn't about him at all. She'd felt restless and trapped for several months. For a while she'd thought the feeling would pass, but now she wasn't so sure. Joel was steady, hardworking, honest and funny. They enjoyed each other's company. She wanted to tell herself that was enough. She wanted to believe that craving more was just plain greedy. Unfortunately, she wasn't sure.

''So you didn't like the movie,'' Joel said.

Cassie blinked. ''What?'' Hadn't he just been talking about work? ''The movie was fine.'' They'd seen a spy thriller with a strong romance woven through the action scenes. Something for both of them.

Joel finished his pie, then pushed his plate away. He took a sip of his coffee and looked at her. ''What's wrong, Cass? You're not really here tonight, are you?''

She shook her head. She wasn't surprised by his observation. After all, they'd been together nine years. Of course Joel knew her.

''I have a lot on my mind,'' she told him, then cleared her throat. ''Actually, I've been thinking about Ryan.''

He nodded as if he'd suspected as much. ''He's an interesting man. What does he do?''

She was a little surprised he wasn't angered by her confession. ''Ryan owns a computer software design firm. They put out a few games of their own, but mostly they do subcontract work from large companies. He started it himself when he was barely out of college.''

She paused as she wondered if she should tell him that she'd actually learned all this during the past year, from Helen, Ryan's sister-in-law, rather than from the man himself. In the week she'd been working for him, she and Ryan hadn't had a personal conversation. Nearly everything they talked about revolved around Sasha.

Joel frowned. ''This has to be a really tough time for him, what with losing his brother and all. I'm sure he appreciates your help.'' He reached across the table and squeezed her fingers. ''*I* appreciate that you were willing to drop everything and move in there to lend a hand. It shows the kind of person you are.''

Cassie wanted to scream. ''I'm not a saint,'' she said testily. ''Sasha is a sweet little girl and I like taking care of her. Looking after one child is much easier than watching six and Ryan's paying me a lot more than I make at the preschool. There isn't much that's noble or self-sacrificing about what I'm doing.''

"You're too modest. Most people wouldn't have bothered to offer their services in the first place."

"I know, it's just..." She glared at him. "Aren't you the least bit jealous or concerned about the situation?"

Joel released her hand and straightened in his seat. "What situation?" he asked in genuine bafflement.

His confusion only added fuel to her temper. "I'm living with a very attractive, very single man. He and I are alone in that house, day after day. A twenty-six-month-old toddler isn't much of a chaperon."

Joel stared at her for a couple of seconds, then started laughing. At first it was just a chuckle, but the sound grew. He slapped both hands on the table. "Jealous? Oh, Cass, don't worry about that at all. It's nice that you're concerned about what I'm thinking, but don't be."

She thought about strangling him but knew she didn't have the physical strength. There weren't any weapons close at hand, not even a fork—the waitress had cleared away Joel's plate and flatware. Which left her glass, a straw, his cup and a spoon. Nothing lethal there. She settled on glaring.

Finally he stopped laughing enough to give her a lopsided smile. "Really. I'm not worried. A man like Ryan would never be interested in a woman like you."

It wasn't anything she hadn't told herself a dozen times in the past week. But whispering it in the quiet of her mind was very different than hearing someone else say it out loud.

"I see," she said sharply. "So I'm not sophisticated enough. My job isn't intriguing, and I don't go to the right parties or know the right people." *I'm not pretty enough,* she thought, but she couldn't bring herself to say that one aloud.

"Exactly."

She looked away and concentrated on keeping her hurt from showing. She knew she wasn't anything like the women in Ryan's world. If she were more like her sister, the situation would be different. Chloe was tall and beautiful. As a journalist, she had a glamorous profession. She could talk to anyone in any situation. She wasn't a preschool teacher whose idea of a hot night on the town was a movie with her boyfriend of nine years.

"Cassie, what's wrong?"

"Nothing." Blinking back tears, she kept her gaze firmly on the collection of plants in the bay window to her right.

"I can see you're upset. Did I say something?"

She turned back to face him. "Nothing but the truth. You're right—a man like Ryan wouldn't be interested in me. I know that, but it's not the point."

He looked bewildered. "Then what is?"

"You're supposed to be worried," she told him. "You're supposed to care that I'm living with another man, that we're in close proximity all day long. You're supposed to think that I'm special enough to tempt anyone. But you don't."

The last three words came out softly as she tried to control her suddenly quivering lower lip. He stretched his hand across the table. "Cassie, don't. I think you're very special. You're a wonderful young woman and I'm lucky to have you."

She waited, but he didn't say anything about how a man like Ryan could be interested in her. Obviously he hadn't changed his mind on that one. He didn't see the problem and she wasn't going to explain it to him.

"Are you angry?" he asked.

She shook her head. "It's late. Let's go."

The drive back to Ryan's was silent. Cassie saw Joel darting her little glances as he tried to assess her mood. Part of her felt guilty for being angry with him, while the rest of her felt it was justified. She didn't understand what was going on or what she was feeling. She just knew she wanted things to be different.

When they pulled into the driveway of the old Victorian house, he put the car in Park and looked at her. "Do you want me to walk you to the door?" he asked, his tone cautious.

She shook her head. "Don't worry about it."

He leaned close and kissed her cheek. "I had a good time tonight. I hope we can get together soon. I miss you."

The streetlight didn't offer much illumination and she could barely make out his familiar features. *Do you really miss me?* But she only thought the question instead of asking it. She wasn't sure anymore.

"Why don't you ever just take me?" she asked suddenly.

"Take you where?"

She nearly groaned in frustration. "Sex, Joel. I'm talking about sex. We never do more than kiss and most of those are chaste. Don't you ever want to rip my clothes off and do it right here in the car?"

He glanced at the narrow bucket seats, then at her. "There's not much room."

She made a low strangled sound in her throat. "Never mind."

But he grabbed her arm before she could reach for the door handle. "What's going on? Are you unhappy with me or the relationship?"

"I don't know."

He stared at her. "I thought this is what we both wanted. I thought we agreed to take things slowly."

"It's been nine years. You've never even touched my breasts. Does that seem natural to you?"

Joel shifted until he faced front. He tightly gripped the steering wheel. "I respect you. Of course I've thought about us…well…being together…that way. After we're married.

I am more than just my animal passions. I thought you were, too.''

She ignored the judgment inherent in his comment. ''Not all the time. Sometimes I want to be swept away and I've always wanted you to be the one doing the sweeping. Please, Joel.''

He swallowed hard. ''Please what?'' He sounded faintly panicked.

''Just kiss me like you mean it. Please.''

''All right.''

He turned toward her and drew in a breath. They reached for each other, but their arms tangled, and with the awkward angle, not to mention the hand brake between them, they couldn't find a comfortable position. Finally Cassie simply grabbed the front of his jacket and hauled him close.

''Kiss me,'' she ordered.

He pressed his mouth to hers. She angled her head and parted her lips. He neither moved more nor responded to the invitation. Instead he froze in place, not kissing her back, not putting his hands on her body, just sitting there. Like a fish, she thought sadly and slowly straightened.

''Enough?'' he asked.

At first she thought he was being sarcastic and punishing her, but then she remembered this was Joel and that wasn't his style.

''Thank you,'' she whispered. Sadness swept through her and she knew tears weren't far behind.

''It's better this way,'' he said kindly. ''We really should wait.''

''I know,'' she said as she collected her purse and opened the car door. ''Good night.''

She stood on the porch and watched him drive away. What had seemed so right for so long now felt very wrong.

It wasn't that she objected to waiting to make love. She

thought it was important to choose one's partners carefully. Given the choice, she would rather just have one lover for her whole life. But she wanted passion in addition to affection and respect. Was that so wrong?

She also didn't remember talking to Joel about putting off intimacy until after marriage. From what she could recall, he'd made that decision all on his own. She wouldn't mind so much if only she could be sure it was all going to work out when they finally did it. But she wasn't sure. Shouldn't they be having trouble keeping their hands off each other? Shouldn't they be breathless and aching with desire? That's what she'd always read about. That's what Chloe talked about when she shared bits and pieces of her relationship with Arizona.

Cassie unlocked the front door and stepped into the silent house. Ryan had left on a light by the stairs. She moved toward it and sighed. Maybe passion wasn't in the cards for her. Maybe she was better off settling. Joel loved her and she loved him. Maybe it was wrong to look a gift horse in the mouth.

But in the darkness of her bedroom, she searched her heart and found that this was too important an issue on which to compromise. She deserved more than just settling…and so did Joel.

The next morning, Ryan hurried down to breakfast. He told himself he wasn't actually interested in Cassie, and he certainly wasn't going to ask about her date, except in the most general, socially correct way. A pleasant "how was your evening?" was expected, even welcome, in most work situations.

He entered the kitchen and paused, taking in his niece and Cassie along with the swept floor, the clean counters and empty sink. Except for the bits of hot cereal on Sasha's face, hands, arms and the front of her bib, not to mention the tray of her high chair, the room was perfect. Nothing like the disaster he'd been living in before Cassie had shown up to straighten out his and Sasha's lives.

He stood in the doorway unobserved. Cassie was back in jeans and a sweatshirt. Her thick short hair swayed with every movement. She'd pulled up a chair next to Sasha's high chair and encouraged the child to keep eating, all the while sipping on a cup of coffee.

She'd come in much earlier last night than he had expected. It had been barely ten-thirty. Not that he'd been watching the clock, he assured himself. He'd just happened to go up to his room to read, and had heard the front door opening. He had thought she would stay out much later. Not that he cared, of course. His was only the most passing of interest in a trusted employee's well-being.

Ryan grinned. Even he was having trouble buying that line. Okay, he could admit it to himself. He was dying to know if Cassie and Joel had made love last night. Probably because it had been so long since he'd had the pleasure of being with a woman, he told himself. He was intrigued by Sasha's nanny. But just because he'd finally noticed her didn't mean—

"Unk Ryan!"

He glanced up and saw Sasha had spotted him. Her baby face split into a grin and she waved her spoon at him.

"Hey, kid."

Cassie turned. "Good morning," she said as she rose to her feet. "The coffee is fresh."

"Thanks."

He quickly glanced at her face, but couldn't see anything lurking in her eyes. No shadows to indicate a restless night, no telltale love-bite marks on her neck.

Sasha held out her cup. "Mill," she said.

He'd already figured out that "mill" really meant milk. "Is she offering me some of hers or asking for more?"

Cassie poured his coffee and grinned. "Why don't you find out?"

He'd actually been hoping for a recap of last night, not a lesson in child rearing, but she'd been right when she told him he was going to have to figure out how to get along with his niece. Tentatively he moved close and took the offered cup. He shook it; it was empty.

"More milk," he said and walked to the refrigerator.

When he handed Sasha back her cup, she beamed at him. Her slight "t" sound could have been an expression of pleasure or thanks. He found he didn't really mind which. With Cassie around to protect him from making a hideous mistake, he sort of liked being with the kid.

"What can I get you to eat?" Cassie asked as she set his mug on the table. "We have cereal and fruit. There are frozen waffles, or I could make you eggs or even pancakes."

Tentatively, prepared to spring up at any moment, he took the seat next to Sasha's high chair. She gave him another grin, then dropped her spoon into her cereal and began eating again.

"You don't have to feed me," he said, not taking his gaze from his niece. She wasn't exactly coordinated, he thought as a bit of cereal went flying, but she got the job done.

"I know it's not technically one of my responsibilities," Cassie told him, "but you have to eat something. Not only is breakfast the most important meal of the day, but Sasha is going to mimic just about everything you do. If you refuse food, she's going to do the same."

There was no fighting a woman when she'd made up her mind about something. He'd learned that lesson early and well. "Cereal," he said. "With a banana. And after today I'll get my own breakfast."

"Whatever you'd like. You're the boss."

Her tone was sweet, but he didn't buy it for a second. She was in charge here, and she knew it.

As Cassie prepared his cereal, Sasha finished hers. Every couple of bites she offered him the spoon. He finally figured out she wanted him to feed her. "Okay, I can do some of the work."

He scooped out a small amount of the warm, rice cereal. Sasha opened her mouth, then looked at him as if to say "Aren't I too clever for words?" He found himself smiling at her. If it had been this easy when he'd first been alone with her, he wouldn't have panicked so much.

When she'd finished eating, she drank the last of the milk, then said, "Down."

Ryan looked at Cassie. "She wants out."

"If she's finished eating, that's fine."

He glanced from her back to Sasha. That hadn't been the answer he'd expected. He'd thought that Cassie would come over and take care of things. Okay, so she was giving him practice. He could handle this.

He crossed to the sink and fished a clean dishcloth out of the drawer, then dampened it and returned to the high chair. After removing the bib, he cleaned the toddler's face, hands and arms, then unhooked the tray and put it on the table. Sasha held out her arms.

Ryan bent over and lifted her from the seat. But instead of leaning down toward the ground, she pressed a wet, cereal-scented kiss on his cheek. "Unk Ryan," she explained.

"Yes, I know," he said, somewhat at a loss as to his next move. Finally he set her on her feet. She giggled once, then scampered out of the room.

"You've won her over." Cassie set his breakfast on the table. After picking up the dirty high chair tray, she carried it to the sink.

"I don't think it was the clear victory of the campaign," he admitted, "but it was a pleasant encounter."

"If this is a campaign, then you must be the general in charge?" she asked.

"You have to ask?"

"Five-star?"

"If they come with that many, sure."

She smiled at him as she returned to the table and took the seat opposite his. He glanced at his cereal, the neatly sliced banana and the plate of toast sitting together on the place mat.

"Thanks for doing this," he said. "I meant what I said. I'll take care of it from now on."

"Whatever you'd like."

He started his breakfast, all the while trying to ignore the unusual domesticity of the situation. He rarely had women over to his place because he wasn't comfortable with them spending the night. Actually it wasn't the nights he minded as much as the awkward mornings. So he did his thing and escaped as gracefully as he could. Besides, the women of his acquaintance had to be at work as early as he did, so there was no time for idle chitchat.

It occurred to him that Cassie was *already* at work and that for her, this was simply a part of her job. The thought unsettled him although he couldn't quite say how.

Sasha ran into the room and handed him a red ball. He took it, but before he could say anything, she was gone again.

"Oh, we're going to play that game again," he said and patted his front pockets. "I don't have any spare change."

"There's some over here," Cassie said, rising to her feet. She crossed to the counter and pulled a white envelope out of a drawer. "It's the remaining grocery money." She fished out several pennies and two nickels. "This should keep her happy.'' She placed the money next to him and took her seat.

Morning light spilled in through the big, lace-covered window. Cassie looked freshly scrubbed and well rested. Except for the heart-shaped earrings she usually wore and her promise ring, she didn't have on any jewelry. Her clothes were as casual as his. Yet there was something about her…something sexy.

He cleared his throat. ''So, how was your evening?''

Her gaze lowered. ''Very nice. We went to a movie, then stopped and had dessert.''

''Were you out late?''

He was a fraud, he thought even as he asked the question. He knew exactly what time Cassie had gotten home. With a quick calculation of the time needed to drive to the theater, watch the movie, then order and eat dessert, unless they did it in less than fifteen minutes, it was unlikely Cassie and Joel had made love the previous night.

The realization pleased him and he refused to consider why.

''I think I got back about ten-thirty,'' she said.

''Oh. I was reading in my room last night. I didn't hear you.'' The lie slipped easily off his tongue and he had a moment of guilt. Then Sasha returned with her favorite stuffed bunny and distracted him. He gave the girl a penny, which she took with a squeal of delight, then raced out of the room again.

''So you had fun?'' he asked, not sure why he was pursuing this particular topic.

She hesitated. ''Of course.''

''You must be very comfortable with Joel. Having dated him for so long. I mean that in a good way,'' he added quickly when she glanced at him.

''We're…'' She hesitated. ''Can we change the subject?''

"Of course. I didn't mean to pry."

"It's not that. It's just I have lot on my mind."

What? he wanted to asked, but knew it wasn't his business. Still, his mind raced. Was it Joel? Had they fought? Were they—

Sasha came back, this time carrying a long, pink dress. Instead of offering it to him, she held it up in front of herself. "Kern," she said, her expression serious. "Unk Ryan, me kern."

He turned to Cassie. "This would be an excellent time for you to translate."

"There's a big assumption there," she said. "I'm not sure what she's asking. Sasha, what's that you're holding?"

Sasha came around to her side of the table and held out her dress. "Oh, it's your dress for Halloween." Cassie motioned to the garment. "Sasha is going to be a princess, aren't you, honey?"

Sasha nodded vigorously. "Me kern."

"Kern," Cassie repeated thoughtfully.

"Isn't a kern a kind of bird?"

"Maybe, but I doubt that's what's on her mind." She leaned toward the toddler. "What's a kern, sweetie? What do you want?"

Sasha huffed out a breath. "Kern," she repeated and patted her head. "Pinccss kern."

Ryan searched his memory for something like a kern, then got it. "She means crown. She wants a crown so she can wear it with her princess dress."

Sasha rushed to him and chattered on about kerns and pincesses and Lord knew what else. Ryan felt as if he'd just aced an IQ test. He stroked the girl's hair, then touched her cheek. "We'll get you a crown. The prettiest crown ever." He glanced over at Cassie. "Do they sell them?"

"No problem. I'll take her by the party-supply store on

our way back from preschool. She can pick out her own. They're made out of cardboard, so they're easy for the kids to wear."

"When is Halloween?" he asked. He hadn't thought of that particular holiday in years. His condo was a secure building, so they didn't get any foot traffic, and it wasn't the kind of place that welcomed children.

"Monday. I haven't bought any candy. I'll do that when I do the grocery shopping."

Ryan reached into his back pocket and pulled out his wallet. He passed over one of his credit cards. "Use this for anything you need. Expenses for the house, whatever. Does she need clothes?"

"Not right now. She doesn't seem to be in a growth spurt, so we're fine. However, kids her age can shoot up, almost overnight, so I'll let you know if anything gets small or tight."

She nodded at Sasha who had left her dress draped over Ryan's lap and was quietly playing on the floor, between her uncle's feet. "You're doing well with her."

"Thanks." He fingered the soft cotton of the princess dress. "You were right last night. I *do* need to spend more time with her. I appreciate you caring enough to say something."

"Just doing my job."

"It was more than that. I'll admit to being a little nervous about the whole thing, but I'm determined to give it my best shot."

"She can't ask for more than that." Cassie paused. "It would be great if you took Sasha out trick-or-treating on Halloween."

"Sure, if you'll come with us."

"No problem. I can ask my sister to hand out candy here while we're gone. She and her husband are going to a party, but that's not until later in the evening. Sasha won't want to go to more than a dozen or so houses. When she gets tired, we can come back here, then she can give out candy."

"Sounds like a plan."

Cassie glanced at the clock above the stove. "Sasha, time to go to school. Let's put your toys away really fast, then we can leave, okay?"

The toddler scrambled to her feet, then bent over and grabbed her bunny. Ryan handed her the dress. While Cassie took care of his niece, he took his dishes to the sink.

He listened to the sounds of them getting ready. He'd grown accustomed to the chatter of voices and the thumping footsteps. Maybe this wasn't going to be so terrible, he thought. Maybe John hadn't made as huge a mistake as Ryan had first thought.

It was Cassie's influence, he realized. She was very special. Honest and giving, an old-fashioned sort of woman.

She stuck her head into the kitchen. "We're outta here. See you later." She hesitated. "You have the most peculiar look on your face. Is something wrong?"

"Not at all." He couldn't tell her what he'd been thinking. She wouldn't understand and he didn't want to do anything that would make her uncomfortable. "I was thinking that Joel is a very lucky man."

Her smile faded slightly and her eyes took on a haunted quality. But before he could ask, her expression returned to normal. "Thanks. I'll be sure to tell him the next time I see him."

Chapter Six

Cassie greeted her sister at the front door. Chloe handed her a large paper shopping bag, reached down and grabbed two more from the porch, then stepped into the Lawford house.

"I don't know why I thought this was going to be a great idea," Chloe said and laughed. "It didn't seem like such a big deal to show up at the party in costume. I conveniently ignored that step in the middle, the part where I actually had to put it all together." She bent forward, her round belly making her awkward, and gave her sister a kiss on the cheek. "I really, really appreciate you offering to help me with this."

"My pleasure." Cassie closed the door behind her and led the way to the kitchen. "I thought we could work in here. Sasha is down for her nap. Apparently they played outside at preschool, so she's exhausted from all the running and jumping. I figure she'll have about an hour and fifteen minutes of honest sleep, then maybe she'll spend another thirty minutes quietly playing in her bed."

Cassie set the shopping bag on a chair and began emptying the contents. "To try and stack the odds in our favor, I went to her room a couple of minutes ago and put her favorite doll in with her."

"Clever," Chloe said as she, too, dumped yards of green, yellow and white fabric onto the table. "I like that in a woman. Now if only you can be equally creative with this mess."

She dug around until she found several of the larger pieces that she'd already sewn together. "Where's Ryan? I don't want to expose my pregnant self to him. I think the poor man is probably traumatized enough in his life."

"Don't give me that," Cassie told her sister. "You look amazing. The problem wouldn't be Ryan, who would be instantly smitten, it would be your husband's insane jealousy."

Chloe tossed her head, causing her ponytail to dance. "Arizona's not insanely jealous. He just keeps a close eye on me when we're out."

"That's because he knows you're the most beautiful woman in the world and he desperately wants you."

Chloe's smile was content. "I don't know about thinking I'm that beautiful, but he does like to keep me around."

"An intelligent man."

"Obviously."

The two sisters laughed. "Do you want something to drink?" Cassie asked. "I have milk and juice."

"Milk would be great." Chloe rubbed her belly. "I'm trying to get all my calcium naturally, which means at least two glasses of milk a day, sometimes more. So while the baby is growing, leaving less and less room for my bladder, I'm drinking more and more. I swear, there are some days I just want to set up my laptop by the bathroom to save myself the time of walking back and forth.'' She took the glass Cassie offered. ''It's only going to get worse before it gets better, too.''

''But it will be worth it.''

''I know.''

Cassie looked at her sister, noting the glow to her skin and the light in her eyes. Chloe had always been the tall, slender, pretty one, but now she was radiant. Arizona's love filled her with a joy she'd never known before. Pregnancy agreed with her, she was working hard on a book about her husband's travels, and she'd never been healthier or happier.

''I'm glad for you,'' Cassie said, meaning it with all her heart. She believed there were enough good things out in the universe for everyone. The fact that Chloe had found what she wanted in life meant that it was possible for Cassie, too.

''So Ryan's working?'' Chloe asked.

''Yes, and unlikely to surface anytime soon. You're safe.''

''Good.'' Chloe unbuttoned the oversize shirt she'd worn that afternoon. Underneath she had on leggings and a sports bra. ''I can't get any part of this costume to work,'' she said as she slipped into the long green sleeves. ''If you could just help me pin it together, maybe baste it in a few key spots, I can sew it when I get home.''

Cassie stepped back and appraised her sister's attire. The invitation to the university's Halloween party stated that attendees were to dress like famous couples in literature. Chloe's advancing pregnancy had prevented her from wearing anything formfitting. She'd toyed with the idea of Romeo and Juliet, but she'd decided that was too obvious. Not to mention the fact that Arizona had refused to wear tights.

''I think you two are going to be the hit of the party,'' Cassie said as she found the layered front of the costume.

Chloe had sewn yellow on the lower part of the belly, with white up by the throat. "The crocodile and Captain Hook are perfect."

"Like I said, I thought it was brilliant until I realized I didn't know how to sew a crocodile costume. I want the puffy-out belly part to skim over my stomach. At least then the pregnancy won't be obvious, but I'm not sure it's going to work."

Cassie stepped close and held up the midsection. "It's not sticking out enough," she said. "And the pocket for your tummy has to be lower. Let me rip out the center seam and insert about six more inches of the yellow cloth. Then we'll use ribbing to give it a little more shape on the side."

"Is that what's wrong?" Chloe asked, then shook her head. "I should have asked for you to help me from the beginning. You always were better than me at this domestic stuff. I've been tearing up pieces for a week and getting nowhere."

"We have different talents," Cassie said as she started separating the layers of fabric.

Growing up, she and her sister had sometimes sewn dresses, but usually Chloe didn't have the patience. She'd always been going and doing. Cassie was the one who liked to stay home and take care of things there. They were so different, Cassie thought. Probably because they had different biological parents. Being raised in the same home could only do so much.

As she worked, Chloe talked about her life. Cassie listened and tried to ignore the faint whisper of envy that drifted through her. She was glad for Chloe and her happiness, and she reminded herself there was still plenty of time for her own dreams to come true.

"Arizona is completely crazed about the plans for next summer," Chloe was saying. "He's received invitations from all over the world. Everyone wants him to come speak. The baby will be six months old, so I told him my requirements were for a relatively short flight, decent facilities and no luggage restriction.'' She rolled her eyes. ''Do you have any idea how much stuff babies require? The more I read about that, the more it amazes me.''

''So you'll be staying in the country?''

''Maybe. I don't know.'' She spread her arms so Cassie could pin on the modified front panel. ''Two universities in England have made fabulous offers, so he's talking about lecturing for a few days in New York or Washington so we get adjusted to the change in time and the plane ride isn't too awful. Then we would take the Concorde to England and spend the summer there.''

''Sounds like fun.''

''I hope so.'' She looked sheepish. ''He's already talking about a second baby, timing it and everything so that we're always free to travel in the summer. He's very concerned that I don't get overwhelmed with all of it and—''

Chloe pressed her lips together. ''I'm sorry. You don't want to hear about all this.''

Cassie stopped pinning and stared at her sister. ''Why not? I *want* you to tell me about your plans. Just because you're married doesn't mean we've stopped being friends.''

''I know. It's just I feel as if I've gotten everything and you don't have…as much.''

Cassie knew the pause had been because Chloe had started to say ''anything.''

''I appreciate your concern about my feelings,'' she said. ''But I do have a lot. Maybe it doesn't seem like it to you, but you and I have never wanted the same things. You're a great reporter and a terrific writer. You've always wanted to travel and you've married a wonderful man who adores you and wants to show you the world. Everything is working out. That makes me happy. But my path is different.''

''I know.'' Chloe touched her arm. ''I'm not being critical. In the past we've argued about your career choice, but I finally understand.'' She rested her hand on her stomach. ''When the baby kicks, I can feel the life growing inside of me. Until that happened I didn't know why you would want to 'waste' your life with children. Now I see it's the most amazing thing you can do with your time. I respect that and I admire you for realizing it before you had a child of your own.''

Cassie was a little embarrassed by the praise. ''Wow, you make me sound like a saint or something. I'm not.''

''Hey, I know that—I'm your sister, remember. But you're a good person who pays attention to what is right. I just wish…''

Her voice trailed off. She fingered the front of her costume. ''I think this is going to work, don't you?''

As subject changes went, it wasn't a very smooth one. Cassie knew what her sister had been about to say. ''You just wish I would break up with Joel.''

Chloe drew in a deep breath. Her mouth twisted down on one side. ''You've tried to explain it to me a dozen times and I still don't understand what you see in him. Yes, he's very nice and he's honest and hardworking, but Cass, you could do so much better. You're bright and funny, you care.'' Her tone softened. ''I want you to find a man who understands that you're an amazing prize and that he's lucky as hell to have you. Not some guy who thinks of you as little more than a housekeeper and broodmare.''

''You're not being fair to Joel,'' Cassie said, but her reply was automatic. She was too conflicted about her feelings to try and explain them to her sister.

''Does he make you laugh?'' Chloe asked. ''Does he

make your heart beat faster just by walking in the room? Does he have a certain way of looking or smiling or have a phrase that makes you realize that if you never heard it again or saw it that you would just die?'' She caught her sister's gaze. ''Do you think about spending the rest of your life with him and know, deep down in your heart, that if something happened to him, you would be happier being alone rather than trying to find someone else?''

Cassie dropped the pins onto the table and sank into a chair. ''I don't know,'' she said quietly. ''I just don't know anymore. I wish I could tell you yes to all of those questions, but I can't.''

Chloe took the chair next to her and placed a hand on her shoulder. ''I'm sorry. I didn't mean to upset you.''

''I'm not upset, I'm confused. I used to be sure. I thought that Joel was exactly right for me, but something's different. I don't know if it's him or me or circumstances.'' She looked at her sister. She had to know. Of all the people in the world, she knew that Chloe would tell her the truth.

''Is passion real?'' she asked. ''Is it like in books and movies? Can it really sweep you away until you can't imagine anything else ever being so wonderful?''

Chloe stared at her for a long time. Finally she nodded. ''It's exactly like that.''

Cassie hadn't realized she was holding her breath until she released it. ''I was afraid of that.'' Her shoulders slumped forward. If passion was real, then she and Joel were doing something very wrong. Maybe they weren't right for each other or meant to be together. As much as she wanted to believe otherwise, she doubted it was suddenly going to flare between them. So she had to decide if she could live her life without experiencing that kind of fire, or if she had to leave the security of the only man she'd ever dated.

''You have to be sure,'' Chloe told her. ''It's been nine

years, so it's not going to hurt if you wait a little longer until you get engaged to Joel, but please promise me you won't settle. If you think it over and believe in your heart that Joel is the man who is going to make you happy for the rest of your life, then I swear I'll be the sweetest sister-in-law ever. But don't make a mistake. Marriage is tough enough, even with love."

Cassie looked at her sister, at the affection and concern on Chloe's face. "I appreciate the kind words and the fact that you worry about me. You're the best sister ever."

"I know," Chloe said and laughed. She stood up and put her hands on her hips. "Enough of this emotional nonsense. Let's get this costume finished."

"Absolutely." Cassie picked up the pins and went back to work.

"How's Ryan doing with Sasha?" Chloe asked as she raised her arms so Cassie could pin the front panel to the sleeves.

"Better. Obviously it's going to take time, but our talk went really well. He seems to intuitively understand how Sasha needs him. They're spending more time together. He joins us for breakfast, he's reading to her before she goes to bed. Considering their shaky start, I'm impressed. Ryan's a quick study and the situation is helped by the fact that he's bright and has a great sense of humor. All important factors for good parenting. Plus, he's kind. He makes me feel like part of the family."

Cassie finished pinning and stepped back. The top and bottom of the costume were unfinished, but there was definitely a crocodile-like shape to the strips of yellow and white down the front. "Maybe a clock," she said, half to herself as she eyed her sister. "Hadn't the crocodile in *Peter Pan* swallowed a clock? We could make the face of a clock out of fabric and sew it on in front. Or maybe you could find a pocket watch somewhere. There's always..." Her voice trailed off as she realized her sister was staring at her.

"What?" Cassie asked. "You've got this weird look on your face."

Chloe broke out into a smile. "Cassandra Bradley Wright, you have a thing for your boss! Why didn't you tell me?"

Cassie desperately wanted to deny her sister's claim, but she could already feel the heat crawling up her face. She ducked her head. "I do not." The statement sounded lame, even to her.

"You do. I can't believe I didn't get this before. Is there anything going on?" Her teasing tone grew serious. "He's not taking advantage of you or the situation, is he? Geez, Aunt Charity and I should have checked the guy out before letting you come stay here. Has he—"

Cassie raised her hand to cut off her sister. "Stop right there. Don't get all worked up about nothing. I swear Ryan isn't taking advantage of me." Not that she would mind if he did, a little voice whispered in her head. Cassie tried to ignore it and the faint warmth that swept over her at the thought.

"Are you sure?" Chloe asked, sounding skeptical.

"Taking advantage of someone requires knowing that person is alive. While I don't doubt that Ryan is aware of my existence, as far as he's concerned, I'm just a helpful household appliance. He has no clue I'm female."

Chloe looked at her and shook her head. "I can't buy that. You're very pretty."

"Get real. I'm a good person, I'm amusing when I'm in a situation where I'm comfortable, I'm reasonably intelligent and I'm honest and have a way with kids. But I'm not his type. Why do you think Joel isn't jealous, and please don't say anything cruel about him. The truth is, a man like Ryan could never be interested in a woman like me."

"Why on earth not?"

Cassie was so startled by the question it took her a minute to figure out how to answer. "There's the age difference," she said at last.

"What is it, five years?"

"Almost nine. He has a successful business, and as you so like to point out, I work in a preschool. What would we talk about?"

"What do you talk about now?"

"Sasha."

"So you have *something* in common."

Cassie reached for the bag and fished out the long length of fabric that would serve as Chloe's tail. "You're pushing this because you think it might be a good way to get me away from Joel."

"Is that so terrible?"

It could be if the crush became something more, Cassie thought. She wasn't looking to get her heart broken. "Maybe," she said, then stopped when she heard footsteps in the hallway.

Chloe glanced toward the door and groaned. "This is *not* how I planned on meeting your boss."

"You look cute," Cassie told her and knew she was telling the truth. Chloe had pulled her dark red curls into a ponytail at the top of her head. Makeup accentuated her big eyes, while pregnancy added a glow to her cheeks. She looked like what she was—a radiantly beautiful woman in the prime of her life.

"Cassie, is there..." Ryan's voice trailed off as he entered the kitchen and saw her company. "Sorry, I didn't mean to interrupt." He glanced over the partially completed costume and raised his eyebrows. "So people *do* dress differently in Bradley than in other parts of the country."

Cassie smiled. ‘‘Not exactly. Ryan, this is my sister, Chloe Smith. Chloe, this is Ryan.’’

The two shook hands. ‘‘You have me at a disadvantage,’’ Chloe said, motioning to herself. ‘‘I don’t like making a first impression in costume.’’ She told him briefly about the party she and Arizona were to attend, then rested her hand on her stomach. ‘‘I figured my choices were limited if I didn’t want to spend the night as ‘pregnant’ Cleopatra and Mark Antony, or ‘pregnant’ Scarlett O’Hara and Rhett Butler.’’

‘‘It’s very original. I suppose pregnant Wendy was out of the question.’’

Chloe laughed. ‘‘I thought about it, but my husband refused to consider anything that involved wearing tights.’’

‘‘Smart man,’’ Ryan said. ‘‘I can’t say that I blame him.’’

Cassie smoothed the tail to pin it in place, but Chloe stopped her. ‘‘I’ll have to do that at the last minute. Aunt Charity can help me. Otherwise, I’ll never fit everything in the car.’’

‘‘I hadn’t thought about that.’’ Cassie turned to Ryan. ‘‘My sister drives a little BMW Z3 roadster. Cute car, with absolutely no trunk.’’

‘‘Very little room for my tummy, either.’’ When Chloe indicated she needed to step out of the costume, Ryan politely turned his back. ‘‘I’m going to have to start trading cars with Arizona so that there’s room between me and my steering wheel.’’

Cassie folded the fabric. ‘‘Are you sure we did enough? I don’t mind working on this some more.’’

‘‘It’s fine,’’ Chloe told her. ‘‘If I have any trouble, I’ll call you to come rescue me.’’ She waved goodbye to Ryan and left.

Ryan waited in the kitchen while Cassie walked her sister to the door. When she returned, he pointed to the scraps of material on the table and floor. "I didn't know you could sew."

"I used to do it more. When I was in high school, I made a lot of my clothes. Not because we couldn't afford to buy them but because I couldn't always find things I liked." She shrugged. "I can handle most of the domestic arts. Cooking, child rearing, sewing. I'm a decent baker and pretty handy in the garden, but I don't like cleaning. Given the choice, I would rather pay to have someone else do it." She glanced at him out of the corner of her eyes. "Most women are well versed at several of these same activities. You don't have to act surprised that I've conquered them."

"It *is* surprising," he told her as he leaned one hip against the kitchen counter. "At least for me. The women I date are more interested in their careers than what they plan to serve for dinner. I'm not saying either is right," he added quickly, not wanting her to think he was judging.

"Agreed," she said. She finished picking up the scraps and carried them to the trash. "Times have changed, but what about when you were growing up? Did your mom bake or sew?"

He shook his head. "She put on patches when we tore out the knees of our jeans, but that was about it. As for baking—" He tried to remember coming home to the smell of brownies or a cake. On birthdays she'd usually bought something day-old from the bakery. "She worked two jobs. There wasn't a lot of extra time."

Cassie's expression softened with compassion. "It must have been really tough for her, having to work so much and still try to raise you and your brother. I'm sure she was really conflicted about the situation."

Ryan couldn't answer that. If his mother had had doubts, she'd kept them to herself. "She taught my brother and me to be hard workers, like she was. She always told us that rich was better than poor. That we were to get good educations and work hard. I've respected that.''

''You've done both,'' Cassie told him.

''Agreed. On the down side, she never spent much time with us. Some of it was because of her long hours at work. For the rest of it, I'm not so sure.'' He wasn't about to tell Cassie that he'd always felt his mother had seen her children as getting in the way of her goals. That if she'd been alone, she would have done much better. Still, he couldn't fault her on her day-to-day care, or for inspiring John and him to get ahead. That had to count for something.

''There wasn't much fun in our house,'' he said at last. ''No money and not enough time.''

''You can have fun with Sasha,'' Cassie told him. ''Little kids need lots of attention and lots of fun.''

Her smile was easy, her posture relaxed. She was completely comfortable with him, and very pretty, he thought, wondering for the thousandth time how he'd managed to not notice her for nearly a week. Now he was having trouble being in the same room without finding something new about her that appealed to him. Sometimes it was her laugh, sometimes a comment she made. Once he'd been caught up in the play of light on her thick, shiny hair.

Telling himself she was completely wrong for him didn't help. Reminding himself that she was not only his employee—and therefore deserving of his respect—but also involved and committed to another man, only intrigued him. He couldn't remember the last time a woman had haunted his thoughts and he found he liked having something other than work on his mind.

Cassie glanced at the clock. ''Sasha should be waking up soon,'' she said. ''I have just enough time to get the cookies in the oven.''

With that she walked over to the refrigerator and pulled

open the door. Ryan was about to excuse himself when she bent over and retrieved a bowl sitting on the bottom shelf. He told himself he was worse than a kid in high school, but he couldn't help looking. Her jeans tightened around her rear end, making him want to go over and pull her close against him. He could imagine how she would feel next to him, under him, naked and....

"Ryan?" Cassie asked as she straightened and caught him staring. "Are you all right?"

"Fine," he said, sounding only a little strangled. "I, um, I think I'll go back to my office." He turned away quickly, hoping she hadn't noticed the rather obvious manifestation of his wayward thoughts.

He was slime, he told himself. Lower than slime. He was the single-celled creature that slime fed on. Because even though it was wrong, even though he was violating fifteen different kinds of moral conduct, he liked that she turned him on. Being around Cassie reminded Ryan that he was alive.

"That one," Sasha said as she pointed at the candy. "This one, too."

Ryan obligingly picked up the two pieces of candy in question and dropped them into the small, clear plastic bag decorated with grinning pumpkins. "She's a tyrant," he complained good-naturedly.

"You're the one who told her she could pick what to put into the bags," Cassie reminded him as she slid ghost-shaped sugar cookies onto the cooling rack. "Don't come crying to me, now."

"I know. How many of these bags do we need to do?"

She settled the last of the cookies in place, then put the empty sheet into the sink. After removing the oven mitts from her hands, she crossed to the kitchen table.

It had been a very good few days, Cassie thought happily. Ryan had responded well to her suggestion that he spend more time with his niece. They were getting to know each other and finding pleasure in each other's company. On a personal level this meant she also spent more time with the man, but she wasn't about to comment on that. Despite her crush, she knew that Sasha was the important one around here.

She counted the filled plastic bags. "You've done eighteen. We need twenty-four." She bent down and hugged the toddler. "Are you helping?"

Sasha nodded, then pointed at Ryan. "Work!" she commanded.

He laughed. "Yes, ma'am. Gee, give the woman a little power and she's ready to take over the world."

"Must be genetic," Cassie said casually, then laughed and jumped back when Ryan glanced at her sharply.

"Are you saying I'm a tyrant?" he asked, his gaze narrow in mock anger.

"I've heard bits of your phone calls, when I've brought you dinner," she said. "You like ordering people around. I think it's in the blood."

"Did you hear that?" he asked Sasha. "She's called us bossy. I don't think that's true. Just because we know what's best for everyone. Right?"

Sasha blinked a couple of times, then planted her hands on her hips and looked at Cassie. "Right!"

"I've been outvoted. Fine. I'll start making the icing for the cookies."

As she collected ingredients, she had to hold in a sigh of contentment. Sasha and Ryan were doing great. She was thrilled that he'd offered to stay in the kitchen after dinner and help with the Halloween bags needed for the party at Sasha's school. She ignored the fact that his actions played into her private fantasy that this was all actually real. It wasn't, of course. It was play, and as long as she didn't forget what was going on, she was allowed to enjoy pretending for as long as the situation lasted.

Abruptly, Ryan pushed back his chair and rose. "I've got work in my office," he said without warning and left.

"Unk Ryan?" Sasha slid off the seat onto her feet and started after him. "Unk Ryan? Back! More work."

Cassie put down the bowl she'd been holding and hurried to the toddler. She caught up with her in the hallway. Sasha stood staring at her uncle's closed office door.

"He's busy," Cassie said quietly. "He'll help us again tomorrow." She glanced at her watch. It was nearly bedtime. "Let's go give you a bath, then I'll read you two stories."

For a second Sasha's lower lip quivered and Cassie was afraid she wasn't going to allow herself to be distracted. But she finally held out her hand and Cassie led her away.

Two hours later it was Cassie's turn to pause outside Ryan's closed door, but unlike his niece, she knocked once, then entered. Ryan stood in front of the window, staring out into the darkness of the night.

There were several lamps on in the room and they reflected in the glass, creating a mirror effect. She could see his face, the pained expression and his closed eyes.

She hesitated, not sure what to say.

"I'm sorry," he told her, his voice tight.

"What happened?"

"Nothing. I had to leave. I'll explain it to Sasha tomorrow." He opened his eyes and met her gaze in the window. "Is she all right?"

She nodded. "She's asleep. I told her you were busy."

"Thanks."

He looked away as if expecting her to leave.

"What happened?" she repeated.

"I'm fine."

She drew in a deep breath. Was she crossing the line? Did it matter? After all, she wasn't about to back down. "I'm not going away."

He turned toward her. "You never told me you were stubborn."

"You never asked."

He nodded, then motioned for her to take the seat opposite the desk. She did. He settled into his chair. "It's going to sound really stupid," he warned her.

"I doubt that, but I promise to listen anyway."

He leaned back and stared at the ceiling. "It was Sasha. She tilted her head a certain way and in that split second, I saw my brother in her."

"She's his daughter. Why does that surprise you?"

"Because I never got it before. I knew in my head that she was John's child and my niece, but I hadn't internalized the information. I'd always thought of her as a person in her own right."

His gaze slid down until it met hers. "I never bothered to come visit them," he said quietly. "They lived less than two hundred miles away, but I was always too busy. I thought there would be time. So birthdays and anniversaries and Christmases went by, all without me. And now it's too late."

Cassie's heart ached for him. He'd finally realized his brother was really and truly gone. "I'm sorry," she murmured.

"Thanks." He paused. "I wish I'd done things differently."

The light from the floor lamps added depth and shadows to his strong face. His eyes were haunted by the pain of actions that would never be.

"You still have Sasha," she said, knowing it was a small comfort, although it was the only one she had to offer.

"I know. I still don't think I'm the right choice, but I'm glad they didn't leave her to anyone else. She's all that's left of my brother."

"No," Cassie told him. "You have all the memories you carry around inside yourself. Those will always be with you."

He leaned forward. Some of the tension left his body. "You're right. I hadn't thought of it that way, but it's true." He smiled. "Thank you, Cassie. You're very insightful."

It was, she knew, her cue to leave. So she wished him good-night and walked out. After closing the door behind her, she leaned against the thick wood and reminded herself it was just a crush. Nothing else. But at this moment, still feeling empathy for his pain, it felt like much, much more.

Chapter Seven

"Can you smile?" Ryan asked as he adjusted the focus on the camera.

Sasha obliged him by placing one hand on her hip, gazing up at him and giving him a big grin.

"Very nice," he told her. "You're a beautiful princess."

Sasha twirled around, then settled to the floor in a cloud of pink fabric. "Pincess! Me pincess."

"Yes, you *are* a princess," Cassie said, moving forward and straightening Sasha's glittery cardboard crown. "The loveliest princess who ever graced a Halloween evening. Look at Uncle Ryan. He wants to take more pictures."

Instead of following instructions, the toddler held out her arms for a hug. Cassie knelt down and gathered her close. "You're going to have fun tonight," she told the child.

Ryan looked through the viewfinder of the camera and took three quick photos, then chose not to look too closely at his motives for doing so. Why would he want photographs of the nanny? Except he knew deep down inside that Cassie was more than that. Over the past few days, she'd also become a friend.

His conscience battled it out over conflicting needs and moral obligations. As his employee, Cassie was entitled to his consideration. As a friend, the same rules applied. The fact that he saw her as a desirable woman put a difficult spin on everything. He still respected her and wanted to pay attention to what was right, but he couldn't stop noticing her, thinking about her, *needing* her.

She didn't wear perfume, but a soft, clean feminine scent clung to her and drove him crazy. During the day he could hear her moving around the house and he wanted to go find her and be with her. He thought about her when he was supposed to be concentrating on work. The more he tried to dismiss her from his mind, the more she seemed to invade his every thought.

If she'd been just a pretty face, he probably could have forgotten about her fairly easily. But she wasn't trying to get his attention. Most of the time he figured she thought of him as *her* uncle Ryan, as well as Sasha's. She treated him like a much older, distant relative. Obviously the nearly nine-year age difference meant a lot more to her than it did to him.

So even as he took a couple more quick pictures of her, he told himself he had to let this fantasy fade. It was nonproductive and only left him aroused and restless.

"Where's your pumpkin?" Cassie asked as she pulled Sasha to her feet and gave her costume a quick once-over. "Wasn't it right here?"

Sasha frowned. "Pun'kin?"

"Yes, the plastic pumpkin Uncle Ryan bought you so that you can take it when we go trick-or-treating and get candy.

It's about this big.'' Cassie demonstrated the size with her hands.

''Me know,'' Sasha said, then dashed out of the room.

Ryan lowered the camera and stared after her. ''Do you realize I've never seen that kid walk? She runs and skips, sort of, and races everywhere.''

''Excess energy. Too bad we can't suck a little of it out of her each morning. Think of how much work we could both get done that day.''

''Interesting thought.'' He returned his attention to her. Cassie had dressed in black jeans and a multicolored sweater. Her usual heart-shaped earrings dangled, catching the overhead light.

''You look nice,'' he told her.

She glanced at him. A slight flush climbed her cheeks. ''Thanks. I wanted to be warm. It's going to be cool tonight. I knew that Sasha wouldn't want to wear a coat over her costume so I put her in two long-sleeved T-shirts and long pants underneath her dress. She's a tad bulky to fit in with the royal set, but otherwise, she's the perfect princess.''

She didn't quite meet his gaze as she spoke and the flush lingered. He made her nervous, he thought with some surprise, incredibly pleased by the fact. Maybe Cassie wasn't as immune to him as he'd first thought. Then she raised her hand to tuck her hair behind her ear and he caught sight of the ring on her left hand. Joel's ring.

She was already committed to someone else, he reminded himself. He had no right to mess with her life.

He set the camera on the counter. ''You don't have to come trick-or-treating with us tonight,'' he told her. ''You haven't been out with Joel in several days. Don't the two of you have plans?''

She shook her head. ''Bradley Discount is having a big celebration, with candy for kids and several departments offering special sales. Joel is in charge of all that, so he couldn't get away. Besides, I *want* to come out with you and Sasha. I doubt she remembers last year, so this will practically be her first time. She's going to have fun."

"If you're sure."

Her gaze met his. "I am."

He was too, sure that he wanted her. He could feel the heat rising inside him, the need growing. One of these days he was going to have to start dating again, he told himself. He couldn't keep having fantasies about inappropriate women—they were starting to interfere with his work.

Sasha raced back into the kitchen. She held out her plastic pumpkin and grinned. "Me find!" She handed the container to Cassie, then walked over to her uncle and raised her arms. "Up."

Ryan bent over and gripped her, pulling her into the air and toward him in one, smooth motion. Her little arms went around his neck. He settled her at his waist, his forearm supporting her butt.

"Hey, kid, you ready to go out trick-or-treating?"

Sasha nodded. "Me pincess."

"You're right. I shouldn't have called you a kid. Are you ready to go trick-or-treating, your highness?"

The toddler giggled.

The doorbell rang and she pointed. "Go see."

"Oh, so I'm transportation now, am I?" Ryan asked, although he didn't really mind. He liked that his niece was comfortable with him and that he enjoyed being around her.

Cassie beat both of them to the door. She pulled it open, allowing her sister, in crocodile costume, and a man dressed as a pirate to enter. Sasha took one look at them and buried her face in Ryan's shoulder.

"It's okay," he said softly as Cassie greeted her sister and brother-in-law. "You know Chloe, don't you? Cassie's sister? You like her. And that man is her husband. I'm sure he would really like to meet a real princess. Especially one as pretty as you."

Sasha raised her head slightly, gave a squeak and hid away again. Cassie smiled at him. "She's gone shy, has she?"

Chloe glanced down at herself. "Do you blame her? I think the theory of the crocodile costume was a good one. While I don't look hugely pregnant, I also don't look much like a normal crocodile. Maybe one that has pigged out over the weekend and is a little bloated."

"You look spectacular as always," her husband said. He glanced at Ryan. "I'm Arizona Smith. You must be Ryan. I've heard a lot about you."

They shook hands.

"Great costume," Ryan said, motioning to the other man's black wig, fitted blue jacket with a matching hat and the fake pistols strapped to his waist.

"I left my hook in the car. I thought it might scare Sasha. I see we did that anyway." He touched the child's arm. "Sorry, little one. Adults are strange creatures and you're going to have to get used to that."

She raised her head slightly. Arizona gave her a big smile, then an exaggerated wink. Ryan felt her relax in his arms.

"You're a very beautiful princess," Arizona told her.

Sasha nodded, as if to say she already knew that much and did he have anything new to tell her. Cassie and Chloe laughed.

If Ryan hadn't known Cassie was adopted, he would have wondered how the same family could have produced two such dissimilar daughters. Chloe was tall and elegant, even pregnant and dressed as a crocodile. She had the kind of sparkle about her that caused men to drop what they were doing just to watch her walk by. Cassie was several inches shorter, curved where her sister was lean, with a quieter beauty that Ryan found all the more appealing for its subtleties.

"We really appreciate you doing this," Cassie told her sister. "We won't be out long. Sasha will get tired pretty quickly."

Sasha began to wiggle. Ryan set her on the ground. She walked over to Cassie and put her hands on her tiny hips. "Me not tired."

"I know, sweetie. You're a big girl. You're going to have a lot of fun." Cassie straightened her crown, then returned her attention to her sister. "The candy is there," she said, pointing to a bowl on the table by the front door. "As I said, we'll be back in plenty of time for you to head out to your party."

Ryan glanced at his watch. "If you want to leave before we're back—"

Chloe cut him off with a shake of her head. "The university party doesn't start for over an hour and it goes practically all night. Take as long as you'd like." She touched her stomach. "Arizona and I are thinking of this as practice for the coming years."

"Absolutely." Arizona stepped next to his wife and put his arm around her. Chloe shifted closer.

They stood together as if they'd been a couple for decades instead of less than a year. Their love for each other was as obvious and real as their costumes. Ryan felt a twinge of envy inside. Was this what his brother and Helen had experienced in their marriage? He'd never been around them enough to notice, and even if he'd visited, he doubted he would have bothered to pick up on the small signals all couples sent and received.

What a waste, he thought grimly. He could have been a

part of a very special family...his family. Instead he'd wasted his time with too much work.

"Then I think we're ready," Cassie said. "Oops, Sasha's pumpkin is in the kitchen. I'll go get it."

She walked down the hall. Sasha trailed after her.

"So what do you think of Bradley?" Arizona asked.

"It's a great town," Ryan told him and knew that wasn't the question Arizona really wanted to ask. He decided to make it easier on the other man. After all, he was looking out for a family member. Ryan respected that.

"I regret that it took a tragedy to bring me here," he said. "Without Cassie's help, I wouldn't have made it through these past couple of weeks. She's terrific with Sasha and a wonderful person to have around. I have the greatest respect for her."

"We think she's special," Arizona said, his gaze steady.

"As do I. It's fortunate that she has family close by. If anything were to happen, she would have plenty of support."

"I'm glad you recognize that," Arizona said.

Cassie and Sasha returned to the foyer. "We're ready." She paused. "What are you two talking about?"

"Nothing special," Ryan told her. "Let's go."

They called out their goodbyes and stepped into the clear, cool night. When the door had closed behind them, Cassie looked at him. "You're not getting off that easily. I could smell the testosterone in the air. Was that some kind of male dominance contest?"

"Not at all." He bent down and smiled at Sasha. "Would you like me to carry your pumpkin for a while?"

Sasha nodded. He took it from her, then held out his hand to his niece. Cassie took her other one and they walked to the sidewalk and turned right. Already there were dozens of children and adults out for the festivities. As they passed a group of boys dressed like monsters, Sasha shrank against Ryan. He squeezed her hand reassuringly, then continued his conversation with Cassie.

"Your sister and brother-in-law are concerned about your safety while you're living alone in my house. They wanted to make sure that I understood they were looking out for your interests. I assured them that I respect you as a person and would never do anything to make you uncomfortable."

"I'm impressed you two got all that said. After all, I wasn't gone that long."

"Guys read between the lines. He understood, as did I."

"If you say so. You would have more experience with the guy thing than me." She paused. "Why wouldn't they trust you? I do."

His first thought was to tell her that was because she was so young. She didn't have enough life experiences to know that she should be wary. But then he realized it wasn't about age at all. It was about Cassie. She was one of the most open people he'd ever met. She would be this trusting at eighty.

"You take the world at face value," he said. "That's not always a good thing. Be grateful you have family watching out for you."

They'd reached the first house. Cassie dropped to one knee and straightened Sasha's crown. "Do you remember what we talked about this afternoon?" she asked. "About trick or treat?"

Sasha nodded.

"Okay, then all you have to do is walk up to that door and knock. When the people come out, hold out your pumpkin, say 'trick or treat' and they'll give you candy."

Sasha hesitated.

"We'll go up with you," Ryan assured her.

With Sasha leading the way, the three of them moved

toward the front door. The porch light was on and more light spilled from the open windows.

"Go ahead and knock," Cassie said.

Sasha stood immobilized.

"I guess this is a bigger moment than I'd realized," Ryan said. He leaned forward and rapped his knuckles on the door.

When it opened a large, older woman peered out. "Oh, look, Martin, this one is so precious. Aren't you just the prettiest thing." She beamed at them all. "What a lovely family. Can you say 'trick or treat'?"

Sasha opened her mouth, but there wasn't any sound.

"Next year," the woman said kindly. "She'll be demanding seconds for sure. Here you go, hon." She dropped a small candy bar into Sasha's pumpkin. "You have a good time tonight and don't eat too much sugar."

They thanked the woman and left. As they walked down the path, Sasha fished the candy out of her pumpkin and held it up to both of them. "Look," she said.

"I see." Cassie took it from her and put it back in the container. "We're going to wait until we get home before we eat any. You want to go to another house and try again?"

"More," Sasha said.

Ryan smiled at Cassie over the girl's head. "I think she's getting the hang of this."

At the next house they had to wait while the group in front of them collected candy. Sasha held out her pumpkin. She still didn't say "trick or treat," but she managed a faint "tank you" when a candy bar was placed in her container.

"More!" she called out. "More and more and more."

"Ah, the greed is setting in," Cassie said with a laugh. "It sure doesn't take long." She bent down and swept the girl into a hug. "Yes, we'll get you more. Unfortunately you won't eat very much of it, so that means I'll have to help.

Like I need more chocolate decorating my hips, thank you very much, young lady.''

Against his will Ryan found his gaze focusing on Cassie's hips. They were round and womanly. Did she really think there was something wrong with them? He loved the shape of her hips. He'd spent many pleasant moments thinking about touching them, of having her on top of him and grabbing those perfect hips to guide her up and down on his....

''Unk Ryan, there.'' Sasha pointed to the next house.

''As my lady wishes,'' he said, forcing his mind away from his passionate, albeit inappropriate, thoughts.

This time Sasha raced up to the house and eagerly knocked on the door. When it opened she held out her pumpkin. ''Candy,'' she said.

The man at the door laughed. ''Not the traditional greeting, but it gets the point across.'' He dropped two wrapped pieces into her pumpkin.

Sasha smiled at him, set her container on the ground, then carefully took out one candy bar and handed it back to him. He took it and winked.

''You don't have this thing figured out yet, do you?''

''Candy!'' Sasha said loudly. ''Candy, candy, candy. Tanks!''

With a little wave, she turned and headed for the street.

''What about this?'' the man asked, still holding the treat she'd given him.

''I think she wants you to have it,'' Ryan told him. He took Sasha's free hand. ''How long do you think she'll hold out?''

They ducked around Darth Vader, a ghost and a kid in a really ugly slobbering-monster mask.

''I thought we'd go to the end of the block,'' Cassie said, pointing to the stop sign three houses up. ''We can cross over and come back on the other side of the street. She should be tired by then."

They continued to walk from house to house. Sasha collected more candy than she handed back. Around them the sidewalks filled with more families. Ryan saw parents with their children, groups of kids alone. Several people stopped to tell Sasha that she was a beautiful princess. The child beamed with each compliment and Ryan felt an odd sense of pride, even though he had nothing to do with Sasha's appearance.

He felt a sense of community that was as tempting as it was unfamiliar. He wanted this all to be real. For the longest time he'd thought his brother was a fool, that John had sold out for something insignificant and that he would live to regret cutting back on his hours so that he could spend time with his wife and daughter. Now Ryan knew that John had made the right decision. He'd had no business judging his brother's actions.

Cassie and Sasha chatted with each other, occasionally drawing him into the conversation. But he was content to mostly listen while he mulled over his own thoughts. They turned up another walkway. Sasha was a couple of steps ahead when Cassie tripped over an uneven flagstone. Ryan grabbed her around the waist to keep her from falling. She clutched his arms.

Their combined actions brought her up against his chest. He felt the pressure of her breasts against him. One of her thighs slipped between his and bumped his rapidly swelling arousal.

The need was as instant as it was unexpected. One minute they'd been talking about upcoming movie releases for the holidays and the next she was in his arms. It took all his self-control to keep from hauling her closer and kissing her until they both forgot all the reasons they had to maintain distance in their relationship.

"Ryan?"

It was too dark for him to read her expression, but he heard the question in her voice. What the hell was he doing?

"Are you okay?" he asked, trying to sound casual. He released her and, when he was sure she'd regained her balance, stepped back a few feet. "You nearly took a header there. That path is pretty rough. Watch your step."

She drew in a shaky breath. "I will. Thanks."

For a second he thought she was going to say more, but thankfully she turned away. "Sasha?"

The little girl had paused halfway up the path. Now she waved and headed toward the front door. "Candy," she called over her shoulder.

"That's right," Cassie told her. "You can..." She groaned. "Sasha, wait. Don't go there."

Ryan heard the concern in her voice. He scanned the front porch and saw what had alerted Cassie.

Fake cobwebs hung from the eaves of the porch. Candles flickered on the porch railing and in the corner two masked kids giggled together as they watched Sasha approach. Spooky music rose to a crash of cymbals, drowning out Cassie's plea that they not scare the little girl as she approached.

Unsuspectingly, Sasha trotted right up the front steps and headed for the door. Ryan raced after her, passing Cassie in three strides. Even so, he was too late.

Sasha innocently reached for the bell beside the door. As she did so, the two monsters sprang toward her, yelling and waving their arms. Sasha let out a screech that took ten years off Ryan's life, dropped her pumpkin and fled down the stairs. In her haste, she lost her balance. Ryan scooped her up before she tumbled to the ground.

"Hush, sweetie, it's okay," he said.

Sasha screamed and sobbed, clinging to him. Cassie rushed over and hugged the child. The three of them stood huddled together, the two adults murmuring promises that nothing bad was going to happen to her. Ryan could feel the tremors rippling through her.

''We're really sorry,'' a young voice said. ''We were just playing. We do this every year. Most people know to keep the little kids away if they get scared. We're sorry, mister.''

Ryan saw the two ''monsters'' in question had pulled off their masks and were maybe eleven or twelve. The boys looked as shaken as Sasha, probably because they were under orders not to frighten small children. One of them held out Sasha's pumpkin.

''Here's her candy. We gave her a couple of extra pieces.''

''Thank you.'' Cassie took it, then smiled at the boys. ''It's not your fault. She's only two and doesn't really understand what's going on. We know you didn't scare her on purpose.'' She kissed the top of Sasha's head. ''Let's go home.''

Ryan nodded. The toddler's tears had slowed, but she still trembled. ''I'm glad you spoke to those two boys. I wanted to blister their hides and I would have overreacted.''

''I don't think they were being deliberately cruel. I saw the cobwebs and candles when we were walking toward the house. I should have realized what was going on.''

''It's not your fault,'' Ryan told her. He shifted Sasha. ''Should you be holding her instead of me? I mean, I got to her first, that's why I grabbed her.''

In the dim light from the streetlamps, he saw her smile at him. ''She's *your* niece. You should be the one holding her. I think it's great.'' She turned her attention to the child. ''Better?'' she asked.

Sasha nodded. ''Bad boys,'' she said.

"Not bad, just playing. I'm sorry you got scared. But you're safe now and we're not going to let anything happen to you. Okay?"

Sasha nodded.

She was so damn small, Ryan thought as he carried the toddler the rest of the way home. The world was a large and difficult place. He would have to protect Sasha as much as he could, all the while teaching her how to survive. The enormity of the responsibility made him shudder, but he couldn't back away from it now—he was all Sasha had.

When they arrived at the house, they said quick goodbyes to Chloe and Arizona. The doorbell rang again and again as more children stopped by for candy. With each cry of "trick or treat," Sasha clung tighter to Ryan's neck.

"She's not having much fun anymore," Cassie said. "Why don't you put her to bed while I man the door."

"Me?" Ryan shook his head. "You know how to do that stuff. I'll—"

Before he could finish his sentence, Sasha raised her head and looked at him. "Unk Ryan," she said. Tears stained her face; her eyes were puffy from crying.

How was he supposed to say no to her?

"You need to do this," Cassie told him. "She doesn't need a bath. I even brushed her teeth before we went out and she hasn't had anything to eat since, so don't worry about that. Put her in a nightgown, get her in bed, then read to her. She looks tired and I'm sure she'll fall asleep fairly quickly."

He wanted to protest that he wasn't ready to handle this sort of thing. Instead he nodded and carried his niece upstairs to her room. It only took a couple of minutes to get her out of her costume and put her into her pink kitten pajamas. Then she was tucked in bed and he was searching for the right story.

''Unk Ryan?''

He looked up from the bookcase. Sasha's big brown eyes were filled with tears again. ''Me don't like monsters.''

''I know, sweetie.'' He sat on the edge of the mattress and pulled her close. ''I'll protect you. I promise to check the whole house tonight. Every closet, every door. You'll be safe. Uncle Ryan will keep you safe.''

He didn't know how much she actually understood. At first he thought he'd gotten through to her because she was quiet, but then he realized she couldn't talk because she was crying too hard. He drew her up onto his lap and rocked her. She cried as if her little heart was breaking. Finally she murmured a single word.

''Mommy.''

Now Ryan felt tightness in *his* chest. None of this was fair.

''I know,'' he murmured. ''I know you miss her. I know I'm a poor substitute for both your parents. I wish I could offer you more, but I'm it. I don't know how to do things, and to be honest, kid, there are times when you terrify me. But I'm not going anywhere. We'll figure this out together.'' With a lot of help from Cassie, he reminded himself. He wouldn't have survived this without her.

Sasha continued to cry and he continued to hold her. Eventually she fell asleep. Carefully he lowered her into her bed and pulled the covers up to her chin. Then he sat in the darkness and wondered what the hell he was supposed to do now.

Chapter Eight

The last of the trick-or-treaters had rung the doorbell about a half hour before. Cassie moved restlessly in the living room and wondered what Ryan was doing. He'd been in with Sasha for so long that if he hadn't had to come down the stairs—which she could see clearly—she might have thought he'd slipped into his office. But he hadn't. He was still with his niece.

She moved to the front door and stared out through the beveled glass. The darkness seemed thicker than it had before when costumed children had brightened the sidewalks. She sank onto the wooden bench there, then sprang back to her feet. She wanted to be doing something, but she wasn't sure what—nothing felt right.

Part of the problem was her concern for Sasha. The poor girl hadn't needed a scare like the one she'd experienced. It wasn't a fun way to end her night. Cassie knew the boys had only been playing, but Sasha was too young to understand. At least she would probably forget between this year and next.

The good news was that in her time of need, she'd turned to her uncle and Ryan had been there for her. Slowly, uncle and niece were forming a family.

This was what she wanted, Cassie reminded herself. This was what she would have chosen for Sasha. She was pleased and relieved. At least she wasn't going to have to worry when Ryan took the girl back to San Jose, or whatever he decided to do with her. But the knowledge that they were bonding also left her feeling like an outsider.

Cassie leaned her forehead against the cool glass. Telling herself that everything was happening the way it was supposed to didn't help. Everything was mixed-up. She knew in her head that Ryan and Sasha had to form a family unit. Originally she'd been concerned that he would simply ignore the toddler and not want anything to do with her. But when she'd reminded him of his responsibilities, he'd come through like a seasoned parent.

So what was the problem? Maybe it wasn't about Ryan and Sasha at all, but about Ryan himself. The man had no flaws. Oh, he could get caught up in work and he liked to think he was the center of the universe. On a good day, he wanted to be treated as such, but Cassie wasn't talking about the details. She meant the inner being that made up the essence of Ryan Lawford. He'd resisted dealing with Sasha, but when push came to shove, he'd been there. Now, only a few short weeks into the relationship, he was terrific with her: patient, caring, making the little girl feel that she was the most important part of his life. Acting as if she was. How was she, Cassie, supposed to resist that?

It's just a crush, she reminded herself. Her feelings, whatever they were, had no basis in reality. In fact—

The sound of footsteps broke through her thoughts. She

turned and saw Ryan heading down the stairs. He looked tired and drawn.

She crossed the foyer and touched the curving end of the banister. ‘‘Is everything all right?’’ she asked. ‘‘Did Sasha have trouble falling asleep?’’

Dark emotions filled his green eyes. ‘‘At first she was worried about the monsters. I told her I would protect her, but I don't know if she understood what I was trying to say. Then—’’ He cleared his throat. ‘‘She was asking about her mother.’’

His expression turned haunted and he swore under his breath. ‘‘How am I supposed to deal with that? I can't fix her problem. There's nothing I can say or do to make it better.’’

‘‘You're right,’’ Cassie said gently. ‘‘You can't fix it. No one can. You can only be there to help her get through the tough times.’’

‘‘Maybe.’’ He shrugged. ‘‘I held her. I rocked her in my arms and let her cry her little heart out. I thought I was going to go crazy listening to the sobs. I didn't know what else to do. I'm useless.’’

‘‘No. You're exactly what she needs.’’

‘‘Yeah, right. What with all my experience with kids.’’ His mouth twisted. ‘‘I'm screwing this up.’’

His pain called to her, making her want to step closer and offer him comfort. Knowing that he would refuse, she held back. ‘‘You're doing everything exactly right. There *are* no set rules. Every parent has to find his or her way in the dark. Sasha isn't going to understand any complicated explanation about what happened to her folks. She only knows that she misses them deeply. Most of the time, when she's happy, she's fine, but when something rocks her world, she cries out for them. That doesn't mean you're doing anything wrong.’’

"I guess." He sank onto the bench by the front door. A bowl of candy sat on the small table next to him. He reached in and pulled out a small candy bar, then held it out to her. "Want one?"

"Sure." She took it, then settled into the seat opposite his.

Ryan unwrapped a piece of chocolate for himself and ate it. When he was done, he leaned forward and rested his elbows on his knees.

"I didn't think it would be like this," he said. "Dealing with Sasha, I mean. When I found out John and Helen had made me her guardian, I was annoyed and frustrated, but I never got how big a responsibility it was."

"It's a challenge," she agreed. "But it's worth it."

He raised his head and met her gaze. "I didn't understand that part, either. But I do now. She's kind of like a tick that burrows under the skin. First you notice a bump and don't think much about it. The next thing you know, you've got a raging infection all through your body."

He grinned. "Sorry, that was kind of gross, and I didn't mean it in a bad way. It's just that for the first couple of weeks, I thought of Sasha as a responsibility I didn't want to deal with. I was very happy to pass her on to you. Now I look forward to spending part of my day with her. The little kid has gotten under my skin."

His words created a warm feeling in Cassie's stomach. Ryan had come to care about his niece. They would do well for each other, she thought, pleased that the sweet child would always have a family of her own. Someone who knew her history and could, in later years, tell her about her parents. Roots were important—Cassie knew that firsthand.

Ryan fished another candy bar out of the bowl. He offered it to Cassie, but she shook her head. He opened it and took a bite. After he'd swallowed he said, "I was thinking about my brother earlier. He was about ten years older than me. We had different fathers, but that didn't matter to us. We were really close. Apparently my mother had bad taste in men because neither of our dads bothered to stick around long enough to see us born."

He made the statement lightly, but Cassie caught the tension in his body. She knew exactly what it felt like to be abandoned by a parent, but she kept her compassion to herself. She had the feeling that at this moment in time Ryan needed to talk more than he needed to listen.

"Our mother worked hard." He shrugged. "She was always urging us to get ahead. John became a doctor." He gave her a quick smile. "Mom was really proud of him. I was, too. It's tough to get through all the training but he did it. Then he turned around and paid back his loans in record time."

He straightened on the bench and leaned his head against the wall. "About five years ago John called me to tell me he'd met Helen and they were getting married. I was a little surprised. In our family we were big on work, but relationships had never been that important. When I pointed that out John said he didn't care. He'd fallen in love and he wanted to get married. He told me that he and Helen had also talked about starting a family. That one really threw me."

"You've never thought about doing that yourself?" Cassie asked before she could stop herself.

Ryan shrugged. "Not really. I never saw the point. There have been women in my life, but no one I wanted to marry."

Cassie wasn't sure what to make of that statement. He'd had women. Did that mean they'd all been lovers? Did he take women to his bed for a few times, then send them on their way? Or was it a mutual decision? Was that what other people did? She couldn't even imagine.

"He told me he wanted to slow down," Ryan continued. "I remember staring at the phone not believing what he was saying. I'd just started making a success of my own company and I was working eighteen-hour days. Who had time to slow down? I couldn't believe he meant it. Worse, I thought he was selling out."

He drew in a deep breath, but he didn't speak. Cassie observed him, watched the play of light on his strong face, the twitch of a muscle as he clenched his jaw. At times she still didn't understand Ryan, but right now she knew exactly what he was thinking.

"You understand now," she murmured. "His actions didn't make sense five years ago, but you're starting to understand what he was trying to tell you."

He nodded slowly. His gaze was steady and direct. "What I remember most about my mother is how hard she worked. She'd been poor for a long time and I understand that it's difficult to let go of the past, but the last few years of her life, she could have slowed down some. She had two sons who were sending her money every month. But she wouldn't spend it. We sent her nice clothes and things for the house. When she was gone, we found all of them, still in their boxes. She never wore them or used them. I don't understand that."

Cassie didn't either. "Do you think she was saving them?"

"I don't know. Sometimes I think she forgot what she was working for. The process became important and she lost sight of the goal." He shook his head. "Or maybe it's something else entirely. All I know is that she died too young, surrounded by lovely things she wouldn't let herself enjoy."

He paused. "I wish..." His mouth twisted and he avoided her gaze.

"What?" she asked.

"I wish I'd spent more time with John. He and Helen kept inviting me here for holidays or just a weekend and I kept putting it off. I didn't think it was as important as my work. I thought we'd have more time."

Her heart ached for him. He was in as much pain as Sasha, but in a way Ryan suffered more. He wouldn't cry out or allow himself to be comforted.

A vague feeling of disquiet settled over her. This was dangerous territory for her. Ryan the remote, successful man at the other end of the house was safe. She was allowed to have a crush on him without having to worry about getting into trouble. But this man was someone different. He wasn't remote or hard to understand. If anything, she felt they had a lot in common. They talked and laughed together easily. She couldn't have a crush on this Ryan because he was real. Once he was real, then her heart was at risk.

Don't be a fool, she told herself. *He* might be more real to her, but *she* was still just the nanny to him. He never thought of her as a woman, someone who might interest him.

Ryan glanced out the window. "I guess we're done with Halloween for this year." He looked at his watch. "It's after ten. I should probably let you get to bed."

She nodded, thinking that she should make her way upstairs. Morning came early when there was a two-year-old in the house.

"I don't suppose you'd care to join me for a quick drink," he offered.

Cassie opened her mouth to tell him that wasn't a good idea. Not with the way her body had gone on alert, every cell tingling with breathless anticipation. But her legs were suddenly heavy and the stairs looked too tall to climb right now. It was just a drink, she argued with herself. What could it hurt?

"That would be nice," she said.

He rose to his feet, then started toward the study he'd taken over as his office. "I think there's some brandy in here," he called over his shoulder.

Cassie trailed after him. It was just a drink, she repeated silently. Nothing significant. It didn't mean his feelings about her had changed. Oh, but she wanted it to mean something, she thought to herself as heat and excitement raced through her. Brandy. They were going to have a glass of brandy together. She thought people only did that in the movies.

She followed him toward the back of the house. While he opened the sliding doors that concealed the bar area in the study, she settled onto a corner of the dark blue leather sofa against the wall opposite the bay window.

A large desk dominated the room. Ryan had brought in a new fax machine, a printer, some other computer equipment she didn't recognize and three filing cabinets. There were thick overnight envelopes on his desk and stacks of paper on nearly every free surface.

Ryan poured brandy into two glasses, then carried them over to the sofa. "I haven't had this before," he said as he handed her the quarter-full snifter. "But John always had excellent taste. I'm sure you'll like it." He touched his glass to hers.

He acted as if she did this sort of thing all the time, she thought with some amazement. No way she was going to tell him that she was more of a beer and white wine kind of girl. Cassie didn't think she'd ever tasted brandy before in her life. While Ryan sat down on the opposite end of the sofa, she took a first, tentative sip.

The liquid burned her tongue and her throat, but not in a bad way. It really was exactly like what she'd read about in books—she *could* feel the fire all the way down to her stomach.

"What do you think?" he asked.

She gave him a smile. "I like it." She took another sip and tried to act as if she did this regularly.

Ryan set his drink on the glass coffee table in front of the couch. "I have something I've been meaning to mention before, but there hasn't been a good time until now."

He paused and Cassie's stomach sunk like a stone. What? Was he going to tell her he was dissatisfied with her work? Did he know about her infatuation and did that make him angry? Was it—

"It's about Joel," he said.

She blinked. "Joel?" That didn't make sense. "What about him?"

Ryan angled toward her and rested his hand along the back of the sofa. "You don't see him very much. I'm concerned that your job is interfering with your relationship." He leaned toward her slightly. "I appreciate how great you are with Sasha. You obviously adore her and the feeling is mutual. You work long hours. Again, you have my thanks, but I don't want your personal life to suffer." He gave a quick smile. "If I'm saying this all wrong, please forgive me. To be honest, I've never had this conversation with an employee before in my life."

She wasn't sure what to say. Part of her thought it was really nice that he was concerned about her relationship with Joel. An equal part of her was annoyed that he was concerned about her relationship with Joel. Couldn't the man have even the tiniest hint of jealousy or envy? She sighed. As everyone had pointed out to her, she wasn't his type. He saw her as the hired help, someone to keep happy and treat fairly.

"You're very sweet to worry," she said calmly, knowing he would be confused if she told him what she was thinking. Maybe confused was putting it mildly. He would probably be stunned…and not in a good way. "But there's no reason for alarm. I've been seeing Joel as much as ever."

He frowned. "You've only gone out a couple of times a week since you've come to work for me."

"I know. That's all we ever see each other."

"But it's been nine years."

"We don't need to spend every minute together." She kept her tone pleasant, even though she was feeling vaguely attacked. "This works for us."

"If you're finding each other boring before you get married, then you two are in trouble."

His voice was teasing, but Cassie couldn't smile. Ryan spoke something she hadn't dared to think to herself, but that she could no longer avoid. She stared at him helplessly, not sure what to say, then faked a chuckle as coldness enveloped her, chasing away any lingering warmth from the brandy. Was that what was wrong? she wondered. Did she and Joel already find each other boring?

She dismissed the sense of foreboding that swept over her. It was the night, she told herself. Or maybe the man. None of this was real.

They sipped their brandy in silence. Ryan told himself it was getting late and that he should send Cassie upstairs, but he didn't want to. Not only did he not want to be alone, but he enjoyed her company. She made him laugh; she reassured him; she reminded him that he was alive. And if he was honest with himself, he would be willing to admit that he also wanted *her,* which was completely different from not wanting to be alone. The ache inside of him was very specifically for the woman sitting at the other end of the sofa. He couldn't call one of his female friends and have her stop by to fill the void…not this time.

Unfortunately, the only woman he wanted was the one woman he couldn't have.

He looked at her. The light from the floor lamp reflected on her gleaming, dark hair. She took another sip of brandy. "You're staring at me. Do I have a smudge on my cheek?"

"Sorry." He forced himself to look away. "Not at all. I was just wondering about you. You're very different from anyone I've ever met."

She wrinkled her nose. "I know what that means. I've always been the country mouse. I guess I always will be."

There was nothing mouselike about her, but he couldn't admit that. Not with the night closing around them and his wanting growing...along with other parts of him. If he inhaled deeply, he could almost catch the sweet scent of her body. He wanted to know what she would feel like in his arms. He wanted to explore her generous curves, touch her soft face, kiss her and taste her and...

He had to clear his throat before he could speak. "I meant 'different' in a good way," he told her. "While you've chosen a perfectly respectable path, it isn't one designed to provide you with material benefits."

She chuckled. "That's a polite way of saying I'll never be rich working in a preschool." She shrugged. "I know that, but making lots of money isn't important to me. I grew up in a typically middle-class town. We didn't have tons of money, but there was always enough. When my parents died, they left me a trust fund. While it isn't millions, if I had to, I could live off it for several years. As it is, I'm just letting the proceeds reinvest."

She took a sip of her drink. "I always knew that I wanted to work with kids. I love their energy and enthusiasm. They're so honest with their feelings. Sometimes I wish I could be more like my sister. Chloe wanted a career and made that happen."

"You have a career," he reminded her.

"It's not exactly the same." She stared into her glass.

"Chloe always wanted to get away from Bradley and I always wanted to stay. When she met Arizona she realized that she had everything she needed right here, which is nice. I enjoy having her close. But it *is* ironic. I mean I'm the one who cares about genealogy and the history of the family and the town, but she's the real Bradley. I'm just adopted."

She said the words easily, as if they were simply information. But Ryan sensed something underneath, something hidden. The truth, he suspected, hurt her. She wanted to belong as much as her sister did. But by a quirk of birth, she never would.

"John and I grew up in a series of small apartments," he said. "It must have been nice to have a house that had been in the family for generations."

She flashed him a quick smile. "It was. Our mom would tell stories about the founding of the town, along with tales of the different Bradley women." Her smile faded. "It's been nearly ten years and I still miss my mother. I suppose that's one of the reasons I understand Sasha so well. I know what she's going through."

He nodded. "I suppose there's good and bad to being older when one loses a parent. You remember the good times, but you also remember the loss. Sasha isn't going to have any memories of John and Helen."

"There's no good time to lose one parent, let alone both," Cassie said, and Ryan remembered too late that Cassie had lost family before. Her birth mother had given her up for adoption.

"I'm sorry," he said quickly.

"Don't be. I don't mind talking about this." She looked at him. "Sometimes I think the worst part of our parents' death was the fact that Chloe and I were separated for nearly three years. Aunt Charity was left as guardian, but she was traveling and the lawyer couldn't find her. So Chloe and I were put into different foster homes. I stayed in Bradley, but she was sent to another town. I think meeting Joel is what saved me.''

''Joel?'' What did he have to do with anything?

She nodded. ''He and I went to the same high school. We met our sophomore years. At first we were just friends, but then we started dating.'' She held up her hand. ''Please spare me the psychobabble on what that means. Chloe has been over it a dozen times.''

She piqued his curiosity. ''What's Chloe's theory?''

''Chloe thinks I'm settling. That I suffered a traumatic loss at a formative age and Joel got me through it. Therefore I have misplaced loyalty toward him. She thinks that marrying Joel would be a mistake.''

Chloe was a very sensible woman, Ryan thought, not daring to question his reasons for suddenly liking Cassie's sister. ''What do you think?''

He'd expected a quick response, either telling him that none of this was his business, or saying that Joel was the love of her life. Instead she leaned back into the corner of the sofa and stared at him.

''I don't know anymore.''

Her words hung in the silence. Inside he felt a quick jolt of pleasure, which he instantly told himself he had no business feeling.

''Sometimes it feels so incredibly right,'' she said. ''We've known each other for years. There aren't any surprises, but that's not always a bad thing. We get along, we respect each other. It's comfortable.'' She drew in a breath. ''But sometimes I want the fantasy.''

He knew he probably shouldn't ask, but he couldn't help himself. ''What fantasy?''

''No, you'll laugh.''

''I promise I won't.''

Her gaze skittered away from his and he sensed her sudden tension. More intrigued than he had the right to be, he leaned toward her and pressed for a reply. "I really won't laugh. Tell me. What is your fantasy?"

She drew in a deep breath. "The Bradley family has this magic nightgown."

Ryan stared at her, certain he'd misunderstood. "A what?"

"A magic nightgown. A long time ago, there was this gypsy woman. She was being attacked by a mob of drunken men."

He listened while she explained the legend of the nightgown. "I don't know what to say," he told her when she'd finished. "I've never heard anything like this before."

"I know it sounds strange, but I can show you the nightgown."

"No, that's not necessary. I'm sure it exists."

She ducked her head. "At least you didn't laugh."

He didn't know about spells and gypsy promises, but he did know that Cassie had just shared something very important to her. "Why would I? Just because I don't have a similar family tradition to tell you about doesn't mean that I'd make fun of yours. So you're counting on this legend?"

She nodded quickly. "I want the legacy to be true for me. I want to wear the nightgown on my twenty-fifth birthday and I want to dream about the man I'm supposed to marry. Chloe wore it and dreamed about Arizona. They met the next day and if it wasn't love at first sight, it was the next best thing. I want that, even though I'm afraid it's not going to happen."

Magic nightgowns and a promise of happily-ever-after. She really was an innocent. "Why wouldn't it happen for you?"

"I'm not a real Bradley," she reminded him. "I'm

adopted. I have high hopes, of course, and Aunt Charity says believing is enough, but I don't know.''

He wanted to tell her it was going to be fine, that she would have her special dream on her special night and everything would work out the way she wanted. But what did he know?

''What does Joel think about all this?'' he asked, wondering how any fiancé would feel about the possibility of being usurped by a mystery suitor.

She finished her brandy and placed the snifter on the coffee table. ''Not much. He's very low-key about the whole thing. Joel believes I'm going to dream about him. I suppose he's right, but sometimes I wish...'' Her voice trailed off.

Ryan knew exactly what she was thinking. ''Sometimes you wish he would be a little worried, and other times you wish you could dream about someone else.''

Her eyes widened. ''How did you know?'' She leaned forward and covered her face with her hands. ''I don't want to know what you're thinking. I know that's horribly disloyal and makes me an awful person.''

He moved toward her and placed his hand on her forearm. ''Don't think that for a second, Cassie. You're a sweet, good young woman. Why shouldn't you have a few dreams? You said yourself that you and Joel were waiting until you were sure. Doesn't that mean considering other possibilities? Besides, it's not as if you're acting on these thoughts. I don't see you out dating other men.'' Even though you should, he added silently, thinking that he would like to go to the top of that list.

He pushed the inappropriate desire away. ''Don't feel guilty about what you want. You haven't done anything wrong.''

She raised her head and looked at him. Her smile trembled

a little at the corners, but it was still pretty. She had a lovely smile. Had he noticed that before?

"Thank you," she told him. "You're very kind."

Kind. There was a word every man was just dying to have applied to himself. Kind. Maybe she could throw in loyal and trustworthy. Then he could feel really macho.

This was a mistake, he thought grimly. He was getting involved in something that didn't concern him. Cassie was his employee, nothing more. They shouldn't be having this personal conversation.

"Have you ever been married?" she asked.

He'd been about to stand up and excuse himself, but her question was as effective as a seat belt at keeping him in his chair. "No," he told her.

"Why not?"

"I never wanted to."

She looked shocked. "Are you saying you've never fallen in love?"

The truth was, he hadn't. But admitting that made him feel that there was something wrong with him. "I never had the time," he answered instead. "I was too involved with work, then with starting my company. There was no room for much of a personal life."

"I see." Her gaze was steady on his face and he wondered what exactly it was she saw.

"That's going to have to be different now," she said. "I'm not suggesting you marry for Sasha's sake, but you are going to have to be around to spend time with her."

"I know." Everything was changing—he could feel it. Somehow when he wasn't looking, his life had taken an unexpected turn. "What about you?" he asked. "What's next? Marriage to Joel? To be honest, I'm surprised he's been willing to wait so long. If I were him I would be worried about that magic nightgown and I would want to sweep you off your feet.''

''As nice as that sounds, Joel isn't the sweeping kind.''

She made the statement matter-of-factly, but Ryan thought he could read between the lines. Perhaps Cassie wasn't waiting for her twenty-fifth birthday and the promise of the family legend as much as she was waiting for romance. She wanted Joel to want *her* enough to be unhappy about any delay. How else was Joel letting her down?

Ryan remembered her few dates with Joel since she'd been in his employ. She'd been back before eleven each time. It wasn't his place to speculate and he was probably wrong about everything, but he couldn't help wondering what that meant. Didn't Joel know what a prize he held? On the heels of that thought came the realization that he would side with Cassie's sister any day. To his mind, Cassie was settling.

''You've been with Joel for years,'' he said. ''You were very young when you started dating him. Maybe you should go out and explore the world before getting married.''

''You don't actually mean the world,'' she said. ''You think I should date other men.''

''I think you should be very sure.''

She rose to her feet and crossed to the bay window. The lights from the room made the glass reflect images like a mirror. He could see her face, her thoughtful expression. She folded her arms over her chest as if to protect herself from danger.

''I've had this exact conversation with myself,'' she admitted. ''Sometimes I'm completely sure and others...'' Her voice trailed off.

''How do you know?'' she asked softly. ''I love Joel, but I don't know what kind of love we share. He's easy for me to be around. I like him. I respect him. But sometimes I'm afraid I love him more like a brother than a husband.'' She drew in a breath. ''We're long on conversation but short on passion. I tell myself that shouldn't matter, but I'm just not sure.''

Ryan felt vindicated. So he'd been right about Cassie's feelings of uncertainty. Unfortunately, he didn't have an answer to her dilemma.

''I tell myself there's more to life than passion,'' she continued. ''Do I have the right to want more? Who am I to think I deserve it all?''

Ryan stood up and crossed to stand behind her. Their gazes met in the reflection of the window. ''Everyone deserves it all,'' he said. She more than most, although he wasn't about to speak the last part aloud.

She turned to face him. ''I want to believe you. Sometimes I feel so guilty for not being more grateful to have Joel in my life.''

''You like and respect him. That's what we're supposed to do with friends. But you don't have to pretend to love him if that's not what you feel. You don't have to marry him if you're not sure.''

They were standing too close, he thought suddenly. He could inhale her sweetness and feel the heat from her body. She wore a sweater over jeans, but somehow the simple clothes had become provocative, calling to him, making him want to touch her. Dear God, what was he thinking? This was all wrong.

He told himself to back off. Cassie wasn't interested in him that way. She saw him as an old man…or at the very least an *older* man. She worked for him. He had no right to want her, to want to take her in his arms and kiss her.

Cassie raised her chin slightly. ''I'm not sure,'' she whispered.

He'd waited long enough. Whatever control he'd had disappeared. There was only the night, the woman standing so close to him, and his need. Telling himself it was wrong didn't help. Telling himself she deserved better than he could ever offer was completely true, but it didn't give him the strength to turn away.

"Cassie, I can't—"

His sentence ended in a strangled sound. Cassie stared at Ryan. He was obviously trying to tell her something, although she couldn't figure out what. She wasn't even sure it mattered. After all, fire filled his magical green eyes. A fire that burned so hot, she felt herself going up in flames.

She told herself she should be afraid, that Ryan wasn't like Joel and that she had somehow become tangled in a situation she had neither the experience nor the skills to handle. But she didn't care. This was Ryan and she trusted him as much as she'd ever trusted anyone. Besides, she couldn't move even if she wanted to. Something had happened to her will. Her legs were too heavy to carry her away. She couldn't think, she couldn't move, she could only wait helpless for something to happen…something wonderful.

He placed his hand on her shoulder. "You should head up to bed."

She nodded. "I should." But she wasn't going to. Not until…well, she couldn't say until what, but she wasn't leaving anytime soon.

"I mean it, Cassie. If you stand here any longer I'm going to have to—" He broke off and swore under his breath.

"You're going to have to what?"

He placed his free hand on her waist and drew her closer. So close that her thighs brushed against his. Instantly heat poured through her. Her legs went from heavy to melting. Her breasts ached and swelled and pushed against her bra. She raised her hands and rested them on his upper arms. She could feel the tension in him, the rock-hard strength of his muscles.

"Ryan," she breathed. Dear Lord, if she didn't know better, she might think the man was going to kiss her. Right here in his office, in front of a window, on Halloween. It was magic. It was perfect. *He* was perfect, trying to warn her away and all. Even now she could see the conflict in his eyes as he attempted to talk himself out of the moment.

It surprised her that there was even a question. After all, she wasn't like Chloe. Men had never found her irresistible. But she loved the fact that Ryan, of all men, seemed to think her so. His breathing was harsh, his body tense, his eyes questioning.

She thought about raising herself on tiptoe, just to take enough of the initiative so that he didn't have to feel badly about what he was doing. But she didn't want to. This was her fantasy, after all, and in all the books she'd ever read, the guy was the one who kissed first.

So she waited...and waited...until it seemed as if he was never going to do it.

Finally, when she was sure he was going to come to his senses and realize who she was and know that he could never really want her that way, he lowered his head to hers.

"Tell me to stop if you don't want this."

Those were his last words. She vaguely heard him utter them and had a split second in which to think that was *so* not going to happen. Then his mouth touched her lips and she couldn't think at all.

For a heartbeat there was nothing. Just the sensation of his skin against hers. Then it hit. The heat, the need, the hunger, the incredible desire to be closer, to have their mouths forever joined.

He kept the contact light, which drove her crazy. His hands didn't move. He continued to touch her shoulder and her waist, while a voice in her head screamed for him to put his hands everywhere. Tremors started at her neck and worked their way through her body. Her nipples tightened and ached, while between her legs damp heat made her fear she really was melting from the inside out.

His head tilted slightly so their lips could press together more firmly. She clung to him, afraid he would pull back. Her hands moved from his upper arms to his shoulders, then wrapped around his neck. She couldn't get close enough. She needed more. Desperately.

"Cassie." His voice was low, thick and strangled.

She uttered two words she'd never before in her life said to a man.

"Don't stop."

He groaned, parted his lips and plunged his tongue inside her mouth.

She welcomed his assault, meeting him with one of her own. They touched and stroked, exploring each other, finding pleasure and heat and madness. She worried a little about her enthusiasm until she realized he was holding on to her just as tightly and that the hand on her waist had dropped to her rear and pulled her hard against him.

Speaking of hard...he was. She could feel the ridge of his need pressing against her belly. She'd never felt Joel's arousal before. Of course they'd never stood this close or kissed with such passion.

He broke the kiss, but only to press his lips against her cheeks, her jaw, then down her throat. Her breathing came in gasps. She didn't know how much longer she was going to be able to remain standing.

"Ryan," she whispered.

"I know," he answered. "I feel it, too."

So this was passion, she thought through a fog of desire as he reclaimed her mouth. This was the sensation that sparked the books and songs and poems. It all made sense now. For the past several years she'd thought everyone was lying to her and that this sort of thing didn't really exist. But it did.

Unfortunately, she didn't have any right to be experiencing it with this particular man.

She broke the kiss, turned on her heel and ran from the room.

Chapter Nine

Ryan leaned against the windowsill and closed his eyes. He could still feel the heat of Cassie's body pressed against his and taste her sweetness on his tongue. A tremor ripped through him. It didn't matter that he was fifteen different kinds of bastard, the wanting inside of him was the most powerful force he'd ever experienced.

The sound of her footsteps died away. There was a moment of silence, followed by a door closing on the second floor. She'd run from him. He hated that she'd done that, but he couldn't blame her. What the hell had he been thinking?

He crossed over to his desk and sank into the leather chair. His breathing still came in gasps and his arousal ached. He had a bad feeling he was going to spend the next several hours in a lot of pain. Still, none of that mattered. The real problem was that he hadn't been thinking. He'd been feeling and reacting.

The questions of right and wrong, of what was proper and decent hadn't occurred to him. One minute they'd been talking and the next she'd been so damn close that he couldn't help himself.

He'd lost control. He, Ryan Lawford, who always played the mating game by the rules, had lost control with a young woman who didn't understand there was a game in progress. He'd been blindsided by a virtual innocent. Joel had been the only man in her life, so she should have been the one in over her head. Instead *he'd* been the one to plunge headlong into passion.

Guilt crept through him, seeping into the cells of his body, replacing the wanting with something cold and ugly.

He'd had no right to touch her. She worked for him. He swore again and wondered what had gone wrong. He'd never once flirted with an employee, let alone dated or kissed one. He'd always been able to separate business from pleasure. To be honest, in the past he'd never been tempted to cross the line. The fact that he'd only done it once didn't make him feel any better. What he'd done was wrong. Cassie not only worked for him, she worked for him *in his house.* She was completely vulnerable and at his mercy by virtue of her living under the same roof. He owed her respect. He owed her a work environment in which she felt safe. He owed her the right to get through her day without worrying that she was going to be groped at every turn.

But that wasn't his only sin. There was also the issue of her involvement with Joel. Cassie was practically engaged to the younger man. He, Ryan, had no business trying to seduce her. If she'd been unattached it still would have been wrong, but this made it unforgivable.

What had happened? Why her? She wasn't his type. He ignored the voice inside that whispered he didn't have a type. She was too young, too inexperienced, too different from the women who regularly drifted through his world.

He leaned back in his chair. It didn't matter, he realized. Right type or not, engaged or not, working for him or not, he wanted her. Something had happened between them. Not just tonight, although the kiss had been glorious, but before. He'd noticed her. He'd seen that she was a bright, funny, pretty, charming woman and he'd wanted her. Now he didn't know how to change his feelings so that he didn't get excited every time he saw her or thought about her.

The realization confused him. Something was happening to him—he was changing. He was no longer the man he'd been when he'd first arrived in Bradley to clear up his brother's estate. Some of the changes had come about because of Sasha. He was growing to care about the little girl. But some of the changes were about Cassie's influence on him.

What was happening to him and how could he make it stop? He'd done so well for so long by ignoring his feelings. He didn't want to have to deal with them now. Unfortunately, he wasn't being given a choice.

His world had just gotten very complicated.

He reminded himself that he didn't want a commitment. Unfortunately, Cassie was the kind of woman men married, not the kind they had an affair with. There was also the issue of her engagement, not to mention her employment with him. He didn't have a choice in the matter. He was going to have to apologize and promise that it would never happen again. That wouldn't make it right, but it was the best he could do. Actually it was the best he was *willing* to do. After all, he could offer to terminate her so that she could get back to her regular life.

But the thought of Cassie leaving was physically painful, and it wasn't all about having to deal with Sasha on his own. He knew instinctively that it would difficult for him to go through his day without seeing Cassie. He didn't even want to think about what that meant.

So instead he would apologize to Cassie in the morning and promise that she would always be safe from him. He would hide his wanting; he would stop thinking about her as much. He would attempt to go back to the man he had been before, even though he had a bad feeling it was going to be a nearly impossible task. He'd seen the light and he doubted he would willingly return to the darkness.

The first fingers of dawn crept around the closed drapes. Cassie pulled her knees more tightly to her chest and watched as the room slowly brightened. She'd been awake for much of the night, thinking about *the kiss.*

It was such a simple act, she thought. A type of contact millions of people had every day. Family members kissed hello or goodbye, old friends often greeted each other with a kiss. She'd kissed her sister, her parents, her aunt and, of course, Joel. But nothing had prepared her for the impact of Ryan's kiss. She was still surprised there weren't scorch marks on her hands and face from the heat of their contact. She'd relived the kiss a hundred times in the long night and each time the memory had made her shiver with longing.

Her body had come alive in his arms. She'd finally understood why lovers risked death to be together. She'd read once that when a woman truly bonds with a man that just the idea of being with a different man could physically make her sick to her stomach. Cassie had always thought that was a lot of nonsense, but now she wasn't so sure. She didn't know exactly what steps were necessary to bond a woman to a man. She suspected they first had to make love, to establish a biological as well as an emotional connection. But she understood the part about not wanting to be with anyone else. Just the thought of another man's kiss made her flinch.

The world had become a confusing place. On the one hand, Ryan's kiss had explained so much to her. She felt as if she'd finally seen through a previously closed door. She had shared a common human experience.

Cassie dropped her head to her knees and sighed. But on the other hand, what she'd done was wrong. There were no words to pretty up the truth. She had a commitment to Joel and she'd violated his trust in her. Maybe she'd been a little annoyed because he hadn't been concerned about her living in Ryan's house, but that didn't give her the right to create a situation in which he would be concerned. She owed him her loyalty.

Ryan was just a crush, she reminded herself once again. As such, she owed him nothing. He might be a flesh and blood man, but their worlds were so different, he might as well be a movie star. She had as much in common with him as she did with someone famous. Except...

She raised her head and squeezed her eyes tightly closed. Except somewhere along the way, he'd become real to her. He wasn't just the object of her affection. He was a normal person with moods and opinions. She'd talked with him and laughed with him. She'd watched him change from a distant stranger into a warm, caring man who was coming to love his niece. She'd seen that he cared about different things, that he was honorable and hardworking. She was still smitten with him, but she also liked and respected him.

Now he'd taught her about wanting. He'd held her close and kissed her until everything had changed. Her body had come alive for him. Even this morning when she should be feeling guilty and horrible and figuring out a way to set things right, memories of their kiss intruded. If she thought about it for too long, she found herself getting warm. Her breasts would begin to ache, and that secret place between her legs would tingle and dampen. She didn't know exactly what was happening to her, but she knew she liked it.

However she wasn't a fool. Here, in Bradley, with only his two-year-old niece for company, Ryan might think that she was great fun to be around. But she wouldn't fit into his real world. She wasn't the right kind of woman. He was older and more sophisticated, while she was just a preschool teacher. Maybe if she'd always wanted to be more they might have had a chance, but she didn't. She loved living in Bradley. She'd only ever wanted to work with children. She didn't care about wearing the right clothes or driving the right kind of car. Her idea of heaven would be a family—roots of her own.

Cassie opened her eyes and stared around at the lovely guest room. The large dresser seemed to waver in the morning light. Then she realized there were tears in her eyes. At one time she'd thought she would find everything she'd ever wanted with Joel. They'd been in love once and they'd made plans for a future. But something had happened along the way. She couldn't point to an exact date or incident, but they were different people now. The kiss between Ryan and her had been wrong, but it had forced her to face something she suspected she'd been avoiding for a long time. She had to end things with Joel.

The thought should have terrified her, but it didn't. She held her breath, waiting for the rush of disappointment or sadness, but there wasn't much of anything. Maybe a little relief, which startled her. Should she have broken things off with Joel years ago? There was no way to get that answer, she realized, and no point in second-guessing herself. She would just have to go forward now and do the right thing.

She brushed her cheek with the back of her hand and smiled. Wouldn't it be lovely if she told Ryan what she was going to do and he was so happy he swept her up in his arms and told her he'd loved her from the first moment he'd met her? It was about as likely as winning the lottery, and she rarely bought a ticket. Unfortunately, Ryan wouldn't think anything about her breaking up with Joel. Or if he did, he would most likely be worried that she would expect something from him.

Cassie's smile faded. She didn't want that. She didn't want Ryan to think she was going to pursue him. She would have to play it very cool. As if the kiss was no big deal. Maybe he would think this sort of thing happened to her every day.

That was going to be her goal, to keep it casual. Ryan must never know how very much his kiss had rocked her world.

Ryan hurried through his shower, then shaved and dressed quickly. His hair was still damp when he left his bedroom and headed for the stairs. He wanted to catch Cassie before she got Sasha up.

But when he stepped into the kitchen, the toddler was already sitting in her high chair with a cup of juice in front of her. She beamed when she saw him. "Unk Ryan. Me pincess."

He gave her a quick smile, taking in the fact that she was dressed in her Halloween costume. "So you are. And a very beautiful princess at that."

His gaze swept the room. Everything looked completely normal. Cassie stood at the stove preparing his niece's hot cereal. Sunlight reflected off the linoleum floor. The smell of bacon and coffee filled the room. It was as if nothing had happened. For a second he thought maybe he'd imagined the whole incident. Then Cassie turned toward him.

"I tried to convince her to wear something else, but she

can be quite stubborn, as you know.'' Her smile was just right, her eyes bright, her expression welcoming. There might have been a hint of weariness in the shadows under her eyes, but he wasn't sure. Still it wasn't Cassie's reaction—or lack of reaction—that convinced him last night had been very real. Instead, it was his own.

Desire slammed into him with the subtlety of a truck traveling at four hundred miles an hour. He half expected to be thrown into the wall and fall to the ground in a broken heap. He wanted her instantly. He wanted to pull her close and kiss her hard. He wanted to bury himself inside of her until they both—

''Ryan? Are you all right?''

''What?'' He blinked and realized that Cassie was holding out his mug of coffee. He took it from her and tried to fake a smile. ''Sure, I'm fine. Thanks.'' He raised the mug in salute, then sipped the steaming liquid.

''Have a seat. I thought you might be tired of cold cereal so I'm making pancakes.''

''Great.'' Except he wanted her too much to eat.

He took his usual chair at the table. Sasha banged her spoon against her tray. ''Me hungry.''

''I'm sure you are.'' Cassie crouched in front of the child. ''You can tell me you're hungry and that you want your breakfast, but you're not allowed to bang on the table.''

Sasha's delicate brow furrowed as she struggled to understand the information. She raised her spoon to bang it again. Cassie shook her head.

''No. Don't bang.''

Sasha stared, released her spoon. It clattered to the metal table. Cassie sighed. ''I suppose that's as much of a victory as I'm going to get this morning,'' she said as she rose to her feet and returned to the stove. ''Your cereal is just about ready, young lady. Give me thirty seconds.''

Ryan sipped his coffee. This scene wasn't playing out the way he'd pictured it last night and again this morning when he'd awakened before dawn. Somehow he'd thought Cassie would be more upset by what had happened between them. He stared at her. There didn't seem to be anything wrong. Was she really all right or was she pretending?

She filled a small, plastic bowl with warm cereal and placed it in front of Sasha. "Do you want a piece of bacon?" she asked the girl.

Sasha nodded. "Peas."

Cassie shot him a grin. "One of these days I'm going to forget she has trouble with her *L*'s and actually hand her a bowl of peas. Imagine how shocked she'll be."

He couldn't stand it anymore. He pushed back his chair, rose to his feet and crossed to the stove. She had several strips of bacon frying in a pan. On the counter, the electric griddle heated for pancakes.

"I'll watch these," he said, reaching for the pan.

"Thanks." She stepped to the side and stirred the batter. "You usually want four pancakes. Does that sound right for this morning?"

"Sure. Whatever." As if he cared about food. He stared at the rapidly crisping meat, then at his niece, who was happily eating, getting as much food on herself as in her mouth.

"Are you all right?" he asked, his voice low enough not to carry across the room.

Cassie poured pancakes onto the griddle, then looked at him. "Of course. Why do you ask?"

"You're many things, Cassie, but you're not dumb. You know why I'm asking."

"Okay." She turned her attention back to the pan. "I'm fine and I'm not just saying that."

"Really?" He wanted to believe her. Knowing that she

wasn't suffering any aftereffects would make his whole life easier.

"Of course. You want the truth?" she asked, then continued without waiting for his response. "It was a very lovely kiss. One of the best I've had in a long time. But that's all it was. We didn't rewrite history or change the course of time. We kissed. I don't really understand exactly how we got from chatting about our pasts to a passionate embrace, but this kind of thing happens. We're two adults working in close proximity."

"This is not common practice in my line of work," he said, a little surprised she was being so sensible. Somehow he'd expected her to be upset.

"Mine either." She grinned. "But then as a preschool teacher I would have many less opportunities than you."

"So you're really okay with this?"

"Sure."

She turned the pancakes, then nodded at his pan. The bacon was done. He scooped the pieces out onto a paper towel.

"I'm realistic," she told him. "Aside from Sasha, you and I have very little in common. We had a moment, now it's over. No big deal."

Her attitude annoyed him, even though he knew he should be thrilled that she was so calm about everything.

"We have more than Sasha in common," he said. "We get along extremely well. We read the same kind of books, watch similar movies. We talk easily."

"I suppose." She didn't sound convinced.

"We're intelligent." They were also great together when it came to kissing, but he didn't think he should point that out to her. While he knew he was more experienced than she, he'd never felt the kind of instant fire before.

"And funny," she agreed. "But so what?" She put the

cooked pancakes onto a plate, then poured four more circles of batter onto the griddle. "Face it, Ryan, we're from different worlds. A man like you would never be interested in a woman like me."

"Don't be ridiculous. Of course I would be interested."

He'd spoken without thinking. Cassie glanced at him. "I don't think so."

He cleared his throat. The conversation had gone a lot better when he'd had it alone in his shower. Somehow she wasn't getting her lines right. "What I mean is that we have enough in common that differences in our living styles aren't significant. I'm not making a play for you, I'm just pointing out that your logic is flawed."

"Thank you for sharing."

He saw the glint of humor in her eye and knew that she was laughing at him. He didn't know whether to be offended or join in the joke. In the end, it was easier to ignore either option and plunge ahead.

"My point is," he said, moving closer and lowering his voice, "that you don't have to worry that I'm going to attack you. You're my employee working in my home. You are entitled to my respect and you have it. I promise I will never compromise your position or violate your trust again."

She flipped the pancakes. "Thanks, Ryan, but it never occurred to me that it would be otherwise. The kiss was a one-time thing. Not to worry."

Her casual dismissal made him want to shake her. Or kiss her again. Which showed him how far he'd gone over the line.

"You're safe here," he said.

"I know."

He gritted his teeth together. "Great. Just so we understand each other."

"We do. You can stop belaboring the point."

Her smile took the sting out of her words, but he couldn't help feeling that he'd lost complete control of the situation. When and how had that happened? And why wasn't he happy with everything she was saying? It was exactly what he'd wanted to hear.

But he wasn't happy. He wanted her to be...what? Afraid? He shook his head. That wasn't right. Maybe it was that she'd put the situation out of her mind so easily, when he was finding it difficult not to pull her close and do it all again.

"Everything is ready," she told him. "Go sit down."

He did as she asked. As she put his breakfast in front of him, she spoke. "I have a couple of things I need to do this afternoon. I've checked with Aunt Charity. She can come by and baby-sit Sasha. I hope that's all right."

"It's fine. Take as long as you'd like."

Sasha claimed Cassie's attention and Ryan was left feeling as if he'd missed something very important. Everything had gone his way, so why did it all feel so wrong?

Chapter Ten

Cassie sat at a corner booth in the small fast-food restaurant at the back of the Bradley Discount Store. She resisted the urge to check her watch. After all, she'd looked at it about thirty seconds before, so she wasn't likely to be surprised by the time.

She glanced around at the plastic furniture and wished she could have met Joel somewhere other than here. From her seat she could see out into the store. There were too many people and not enough privacy, but when she'd called Joel that morning he'd said he couldn't spare more than a few minutes for her. Her choice had been to come to the store, or put off their conversation. Cassie had agreed to come to him rather than wait another day.

She took a sip of her soda and wondered what on earth she was going to say to him. She'd practiced several different approaches in the car, but each had sounded more stupid than the last. There was no easy way to do this, but it had to be done. She had to tell Joel the truth. She wanted to be as kind and gentle as possible, but she had to get the message across.

She heard footsteps and glanced up. Joel crossed the black and white floor, moving toward the booth. He wore gray slacks and a pale blue shirt, along with a cartoon-print tie. His hair was neat, his face freshly shaved. He held a clipboard in one hand. He looked like what he was—a busy, albeit harried, manager.

''Hi,'' he said, sliding onto the plastic bench opposite hers. ''Sorry I'm late. There were some problems in housewares.''

''It's fine. I've only been waiting a few minutes.'' She paused. Now what? ''Joel, I have something to tell you.''

''Okay, sure.''

But as she watched, his gaze strayed to the clipboard resting on the table. Trying not to show her annoyance, she reached out and turned it over so he couldn't read it anymore. ''This is important,'' she told him.

''Fine. I'm listening.''

''I...'' Her mind went blank. ''It's just...well...'' Then the words came in a rush. ''You didn't touch me just now. Not even a kiss on the cheek.''

His mouth tightened as his light brown eyes narrowed. ''Is that what this is about? Are we going to talk about our feelings again? I'm willing to do that, Cassie, but not now and not here. It's the middle of my workday. We're in my store. I'm not going to entertain my employees with a passionate embrace. If that bothers you, I'm sorry.''

She took a sip of her diet soda and tried to smile. ''You're absolutely right. This isn't the time or place to talk about feelings and I don't expect a passionate embrace at your place of work. But you didn't touch me at all. I'm not angry,

I'm simply pointing out the obvious. We don't touch anymore. We haven't for a long time."

He sighed heavily, the world-weary sound of a logical male about to be exposed to the irrational thinking of a female. Cassie promised herself no matter what, she wasn't going to lose her temper.

"Don't," she told him. "Don't say anything, just listen."

He frowned, then nodded. "If you'd prefer."

"I would." She took a deep breath. All right. She had his attention. Now what was she going to do with it?

In the car on the way over she'd discarded a couple dozen ways of telling him the truth. She wasn't sure of the correct tone, or proper sequence of the words that would explain what was going on with her. Despite the practice, all she could think of was a bald statement of the facts.

"Working for Ryan has become a problem," she said. "It's not him, it's me. I have feelings for him." She couldn't bring herself to look at him, so she stared at the hard plastic table. "It's just a crush. I mean what else could it be? I barely know the man. But it's there and it doesn't seem to be going away."

"Is that it?" Joel asked.

Cassie raised her head and met his steady gaze. "What do you mean, 'is that it?' Isn't that enough? We've been together for nine years, I confess to having feelings for an other man and that's all you can ask me?"

"Oh, honey, you're making too much out of this. Of course you have a crush on Ryan. What young woman in your position wouldn't? He's older, he's successful, he's sophisticated. I'm sure he can be quite charming. If you hadn't noticed him I would have worried about you. It doesn't mean anything." Joel's smile was warm and friendly. "Is that what all this is about? Have you been worrying yourself over nothing? That's so like you, Cass."

She couldn't speak. She could only stare. Maybe it was her hearing. Maybe some connection to her brain had malfunctioned and words were getting messed up or turned around.

"You don't care," she managed between stiff lips.

"Of course I care. You mean the world to me. But I'm not worried about your crush on Ryan. As soon as he's out of your life, you'll forget all about him."

He was taking this way too calmly, she thought. Maybe he was the one with the broken brain. "There's more," she told him.

"I'm listening."

"We kissed." She waited, but there was no reaction. "It was just once. I mean it was just one event, but during those few minutes we kissed several times."

Still no reaction. Joel nodded as if to show he was listening, but there wasn't any obvious anger or displeasure on his part. For all she knew he was thinking about his problems with the housewares department.

She set her forearms on the table and leaned toward him. "It wasn't like when you and I kiss, Joel. There was no holding back. I felt…I felt things I've never felt before. I wanted him…passionately."

She paused, then realized she was done. What else was there to say? Except maybe the obvious. "I'm sorry," she added in a low voice. "I didn't mean to hurt you."

"Ah, Cass."

He glanced at his watch. She blinked. His watch? Like he was late for something more important? "Joel, I'm telling you that I kissed another man and that it turned me on. I wanted to *be* with him. Do you want to say something about this?"

"I'm not surprised," he told her calmly. "The situation was bound to occur. Frankly, I expected it sooner, but I'm glad it's finally here. We can deal with it and put it behind us.''

One of them was crazy. ''What are you talking about?''

''When we started dating, you were only sixteen,'' he said.

''I'm well aware of that.''

''I was seventeen.''

She felt as if she'd been dropped into a conversation already in progress. ''What does that have to do with anything?''

''I've dated other women, but you never dated other guys.''

He was comparing his few dates in high school to her kiss with Ryan? ''Joel, you don't understand what I'm trying to tell you.''

''Of course I understand.'' His smile was kindly. ''I've been there. When I dated before, I kissed those girls and...well...'' He flushed. ''We did some things together. My point is I've experienced life. I know what's out there in the world. You haven't done that. I'm pleased that you had the opportunity to sow your wild oats and get all this out of your system.''

Okay, so they weren't talking about the same thing at all and Joel didn't get it. Now what? ''This is more than wild oats,'' she said. ''A lot more.''

''I know you believe it is, but don't worry. It's done and now we can get on with our lives.'' He reached out and placed his hand over hers. ''I love you, Cass. You're the one that I want to be with. I still trust you. Isn't that what matters?''

It should, she thought sadly. It should matter a whole bunch, but it didn't.

She studied his familiar face, the shape of his jaw, the curve of his lower lip. Light brown eyes crinkled slightly at the corners. He was so honorable, she thought. So willing to believe the best of her.

"It's not that simple," she said. "I don't want to go back to what we had. It's not enough." She pulled free of his touch, and stared at her fingers. The promise ring glinted in the overhead lights. "I can't keep this anymore," she told him and slipped the slender band from her finger.

"What are you doing?" Joel asked, the first hint of concern filling his voice.

"What it looks like. I'm sorry."

"I see." Joel picked up the ring. "I hope you're not making the mistake of thinking he's going to want you."

She told herself he hadn't meant the statement as cruelly as it came out, but she wasn't sure. "I don't pretend to know what Ryan wants in life, but I'm reasonably confident it isn't me. Our kiss was just something that happened. It didn't mean anything." At least not to him. Unfortunately for her, it had not only been a wake-up call about her relationship with Joel, it had also embedded itself in her mind. She couldn't stop thinking about those few moments in his arms.

"I'm not breaking up with you because of Ryan," she continued. "I'm doing it because of me. I've experienced passion. I know what it's like to want someone so much it hurts." She drew in a deep breath. "Maybe I'm setting myself up for heartbreak. Maybe I'm reaching for the stars. I don't know. But what I *am* sure of is that I want to find this again. I want that kind of passion in my life on a permanent basis."

"It's that important to you?" Joel asked.

"Yes."

He picked up the ring and stared at the tiny diamond. "We could do that," he said without looking at her. "If you wanted to."

If she hadn't been so close to tears, his lack of enthusiasm would have made her smile. ‘‘I appreciate the offer, but no thanks. It’s been nine years and we’ve never even tried heavy petting. It was too easy not to become lovers.’’

She swallowed. ‘‘I’m sorry, Joel. You are a wonderful man and I adore you. In some ways I love you. I’ll always have feelings for you, but they’re not the kind of feelings that a woman should have for her husband. I can’t see you anymore.’’

He closed his fingers over the ring. ‘‘Just like that? It’s been nine years.’’

‘‘I know. It’s what I want. If you look deep inside, I think you’ll find it’s what you want, too.’’

‘‘All right.’’ He slipped the ring into his shirt pocket. ‘‘If you need time, I’ll give you time. We’ll put the relationship on hold for a few weeks. I’m sure once you’ve had a chance to think about it, you’ll come to your senses.’’

She didn’t know whether to scream or cry. Anger, sadness, frustration and pain from the thought of never seeing Joel again all welled up inside of her.

‘‘I don’t want time,’’ she said. ‘‘I want it to be over. I want you to walk away from me without any regrets. I want you to find someone else and experience a little passion of your own. It will change your life forever.’’

She slid out of the booth and tried to smile. She had a feeling she failed pretty badly. ‘‘Goodbye, Joel. Good luck.’’

Then she turned and walked away.

A knock at his office door interrupted Ryan. He called ‘‘Come in,’’ without turning away from his computer screen, then remembered that Cassie had left for the afternoon an hour or so before. He glanced up in time to see an attractive fifty-something woman step inside.

She was about Cassie’s height, with sleek dark hair pulled

back into a fancy bun. Tailored clothes emphasized her trim body.

"You must be Cassie's aunt Charity," he said, rising to her feet.

"Yes. I just thought I'd poke my head in and say hello."

She crossed to his desk and handed him a cup of coffee. As she held another mug in her hand, he figured she was expecting an invitation to join him for a few minutes.

"Have a seat," he said, motioning to the empty chair next to her. Like Cassie's sister, her aunt wanted to check out the man Cassie worked for. He appreciated that her family was so concerned about her well-being.

"Thank you."

Charity sat down and set her coffee on the desk. He did the same.

"Is Sasha asleep?"

"Yes. She was a little hyper from playing," Charity said as she crossed her legs and picked up her mug. "I supposed a game of tag in the backyard wasn't a clever idea right before her nap, but I wasn't thinking." Her easy smile returned. "It comes from not having had children of my own. By the time I moved in with Cassie and Chloe, they were far too old to play games or need naps."

"You're their aunt on their father's side?"

"That's right. So I don't have any connection with the town of Bradley." She took a sip of coffee. "Has Cassie told you that one of her relatives actually founded the town?"

"She mentioned something about it."

"It's quite extraordinary for me to imagine having roots that go down that deep. I've always been something of a wanderer." Her well-shaped eyebrows drew together. "Come to think of it, I've lived in Bradley longer than anywhere else in my adult life. I came here when the girls were nearly eighteen.'' She paused, then gave a small gasp of surprise. ''That was more than eight years ago. Time does get away from us all, doesn't it? Eight years. Who would have thought?''

''There is something pleasant about Bradley,'' he said. ''I'd planned to be here a month or six weeks at most, but now I find myself considering a longer stay.''

''Really?'' Dark brown eyes regarded him thoughtfully. ''There's a lot to like here.''

He wondered if she was still talking about the town or something else. Had Cassie told her aunt about what had happened the previous night? He studied the older woman sitting across from him, but he couldn't be sure.

Charity set her mug on the desk. ''I moved in with the girls as soon as I found out about my brother's death. Unfortunately, I'd been in remote sections of the Far East, so it took the family lawyer three years to find me. I couldn't imagine staying in a small town where the neighbors knew one another. Living with two teenage girls was also a shock. I couldn't wait to leave.'' Her expression softened. ''But slowly, the town and the girls worked their magic. Cassie and Chloe have both urged me to resume my travels, but I find I miss them less and less with each passing year.''

She smiled. ''I stayed at first to make sure the girls got through college. Then there was always some excuse to keep me around. Now I want to stay to see Chloe's baby born. I'm beginning to suspect I've lost the travel bug. Still, I saw a great deal of the world.'' She paused, and leaned forward slightly. ''Is Bradley anything like where you grew up?''

''Not really. My mother, my brother and I lived in different parts of Los Angeles.''

''What about your father?''

''John, my older brother, had a different father. His dad left when John was three or four. My father ran out on my mother when he learned she was pregnant.'' Not much of a legacy, he thought grimly. How could any man turn his back on his child?

''That must have been difficult for all of you,'' Charity said. ''Your mother sounds like a very strong woman.''

''She was. She worked hard. Maybe too hard. There wasn't a whole lot of fun in our house.''

''I've met people like that,'' Charity told him. ''I can't remember the exact old saying but it's something about hard work curing every ill.'' She flashed him another smile. ''And here I'd always thought only chocolate could do that.''

''I don't know about chocolate, but there were things I missed when I was growing up. She never approved of me going away with my friends and their families on camping trips. When I was in high school, she didn't want me spending money on school dances.''

Ryan had nearly forgotten about all of that. He remembered finally getting the courage to ask a girl out, only to have his mother tell him it was a waste of his hard-earned wages. In the end, he'd gone on the date, but hadn't bothered asking the girl out again.

''It was a relief to get away to college.''

''You went on scholarship?'' she asked.

He nodded. ''I worked, too, for spending money.'' It was as if he'd opened a long-closed door. The past flooded over him. How he'd enjoyed being on his own and how guilty he'd been for those feelings. He remembered phone calls from his mother where she'd reminded him to keep up his grades and warned him not to be frivolous by joining a fraternity or getting involved in extracurricular activities. He'd done a few things, but the guilt had always kept him from enjoying them too much.

''A doctor and a successful businessman. Your mother must be very proud.''

''No,'' he said quietly. ''She's gone now, but it wasn't like that.'' He shrugged. ''She never said anything except to keep working hard.''

''And then she died.''

Charity said the words as if she'd actually known his mother. Ryan stared at her. He realized how much he'd revealed in the past few minutes. ''How did you do that?'' he asked.

She didn't pretend to misunderstand. ''It's a gift,'' she admitted. ''People often find me easy to talk with. Plus, with you, I had an advantage. I knew your brother.''

''I didn't,'' he said without thinking, and realized it was true. ''He was ten years older and had left for college when I started third grade. He would come home and visit but it wasn't the same as growing up together.''

''He was a good man. You would have liked him.'' She tilted her head and stared at him. ''More important to you, I suspect, he would have always liked you. Cassie says you're doing very well with Sasha.''

''I can't take any of the credit there. Cassie has been a huge help and Sasha is a sweetheart. We have a great time together.''

''You're making an effort,'' Charity said. ''Many people wouldn't bother.''

He remembered his first few days with his niece. How he'd wanted to avoid her and how desperate he'd been for someone to take away the responsibility. ''Cassie had to shame me into doing my part.''

''I suspect it wasn't all that difficult. You're not the sort of man who walks away from what's important. Cassie thinks too much of you for it to be otherwise.''

The implied approval made him uncomfortable. He

doubted Charity would be as friendly if she knew about the kiss. "Cassie is very accepting. I admire that in her. And she's a natural when it comes to kids." He thought about the laughter that always filled the house. "I've never known anyone like her. She seems to understand exactly what Sasha is thinking all the time."

"She has a college degree in child development and works in a preschool. If she didn't understand children, I would be worried. Yes, some people are better with children than others, but don't discount the training or years of experience. You wouldn't expect a new employee fresh out of school to be an expert in your line of work. Why is it different with Sasha?"

"That's what your niece told me. I guess I should believe her."

"Of course. We can't both be wrong."

"Agreed." He picked up a pen, then set it back on the desk. "The problem is I don't have Cassie's experience or her training. I worry that I'm not going to do the right thing where Sasha is concerned. With her parents gone, I'm all she has."

"Worry is half the battle," Charity told him. "It means you care. Too many people don't. You'll do your best. Sometimes you'll get it right, the rest of the time you'll fake it." She looked at him with compassion. "Believe me, I understand. I came into a household with two nearly grown young women. I wanted to share my life experiences with them, but I had to balance that with their need to find things out for themselves. Sometimes it was hard to bite my tongue, sometimes I wondered how much I was going to get wrong. But I knew I loved those girls and the loving makes all the difference."

Ryan knew that six weeks ago he would have discounted those feelings, but now he knew better. Sasha feeling that she mattered to him was half the battle. "I want to do what's right," he said. "I owe it to Sasha, and to my brother."

Knowing eyes darkened. "Maybe you owe it to yourself as well."

Once again he was surprised by how easily he shared his innermost thoughts with this woman. He'd always held that part of him back, but there was something about Charity that made him think that not only could he trust her but that she would also understand what he was trying to say. "You do have a way of making people talk, don't you?"

"As I said, it's a gift. But you're not to worry. I'm very good at keeping secrets. Speaking of which, Cassie will be turning twenty-five soon. There's going to be a party for her and I would like to put you on the guest list."

"Thank you."

Charity leaned back in her chair. "Has Cassie told you the significance of her twenty-fifth birthday?"

"Yes. She mentioned the legend of the nightgown. I know that she believes it's true. Do you?"

"Of course. I've traveled all over the world and I've seen dozens of things modern science can't explain. By comparison a magic nightgown is rather tame. Besides, Chloe dreamed about her husband when she wore the nightgown. They'd never met before, yet when they ran into each other the next day, she knew things about him that would have been impossible for her to know, unless the dream was real. It was nearly love at first sight for both of them. That's difficult evidence to dispute."

It was a tough story to swallow, he thought, trying not to play the cynic. "Do you think Cassie will dream about Joel?"

"Do you think Joel is Cassie's fantasy, or even her destiny?"

The thought made his skin crawl. "It's really not my

place to say. Besides, they've been together for nine years. Who else would Cassie be interested in?''

Charity stared at him for a long time without speaking, then she rose to her feet and walked to the door. ''I'm sure you're very busy. I've kept you long enough.''

She gave him one last piercing glance, then she was gone. Ryan was left with the uncomfortable feeling that she knew about the kiss…and a few other things he hadn't figured out yet himself.

Chapter Eleven

Ryan spent the rest of the afternoon pretending to work without actually getting anything done. Part of the reason was he couldn't believe all the personal information he'd shared with Cassie's aunt. Spilling his guts to total strangers wasn't his style. Actually he rarely spilled his guts to anyone. How had she done that?

He hadn't been able to come up with a reason and after a while it had ceased to matter because of the second reason he couldn't work—Cassie. Where was she? She'd left in the early afternoon and it was near—he glanced at his watch—four-thirty. She never took much time off to begin with and certainly not in the middle of the day. Had something happened to her?

Even as he contemplated calling the police and local hospitals, he heard the front door open and the sound of low voices. He exhaled in relief. She'd made it home. Now he could concentrate.

But even though he turned to his computer and stared at the screen, he wasn't thinking about the spreadsheet in front of him. He wanted to know where Cassie had been and what she'd been doing. He knew it wasn't any of his business, but he couldn't help thinking it had something to do with what had happened between them last night. Even though it was probably both paranoid and incredibly egotistical, he wondered how much that kiss had changed everything.

She'd seemed all right that morning, he reminded himself. Had she been acting? Maybe he should just accept things at face value. Maybe he should believe her when she said she was fine. It was just a kiss, after all. Nothing earth-shattering. Except that the passion had nearly overwhelmed him. He'd never experienced anything like it before. But that didn't mean she hadn't.

Ryan frowned. He didn't like to think that she and Joel created the same kind of heat. They couldn't have and not bothered to get married. If he had dated a young woman who had made him feel the way Cassie did, he might have changed his ideas about getting involved in a serious relationship.

Not now, of course, he told himself. He was a mature man who understood that there was more to life than great sex. He didn't want a commitment with anyone. Sasha was going to change his life enough without throwing a wife into the mix. And if he did decide to get married, it wouldn't be just for the sex. There were other, equally important issues such as temperament, compatibility, trustworthiness. He would want someone intelligent and caring. Obviously a woman who could love Sasha as if she were her own. But he wasn't looking, nor had he found anyone.

That decided, he told himself to lose the lingering guilt, and get back to work. Before he could, there was a light tap on his door, then Cassie stuck her head into the room.

"I'm back," she said, giving him a warm smile.

He studied her face. Except for the shadows under her eyes indicating she hadn't slept well the night before, she looked fine. "Everything all right?" he asked.

"Perfect. I'd like to invite Aunt Charity to stay for dinner. Is that okay with you?"

"Yes," he said automatically, when he really wanted to refuse her request. It wasn't that he hadn't enjoyed talking with Charity, it was just that he and Cassie had things they needed to discuss. Although at the moment he couldn't quite figure out what they were.

"Great. I'll call you when dinner's ready."

She disappeared and he was left staring at the closed door.

She had seemed like her normal self, he thought. If she had let last night go so easily, he should do the same. She'd accepted his apology and his promise that it wouldn't happen again, and moved on. He told himself he was grateful. He told himself that the lingering memories of the feel of her in his arms would pass in time. He told himself he had to work when in fact he listened intently to the sounds of female voices coming from the front of the house. He told himself he preferred it this way and that he wasn't lonely, even though he longed to be a part of the laughter. And he pretended to work until Cassie reappeared to invite him into the warmth of her company.

"You are a precious angel, aren't you?" Charity said as she stroked Sasha's cheek. "This little one and I had a terrific time together. Feel free to call on me to baby-sit anytime."

Sasha beamed with the additional attention and placed her hands on her high chair tray.

"She's a charmer," Ryan said, from across the table. "She's too cute and she knows it, don't you?"

Sasha held out her arms. "Unk Ryan."

"Yeah, yeah," he grumbled as he pushed back his chair and circled around to crouch by her high chair. Her short arms wrapped around his neck. She squeezed tight while he gently hugged her back. He didn't fool himself about who had the power in this relationship, he thought with a smile. "You've got me pegged, kid. I'm a sucker for your hugs."

Sasha pursed her lips and he obliged her with a quick kiss. Her need for affection satiated, the toddler picked up her spoon and banged it against her metal tray. "Me hungry."

"We know," Ryan said as he took the spoon from her and set it on the large table just out of reach. "Sit there nicely until Cassie brings you dinner. It won't be very long."

She stared mutinously at him. Her lower lip quivered. Uh-oh, the storm wasn't far behind. Time to entertain the troops. He slapped his hand on the tray table and splayed his fingers. "Pick one," he said.

Sasha hesitated.

He faked a hurt look. "Don't you want to play?"

She pulled on his index finger. In response, he bounced the digit several times. Sasha giggled, then pulled on his middle finger. This time he raised his hand until it hovered a couple of inches above the table, all the while humming scary alien music. After a couple of seconds, he let his hand flop back to the table.

Sasha squealed with delight. "More," she demanded and tugged on his thumb.

He flopped his entire hand back and forth, moving very quickly and finishing with a lunge for her side so he could tickle her. Sasha laughed and wiggled, pushing him away, then grabbing him and drawing him close.

"You can't have it both ways, kid," he told her.

"Dinner's ready," Cassie said.

He looked up and saw her standing in the entrance to the dining room. She held Sasha's plastic plate and gazed at him with a bemused expression.

Ryan stepped back hastily. He'd forgotten that he and Sasha weren't alone. A quick glance told him that Charity had been equally amused by his game with his niece.

"She was going to cry," Ryan said defensively. "I wanted to stop that."

"You did a great job," Cassie told him. "I'm impressed." She set the plate in front of Sasha, handed the child her spoon, then patted Ryan's arm. "Everything is ready. Why don't you have a seat?"

He felt oddly embarrassed, as if he'd been caught doing something foolish. But he didn't keep defending himself. Instead he opened the red wine Cassie had set out and filled the three glasses.

"Ryan and I were talking earlier today," Charity said as her niece served tenderloins of beef and steamed asparagus. "Did you know he'd been to college on a scholarship?"

"I hadn't heard." Cassie disappeared into the kitchen, then returned carrying a bowl of mashed potatoes and a tray with French bread.

Belatedly, Ryan rose to his feet and took the serving pieces from her. "Sorry," he said, placing them on the table. "I should have offered to help sooner."

"You took care of Sasha. That was a big help."

He nodded, then held out her chair for her. What was wrong with him? He wasn't usually so socially inept. It was all the distractions, he decided. His concerns from the previous night, dealing with both his niece and Cassie's aunt, not to mention the fact that he rarely entertained at home. He'd been too busy lately, and when he did get together with friends it was usually at a restaurant.

Cassie had placed him at the head of the table with her aunt on his right. As the serving plates and bowls were passed around, Charity picked up the conversation.

"He worked part-time while he was at school, as well. Impressive determination in one so young."

Cassie took a spoonful of potatoes and flashed him a smile. "Ryan has many good qualities."

"He's doing very well with Sasha," Charity said. "He's had no training, virtually no warning, yet they've bonded."

Ryan glanced from one to the other. "I *am* in the room. You can direct some of these comments to me directly, if you'd like."

"Are you feeling left out?" Cassie asked with a grin. She lowered her voice conspiratorially and leaned toward her aunt. "Men are so sensitive."

Charity sighed. "It's a problem with the whole gender. Such delicate creatures. But what choice is there? They're all we have." She patted the back of Ryan's hand. "What would you like to talk about, dear?"

"I'm not a domineering male," he said, enjoying the banter and the feeling of being part of a family. "You can't lay that at my door."

"Of course we can," Cassie said and took a sip of wine. "There are two of us and only one of you. We can say or do anything we like."

"I see. And if I remind you that you work for me and therefore are expected to treat me with, if not reverence, then at least respect?"

"I'll point out that's an extremely domineering remark. Then I would probably take you to task for saying reverence, even in a kidding way. Reverence, Ryan? Do you secretly want to be worshiped?"

"Don't all men?"

Her brown eyes sparkled with laughter. "We'll have to

set up a little shrine in one of the spare bedrooms. Maybe put up your picture. I can come in every morning and light candles.''

''Works for me, but I would prefer a large shrine, not a little one.'' He glanced at Charity and gave her a wink.

''You're a tricky one,'' the older woman said. ''Be careful with him, Cassie. He's charming and they're the most dangerous kind.''

''I'm not worried about Ryan,'' her niece said. ''He's a great boss. I like working for him.'' Then she asked her aunt about a recent play she'd been to, and the conversation became more general.

Still, the feeling of well-being lingered for Ryan. He didn't join Cassie and Sasha for dinner as often as he should. He enjoyed the company. He kept to himself too much, he realized. Maybe it was time to change that.

When Sasha spilled her milk, he motioned for Cassie to keep eating while he took care of the mess. As he returned to his seat, Cassie put her hand on his arm.

''Thanks,'' she said.

''My pleasure.''

His gaze dropped down to her mouth, which instantly made him think of kissing her again. Down boy, he ordered himself, then looked away. At the same time Cassie withdrew her hand. He caught the movement out of the corner of his eye.

A small alarm went off in his head. Something was wrong.

He looked at her face, trying to read her thoughts. Again she looked completely normal. Her clothes were fine, she had on her watch and her—

A cold knife cut through his midsection. He blinked slowly, but the reality didn't change. Dear God, why had it taken him so long to notice? Her promise ring—Joel's promise ring—was gone and in its place was a band of pale skin.

Charity didn't leave until nearly ten that night. It had been the longest evening in Ryan's life. At first he'd tried to think of a way to get Cassie alone and ask her what had happened. Unfortunately he had a bad feeling he knew what had happened. He didn't want to know, but he *had* to know.

She'd told Joel about the kiss. They'd had an ugly fight. They'd broken up. It was the only explanation. Ryan paced back and forth in the hallway, waiting for Cassie to finish her goodbyes. She'd seemed so calm all evening, yet she had to be dying inside. This was all his fault.

No it wasn't, he told himself. All he'd done was kiss her. It had just happened. It wasn't anyone's fault. Or maybe it was both their faults and they should… Except he didn't know what they should do. He didn't know anything.

The front door closed. Ryan moved to intercept Cassie in the foyer. "We have to talk."

She drew in a deep breath and shook her head. "Not tonight, Ryan. I'm tired and I'm getting a headache. I don't usually suffer from them, so I'm sure it will be gone by morning."

He didn't think she was torturing him on purpose, but that was how it felt. "Please, just for a few minutes. I don't want to make your headache worse, but we do need to talk."

Cassie hesitated, then led the way into the living room. Ryan followed on her heels. When she took a seat on the sofa, he thought about settling next to her, but he couldn't imagine being able to stay still a minute longer. Sitting through dinner was nearly the most difficult thing he'd ever done. He glanced down at her, opened his mouth, closed it and began to pace.

Several floor lamps added light to the room. The furniture

was large but comfortable, done in blues and greens, accented by oak tables. Ryan forced himself to take a couple of deep breaths. He walked from the window to the fireplace and back, stopping in front of her.

"You're not wearing your promise ring," he blurted out at last.

A faint smile touched the corner of her mouth. "I know."

"This isn't the least bit humorous to me." His tone was sharp and her smile faded. "What happened to it?"

"I didn't lose it if that's what you're asking," she said. "I gave it back to Joel."

He'd already figured out the truth, even as he'd tried to deny it to himself. He didn't want to hear this. He didn't want to know. The guilt returned and swamped him. She'd given back her ring because of him? He refused to accept that. He paced again, then swore under his breath. They did *not* have a relationship. What the hell was she thinking?

Questions filled his mind. Questions and answers and fears and guilt. "This isn't my fault," he said quickly. "It was just a kiss. I apologized this morning. That's not a reason to break off your engagement. You shouldn't have done that. You weren't thinking."

If he was trying to make it all her fault, he was doing a poor job. Worse, he was practically squirming to get away and that wasn't his style. Ryan forced himself to stand in front of her.

"Don't panic, Ryan. Joel isn't going to come after you with a shotgun. I don't know what you're thinking, but I suspect you're making this more complicated and more personal than it has to be."

She sounded so calm. Her gaze was steady, her body language relaxed. She wore a dark green dress and matching pumps. Her hair curled away from her face, exposing her big eyes and perfect cheekbones. Not to mention her tempting mouth.

He jerked his attention away from her lips. "Then why don't you explain it to me."

"All right. I didn't give Joel back the ring because you and I kissed. I gave him back the ring because of how the kiss made me feel." She held up her hand when he would have interrupted her. "They're not the same thing at all. Let me finish. Joel and I have been together for years. In all that time, through all the kissing and hugging and hand holding, I never once experienced anything close to the passion I felt last night."

He started to tell her that kisses were always like that, but he found he couldn't lie. *He'd* never experienced that kind of wanting before, either.

"So you told him." It wasn't a question.

"I had to. First I told him about the kiss, but he was surprisingly unconcerned."

That startled Ryan into sitting down on the opposite end of the sofa. "What do you mean?"

She recounted her conversation with Joel, sharing her ex-boyfriend's theory about the need to sow wild oats.

"He's crazy," Ryan muttered more to himself than her. If he'd been involved with Cassie and had found out she'd kissed another man, he would have gone wild with rage and jealousy. "So because he wasn't worried or upset, you broke up with him?" He shook his head. "That makes about as much sense to me as the fact that you told him the truth in the first place. You didn't have to do that. It was a one-time thing, never to be repeated."

Cassie stared at him as if he were a particularly slow child. "You're missing the point entirely," she said. "I didn't break up with him because of the kiss, or because he didn't get upset. I broke up with him because I've had a lot of questions for a long time. I couldn't figure out what was wrong with our relationship or why we didn't seem to feel any physical desire for each other.'' She took a deep breath and continued. ''Because I had no frame of reference, I didn't know if there was something wrong between Joel and me or if all those songwriters and poets had been lying. Last night I learned there was a whole world waiting for me. A world of incredibly physical sensation.'' A dreamy expression crossed her face. ''I want that. Not just sex for the sake of having sex, but a relationship that involves an emotional as well as a physical connection. I broke up with Joel because I'm not willing to settle anymore. This time I want it all.''

Cassie had been afraid that Ryan might take her comments too much to heart. He stood up and actually backed away from her. His expression was trapped and his hands came up in a protective gesture. If she hadn't been so tired and vulnerable, she might have found the situation amusing.

But tonight she wasn't feeling especially strong. If only things had been different, she thought. If only Ryan wanted her as much as she wanted him. If only... How many hearts had broken apart on those rocky words?

''Don't panic,'' she said, deliberately keeping her words light. ''I'm not going to beg you to come to bed or ask you to father my child. While you were technically involved in my awakening, passion-wise, this isn't really about you.''

''That's not how it looks from here.''

At least her headache had faded, she thought with gratitude, so it wasn't difficult to think. ''We went over this when we talked this morning, Ryan. We're very different people. I'll agree that there are some similarities as far as our personalities go, but none of this is about having a relationship with you.'' Even though she knew she wanted one.

As long as she kept the truth from him, he would never

feel obligated to try to spare her feelings. That was one thing she didn't think she could bear...Ryan's polite dismissal.

"Then what is it about?" he asked.

She motioned to the sofa and waited until he'd settled down again. "I know that you and I will never have more than a working relationship, and I'm fine with that. The kiss was a fluke. A very nice fluke, but not significant in the scheme of things."

"It was significant enough to cause you to break up with Joel."

Okay, so the man had a point. "Not exactly," she hedged. "It showed me a truth I'd long suspected. I realized I had to make a choice. For years Chloe has been telling me I was just settling for Joel. She told me there was a lot more out there and I owed it to myself to explore the world. I never thought she was right. I thought she had an irrational dislike of Joel."

She wasn't sure but his shoulders seemed to be relaxing a little. "And now?"

"Now I've had my eyes opened. I don't think I was settling for Joel. He's a wonderful man and I'll always be happy that he was in my life. But I want more than he and I can have together. I want to try to have the best of both worlds. Companionship and passion."

"And that's it?"

She nodded. "I'm being honest, Ryan. After nine years of dating Joel, what we shared is gone. When I drove home I kept waiting for the anguish. I thought it would be like losing an arm or something." She pressed her lips together and looked away. She didn't want him to see the tears filling her eyes.

"Are you crying?" he asked sharply.

She sniffed. "Yes, but not for the reasons you're thinking.

All I feel is relief. Not sadness or regret or pain. I thought I would feel more.''

''You might later.''

''I'm sure you're right. But my heart isn't broken and I'm not sorry about what happened. Any of it,'' she added. ''Obviously the kiss has made you terribly uncomfortable with me, and I do feel badly about that. For me it was a call to action. I hope you don't worry that it's anything else.''

''I'm not uncomfortable,'' he said. ''Kissing you did *not* make me uncomfortable.''

Cassie had to suppress a smile. She hadn't meant to offend him, but the male ego was a fragile, albeit complicated, thing. ''What I meant,'' she said carefully, ''is that you have some genuine reasons for concern. I really appreciate that. I don't want to you to think any of this is your fault.'' She drew in a deep breath.

Now came the hard part. This morning it had been surprisingly easy to ''fake'' being okay with everything that had happened…mostly because she found that she *was* all right. She might lust after Ryan and his body, she might think he was brilliant and wonderful and that they would be perfect together. But he didn't think that, and she wasn't foolish enough to try to convince herself otherwise. She would enjoy their conversations and contact while she could, then when it was over, she would do her best to put him behind her.

''I don't want you to worry that I'm going to make a play for you,'' she said. For the first time, she felt a heat on her cheeks and it took all her strength not to turn away from his intense gaze. ''Just as you were worried about me feeling in danger and took the time to reassure me, I want to do the same. I'm not going to spend my day making calf eyes at you.''

His expression didn't relax at all. There was something

odd in his eyes, a strange emotion she couldn't read. "What *are* calf eyes?" he asked.

She smiled. "I'm not sure either, so if I don't know, I can't make them, or do them, or whatever." She turned serious. "I'm not going to be a problem."

"I never thought you would be." He leaned toward her. "I want you to feel free to date. You still have time off in the evening and if you're giving up Joel, there's no reason to wait to 'discover the world' as you put it."

She didn't mind him not sharing her fantasy, but she deeply resented that he was so quick to throw her into the path of other men. "Gee, thanks," she said. "I think I'll wait at least a couple of days to get used to being single again. It's been a long time." She rose to her feet. "It's getting late. I'm going up to bed."

She crossed to the door, then paused and looked back at him. "Thanks for everything, Ryan. For reasons that probably don't make sense to you, I'm very grateful for what you did."

He stood, too. He was tall and broad and she found herself wishing she was standing a little closer to him.

"You make it sound like a big favor," he said. "Kissing you was my pleasure." He flashed her a quick smile. "I mean that."

She told herself to turn away, but she couldn't. If only he would walk over and kiss her again, she thought. Maybe even do more than kiss. But he wasn't going to. She thanked him again and left. At least she would have the memory of their kiss…not to mention all the fantasies about what it would be like if they were to start that fire between them again.

Chapter Twelve

The next week was uneventful, for which Cassie was grateful. There had been enough trauma and change in her life for any month. Not that she would have objected to Ryan showing up unexpectedly in her bedroom, swearing undying devotion and then making passionate love to her for hours. But if she couldn't have that, peace and quiet were a very nice substitute.

Their routine continued, with Sasha in preschool Monday through Thursday morning. Ryan joined them for meals and spent his early evenings with his niece as well. Cassie wanted to believe that her witty company was what drew him, but she knew better. When it was time for Sasha to go to bed, he either took over the duties or let her handle them and disappeared into his office. Either way, once Sasha was down for the night, Ryan left Cassie alone.

"We can't have everything," she said aloud, as she slipped her jacket off its hanger and put it on. They were going shoe shopping for Sasha. In the space of a few days, the toddler's favorite shoes had gotten too tight. Visiting the mall would be a nice change, and for reasons Cassie didn't quite understand, Ryan had agreed to go with them.

She crossed to her dresser and ran a brush through her short hair. She used her left hand to push a wayward strand in place, and as she did so, she glanced at the place where her promise ring used to be. Joel was well and truly out of her life.

She'd thought he might call her. After all, his idea had been that with a little time she would come to her senses. But he hadn't tried to contact her at all. Cassie carefully probed her heart, searching for any signs of hurt or remorse. The only negative emotion there was sadness that something that had lasted so long could be forgotten so easily. She still wasn't sorry that she'd ended things between them. Her only feeling was one of relief and a nagging sense that she should have done this a long time ago.

If there was any regret, it was that this might be causing him pain. She hoped not. Their relationship had been comfortable for both of them, but she doubted Joel had given his heart any more than she had. A smile tugged at the corner of her mouth. All he needed was a hot date with a gorgeous blonde and he would forget all about her, she thought. If only she knew one who was interested in him.

''Cassie, are you about ready?'' Ryan called from downstairs.

At the sound of his voice, her heart rate increased. ''I'm on my way,'' she yelled as she hurried from her bedroom and headed for the stairs.

If Ryan could make her heart race with just the sound of his voice, imagine what would happen if they ever did the naked thing, she thought humorously. Not that they ever would, but a girl could dream. And dream she did. Nothing like having a handsome, single, charming man living under the same roof to give her a little inspiration.

She grabbed her purse and stepped outside. Ryan and Sasha stood by his late model BMW 540i. "I installed the car seat," he said as she approached.

Cassie leaned around the open rear door and stared in to the back seat. The new toddler-size car seat had been strapped into the center. She turned to Sasha. "It's very nice and grown-up. Are you excited?"

Sasha nodded. "Unk Ryan buy for me."

"I know. He cares about you very much and he wants to keep you safe. Isn't that nice?"

Sasha grinned. "Go now."

"We've received our instructions," she told her boss. "Guess we should listen."

"Absolutely." He circled around to the other side of the car. "As this is the first time we're using this particular car seat, I'm guessing it's going to take both of us to get it right." He patted his back pocket. "I have the instruction diagram right here."

She motioned for Sasha to climb into the car. "Wow. A guy willing to read the instructions. I'm impressed."

Ryan didn't return her smile. "This is about keeping Sasha safe. I wouldn't play around with that."

Why did he keep doing that? she wondered. Saying and doing exactly the right thing. He made it very difficult for her to remember her place and keep her perspective. If only he would go back to being the silent man who didn't want anything to do with his niece. Then she would have a chance of getting over her thing for her boss.

Cassie sighed. Even though it meant the potential for more heartbreak for her, she couldn't in all sincerity really wish that Ryan changed back into the man he'd been when he first arrived. She wanted what was best for Sasha, and this new and improved uncle was definitely what the toddler needed.

Sasha crawled into the car seat and got comfortable. Cassie leaned from her side, while Ryan did the same from his. They reached for buckles and straps, occasionally bumping. At one point their hands got tangled together. Sasha thought it was all a great joke and laughed at them. Cassie smiled with her and tried to ignore the tingling that shot up her arm. She was careful to keep her expression pleasantly neutral. Despite her growing feelings for Ryan, she hadn't forgotten the trapped look in his eyes when she'd told him she'd broken up with Joel in order to find what she really wanted. The last thing the poor man needed to know was that his worst fears had come true—that his unsophisticated, much-younger nanny had the hots for him.

Cassie gave the car seat straps one last tug. ''Looks great,'' she said and closed the passenger-side rear door. Before she slid into the front seat, she took a couple of deep breaths. If nothing else, she'd been blessed with the ability to see the truth in any situation. Ryan wasn't interested in her. Therefore she didn't want to make him uncomfortable by swooning or anything else that obvious. That gave her the determination she needed to be calm and pretend disinterest. She was able to slide into her seat and not even flinch when his arm brushed against hers.

Her resolve was strengthened by the humorous image of herself in a dead faint in Ryan's arms, while he ran around the mall begging people to help him make her not be in love with him. No, he wasn't for her, she thought, even though in her heart of hearts, she wanted him to be. But there *was* a man out there. Someone warm and caring, someone who would make her heart beat just as fast. Someone who would appreciate her good qualities. Someone who would love her back. As soon as she finished working for Ryan, she was going to go out and find her mystery man.

"What are you thinking?" Ryan asked.

"Nothing important."

"You were smiling."

"I'm a happy person."

She glanced at him and found him studying her. "Yes, you are," he agreed, his green eyes bright with affection.

She wanted to believe it was more than just friendship...wanted to, but couldn't. If only she weren't such a dreamer.

"So what kind of shoes are we going to buy?" he asked.

"You sound as if you think we get a vote."

He looked startled. "We don't?"

"They're Sasha's shoes."

"She's only two."

Cassie grinned. "You've never shopped with a stubborn toddler before, have you?"

Ryan groaned. "I don't want to hear about it."

"You don't have to. You're going to live it."

Forty minutes later Sasha sat in the shoe store and shook her head. "Pink," she said when Ryan tried to slip a yellow shoe on her foot.

He looked helplessly at Cassie. "The yellow ones are better made. They'll last longer. The only thing she likes about the pink ones is the little kitten on the side."

Cassie resisted the urge to say "I told you so." She leaned back in her chair. "I think you should explain that to her."

"Yeah, right." But he crouched in front of his niece. "Sasha, the yellow ones are very nice. They're pretty, don't you think?"

Dark curls flew back and forth as she shook her head. "Me want pink shoes. With kitty. Like book. Me like pink.

Me like kitty.'' She kicked off the yellow shoe the salesman and Ryan had wrestled onto her right foot. ''No!''

Ryan looked so shocked, Cassie had to bite her lip to keep from laughing. Most of the time he and Sasha got along fine. There hadn't been many tantrums in his presence. Looked like that was about to change.

''What do I do?'' he asked.

''It's your choice,'' she told him. ''Pick your battle. Do you want to fight it out with a two-year-old over these shoes? You have to weigh the costs and benefits. Yes, you're the adult, you're buying the shoes, you have the final say. If you think the yellow shoes are better for her feet then you should insist.'' She met his gaze. ''If it's just that you like the brand name better, then it's less simple. What if she refuses to wear the yellow shoes once you buy them? Do you want to have this fight every morning? Or to be more accurate, do you want *me* to have this fight every morning?''

''She'd really hate them that much?''

''I don't know. She might be fine. She might always remember the pink ones.'' Cassie leaned forward. ''Welcome to parenting, Ryan. There aren't any easy solutions. You do have to decide what's worth taking a stand on because one of the worst things you can do is waffle once you've drawn a line in the sand. So think long and hard before making any pronouncements.''

He picked up a pink shoe, then grabbed the yellow one she'd kicked away. ''They're just shoes.'' The brightly colored footwear looked tiny resting on his hand. He turned his attention to his niece. ''You're too young to be causing this much trouble.''

Sasha held out her arms. ''Hug,'' she demanded.

He obliged, all the while grumbling. ''You're not going to win me over with a little affection,'' he said.

"Why not?" Cassie asked. "Women have been using their feminine wiles to get what they want for centuries."

"I don't think of Sasha as having feminine wiles."

Cassie didn't say anything, but she knew the exact moment Ryan made his decision and she wasn't surprised when he turned to the hovering clerk and said, "We'll take the pink ones."

As he helped Sasha back into her old shoes and socks, he glanced at her. "What are you thinking?"

That he was too cute for words, but she couldn't tell him that. "Nothing much."

"Which ones would you have bought?"

"The pink ones. It's an easy win for her. They're both well-made, she'll outgrow both of them quickly."

"So I did okay?"

His earnest, hopeful expression made her heart melt. "You did great."

"Thanks. Your opinion means a lot to me."

He flashed her a smile that, if she hadn't already been sitting down, would have made her knees collapse.

While Ryan settled Sasha on his hip and walked over to pay for the shoes, Cassie slowly collected their jackets. She needed a minute to calm down. It was difficult to pretend he didn't matter to her when her body was on constant alert. But as long as Ryan didn't figure it out, she could live with the symptoms. At least that was what she told herself.

Feeling and strength returned to her legs and she rose to her feet. As she met Ryan by the door, a young woman with two children in a stroller smiled at them. "Your daughter is very pretty."

Ryan hesitated, then thanked the woman.

When they were in the mall, he turned to her. "I didn't know if I should explain the situation or not," he said. "It seemed easier to accept the compliment. I hope you don't mind.''

''Not at all. It was bound to happen.''

''Thanks for understanding.''

''No problem.''

''So what are we going to do about lunch?'' he asked.

Cassie listened while he and Sasha discussed the possibilities. She reminded herself that she had Ryan's respect and his affection. That was enough. But when the woman had assumed they were a family, something inside of her had flared to life. In that moment she realized that walking away from Ryan was going to be much harder than letting go of Joel. She hoped that there weren't any other parallels—that when she gave her heart to a man other than Ryan, she wouldn't be settling for second best again.

The sound of laughter pierced Ryan's concentration and he turned toward the window. At first it had been easy to block out the sounds of Cassie and Sasha in the house, but that was becoming more and more difficult. He supposed part of the reason was that he enjoyed spending time with them. Given the choice between them and work, there wasn't a choice at all.

He leaned back in his chair and wondered if any of his employees would believe that if he told them. After all, he was known for his long hours, a nearly superhuman ability to focus on the problem at hand, and the need to put work above all else in his life.

That had changed, too, he thought as he saved his work in progress and left the office. The truth was if he was going to stay in Bradley for much longer, he was going to have to look into getting an office. Every week he stayed in the house, he was getting less and less done, while spending more time with Cassie and Sasha.

He stepped out the back door and stood unobserved on the rear porch. The November afternoon was bright, but cool. Sasha sat on the small swing her father had given her for her birthday. Her hair was still tousled from her nap, while the nip in the air added color to her plump cheeks. She was dressed in pink corduroy jeans that matched her favorite new pink shoes, and a jacket. Cassie stood behind her, gently pushing her on the swing.

"More," Sasha called, ever the thrill-seeker.

"This is about all you can handle, sweetie," Cassie told her.

Her life was so simple, Ryan thought, studying his niece. Playtime and nap time, plenty of love and affection. If she was fed and warm and cuddled, her world was right. Adults could learn from that, he thought. His gaze strayed to Cassie. Some already had.

Cassie was one of the most open women he'd ever met. In a world of people being politically correct, she said whatever she thought. She didn't play games, she didn't pretend to care about something, even if the world said she should. She was so pretty, he thought as he stared at her smooth skin and laughing brown eyes. Just watching her made him feel that everything could work out.

He was still in the shadows and hadn't been spotted. Cassie slowed the swing and wrapped her arms around Sasha. "You are the most precious little girl," she said. "I love you very much."

Sasha hugged her back. The child whispered something and they giggled together.

Ryan felt as if he was eavesdropping on something very private, yet he couldn't turn away. At least he didn't have to worry about the person taking care of his niece. Every time he'd come into a room unexpectedly, all he'd found was warm affection and plenty of attention. Cassie treated

Sasha with the same loving concern she would give her own child.

Now, as the two females talked, he wished there was some way to find out what Cassie was thinking. For the past two weeks, she'd acted as if everything was fine with her. As far as he could tell, she hadn't heard from Joel. Did that bother her? Was she really all right, or was she hiding the truth from him? No matter how bright her smile, he couldn't shake the feeling of guilt inside of him. He'd been the one to kiss her, and that had, directly or indirectly, caused her to break it off with Joel. Therefore it was his fault. Therefore he had to fix the problem.

The question was how?

Maybe he could—

"Unk Ryan!" Sasha spotted him and came running toward the porch. "Come pay me."

He chuckled. "I'm translating that as 'come play with me' rather than 'you owe me money.'"

"Have you borrowed any money from her recently?" Cassie asked, her voice teasing.

"No, I think our debts are cleared." He picked up Sasha and swung her around. "What do you say, little one? Do I owe you vast sums of money?"

"More!" Sasha cried out as she moved through the air. "More!"

He tossed her in the air and caught her. Sasha squealed with delight, while he marveled at her ability to trust. Finally he set her on the ground. "I need a break," he said.

"Cassie," Sasha said, pointing at her nanny.

Cassie shook her head. "Thank you, no. I don't want to be thrown into the air and I doubt your uncle wants to be the one to catch me. I would hurt his back."

Sasha frowned.

Cassie crouched in front of her. "I'm too big, sweetie. He can lift you, but he can't lift me."

"Then cull," she said with a sly little grin and rushed toward Cassie.

"What is she talking about?" Ryan asked as Cassie backed away from his niece.

She laughed, then ducked around the swing pole and moved to her left. "You're not going to get me," she cried over her shoulder, walking just fast enough to keep Sasha an arm's length away. "Tickling. She's trying to get me so she can tickle me."

Cassie made a tempting target. Worn jeans hugged her thighs and rounded hips. She wore a red sweatshirt that concealed her generous breasts, but he knew they were there. An intriguing thought occurred to him.

"Sasha, you want help?" he asked.

Sasha stopped and stared at him. Then she grinned and nodded. "Get Cassie."

She ran as fast as her short legs would carry her. He circled around from the opposite side. Cassie laughed.

"This isn't fair. Two against one." She eyed Ryan as he got closer. "Wait. Maybe we should gang up on Sasha. Wouldn't that be fun?"

"Sure, but not as much fun as this," he said as he lunged for her.

She screamed and ducked, then had to leap back to keep from tripping over Sasha. Down she went onto the soft grass. Sasha jumped on top of her and began tickling. Ryan joined the fray.

He knelt on the ground and pulled his niece toward him. As he did so, he tickled her sides. Sasha giggled and laughed, trying to squirm away.

"Thank you," Cassie said as she rose into a sitting position. Her hair was mussed, her eyes dancing with amusement. ''I thought I was—''

He leaned Sasha against his thigh and kept tickling her with one hand, while with his free hand, he reached out for Cassie. She broke off in midsentence and tried to scramble away. But she was laughing too much and couldn't get to her feet. She pushed at his hand.

''Ryan, stop. You can't do this. It's not part of my job description.''

Then, without warning, Sasha turned on him. Her tiny hands found that one sensitive place on his ribs. Instantly he released both her and Cassie. ''No, you don't,'' he said, physically holding her out of harm's way.

But it was too late. Cassie had seen his moment of vulnerability. She lunged toward him and attacked. Then the three of them were laughing and tickling and rolling in a heap.

He pushed hands away, tried to pin them both down, but while Cassie and Sasha weren't that strong, they were definitely squirmy. He was also afraid of hurting them, so he couldn't use his strength against them.

''Truce,'' he called after a couple of minutes. ''Enough.''

'''nuff,'' Sasha agreed and collapsed against him.

''Agreed.'' Cassie took a deep breath and relaxed. Her head was on his shoulder, her body pressed against his.

In that moment, he wanted her more than he'd ever wanted any woman in his life. But that wasn't what scared him. What made him break out into a cold sweat was the realization that this was exactly what he needed. Days like this. With sunshine and laughter, Sasha and Cassie. He needed them to be a family.

Fear came on the heels of desire. Fear and the sense that he was in over his head. As much as he might want to be like everyone else, he knew he didn't have the skills. He could work hard, he could build a company from nothing with only a dream and determination. He could learn that which could be taught, but he didn't know how to be a husband or a father. He'd never seen it done. He allowed himself to get close to Sasha because he had Cassie there to keep him from making any big mistakes. But who would protect her from him if they got involved?

Besides, Cassie wouldn't want a man like him. She would want someone more like herself—open and loving. Someone who believed in family and happily-ever-after. He believed in keeping an emotional distance and working eighty-hour weeks. He had nothing to offer her.

There was only one solution. He had to fix her problem. Somehow, some way, he was going to get her and Joel back together.

"Here's John when he left for college," Ryan said, pointing to a photograph of a serious young man who looked like a shorter and broader version of his brother. "I guess I was about eight or nine. I didn't want him to go. He promised that we'd still do things together, but I knew it was going to be different."

"Was it?" Cassie asked.

He nodded. "He came home for holidays, the first couple of years, then he was too busy."

The evening was chilly, but Ryan had lit a fire in the fireplace. The welcoming scent of wood smoke filled the living room. Cassie picked up her wine and took a sip. Despite the quiet of the dark house around them and the late hour, not to mention the flickering flames, she refused to acknowledge this was the least bit romantic. Ryan had asked for her help in sorting through old pictures. He'd wanted to put a few up for Sasha to see. That was all. She was a hardworking employee helping her boss. The fire, the wine, the night…well, they were just set decorations. As real and as meaningful as a movie backdrop.

At least that was what she kept telling herself, even as her body quivered and her mouth went dry.

They were sitting next to each other on the sofa. Several photo albums were stacked around them. Ryan reached for a pale fabric-covered one and set it on the coffee table. "This is their wedding album," he said.

Helen had been a slight woman, with mahogany-colored hair and big, dark eyes. The first picture showed her and John standing together, their arms wrapped around each other. They were obviously in love. Cassie fought against the envy that swelled inside of her. She wanted that for herself—true love and someone to share it with.

"They look so happy," Ryan said. He leaned forward and rested his elbows on his knees while he studied the photo. "I still can't believe I thought my brother was crazy to cut back his hours. As I look through these pictures, I know he did exactly the right thing. I just wish I'd been able to tell him at the time."

"He knew," Cassie said. She turned several pages. In every one the couple gazed at each other, their love a tangible part of their beings. "It shows everywhere."

There was a picture of a very pregnant Helen at a summer barbecue. John stood behind her, his hands splayed across her belly.

"He loved her," Ryan said. "She meant everything to him, and him to her. I see it all so clearly now. I admire him for being able to turn his back on how he was raised. It's not easy to give up old habits and fears. My mother always told us that if we stopped working, we would lose it all. Yet, he did it anyway."

"His love was stronger than his fear," Cassie said. "But you're right, it is tough to give up old beliefs."

She held her glass of wine in both hands. She understood because she was wrestling with her own demons. She'd nearly forgotten about them in the past few years, but since her breakup with Joel, they'd started visiting her again.

They came in the night and whispered that if she wanted too much, if she tried to get what she really wanted, she would just lose it. Better to take a little less. Then she wouldn't be at risk. She'd come to realize that those fears had been the basis of her relationship with Joel. Chloe had been right—she *had* settled. Wanting Joel wasn't the same as wanting it all. Losing him wouldn't break her heart. So he'd been safe to love. Now she was thinking about going after her heart's desire, the price of which could destroy her.

What if she really fell in love? What if she gave all of herself, then lost it? She'd already been abandoned twice, first by her birth parents, then when her adopted parents had died. She didn't want to risk that happening again.

''What are you thinking?'' Ryan asked.

She glanced at him and saw that he was watching her. ''That no matter how scary it is, we still have to go after our dreams.''

''What are you scared of?''

She shrugged. ''Mostly of not belonging. That's what Joel was for me. An easy way to fit in. Now I'm feeling strong enough to go out and find a way to fit in on my own. Bradley will always be my hometown, but I'm not sure that staying here is such a good idea. I'm not going to magically finds roots. I have to go out and grow them. That might mean trying a different way of life. I need to figure out what's really important to me and then go after it.''

The words sounded brave. She hoped she had the strength of character to do it, despite the demons that whispered she would only fail.

"I admire you," he said. "You're the most honest person I know."

She thought about her secret passion for Ryan. "Please don't make me out to be incredibly virtuous. I'm not at all." She wanted to say more, but he was sitting too close. She could feel his leg lightly pressing against hers. Maybe it was the wine or the fire, but she was suddenly warm.

"I'm glad you're here," he said.

She made the mistake of looking at him and found herself getting lost in his green eyes. A man shouldn't be so beautiful, she thought to herself as all the air rushed out of her lungs. It wasn't fair. How was she supposed to keep her head about her when he looked so incredibly perfect? And why didn't he just take her in his arms and kiss her? Couldn't he feel the tension between them? Didn't he know that she wanted to be with him? The image of them together, touching and tasting, holding and doing all those things she knew about in theory, if not in practice, haunted her.

Their gazes locked. The temperature in the room cranked up yet another notch until she found it difficult to breathe. The night closed in around them, making her feel isolated, but deliciously safe with Ryan. Only Ryan.

He leaned forward. He was going to kiss her. She knew it...believed it...anticipated it. He reached his hand toward her, long fingers that would stroke her skin and leave her....

"It's late. You need to be in bed. Good night, Cassie."

His words combined with his brisk tone to make her feel as if she'd been doused by ice water. She blinked twice, certain she hadn't heard him correctly. He was sending her to bed? Alone?

"Um, sure," she said. She set her wine on the coffee table and awkwardly rose to her feet. She felt like a child being sent away so the grown-ups could enjoy their evening.

"Good night," she murmured as she made her way to the stairs.

Despite her wishes to the contrary, Ryan didn't know she was alive. At least not as a woman. He knew she existed as Sasha's nanny, and no matter how she tried to convince herself otherwise, that wasn't enough for her. She wanted more. Unfortunately, she didn't have a clue as to how to get more.

When she reached her bedroom, she closed the door behind her, then leaned against the cool wood. Letting go of Joel had been incredibly easy. Despite the fact that she'd known Ryan less than two months she had a bad feeling that letting go of him was going to take at least a lifetime.

Chapter Thirteen

Ryan looked out the front window for the third time in as many minutes. He couldn't remember the last time he'd been this nervous. Telling himself he was doing the right thing for the right reason wasn't helping. If only he'd had more time to talk to Joel. But their conversation had been rushed and he'd only had a chance to issue the invitation.

Actually, "issue" wasn't a strong enough word. Joel had practically required a summons to agree to show up for dinner tonight. No doubt the young man was still suffering, Ryan reminded himself. It wasn't every day that a man had to get over someone as terrific as Cassie. And if Ryan had his way, by the end of the evening, Cassie and Joel would once again be back together.

He dropped the curtain in place and checked his watch. Joel wasn't due for about ten more minutes. This was going to be great, he told himself. Sure, Cassie acted as if everything was fine, but what choice did she have? She couldn't really admit that she'd made a huge mistake. Still, Ryan didn't doubt that she had. She and Joel had been together for years. They obviously belonged together. Even if Cassie insisted otherwise. If he hadn't lost control of himself and kissed her, then none of this would have happened. She wouldn't have gotten it into her head that Joel was the wrong man for her. It was his fault they'd broken up and he was going to see they got back together.

But the thought of her with another man, even Joel, annoyed him. Images of them together ripped through his brain, making him want to do some ripping of his own. Like maybe taking Joel apart, limb by limb. He drew in a deep breath and reminded himself of his higher purpose in all this. While he might want Cassie, he couldn't have her. He was emotionally incapable of providing her with all that she needed and deserved. However, Joel could give her that. So they belonged together.

He walked into the kitchen to check on Cassie. Before he got there, he reminded himself he had to act casual about the whole thing. While she knew that he'd invited Joel to dinner, she didn't know that he planned to disappear right after the meal, leaving the two lovebirds to work things out.

Cassie looked up from the pot she was stirring. "I hope you like spaghetti," she said. "Charity dropped off some sauce when she was here a couple of weeks ago, and I defrosted it for tonight's meal. It's the famous Wright family recipe."

"I'm looking forward to it."

He studied Cassie's face, but as usual, she looked calm and incredibly attractive. Her soft pink sweater hugged her torso, outlining her breasts and making his skin twitch. He wanted to touch her. He wanted to hold her and be with her and...

Stop it! he ordered himself. This wasn't about him. He had to remember what was important.

''It was very nice of you to invite Joel for dinner,'' Cassie said. ''I'd been worried that he wasn't getting out much since we broke up. Joel isn't the most social guy on the planet. Work was always his whole life.''

''He seemed a little subdued,'' Ryan said. ''I could tell he hadn't been sleeping much.''

At least that part of it was true. Joel had looked exhausted, although he'd been plenty cheerful.

''You never did say what you were doing over at Bradley Discount,'' Cassie said, setting down her spoon and facing him. ''Had you been there before?''

''I was checking out toys for Sasha. Christmas is less than two months away.'' It was a pitiful excuse, but the best he could come up with under the circumstances. No way was he going to tell her he'd gone to the store expressly to see Joel and had spent nearly an hour tracking the man down. Nor was he going to mention Joel's reluctance to join them for dinner.

Ryan grimaced as he remembered how he'd even taken the time to assure the younger man that there was nothing between Cassie and himself. Despite the fact that he wanted her to the exclusion of all other women.

''You were Christmas shopping? By yourself? In November?'' Cassie asked the questions in a tone of disbelief usually reserved for questioning murder suspects.

''I can if I want to,'' he said, then practically sighed in relief when the doorbell rang. ''I'll get that.''

He made it halfway down the hall, paused, and returned to the kitchen. ''Maybe you should get it.''

Cassie stared at him. ''What on earth is wrong with you?''

''Nothing.''

The doorbell rang again.

"One of us had better get it," she muttered and headed out of the kitchen.

Ryan trailed after her. He didn't want to intrude on their greeting, but he also wanted to witness the event. If things looked like they were heating up instantly, he would hide out in his office and quietly drink himself into oblivion.

Cassie pulled open the door. "Hi, Joel."

"Cassie!" He swept her into a big bear hug.

Ryan had to resist the urge to jerk her out of the other man's embrace, all the while reminding himself that this had been *his* idea. Still, he hadn't thought it would hurt so much to watch her in Joel's arms. He turned away.

"Wow, you're so different," Cassie said. "What happened?"

Joel laughed. "Do you like it?"

Ryan glanced back and saw Cassie staring at Joel as if she'd never seen him before. "You're in contacts," she said and touched his face. "Your hair is styled and you're wearing new clothes."

"It's the new me."

A new look? Great, Ryan thought, trying to muster a little enthusiasm. Obviously Joel was trying to make a good impression. It seemed like everything was going to work out fine. He was thrilled. Really.

He cleared his throat and stepped forward. "Joel, thanks for joining us for dinner. Come on in."

There was the usual flurry and confusion of getting settled and taking drink orders. Cassie excused herself to check on Sasha, who had been put in bed a half hour before.

While she was gone, Ryan searched for something to say to Joel. "How's business?"

"Great. I've been talking to some people and they think I've got a real chance at making it to president of Bradley Discount." He leaned forward and lowered his voice to a confidential whisper. "I've been thinking about making a switch. There are a lot more opportunities with the big chains. I might give that a try. It would mean moving, of course, but that's not a problem anymore. Cassie never wanted to leave Bradley, but I think I would like to see the world. Maybe even move to the Bay area."

Ryan stared at the younger man. He *did* look different. The new hairstyle swept back from his face, giving him a "young executive" look. His clothes were expensive, as was his obviously new watch. Something had happened to Joel in the couple of weeks he'd been single. Something Ryan didn't like at all.

He was torn between defending Cassie's desire to stay close to home and pointing out that a move to the Bay area was hardly seeing the world. Before he could decide, Cassie returned and took her seat on the sofa.

Unfortunately, when they first came into the living room, Joel had taken one of the wing chairs, leaving Ryan and Cassie the sofa. Still, Joel was across from her and eye contact was very powerful. At least it was when Cassie looked at him.

She took a sip of her white wine. "I can't get over the changes. You look terrific, Joel."

"Thanks." He half raised his hand, then put it back in his lap. "I've worn glasses for so long that it's difficult to get used to being without them, but I like the contacts." He cleared his throat. "So how are you doing?"

"I'm fine."

She gave him one of her best smiles, the one that always made Ryan want to rush her into his bed. Joel didn't seem affected. The ungrateful twit.

"I've been keeping busy with Sasha. She's a handful, but such a sweet girl."

Cassie continued talking about her job, and then filled Joel in on news about her family. The other man pretended to listen, but Ryan could tell his attention was elsewhere. Then it hit him. Joel had asked about Cassie's life to be polite, but he wasn't interested in the answer. What he wanted instead was to talk about *his* life.

Ryan took a hefty swallow of beer and wished he'd chosen something stronger, like Scotch. He had a bad feeling about what was about to happen. He opened his mouth, but couldn't think of anything to say. It was like watching two trains on the same track. They were going to collide and all he could do was helplessly stand by.

"So what's new with you?" she finally asked, then smiled. "Aside from the great new look."

He scooted forward in his chair. "A lot. I have to tell you, Cass, when you first broke up with me, I thought you were crazy. All your talk about wanting more, about passion. I figured it was some female thing and you'd get over it in a couple of days."

He shrugged. "The thing was, I couldn't stop thinking about everything you'd told me. It started to make sense, sort of, and then I got this feeling you weren't going to change your mind. I began to realize you'd meant what you said."

"I did," she said. "I'm glad you see that. I think we're both happier this way."

Ryan had to grind his teeth to keep from speaking out. This was *not* how he'd planned their conversation. They were supposed to be talking about how much they missed each other. Maybe he was the problem. If he left the room, at least they would have privacy. But he couldn't think of a smooth way to make that happen, so he hunched down in the corner of the sofa and pretended not to be there.

"I am happier," Joel said, sounding sheepish and proud at the same time. "I got real confused about everything, so

I asked Alice to dinner. She's the assistant manager of the Bradley Discount pet department. Redhead, about so tall.'' He held up his hand, indicating a tiny woman.

A knot formed in Ryan's stomach. The trains were only a few feet apart now. The impact was going to be felt for miles.

''I told her everything you'd said and then asked for her opinion. I figured with her being female and all, she'd have a better idea than I did as to what was going on.''

''What happened?'' Cassie asked.

Ryan closed his eyes. He didn't want to know.

''Well, it was the strangest thing. Partway through the meal, she told me that I should forget all about you. It seems that she's had a thing for me for about two years. She told me she was in love with me. You can imagine how shocked I was.''

Not nearly as shocked as me, Ryan thought grimly. He wanted to groan out loud. He wanted to rant and rave and throw things and beat the hell out of Joel for giving up on Cassie in the first place.

He risked a glance at Cassie. She was nodding intently, as if the story was interesting but didn't have anything to do with her personally. ''What did you say?''

''Nothing. I listened. Then she invited me back to her place.''

Ryan thought about throwing Joel out, but it was too late. What had gone wrong? Why weren't they getting back together? He knew what the other man was going to say next. The trains impacted and the room shook. He seemed to be the only one who noticed.

''I spent the night. Actually, I spent two days there.'' Joel grinned like a kid who'd hit his first home run. ''I even called in sick, which, as you know, I've never done before.''

''That's true. You always prided yourself on your perfect

attendance.'' Cassie's voice was calm. Ryan wanted to crawl under a rock.

''It's just like you said,'' Joel told her. ''With Alice, I feel the passion. It's amazing. We talk about everything. There's so much to say and never enough time. We can't seem to get out of bed.'' He looked at her and grinned. ''Cass, I owe you for this. I've never been happier. Alice is exactly who I belong with. You were right. I should have known. You always were the smart one in the relationship.''

''Joel, I'm happy for you.''

Ryan thought he was going to be sick.

''Is it serious?'' she asked.

''Yeah. We're, uh, sort of living together.''

''Already?'' Ryan asked before he could stop himself. ''Do you think that's wise?''

''Sure. We're getting married. I bought her a beautiful engagement ring. Nearly two carats in diamonds. It's—'' Joel paused and, for the first time, seemed uncomfortable. ''Sorry, Cassie. That wasn't nice, was it? I didn't mean to imply—''

She cut him off with a wave of her hand. ''It's fine. You gave me the promise ring when we were both kids. Now you're a man. Of course you would do things differently.''

Ryan had forgotten about the diamond lint ring. The little piece of animal refuse had cheated Cassie out of a decent engagement ring, too.

''Anyway,'' Joel plunged on as if determined to tell his story, regardless of whom he hurt, ''we're heading over to Las Vegas at the end of the month. This close to the holidays we had a hard time getting four days off together, but I pulled a few strings. We'll be married then. We know we want to be together forever, and don't see the point of waiting.''

He made the last statement with a note of defiance in his

voice, as if he expected someone to tell him that he was acting impetuously. Ryan was more than ready to do it, but he was too stunned by everything that had happened. The evening wasn't supposed to play out this way. Joel was supposed to have taken one look at Cassie and begged her to come back. They would have talked, she would have agreed, end of problem.

"I'm very happy for both of you," Cassie said. She rose to her feet, walked around the coffee table, then bent over and kissed Joel's cheek. "I mean that completely."

"Are you sure?" Joel asked, his weasel eyes searching her face. "I wouldn't have told you if I thought you still cared."

Yeah, right, Ryan thought bitterly. He couldn't wait to gloat. No doubt he figured Cassie would be destroyed by the information, kicking herself for letting him get away. Well, that wasn't going to happen. Somehow he, Ryan, would figure out a way to make it right. Although his track record at fixing things was currently pretty crummy.

"I'm completely sure," Cassie told him. "Joel, we had nine lovely years together. I'll always remember them fondly. I hope you will, too. But at the end we both knew it was time to move on. I'm so pleased that you've found your heart's desire."

"Thanks, Cassie." Weasel-boy squeezed her hand.

Cassie flashed him a smile. "I need to check on dinner. I'll be right back."

Ryan gave her a thirty-second lead, excused himself and raced after her into the kitchen.

"Cassie, I'm so sorry," he said as he burst into the room. "If I'd known that little ingrate had gone and done this, I never would have invited him over. Are you doing okay? Do you want me to send him home? I could beat him up for you."

Cassie glanced up from the tray of garlic bread she was about to place in the oven. She laughed. "What a generous offer. No one has offered to beat up another person for me before. You're being very sweet and I appreciate your concern, but I meant what I told Joel. I'm fine."

She left the garlic bread and crossed to stand by him. "I'm the one who ended the relationship. It was my idea."

"You could be having second thoughts."

"I could, but I'm not."

Ryan wanted to believe her. He stared deeply into her dark eyes, but he couldn't tell what she was thinking. Obviously the pain was too great for her to even conceive of it yet. "I'll go beat him up."

As he turned, Cassie grabbed his arm. "Don't. Joel hasn't done anything wrong. I really am happy about the new lady in his life. I swear." She made an X on her chest. "Just let it be and enjoy the evening. I'm going to."

"Sure," he muttered and stalked out of the kitchen. Enjoy the evening. No problem.

It was the longest two hours of Ryan's life. All through dinner, and afterward, while he sipped coffee and apparently had no plans to leave anytime soon, all Joel talked about was Alicc. Alicc was brilliant, Alice was witty, Alice was charming and insightful and well-read and probably three days away from curing several lethal diseases.

Ryan sipped his brandy and admitted the last thought hadn't been completely accurate. But, dammit, Joel was getting on his nerves. He wanted Weasel-boy out of his house.

"We're going to put off having children for a few years," Joel was saying. "Alice and I want to spend time with each other first."

"Very wise," Cassie said. "Once the little ones start coming, everything changes."

As she'd been all evening, Cassie was the picture of poise. A lovely and gracious hostess. Ryan ached for her and wished there was something to do to help her feel better. In his arrogance, he'd tried to fix her life. Instead he'd made it worse. She must feel as if she was trapped in hell.

Finally, a little after ten, Joel pushed back his chair and stood up. "I should head home."

About time, Ryan thought. Don't let the door hit you in the ass on your way out. But he didn't say that. Instead he offered the other man a tight smile and led the way to the foyer.

They said their goodbyes quickly. When he was gone, Ryan closed the door behind him and leaned against the frame. "I'm sorry," he said.

"You've already apologized. I told you then there was no need. There still isn't."

She walked back into the dining room and started clearing the table. Ryan trailed after her. "I don't believe you. You have to be in pain. This is awful and it's all my fault. I was an arrogant fool who thought he could fix everything. All I've done instead is make the situation worse. I'm sorry."

Cassie sank down into a chair and wondered how offended Ryan would be if she started laughing. He obviously believed her heart was breaking and that she was within a hairbreadth of losing it completely.

"I appreciate the concern," she said as she stared at him. "You are a very kind man to worry about me. But as I said before, I'm fine."

"Cassie, a month ago you were going to marry Joel. Now he's living with someone else who he plans to marry at the end of this month. You can't tell me that doesn't matter."

"You have a point," she said. "I feel strange hearing about the changes in Joel's life. As a friend, I'm a little worried that he's moved so quickly. But deep down inside,

I don't feel anything. I'm not sorry I ended our relationship. I don't wish he were marrying me instead.'' She allowed herself a small smile. ''I'm a little bitter about the engagement ring—it sounds beautiful. However, I would like to point out that if my biggest worry is that he spent twenty times more on her ring than mine, then I'm obviously not going to be destroyed by all that's happened. I don't have any regrets.''

He studied her face. ''I wish I could believe you.''

''You can. I'm telling the truth.'' She clasped her hands together. ''You're forgetting that I was questioning my relationship with Joel for a long time before I ended it. I didn't make that decision lightly. I know you feel responsible because of what happened between us, but I wish you could let that go. I have.''

Okay, so that was a lie, but in the scheme of things, it wasn't a very big one. She hadn't let the kiss go. If anything, she thought about it more than ever, but only because her feelings for Ryan had changed.

The entire time Joel had been talking about Alice, she'd been thinking about Ryan. She'd realized she didn't have a crush on her boss anymore. She'd fallen in love with him.

Everything Joel had said about what it was like to spend time with Alice had made her wish it was that way for her and Ryan, too. She'd wanted to experience those things with him, she'd wanted him to return her feelings. She wanted them both to fall madly in love, to be swept away by fire and passion, and live happily ever after.

She drew in a deep breath. Unfortunately, that wasn't in the cards for her. Ryan liked her and respected her, but it wasn't love. The truth didn't have to be pleasant, but she did have to accept it. There was no point in planning on something she was never going to have. So, despite the ache in her heart, she would be sensible.

She would go out and find a place in which to belong. She would find someone she could love and who wanted to love her back. She would make sure that this time there was passion as well as friendship. And eventually, she would forget Ryan and all that he'd meant to her.

But not just yet. For the next few weeks she would stay here in Bradley, in Ryan's house, and collect as many memories as possible.

"You're not even listening," he complained.

Cassie blinked. "You're right. I'm sorry. What were you saying?"

He crossed to the chair and grabbed her hand. After pulling her to her feet, he cupped her face.

"I'm more sorry than I can tell you. You've been so great and all I've done is mess up your life. I didn't mean to upset everything by kissing you. Now, by inviting Joel over, I've only made things worse. I thought that if the two of you spent some time together, everything would work out."

She loved the feel of his palms against her skin, but instead of savoring the moment, she grabbed his wrists and pulled him away. "You have an incredible ability not to hear what I'm saying. It's a gift, isn't it?" She took a deep breath. "I'll speak slowly so that you can understand. I don't want Joel. I don't miss him. I don't want to be with him anymore."

His green eyes darkened. "Really?"

Was she actually getting through to him? "Yes, really. I would rather be alone than be with someone I don't love. I don't love him."

"Cassie, I—"

She held up her hand. "If you apologize one more time I'm going to ask you to beat up yourself."

He grinned. "Okay, I won't. I'm just concerned."

"And I'm just fine. I mean that."

"All right. I'll let it go, but only after I tell you that Joel is a stupid man. He had a real prize in you."

His words warmed her. Without thinking, she leaned forward and kissed his mouth. "Thank you. That's so nice. You really—"

But she couldn't finish her sentence. Not when she saw the heat flaring in his eyes. Heat that ignited a matching fire in her body. "Ryan?"

He swore under his breath. "I promised I wouldn't do this again, Cassie, and I meant it. But you do things to me." His jaw tightened. "Just walk away. Go to bed. Leave the house if it scares you too much." He swore again. "I didn't mean for you to ever find out. I'm a real bastard. I'm sorry."

She stared at him. "You want me," she said, not quite able to believe the words even as she spoke them. Wonder filled her. Wonder and longing.

"Of course. Who wouldn't?"

She could probably come up with dozens of names, but right now that didn't seem important. He didn't love her, but he wanted her. It shouldn't be enough, but it was. She would rather have a little bit of magic with Ryan than have a lifetime of almost with someone else.

"I'm not afraid," she told him. "You're not a bastard. I'm not leaving the house. In fact, I don't think I'm going to bed for a long time."

"One of us has to be strong."

It took all her courage, but she took a step toward him and placed her hands on his shoulders. He tensed. She leaned a little closer and felt his arousal pressing into her belly.

"I'm not feeling especially strong," she told him. "Guess it's up to you."

They stared at each other. She thought he might back off, or push her away. Instead he sucked in a breath, wrapped his arms around her and kissed her.

Chapter Fourteen

This kiss was better than the one she remembered. Cassie let herself lean into him, absorbing the heat that flared instantly. His mouth was hot and firm against hers, his body hot and hard. Passion swept through her, like a rush of light, filling every pore, every cell. She couldn't think, couldn't breathe, couldn't imagine ever wanting to stop. All she could do was kiss him back.

Ryan brushed her lower lip with his tongue. She shivered as she parted to admit him. He moved inside, stroking her, circling around, exploring and teasing. He tasted of wine and himself, a potent combination that left her light-headed.

His hands were everywhere. On her back, slipping down to her waist, then cupping her hips. He squeezed her derriere and pulled her against him so that she could feel all of his arousal, then brought his hands up her arms and began the journey again. In turn, she allowed herself to rest her fingertips on his broad shoulders. He was so strong. Every muscle tightened as she traced a pattern down his back. She could feel his rippling tension.

What was that old line? "If this is madness, then let me live with the insane." Or something like that. It didn't matter. The concept captured her feelings perfectly. She wanted to be crazy, if it meant sharing this incredible moment with Ryan. Her breasts ached and swelled until she wanted to beg him to touch her there. Her legs trembled. Between her thighs, that most private part of her dampened. She could feel a heaviness low in her stomach and it took all her strength not to rock her hips against him.

Ryan cupped her face. He trailed kisses across her cheeks and nose, along her jaw to her ear. There he nibbled on her earlobe. Her breath caught as the impact of his teasing made her softly cry out. It was too delicious, too incredible, too unlike anything she'd ever experienced.

"Ryan," she breathed, wanting to say his name again and again so that she could know this was really happening.

He pulled back and stared at her. The fire she'd seen before had exploded into a raging storm. If she hadn't known better, she would have sworn that his hands trembled as he held her face. She noticed that his mouth was damp...from *her* kisses! *She* had done that to him. Somehow, despite her inexperience, she'd managed to arouse him and his passions.

"I want you," he said, his voice low and husky. "I want you, Cassie. In my bed. I want you naked, underneath me. I want to touch you and taste you everywhere, then I want to bury myself inside you and make you mine."

His words created an image that took her breath away. She couldn't do anything but stare at him. She'd never been naked in front of a man before, nor had a man touched her intimately. She waited for a feeling of nervousness or a voice to whisper that what they were doing was wrong, but there was only the silence of expectation.

"I want you, too," she murmured, then ducked her head as she blushed. Had she really said that?

He touched her chin and forced her to look at him. "No regrets?" he asked. "I can stop now, if you want me to." He gave her a crooked smile. "I'll want to die, but I can stop. I need you to be sure."

She knew what he was trying to say. That he wanted to make love with her, but nothing else about their relationship was going to change. He hadn't suddenly fallen in love with her. He wasn't promising her anything more than a night in his bed.

Cassie stared at his face, at the handsome lines and the need tightening his mouth, at the light in his eyes. For her it was a question of regret. Which would she regret more? Turning him away or being with him, knowing that it would never be more than a physical relationship.

She waited for the debate to begin, but there was only silence in her head. She loved Ryan. She knew him to be a good man. Despite his attempts to keep their relationship completely professional, he had stolen her heart and there was no way for her to get it back.

She'd already felt the passion of their kisses. Now she wanted to know the rest of it. She wanted to be with him in the way women had been with men since the beginning of time. As he didn't want a romantic relationship, she had to remember that this wasn't going to mean the same to him as it did to her. Eventually, she would have to get over him and find someone else. He wasn't going to be the last one...was she willing to let him be the first?

"No regrets," she said.

He brought her hand to his mouth and kissed her knuckles, then he led her to the stairs and up to his bedroom.

The room they entered was large and dark. "Stay here," he said.

He moved through the shadows. A lamp clicked on by the king-size bed, casting dim light in all directions. Cassie stared at the bed, then at Ryan. They were really going to make love. She and Ryan. She wasn't sure she believed this was happening.

"Why do you want me?" she blurted out. "I'm nothing like the women in your life."

He returned to her side. "What do you know about the women in my world?"

"Just that they're nothing like me. They're in business, or computers. They travel, wear sophisticated clothes, go to the theater and understand about wine. That's not me."

He took her hand again and pressed his mouth to her palm. "Maybe that's what I like about you," he told her. "That you're not in competition with me, that you care more about making Sasha happy than being seen in the right kind of restaurant. Maybe I like that you're honest and good, and that you don't even know there's a game, let alone understand the rules."

Game? "What game?" she asked.

He licked her palm. A shiver rippled through her and she thought she might have to sit down.

"My point exactly. I'm not claiming to understand you completely, but all the surprises have been positive ones. You're a good person. I enjoy your company, and you're sexy as hell."

She grinned. "Really?"

"I swear."

Sexy, huh? She'd never thought of herself that way. She was just plain Cassie Wright. Nothing special. Except now, with Ryan nibbling on the inside of her wrist and her whole body threatening to go up in flames, she felt very sexy and alive.

He dropped her hand and hauled her hard against him.

Before she could catch her breath, his mouth was on hers, his tongue plunging inside. She met him and gave back all that he offered. When his hands slipped under the bottom of her sweater and started moving up, she didn't think about being shy or afraid. All she could do was hold herself away a little so that he could slide up to her breasts.

She'd waited for this for so long, she thought as his fingers stroked her skin. She felt him trace her ribs, then the band of her bra. At last his right hand moved up and cupped her breast.

The contact was different from what she'd expected. Firm, yet gentle, and certainly better in every way. He squeezed, then took her tight nipple between his thumb and forefinger. He rolled the beaded tip and sent jolts of pleasure through her. Her knees threatened to buckle, her thighs were on fire. She had to hold on to him to stay upright.

"Ryan," she whispered against his mouth. "Oh, Ryan."

"Tell me about it." His voice was thick. "I can't believe what you're doing to me. I want you so much, I'm about to explode."

He stepped back and with one quick, practiced movement pulled her sweater up over her head. The night air was cool on her bare skin. Cassie didn't even think about covering herself, despite the fact that Ryan was obviously staring.

"You're so beautiful," he said and stroked the valley between her breasts. "I thought you'd be perfect and I was right."

He'd thought about her? Naked? She felt a shiver in her tummy.

He took her hand and drew her to the bed. Once she was seated, he crouched down and removed her shoes and socks. He quickly did the same to himself, then settled next to her. As he kissed her, he lowered her to the mattress.

Her left arm was trapped between them, so she reached

around with her right one. She explored his cheek and his ear, then ran her fingers through his hair. All the while they kissed as if they couldn't get enough of each other.

Cassie felt his hand on her belly. His splayed fingers moved in a lazy circle. He moved up and stroked her breasts with long, slow movements that had her arching like a cat. The need grew inside of her. She wanted...only she wasn't sure what. Every time he brushed against her tight nipples, she gasped. Between her legs a steady ache pounded in time with her heartbeat. She wanted him to touch her *there* but she was also a little scared, so she didn't say anything.

He continued to brush her skin, from her shoulder to her waist, pausing at her breasts with each trip. On one of the journeys, he unfastened the hook at the front of her bra. The lace fabric fell open.

He trailed kisses down her chin to her throat, then lower, toward her breasts. Her breath caught. Was he really going to kiss her nipples? Apparently he was, she thought as he nudged aside her bra and licked the hollow. The damp trail moved up the curve, then he took the peak in his mouth.

The pleasure was so intense, she made a soft whimpering sound and gripped his upper arm. It was too wonderful; she would never survive. But she didn't want him to stop. She wanted the moment to go on forever.

"Oh, Ryan, please," she begged, not sure what she asked for.

He raised his head and blew on the damp skin. The quick chill made her shiver, but before she could register discomfort, he took her in his mouth again and sucked.

A ribbon of need wove its way between her breasts and her feminine place. When his hand slid down her belly toward that spot, she didn't protest. She trusted him. Equally important, she wanted him. All that he had to offer.

His fingers pressed against the seam of her jeans. He

rubbed back and forth. She shifted slightly, enjoying the pressure. It was nicer than she would have thought, even though—

A jolt ripped through her. She half sat up. ''What was that?''

''The promised land,'' he said and grinned a very satisfied male smile.

Before she could ask any questions, he began tugging off her jeans. He peeled away her panties, too, and she was naked.

Any nervousness quickly disappeared as he returned his attentions to her breasts. He kissed her curves, loving her until she nearly forgot to breathe. His hand was once again on her stomach, but this time she could feel the faint roughness of his skin, along with his warmth. His fingers followed the same trail they had before, but it felt very different on bare flesh. She quivered and jumped, but didn't protest as he made his way down to the dark curls. He slipped through them slowly, almost tickling her. Almost. There was too much anticipation for her to laugh. She wanted...so much.

He raised his head. ''Cassie, look at me.''

She opened her eyes, not actually remembering closing them, and stared into his face.

''I want to see you,'' he said. ''I want to know I'm getting it right.''

She couldn't imagine him doing anything wrong, but for some reason she couldn't speak right now. Not with his fingers actually sliding down from the curls into her waiting woman's place.

He stroked her lightly. ''You're so wet and ready,'' he said with a groan. ''I want you so much. But first I want you to want me.''

She started to tell him that she did. But it was hard to think of anything except the feel of him as he discovered her. He slipped inside. She felt herself clamp tightly around him.

"Oh, I…" She trailed off, not sure what she apologized for, but sure she'd done something wrong.

"No!" he said as he stared at her intensely. "I love that you want me. Don't hold back. I want to hear you."

Cassie nodded, even though she didn't have any great plans to be chatty during the event. It was going to be difficult enough pretending this *wasn't* her first time. She was hoping that Ryan wouldn't figure that out. He'd felt so responsible just for kissing her, she could only imagine what he would put himself through if he found out she was a virgin.

His finger moved in and out of her, creating an irresistible rhythm and tension. She found her attention focusing on what he was doing and all other thoughts faded. Her hips moved of their own accord, pulsing slightly to meet his every thrust. When he withdrew, she wanted to protest, but he brought his fingers a little higher, probing gently until he found a spot that made her want to cry out.

Instead she tensed and made a grab for his wrist as her eyes fluttered closed.

"There?" he asked.

She wasn't sure of the question, but she knew he had to keep touching her. If he didn't, she was going to die. "I don't know," she gasped.

He chuckled in her ear. "I do. How do you like it?"

He circled her slowly, occasionally brushing over the sensitive spot. Then he pressed a little more, went a little faster. She found herself caught in a process she didn't understand. "Like…that," she managed.

"Relax," he murmured. "We've got all night. I want to make this good for you."

His words made her uncomfortable. He was talking about

that whole pleasure thing. She'd read about it, of course. For most guys it was a sure thing, but for women it could be complicated. Worry distracted her from the intense enjoyment. How was she supposed to know if it was happening to her? What would it feel like if it did? How long would it take? She didn't even know enough to fake it.

Cassie pressed her lips together. For now, what he was doing to her was amazing. She felt as if she were being carried toward the sun. Heat flooded her body, as her muscles tensed. She dug her heels into the bed and raised her hips toward him, urging him to continue.

She would let him do this for a few more minutes, she decided. Until he was probably bored, then she would plead exhaustion or nerves or something and get him to stop so they could get on with it. Yes, that was it. She would tell him to stop. Just not yet.

He continued to touch her. Occasionally he slipped his finger inside of her. Her breathing became rapid and she tossed her head back and forth. It was perfect, just like this. The rubbing, the closeness, the tension that spiraled higher and higher.

"You're getting ready," he told her. "Go for it."

She was about to tell him she didn't know what the "it" was, but she couldn't speak. A fine thread seemed to be unraveling inside of her. Heat radiated from that place in the very center of being. Heat and an odd pressure.

"Please," she breathed, hoping he would understand that she needed him not to stop.

Apparently he did because he moved faster and lighter, now directly over that one tiny point of sensation. She could feel herself gathering, reaching, straining. She clutched at the bedspread and splayed her knees wider.

"Cassie, look at me."

She opened her eyes and found herself drowning in his

gaze. She clung to the edge of sanity. She was almost there...even though she wasn't sure of her destination.

He stopped moving. Her breath caught in her throat. One heartbeat, two. Then he resumed, circling and circling, faster and faster until her body peaked.

She remembered crying out his name as the ripples of release rode through her. She remembered his lips on hers and the feel of his tongue in her mouth and how he'd kissed her at the exact moment when she'd wanted to be kissed. She remembered how he'd held her afterward, hugging her close and murmuring about how beautiful she was.

Finally, when her heartbeat was nearly normal, she looked up at him. "Wow."

"Yeah? I'm glad." His pleased smile faded. "I want you."

In his arms, having just experienced the ultimate pleasure for the very first time, she found herself feeling a little bold. "I want you to have me," she said perkily.

He kissed her with a passion that made her toes curl. While he fumbled with his belt and slacks, she worked on his shirt. It was tough to undress a man, all the while still kissing him, but she liked it. It made her feel sexy and worldly.

When he was finally naked, he rolled away, opened his nightstand drawer, dug out something and closed the drawer. Then he turned back and propped himself up on one elbow.

She let her gaze drift down his broad shoulders and bare chest. While they were incredibly lovely and later she would want to look her fill, right now she was far more interested in seeing a naked, aroused man. Except for some brief, shadowy glimpses in the movies, she'd never actually seen *it*.

And *it* made her gasp. "It's so big," she blurted out.

Ryan grinned. "Why, thank you, my dear. I'm glad you approve."

Approve wasn't the word she would have chosen, Cassie thought. Suddenly fear threatened. Maybe this was a bad idea. Maybe she should tell Ryan she'd changed her mind. Maybe...

She glanced up at his face, at the wanting in his eyes, at the tender-hungry expression that made her love him more. Of course she wanted this. She wanted to finally know, and she wanted to learn it all with Ryan. She trusted him and she loved him.

He slipped on the protection, then kissed her. As his tongue plunged in deeper, his hands stroked her breasts. She hadn't thought she could want him again, but she did. Her body tensed. Between her legs, she felt the heat and swelling. Could she experience that wonderful release again? At least this time she knew what to expect.

He slipped one hand down and rubbed against her until she was breathing hard. She rocked her hips in rhythm with his movements and felt herself reaching for that perfect pinnacle. Then something hard probed at her. He pressed in slowly.

Cassie told herself not to stiffen. She took deep breaths and tried to go with what was happening. He filled her, inch by inch, stretching her. It wasn't exactly painful, but there was a little discomfort. She concentrated on the unfamiliar weight of him on top of her and how safe that made her feel. She inhaled his scent and promised herself she would remember this forever.

Ryan raised his head slightly. "You feel incredible."

His face was all harsh lines and need. His eyes opened briefly, then sank closed as he slid in deeper. He paused, flexed his hips, then looked at her again. "There's something wrong," he told her.

She'd been afraid of that. There was physical proof of her virginal state. He couldn't stop now. She was close to having all she'd ever wanted. "Everything is fine," she said and placed her hand on his hip. "Be inside of me. All the way." When he still hesitated, she pulled him close. "I want this," she whispered, then kissed him.

She felt his questions and his concern, even as she nibbled on his lower lip and plunged her tongue inside of his mouth.

"How the hell am I supposed to resist you?" he asked with a groan.

"You're not." She looked at him. "Unless you want to."

"The only thing I want is to make love with you."

She smiled. "We seemed to have undressed for the occasion and assumed the position."

"That we have."

He thrust inside with a force that made her gasp. The sharp pain faded as quickly as it had appeared. Ryan froze.

"Don't stop," she said. Then she raised her hips, offering herself to him.

For a second, he didn't move. Cassie was terrified he was going to stop. She wouldn't be able to stand that. She wanted to know. She wanted to make love with him. She wanted him to experience the same release she had.

Acting on instinct, she clenched her muscles tightly around him, then relaxed. After she repeated the action twice more, he groaned low in his throat and began moving. He withdrew only to fill her again. Her body stretched and welcomed him, the last of the discomfort faded.

"I want you," he growled. "I want to be in you, even though I shouldn't."

She touched his face, his arms, then boldly reached down and cupped his rear. "It feels too right to be wrong. Make love to me, Ryan. Show me what all the fuss is about."

"A challenge?" A faint smile tugged at his lips.

"Absolutely."

Then the smile faded and he was kissing her—the same

deep, soul-touching kiss that first changed her life. He slipped his hands under her back and hauled her closer, all the while moving in and out of her. She felt herself reaching for release again, in that strange way that had happened before, except this time it was different. This time....

He tensed in her arms. "Cassie!"

The way he said her name made her shiver with incredible delight. Her body began to convulse around his. She felt the pleasure, the rightness, then he was shuddering and kissing her and the moment was as perfect as she'd known it was meant to be.

Ryan held Cassie close and prayed for inspiration. Nothing in his life had prepared him for this moment. What the hell had he done? It wasn't only that he'd destroyed her life by causing her to break up with her boyfriend of nine years and then put her in a position where she'd had to hear about *his* new fiancée, but he'd just stolen her virginity. The fact that their lovemaking was the best he'd ever experienced in his life was no excuse.

"Someone should shoot me," he said, releasing her and rolling onto his back. "That's about what I deserve."

"Is this about the lovemaking not being very good or something else?" she asked.

Her voice was low and soft, laced with concern. Ryan looked at her. Cassie was as beautiful naked as he'd imagined. Now, with her hair mussed and her mouth swollen from his kisses, he couldn't imagine ever wanting to be with anyone else. Despite the fact that he'd just finished, his body stirred at the thought of being with her again. Which meant he was lower than slime. He was a single-celled creature that aspired to *be* slime.

He touched her face. "The lovemaking was wonderful. I swear." He tightened his jaw.

"But I should have told you that I was a virgin."

He'd known, of course. He'd felt the barrier, then broken through it, but still, hearing the word spoken aloud made him wince. "Yeah, you should have told me."

She flashed him a quick smile. "There wasn't much time for meaningful conversation. Besides, I didn't want you to stop."

He couldn't deal with this. Nothing made sense. "You were together with Joel for nine years. In all that time you never...."

"Obviously not. Actually, we never did anything. Not even heavy petting. I told you, there was no passion. That's one of the reasons I ended the relationship."

She rolled on her side and faced him. "Don't worry, Ryan. I'm not some innocent teenager."

"No, you're an innocent twenty-four-year-old nanny. What the hell was I thinking?"

"I'm almost twenty-five."

As if that made any difference, he thought grimly.

She touched his cheek. "Don't worry. I understand exactly what's happened here. We made love. I don't have much experience, but I can tell you it was amazing for me. It probably wasn't really smart, but it's done. I'm not going to take advantage of the situation. I'm not going to demand a relationship with you. I still work for you and I think with a little bit of effort on both our parts, we can get back to just being friendly co-workers." Her smile returned. "Just not this friendly."

He stared at her. "That's it?"

"Sure."

She was saying everything he might have said, if he'd been thinking. Why did it sound so wrong coming from her?

"Cassie," he started.

She leaned over and kissed his mouth. "No, I won't talk

about this anymore.'' Then she stood up and gathered her clothes together. After slipping into his robe, she turned to him. ''I'll return this in the morning. Good night.''

With that, she was gone.

Ryan stared after her. Cassie had said everything just right. He *should* believe her. The only problem was he suddenly didn't want to.

Chapter Fifteen

As Cassie gave Sasha her breakfast, she listened for the sound of footsteps on the stairs. No doubt Ryan would want to have yet another heart-to-heart talk when he came down this morning, so she had to be prepared.

She'd spent most of the night going over what she would say to him. He would be worried that she was all right, and probably worried that she would expect a real relationship. She would have to reassure him on both accounts. The first would be easy, because she was all right. In fact, she felt terrific. Ryan had made her first time wonderful. She knew she would remember everything about their being together for the rest of her life. Thinking about it now sent a shiver through her tummy. She wanted to be with him again, be held close and feel him inside her. She had a feeling that there was a lot of potential there.

Convincing him of the second issue would be a lot more difficult. Not only *did* she really want a relationship with him, but she was in love with him. She didn't know how much she was going to be able to fake about all that. At least she had a little practice at not showing her feelings, even though she wasn't sure it was going to be enough.

She wanted to be with Ryan, but only because *he* wanted it, too. She would rather be alone than have him with her out of guilt or mercy. So she was going to have to convince him that she felt only a passing interest and that she could easily walk away without a backward glance. She sighed. It sounded simple in theory—but was she going to be able to pull it off?

She stiffened as she heard his footsteps, then smiled at Sasha. "Can you eat that by yourself? I have to go tell Uncle Ryan something, then I'll be right back."

Sasha nodded and continued to eat her breakfast. She mumbled something that sounded like the two-year-old version of "big girl." Cassie kissed the top of her head.

"Yes, you are a big girl, and very special. I'll just be a minute."

She headed out the door and intercepted Ryan in the hall. From here she could keep an eye on the toddler, but not be overheard.

"Good morning," he said when he saw her.

She took in the stern set of his face, the signs of sleeplessness, the lack of a smile and knew that she'd been right. They were going to have a serious talk. She drew in a deep breath. "While I don't mind having these talks with you, Ryan, it would be nice if all of them didn't have to happen before I've had my second cup of coffee."

He shoved his hands into his slacks pockets. "Sorry about that, but this one can't wait."

"Oh, I know." She could see him gathering himself for whatever speech he'd prepared. She didn't think she could bear to listen to his carefully worded dismissal, so she decided on a preemptive strike. "I know what you're going to say."

He raised his eyebrows in surprise. "Do you?"

"I can't be sure, but I have a fair idea. You're concerned that I'm upset about last night and that I blame you. You're worried that I'm going to quit or at least sulk. You're also a little worried about my assumptions that we now have an emotional relationship. You want to know my expectations. Does that about sum it up?"

She'd said everything without her voice trembling or a single slipup. There was something to be said for practice.

He stared at her for a long time, then nodded slowly. "That about sums it up."

"Good. Then let me address your concerns. First, I'm an adult. Last night I was a consenting adult. I wanted to make love with you. I'm not sorry we did it. Yes, I was a virgin and maybe I should have told you, but I didn't. I still don't have any regrets. Except for your reaction, there's nothing I would have changed about what we did."

He shifted. "It's not that I didn't enjoy it, it's just..."

"You feel guilty," she told him. "I understand that. If I were in your position, I would probably feel the same way. But it's not necessary. I wanted to be there. You gave me many opportunities to back out or to ask you to stop. I didn't. I take responsibility for that. I'm glad we made love."

She paused to catch her breath. "I think that covers your first few concerns."

"You're being very logical."

"It's a gift." She smiled. "Now, for the rest of your worries. I'm not expecting a proposal of marriage. I'm not even expecting a relationship. But I will admit things have changed."

Ryan's expression had cleared some, but now his eyebrows drew together again. "I don't dispute that, but I would like you to clarify what you mean."

"There have been a lot of changes in my life in the past couple of months. I've come to work for you, I've broken up with Joel, I've done the wild thing." She cast a quick glance over her shoulder to check on Sasha. The little girl was happily eating her cereal.

"I've made some decisions about what I want," she continued. "The only decision that affects you directly is that I can only work for you another month."

She felt her throat closing. This was harder to tell him than she'd first thought. She wanted to promise to stay as long as he would have her around, but she couldn't. She owed it to herself to be stronger than that. She deserved to love someone who loved her back. That person wasn't Ryan. She could allow herself to stay for a short period of time and be with him, but then she would have to move on. She needed to get the broken-heart part over with so she could begin healing, then get going with her life.

"You're leaving me?" He sounded stunned.

"I have to. A month gives you plenty of time to make other arrangements. If you're going to stay in Bradley, I'll help you find reliable day care. If you're going back to San Jose, then you need to start contacting places there."

She drew in a deep breath. Now for the really scary part. "I have no expectations for the time we have left. My preference is that we continue to be friends. I enjoy your company and I think you feel the same way about me."

"Of course I do. You know that."

"Good. As to our physical relationship—" She had to clear her throat before continuing. "I wouldn't object to us being lovers for the next month. We would have to be discreet. I wouldn't want to confuse Sasha or start any rumors in town.'' She didn't know what else to say. ''It's up to you.''

He looked a little stunned. ''You've thought of everything.''

''I tried to.''

She forced herself to maintain her calm, but it was difficult. She wanted to throw herself at him and beg him to love her back. She wanted him to declare undying devotion, or at least a general fondness. She wanted him to beg her to stay forever, telling her that he couldn't possibly live without her.

''What do you get out of all this?'' he asked.

''Working for you or being in your bed?''

''Being my lover.''

She shivered. It was one thing for her to say the ''L'' word out loud, but quite another for it to come from him. ''I want to be there,'' she answered honestly.

He sucked in his breath. ''You lay it all on the line, don't you? I admire that about you, even though it terrifies me.''

''I don't understand.''

''I know. That's part of your appeal.'' He took a step toward her and tucked her hair behind her ear. ''Work for me as long as you would like. I won't ask you to stay past your deadline, even though I want to. You've been more than kind in accommodating me and I don't have the right to mess with your life more than I have. As for having you in my bed, it would be my honor and privilege. But I want you to think about it a little longer. I want you to be sure this is what you want. When you leave, I want all the memories of your time here to be good ones.''

''All right, I'll think about it,'' she told him, because that was what he wanted to hear. She didn't have to think. She already knew. But it would probably look better if she waited a couple of days before she walked into his room, ripped off her clothes and begged him to take her.

Then, when her month was up, she would walk away. Because if she couldn't have Ryan, she would have the next best thing—a life of her own.

Ryan poured a drink for himself, then for Arizona. Chloe was out in the kitchen with her sister, and Sasha was down for the night. This was the second time he and Cassie had had someone from her family over for dinner, with Cassie's Aunt Charity being the first. He found he liked being the host and had looked forward to the evening. Unfortunately now that it was here, he couldn't concentrate on what Arizona was saying.

"I've gotten boring in my old age," Arizona said as he sat on the couch and sipped his Scotch.

"Not at all." Ryan took the wing chair opposite the sofa. "I apologize for not paying attention. I have a lot on my mind these days. I'm still putting my late brother's affairs in order. Then there's Sasha. She's a handful. I also have to decide if I'm going to stay here in Bradley or go back to San Jose."

Time was ticking away. Already a week of Cassie's month was gone. If he stayed here, he would have to relocate his business. If he left... He shook his head. He couldn't think about leaving. Not yet. Bradley was the only place he'd ever felt he belonged. Besides, if he left he would never see Cassie again. He had to see her. She was— He swore silently. He didn't know what she was to him, but he couldn't imagine living without her.

"That's not all," Arizona told him. "There's also the issue of Cassie."

Ryan thought about denying it, but figured there was no point. "There is that," he admitted.

He didn't understand what was going on. For one thing, she was handling their relationship a lot better than he was. For the past four nights, she'd stayed in his room. They'd made love until dawn, then she'd quietly crept away. He told himself he had it all—great day care for his niece and an incredible lover in his bed. What man was lucky enough to find a woman as special as Cassie, who would be with him, then at the end of a month, walk away without a second thought?

At first he'd thought she was kidding about her offer, but she was keeping to it with no apparent problem. Not once had she hinted about taking their relationship to the next level. She seemed very content to take care of Sasha during the day and him at night. She'd never once mentioned emotional entanglement.

Ryan took a swallow of his drink. He was a first-class jerk. He didn't deserve Cassie, and if he had any kind of moral character, he would break things off with her instantly. Except he couldn't imagine a world without her. Not that he was falling for her. He didn't know how to love anyone, nor did he want to learn. Love meant being vulnerable. He didn't trust emotion. Now hard work he could depend on.

"You've got it bad," Arizona said. "I recognize that fierce look."

Ryan glanced up. He'd completely forgotten the other man was in the room. "I don't have anything," he said quickly. "Cassie and I work together."

"Sure you do. And Chloe was just some reporter doing an interview." He leaned back in the sofa and rested one ankle on the opposite knee. "I'd spent my whole life going from place to place, never spending more than a few weeks under any one roof. I couldn't imagine settling down, having children. Roots didn't matter to me. Then I met Chloe and everything changed. I couldn't see it at first. All I knew was that I felt different around her. Suddenly it wasn't so easy to imagine my life the way it had been before we'd met. I told myself I didn't believe in love, and that happily-ever-after only happened in books and movies.''

Arizona looked up. Ryan heard the light footsteps, too. Chloe came in with a tray of dip and crackers. ''This is to keep your strength up until dinner is ready.''

She placed the food on the coffee table, flashed her husband a quick smile and left.

Ryan stared after her. At nearly seven months pregnant, she glowed. ''You make her very happy,'' he told the other man.

''She does the same for me. I never had anyone I could depend on in my life. It took me a while to realize that's what I'd been searching for all along. Sometimes it's hard to recognize the truth.''

''I'm not in love with Cassie,'' Ryan said flatly. ''If that's what you and Chloe want, I'm sorry. It's not going to happen.''

Arizona grinned. ''Famous last words.''

Ryan didn't know how to answer. Cassie wasn't part of his plan. He wanted— He paused and realized he didn't know what he wanted anymore. Too much was different.

''I need time to figure this out,'' Ryan said.

''So take it. Cassie's not going anywhere.''

But Arizona was wrong. In three weeks Cassie would be leaving. Ryan didn't doubt her intention to keep to her plan. She was strong and bound by her word. Unless he found some way to keep her, she was going to walk out of his life. He told himself he would be fine, but in his heart, he was starting not to believe it.

Chloe closed the door to the kitchen. ''I took them food. That will keep them quiet long enough for you to tell me what exactly is going on.''

Cassie checked on the roast and the scalloped potatoes, then leaned against the counter. ''I've told you I broke up with Joel,'' she said.

''I thought you two had a fight. I didn't know he was already engaged to some woman from his store.'' Chloe looked furious. She crossed her arms above her swelling belly. ''They're going everywhere together, which is surprising considering they can't keep their hands off each other. They should just stay home and not subject others to their displays of affection.''

''I distinctly remember you and Arizona going through a stage like that, not too long ago. In fact, it sort of explains your pregnancy.''

''That was different. Joel was involved with you for nine years. Now he's rubbing your nose in the fact that he's marrying someone else. I want him to stop.''

Cassie walked over to stand next to her sister. She touched her shoulder. ''I appreciate the show of support. Really, it's very sweet. But it's not necessary. I don't care about Joel in that way. I wish you would believe me. I'm not hurt by anything he's doing. He's not rubbing my nose in anything—he can't. I broke up with *him.*''

''I'm worried about you,'' Chloe admitted. ''How can this not bother you?''

''It just doesn't.'' Cassie got down two glasses. She poured her sister some juice, and wine for herself, then led the way to the table.

''I'll admit to feeling a little strange,'' she said when they were both settled. ''Joel and I were involved for years. Sometimes I think I should miss him more, but I don't. I'm genuinely happy for him. I wish him and Alice the best of everything.''

She stared at her sister's familiar face. "I should have listened to you when you told me I was settling. I see that now. I wanted so much to belong to someone that I stayed in a relationship that didn't have a future. I was afraid to ask for it all. I thought if I kept my hopes and dreams small enough that they would have a chance of coming true, but that if I wanted too much, I would lose everything."

Chloe leaned forward. Her long red curls tumbled over her shoulder and brushed against her forearms. "You *do* belong. You're a very special member of our family. Just because you're adopted doesn't mean you don't belong."

"It's not the same, Chloe. I have you and I have Aunt Charity. I know you both love me very much. But I wanted something of my own. I wanted to start building a history. I wanted to be married and have a family. I still want that. The difference is I've finally learned I have to take a chance on my heart's desire. I'm not going to settle again."

Chloe searched her face. "That all sounds good. So why do you look so sad?"

Cassie drew in a deep breath. She hadn't decided if she was going to tell her sister everything that was going on, but now she realized she needed the advice.

"I'm in love with Ryan."

Chloe smiled. "No big surprise there. Your crush evolved as you got to know him. He seems great. He's smart, a hard worker, Aunt Charity says he's devoted to Sasha, which means he'll be a good father. There's a slight age difference, but that shouldn't matter. What's the problem?"

"He doesn't love me back." She told Chloe about the kiss and Ryan's reaction when she broke up with Joel. "He panicked. He thought I was going to lay claim on him. It got worse when he invited Joel over for a reconciliation dinner and Joel sprang the news about his engagement to

Alice.'' She took a sip of wine. ''Ryan's never been in love. I think the emotion scares him to death.''

''So there's nothing between you?''

''Not exactly.'' She felt herself flushing. ''We're lovers.'' She explained how that had come to be and that she'd given herself one month with Ryan. ''Then I'm leaving. I have to. If I don't go while I can, I could waste my life here. I refuse to do that again. While having Ryan love me back would be wonderful, working for him and sleeping with him without any kind of commitment is just settling.''

''Do you think he'll let you go?''

The question surprised Cassie. ''Of course he will. Why wouldn't he?''

''The man shows all the symptoms of someone who has it bad.''

''You're mistaken,'' Cassie told her sister. ''He likes me well enough, and I'm convenient, but I don't fool myself into thinking he wants more.''

''I think you're selling yourself short. I don't think Ryan is going to give you up as easily as you think. You're everything he could possibly want in a woman. You're intelligent, you're funny, you're great with kids, and I'm going to assume the sex is amazing.''

Cassie ducked her head and nodded. ''*I* like it.''

''Then he would be a fool to lose you and Ryan isn't a fool.''

Cassie looked at Chloe. ''I don't think he wants to love me—or anyone.''

''People don't always get a choice in the matter. Sometimes love just happens. Don't be so quick to write him off. I agree that if nothing changes, you have to stick to your plan.'' Chloe gave her sister a quick hug. ''I admire your ability to stand up for what you believe. I'll support you in any way I can. But don't be surprised if things start to happen. Ryan is confused right now, but I'm betting he's going to get it figured out in time.''

''I can barely stand to think about that,'' Cassie said. ''I want to hope, but I'm so afraid he's going to let me go. I know I'll survive without him, but I would rather not.''

''Have faith. You're due for some good fortune.''

Cassie smiled. ''You're right. And if nothing else, there's always the nightgown. It's practically my twenty-fifth birthday. Maybe I'll dream about someone wonderful.''

She rose to her feet and went to check on dinner. Chloe changed the subject, but Cassie was still thinking about Ryan. It *was* nearly her birthday and she *would* wear the nightgown, hoping the family legend would work for her. But in her heart of hearts the only man she wanted to dream about, the only man she wanted to be with, was Ryan.

Chapter Sixteen

They called out their last goodbyes and closed the door behind their guests. Cassie gave Ryan a big smile. "That was a lot of fun. Thanks for suggesting we invite my sister and Arizona for dinner."

Without thinking, he put his arm around her and pulled her close. "You're welcome. I had a good time, too."

Cassie slipped easily into his embrace. She was warm and willing as she leaned against him. Already he could feel the passion igniting inside of him. He didn't have to be around her very long before he found himself wanting her. He kissed the top of her head, then led them both up the stairs.

"I'm really enjoying Chloe's pregnancy," Cassie was saying. "It's a first time for both of us. I like hearing about all the details without actually experiencing it."

"Preparation for when it's your turn?"

"Something like that."

He tensed slightly. It was the perfect opening for her. Now

she could casually mention something about the future, or ask if he wanted a child of his own. But she didn't. Instead she walked down the hall and checked on Sasha.

Ryan trailed after her. If Cassie were a different kind of woman, he might think that she was playing a game with him. Except that wasn't her style. She was simply being herself. She could talk about Chloe's pregnancy, or her future life, or any number of potentially awkward topics and not give it a moment's thought. She'd told him what she wanted from him and she wasn't pushing for anything more.

As she disappeared into the darkness of his niece's room, Ryan stopped in the center of the hall. Maybe the reason Cassie wasn't pushing for more with him was because she didn't want more. Maybe she wasn't interested in him for more than something temporary.

He was glad he was standing there alone because he was sure he had a stunned look on his face. All this time he'd been worried about her coming on to him when in fact she might not find him the least bit desirable. Oh, sure, she was willing to sleep with him, but was he the kind of man a woman like her would want to marry? He had no history of making relationships work. At first he hadn't wanted anything to do with his niece. While he and Cassie got along, and he was reasonably confident that she liked him, liking wasn't the same as respecting…or loving.

Cassie stepped back into the hall. "She's fine. Sleeping like the angel she is." She walked up and wrapped her arms around his waist. "What about you, Ryan? Are you tired or would you like some company?"

He stared at her, then touched her face. Less than ten days ago she'd been a virgin. Now she was asking if he wanted her in his bed. It wasn't that Cassie was arrogant or pushy, she simply had a strong sense of self. He admired that about her. He admired so many things.

"You have an odd look on your face," she said. "Did I say something I shouldn't have?"

"Not at all." He kissed her. "I was just thinking how perfect you are."

She wrinkled her nose. "That's not true, but thanks for the compliment." She took his hand and led him toward his bedroom. "I was reading an article in this women's magazine and they mentioned something I thought we could try."

"Like what?"

She gave him a coy smile over her shoulder. "You'll just have to wait and see."

Two hours later, Cassie lay sleeping in his arms. His body was sated and pleasantly tired, but his mind wouldn't let him rest. He couldn't stop thinking about Cassie…and about what she wanted. Realizing that it might not be him had changed everything.

He stroked her short, dark hair and wondered how he was supposed to figure out what was right for either of them. He knew that in three weeks she was going to leave him and that he didn't want her to go. That much had become clear. But did he have the right to keep her? He wanted what was best for her. Could he be that? Was he capable? Or would it be kinder to simply walk away and get over her. Except he didn't think he could.

No other woman had changed him the way she had. No one else understood him or made him happy. But it wasn't all about him, either. He'd never thought about someone the way he thought about her. He wanted to make *her* happy. He wanted to help her achieve whatever she wanted in love. He wanted…

He wanted to love her.

Ryan stared into the darkness and knew he'd found a truth. He wanted to love Cassie the way she loved everyone in her world. He wanted to feel those emotions and be able to express them. But he didn't know *how* to love or to tell her that he loved her. He didn't know how to be a good husband or father. He was better with machines than people. Didn't Cassie deserve more than him?

He ran the thoughts over and over in his mind until near dawn, then he finally slept. His dreams taunted him with visions of a future he wasn't sure he could ever have.

"Catch me! Catch me!" Sasha cried as she ran around the backyard.

Ryan walked after her, careful to stay close enough to keep her safe, but not so close that he could reach her.

They'd been playing tag for nearly an hour and the toddler showed little sign of getting tired. Ryan couldn't say the same for himself. He hadn't gotten much sleep in the past couple of nights. He'd been too busy trying to figure out how he was going to tell Cassie all he'd been thinking about. He wanted her in his life. Of that much he was sure. The question was how did he say it? How did he make the offer so desirable that she couldn't turn him down? So far he hadn't come up with the perfect combination of words, but he was working on it.

Sasha dashed around the swing set. Ryan went after her. She made a darting move to her right, surprising him. He turned, tripped on a ball and tumbled to the ground.

"Smooth," he muttered as he lay staring up at the cloudy afternoon sky. "Very smooth."

"Unk Ryan!" Sasha rushed to his side and threw herself on top of him. "Kay?" she asked. "Me kiss boo-boo."

"I'm okay," he told her and shifted her so she sat astride his waist. Her short legs stuck out. "Thanks for worrying. I tripped but I'm not hurt."

Sasha nodded, then leaned forward and rested on his chest. "Me tired."

Ah, so the running around had finally caught up with her. "Are you going to take a nap on me? Right now?"

She giggled and tried to fake sleep. But she kept peeking up at him to see if he was watching. Every time she showed her face, he growled at her. She giggled and retreated, only to try it again.

Suddenly, she wrapped her little arms around his neck and squeezed tight. "Me love Unk Ryan."

His throat tightened with unexpected emotion. "I love you, too, Sasha," he managed, although his voice was a little thick. "I love you very much and I'll always be here for you."

Wise toddler eyes stared at him. "Me know," she told him solemnly, and at the moment he believed she *did* know that she could trust him.

Was that all it took? he wondered. A heartfelt declaration? Could he just tell Cassie that he loved her and wanted to marry her? Would that be enough? It would have to be, he thought. He didn't have anything else to try.

Tonight, he decided. Tonight, when they were in bed together, he would tell Cassie the truth. He would explain that he didn't know how to do any of this right, but that he would always try to do what she wanted. That making her happy was the most important part of his life. Then he would confess his feelings and propose.

Before he could figure out if it might work, a voice cut through the afternoon. "Ryan? Are you out here?"

He grabbed Sasha around her waist and set her on the ground, then stood up himself. Cassie's Aunt Charity came into the backyard. She smiled when she saw him. "Cassie said you two were playing." She walked over and gave Sasha a hug. "How's my best princess?"

Sasha giggled.

"I'll take that as a good report," Charity said, then

straightened. "I'm just here for a second to say hi. I had a few last-minute details to work out with Cassie for her birthday party and I needed to drop off the nightgown."

Cassie's twenty-fifth birthday was at the end of the week. "She's really looking forward to the party."

"I'm sure it will be fun," Charity said. "I've even hired a high school girl to look after Sasha so you and Cassie can relax. Seven o'clock on Thursday."

"I'll get her there."

With that, Charity was gone. Ryan stared after her. Should he buy an engagement ring first, or wait until he talked to Cassie? She might want to pick it out herself, especially after nine years of wearing diamond lint.

Sasha tugged at his hand. "Drink, peas."

"Sure thing, kid." He picked her up and carried her inside.

Cassie sat at the kitchen table, reading a cookbook. She glanced up when they came in. "I saw you two out there. You were having a good time."

Her face was practically free of makeup, her clothes were sensible rather than glamorous, her hair slightly tousled. Yet Ryan thought she was the most lovely, incredibly attractive woman he'd ever seen. It was all he could do not to declare himself right there.

"We were," he said, and had to clear his throat. "Ah, Sasha wanted a drink."

"I'll get it," she said and stood up. As she crossed to the refrigerator, she passed a large white box. "It's the magic nightgown. Want to see?"

Ryan couldn't answer. He'd completely forgotten about the Bradley family legend and Cassie's hope that when she wore the nightgown on her twenty-fifth birthday she would dream about the man she was destined to marry. She'd waited for this night nearly all her life. He knew she thought of herself as an outsider in the family. Her adoption had left her feeling different. If the nightgown worked, then she would truly belong.

He told himself the nightgown wasn't really magic. She wasn't going to dream about anyone. But he also knew that his opinion didn't matter…it was Cassie's fantasy and he had no right to interfere. So he would wait until after her birthday. He would let her dream, perhaps even about another man. Then he would win her for his own.

By the middle of the week Cassie knew she wasn't imagining things. She drove back to the house determined to have it out with Ryan. Sasha was in preschool for two hours. That should give them plenty of time to deal with whatever was going on with him.

For nearly a week, he hadn't been himself. She kept turning around and finding him staring at her with a really strange look on his face. He would start conversations, then simply walk out of the room. Something had him distracted and she was determined to find out what.

She had a bad feeling she already knew the answer. He was ready to end their affair. No doubt he was concerned that she was getting too emotionally attached to him and he didn't want to be responsible for hurting her. So he would end it before she completely fell for him. Good thing he didn't know she was already in love. There would be no avoiding the pain this time.

She parked in the driveway, then walked purposefully into the house. It would be easier to avoid the situation, but that had never been her style. So she squared her shoulders, dug up all the spare courage she could find, then headed to his office and knocked on the door.

"Come in," he called.

She stepped inside. "Ryan, we need to talk," she began,

then stopped when she saw he wasn't at his desk. Instead he stood by the window, staring out at the backyard. "Is everything all right?" she asked.

He turned toward her. "Sure."

But despite his neutral expression, she didn't believe him. "No. Something has been bothering you for several days and I think I know what it is."

He smiled. "I doubt that."

Okay, here went nothing. "You're worried about me. You're concerned that I'm going to get emotionally attached to you because we're lovers and women tend to bond when they make love with someone. I want you to know that I understand and I'm—"

"They do?" he asked, interrupting her.

"What?"

"Women bond when they make love?"

"Yes. Most of the time. If they have feelings for the man. It's pair bonding, like wolves or swans. But that's not the point. I don't want you to be concerned about me."

"Because you haven't bonded?"

This was the tricky part, she thought. She didn't want to lie, but she was afraid to tell him the truth. She took a step toward his desk. "I'm a mature person. I can handle my feelings."

"So you *have* bonded."

"I didn't say that." Except by avoiding the question, she sort of had.

He moved toward her, stopping less than two feet away. His green eyes were alight with an emotion she couldn't read. "It's one or the other. Either you've bonded or you haven't. But if it makes answering the question any easier, I can tell my bonding story."

"Okay." What was he talking about? Her stomach got all

quivery and she felt both hot and cold. Dear Lord, please don't let it be bad.

He took one last step forward, then kissed her gently. "I've bonded with you, Cassie. Even before we made love, I found myself falling in love with you. I didn't recognize it at the time, probably because I've never felt this way before. You mean everything to me."

She couldn't speak. She wasn't sure she was even breathing. Was this really happening? Was Ryan actually saying these things to her?

He touched her cheek, traced her mouth, tucked her hair behind her ears and gave her a shaky smile. "You deserve so much more than I have to offer. I don't know how to be what you need, but I'm too selfish to let you go. I love you. I want to marry you. I want us to raise Sasha along with a couple dozen kids of our own. I want to make love with you every night, I want to hold you while you sleep and I want to watch you smile when you wake up in the morning."

He clutched her hands tightly in his. "Just tell me what *you* want. I can learn to be a better man, if you'll help me. I want to make you happy. I want to make all your dreams come true."

He was saying everything she wanted to hear and more. So much more. The odd light in his eyes was love, she realized. He loved her. "You *have* made all my dreams come true."

"Then why are you crying?"

She pulled one hand free and touched her face. It was wet. "I'm so happy." Her head was spinning. "Is this really happening? Did you just propose to me?"

"Not exactly."

Her heart plunged to her toes and then broke.

"No, don't!" he said quickly. "I want to marry you. I want to elope with you tonight. But I know how important the family legend is with you. So I'm going to ask you to marry me, but I don't want you to answer. Wear the nightgown tomorrow night, then answer me in the morning.''

''I don't understand. What if I don't...'' She couldn't finish the statement. But he knew what she was thinking.

''What if you don't dream about me?'' he asked. ''If you dream about another man, I'll win you from him because I know you're my destiny. I'll sweep you off your feet with passion and devotion until you can't imagine being with anyone else. I'll earn you, and once I have you, I'll never let you go.''

''I want to marry you,'' she said and kissed him.

''Tell me that again in forty-eight hours.''

Cassie's fingers trembled as she unfolded the nightgown, then slipped it over her head. She climbed into her bed and pulled the covers up to her chin.

Ryan sat down beside her and smiled. ''Don't look so scared. It's going to be fine.''

''I know, it's just so strange. All my life I've wanted the nightgown to be magic, and now I don't.''

''You're going to dream of me. I know it. And if you don't, hey, I have a plan. Either way, I love you and want you in my life.''

''I love you, too,'' she whispered back.

They talked for a few more minutes, then he left her alone. Cassie fingered the lace at her collar and cuffs, then turned on her side. The bed felt odd. She hadn't slept in it since she and Ryan had become lovers.

She closed her eyes, then opened then. After twenty-five years, it was finally her turn to wear the family nightgown, and now that the moment was finally here, she was afraid to go to sleep.

''This is dumb,'' she told herself aloud. ''Ryan is a wonderful man. I love him. I want to marry him. I should just go accept his proposal.''

Except she'd tried that several times over the past couple of days and every time he told her to wait. He wanted her to have her night of magic.

She tried to relax. In an effort to distract herself, she thought about her wonderful party. All her friends had been there. Ryan had fit in with everyone. He'd made her feel so special.

Gradually, her eyes grew heavy. She fought against sleep because she was afraid, but at last it claimed her. She drifted for a while, then found herself standing on the porch of the Bradley house, staring at the wide lawn. A man appeared in the shadows. Her heart pounded in her chest. She was having a magic dream. The nightgown was about to reveal her destiny.

Even in her sleep, she found herself calling out for Ryan. She needed it to be him. She loved him.

The man continued to walk toward her. His figure was indistinct, then suddenly he was in front of her. All five feet four inches of him. She recognized the gray hair, the craggy face and the scowling expression. Old Man Withers, their caretaker for longer than she'd been alive, glared at her.

Cassie woke up with a start. She sat up and hugged her knees to her chest. She'd dreamed about Old Man Withers. What a joke. The nightgown wasn't going to work for her.

''It's better this way,'' she whispered to herself. ''I love Ryan.''

But the sadness inside her didn't have anything to do with loving Ryan. It was about really belonging to the Bradley family. She was adopted. There wasn't a legend for her.

Coldness swept through her and she shivered. She didn't want to be alone so she got out of bed and walked down the hall. Ryan stirred as she opened his door. He raised himself on one elbow. ''Good news?''

His eyes were sleepy, his hair mussed. She knew that under the blankets and sheet, he was naked and if she crawled in beside him and touched him, he would want her. He loved her and she loved him back. He'd changed in the time she'd known him. He was a wonderful father to Sasha and he would be an equally wonderful husband.

All her life she'd wanted to belong. She suddenly realized that being a part of something wasn't about a place. It didn't matter where she'd been born or who had given birth to her. Home was a state of mind. Home was where her heart was welcome. Home was with Ryan.

She smiled. ''The best news,'' she said and slipped in beside him.

He wrapped his arms around her. ''I knew you'd dream about me. Now you *have* to marry me.'' His voice was sleepy. ''I was gonna win you no matter what, but this is better. Let's get married soon.''

''I'd like that,'' she said.

''Good.'' He kissed her cheek.

He was, as she'd suspected, completely naked. And he was half-asleep. She really should let him get his rest. Except she found herself wanting him. Not because she'd lost her dream, but because she'd finally found where she belonged—where she'd always belonged. First with her adoptive parents and Chloe, and now with Ryan.

So even though his eyes were slowly closing, she rested her head on his shoulder, then slipped her hand down his body. He made a low sound of pleasure.

''You're not going to let me get right back to sleep, are you?'' he asked lazily as her hand closed over him. He was aroused in a matter of seconds.

"Pay no attention to what I'm doing," she told him in a whisper. "I'm just trying to relax you."

"Oh, yeah, it's very relaxing."

She continued to stroke him, moving up and down in that slow steady pace he enjoyed. Then, without warning, he rolled over, taking her with him, until she was on her back, staring up at him.

"I love you," he said, his green eyes bright with a combined blaze of love and passion. "You are mine and I'm going to spend the rest of my life convincing you that you've made the right decision."

"I already know," she assured him.

"Do you? I think I should start making you sure right now."

He lowered his head and kissed her. His tongue swept against the seam of her lips before slipping inside to tease and torment her in the most perfect way. They'd learned so much about each other's bodies in the past several weeks. They'd learned about the pleasures they most enjoyed together. He knew how to touch her to make her sigh, to make her catch her breath, to make her aroused. She knew how to bring him to his point of release in a matter of seconds. There were still wondrous discoveries, but already they were finding their favorite ways to make love.

He sat up and pushed down the covers, then pulled her into a sitting position and tugged off the nightgown. With her body bare to his gaze, she relaxed back onto the bed, drawing him with her. He kissed her deeply, then broke that kiss to touch his mouth to her forehead, her eyelids, her cheeks and her nose. He left a damp trail down her neck, then loved her breasts with mouth and tongue and teeth until she was shaking beneath him.

"I want you," he breathed against her heating skin. "I want to be with you and in you. I want to make love with you so much that we really become halves of the same whole. I want to be deep inside you—and I want you to have our children. I will always love you, Cassie. No matter what. Forever. I promise.''

She felt the wetness of her happy tears as they trailed down her temples and into her hair. She felt her body ready for him.

''I want you, too,'' she whispered. ''I want your babies and your arms around me at night.''

She had more to say, but he was moving lower, kissing her belly, then kneeling between her legs so that he could give her the most intimate kiss of all. He parted the soft folds of her feminine place and touched his lips to her center-most place. Pleasure shot through her. Pleasure heightened by the realization that Ryan loved her as much as she loved him, and that they'd committed to each other. No matter what, they would always be together.

Then she was unable to think at all. She could only feel the sweep of his tongue against her and the pressure of the finger he'd slipped inside her. He moved in a matching rhythm designed to take her to the edge of madness and beyond. She parted her knees more to allow him to get closer, then dug her heels into the bed. As she neared her release, she half sat up to watch as well as feel his magic. She stroked his head with her fingers, giving a quiet moan as the pleasure intensified.

Then she was lost in the perfection of the moment, caught up in a storm that rearranged the universe, then delivered her safely to her lover's arms. Ryan caught her as she fell and entered her while she was still quivering. Long, deep incredible thrusts filled her woman's place and took her back up on that wonderful journey.

They opened their eyes at the same moment and stared at each other. She could not say who held the other tightest.

They were so joined that she could feel his own need as well as her own—she knew the exact moment when he would find his release.

Her body shattered with his. They loved and gasped together as if they'd been born to be lovers. Perhaps they had been, she thought drowsily.

When their bodies had calmed, Ryan kissed her gently, helped her pull on her nightgown, then settled her next to him in their wide bed.

"I love you," he murmured, already half-asleep.

"I love you, too," she told him.

She fingered the lace on the nightgown and knew that despite the legend, she'd found her home and her destiny. She and Ryan were going to do well together.

Contentment filled her, warming her from the inside out. She found herself dozing off, safe in the comfort of his arms.

The dream returned. Cassie stood on the porch of the Bradley house, staring at a man walking out of the shadows. Old Man Withers appeared in front of her and glared.

"Not me, you ninny," he growled and stepped aside. "Him!"

She hadn't seen the second man before, but there he was, moving into the sunlight. "Ryan!"

In her sleep, Cassie smiled and reached for her husband-to-be. In his sleep, he pulled her close. In the morning she would tell him the truth about the dream, and that would only make him love her more.

Epilogue

Cassie held her breath until Sasha made it all the way down the aisle. The little girl had managed to sprinkle rose petals *and* walk on the white runner. The fact that she'd wandered a little from side to side didn't really matter.

The organ music swelled. Chloe sniffed. "It's not enough that I'm nine months pregnant," she said. "Now I'm going to cry and my face will swell up enough to match my stomach." She gave Cassie a watery smile. "At least everyone will be looking at you instead of me, so it doesn't matter."

"You look wonderful. Radiant, in fact."

"So do you. I'm glad you're marrying him."

"Me, too. Now walk down that aisle so I can follow you and get married."

Chloe made her way toward the front of the church. Her peach dress swayed with every step. Cassie waited for the music to change to the wedding march, and then it was her turn.

She still had trouble believing this had happened to her.

She and Ryan had pulled together a wedding in less than a month. Fate had been on her side. Her local church miraculously had a free Saturday and could recommend a caterer who was also available. Her wedding gown had been hanging in a display window, and had fit perfectly, without a single alteration. The weather was flawless, the pews filled with family and friends. She had the oddest feeling that someone was looking out for her and Ryan.

She looked up and saw Ryan waiting for her. He was so handsome in his tux. For reasons she still didn't understand, he loved her and wanted to be with her. She knew that she loved him with all her heart. They were going to have a wonderful life together.

She was still several feet away when she heard a familiar little voice demanding, ''Unk Ryan.''

He walked across the aisle and picked up Sasha. They were both waiting when Cassie reached the altar.

''She wants to be with us when we're married,'' Ryan said. ''Do you mind?''

The toddler rested on her uncle's hip. Sasha grinned and leaned forward for a kiss. Cassie obliged her. ''I don't mind,'' she said. ''It's exactly right.''

Ryan took her hand in his and the three of them faced the minister, where they were joined together as a family.

Somewhere, in a place some on earth might not quite understand, an old gypsy woman smiled down at the couple destined for a life of happiness.

The legend of the nightgown had once again come true.

* * * * *

This June, look for LONE STAR MILLIONAIRE by Susan Mallery—part of Silhouette's exciting WORLD'S MOST ELIGIBLE BACHELOR continuity series.

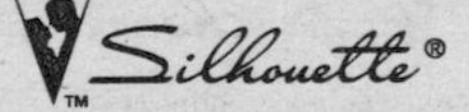
Silhouette®

CLINICAL COMPANION FOR

Fundamentals of Nursing

7th EDITION

VERONICA "RONNIE" PETERSON

BA, RN, BSN, MS

Manager of Clinical Support,
University of Wisconsin Medical Foundation;

Adjunct Clinical Instructor,
University of Wisconsin School of Nursing,
Madison, Wisconsin

with 93 illustrations

ELSEVIER

11830 Westline Industrial Drive
St. Louis, Missouri 63146

CLINICAL COMPANION FOR FUNDAMENTALS OF NURSING, SEVENTH EDITION ISBN: 978-0-323-05482-9

Notice

Knowledge and best practice in this field are constantly changing. As new research and experience broaden our knowledge, changes in practice, treatment and drug therapy may become necessary or appropriate. Readers are advised to check the most current information provided (i) on procedures featured or (ii) by the manufacturer of each product to be administered, to verify the recommended dose or formula, the method and duration of administration, and contraindications. It is the responsibility of the practitioner, relying on their own experience and knowledge of the patient, to make diagnoses, to determine dosages and the best treatment for each individual patient, and to take all appropriate safety precautions. To the fullest extent of the law, neither the Publisher nor the Author assumes any liability for any injury and/or damage to persons or property arising out of or related to any use of the material contained in this book.

The Publisher

Previous editions copyrighted **2005, 2003, 1999, 1995**

Library of Congress Control Number 2007941311

Acquisitions Editor: Susan R. Epstein
Senior Developmental Editor: Maria Broeker
Editorial Assistant: Mary Jo Adams
Publishing Services Manager: Deborah Vogel
Associate Project Manager: Brandilyn Tidwell
Designer: Amy Buxton

Printed in the United States of America

Last digit is the print number: 9 8 7 6 5 4 3 2 1

Reviewers

Patricia C. Buchsel, RN, MSN, FAAN
Clinical Instructor,
Seattle University College of Nursing
Seattle, Washington

Gale P. Sewell, RN, MSN, CNE
Assistant Professor of Nursing
Indiana Wesleyan University
Marion, Indiana

Preface

When I began my first student clinical experience, I felt overwhelmed. There just wasn't time to memorize lab values, metric conversions, or the dozens of other facts I needed to know. So I compiled a small notebook of this information and carried it with me everywhere. Later, as a graduate student pursuing my master's degree, I taught nursing students who were experiencing the same problem.

For them, and for you, I have compiled those hard-to-memorize charts, graphs, numbers, and abbreviations that you must know, even in your first clinical experience. I've added some handy checklists for physical assessment and an assortment of other useful bits of information.

Clinical Companion for Fundamentals of Nursing, seventh edition, is designed to be a portable, quick reference for facts and figures, focusing on adult health care. I hope you will find this as handy a resource during your clinical work as I did.

Ronnie Peterson

Contents

Chapter 1

Health Care Terminology

For an in-depth study of health care terminology, consult the following publications:

Austrin MG, Austrin HR: *Learning medical terminology*, ed 9, St. Louis, 1998, Mosby.

Birmingham JJ: *Medical terminology: a self-learning text*, ed 3, St. Louis, 1999, Mosby.

Brooker CG: *Mosby's nurse's pocket dictionary*, ed 33, St. Louis, 2005, Mosby.

Mosby: *Mosby's medical, nursing, & allied health dictionary*, ed 7, St. Louis, 2006, Mosby.

Thibodeau G, Patton K: *Structure and function of the human body*, ed 12, St. Louis, 2003, Mosby.

ABBREVIATIONS*

a before
aa of each
AA Alcoholics Anonymous; ascending aorta
AAA abdominal aortic aneurysm
abd abdomen; abdominal
ABG arterial blood gas
abn abnormal
abp arterial blood pressure
ac before meals
ACTH adrenocorticotropic hormone
ad lib as desired
ADH antidiuretic hormone
ADLs activities of daily living
AIDS acquired immunodeficiency syndrome
AK above the knee
AKA above the knee amputation
ALL acute lymphocytic leukemia
ALS amyotrophic lateral sclerosis
am morning
ama against medical advice
amb ambulatory
AML acute monocytic (myelogenous) leukemia
amp ampicillin; amputation
amt amount
ANS autonomic nervous system
A&O alert and oriented
AODA alcohol and other drug abuse
A&P auscultation and percussion
appy appendectomy
Aq water
ARC AIDS-related complex; American Red Cross
ARDS adult respiratory distress syndrome
ASA aspirin
ASAP as soon as possible

*Standard abbreviations may vary by institution.

ASL American Sign Language
AV atrioventricular
AVR aortic valve replacement
A&W alive and well

Ba barium
BAC blood alcohol concentration
BB breakthrough bleeding
BBB blood-brain barrier; bundle-branch block
BBT basal body temperature
BE barium enema
bid twice per day
BK below the knee
BKA below the knee amputation
BL bleeding; baseline; blood loss
BLE both lower extremities
BM bowel movement; body mass; bone marrow
BMR basal metabolic rate
BP blood pressure; bathroom privileges; birth place
BPH benign prostatic hypertrophy
BRBPR bright red blood per rectum
BR bed rest
BRP bathroom privileges
BS blood sugar; bowel sounds; breath sounds
BSA body surface area
BT bleeding time; brain tumor; bladder tumor
BUE both upper extremities
BUN blood urea nitrogen
BV blood volume
BW body weight; birth weight
Bx biopsy

c̄ with
C Celsius; calorie; Caucasian
CA cancer
C&A Clinitest and Acetest
CABG coronary artery bypass graft
CAD coronary artery disease

CAT computerized axial tomography
cath catheter; catheterization
CBC complete blood count
CBI continuous bladder irrigation
cbr complete bed rest
CBS chronic brain syndrome
CC chief compliant
CCU coronary care unit
CD cadaver donor; cardiac disease
CDC Centers for Disease Control and Prevention
C-diff Clostridium difficile
CEA carotid endarterectomy
CF cystic fibrosis; cardiac failure
cg centigram
CHD coronary heart disease; congenital heart disease
CHF congestive heart failure
CHO carbohydrate
CIS carcinoma in situ
cl clear liquid diet
Cl chlorine
CLD chronic liver (lung) disease
cm centimeter; costal margin
cm^3 cubic centimeter
CMV cytomegalovirus
CNS central nervous system
c/o complains of
CO carbon monoxide; cardiac output; castor oil
CO_2 carbon dioxide
comp complaint; complication; compound
COPD chronic obstructive pulmonary disease
CP cerebral palsy; closing pressure
CPK creatine phosphokinase
CRD chronic renal disease
CRF chronic renal failure
crit hematocrit
c-sec cesarean section
CS central supply/central service; coronary sinus

C&S culture and sensitivity
CSF cerebrospinal fluid; colony-stimulating factor
CST convulsive shock therapy
CSW certified social worker
CT computed tomography
CV cell volume; central venous
CVA cerebral vascular attack
CVP central venous pressure
CVS cardiovascular system
CXR chest x-ray
cysto cystoscopy

d day
DAT diet as tolerated
dc discontinue
D&C dilatation and curettage
D/C discharge
DDS Doctor of Dental Surgery
DG diagnosis; diastolic gallop
DIC disseminated intravascular coagulation
diff differential blood count
DJD degenerative joint disease
DM diabetes mellitus; diastolic murmur
DNR do not resuscitate
DOA dead on arrival
DOB date of birth
DOD date of death
DOE dyspneic on exertion
DPT diphtheria/pertussis/tetanus
DTR deep tendon reflex
DU duodenal ulcer
DVT deep vein thrombosis
DW distilled water; dry weight
D5W 5% dextrose in water
Dx diagnosis; dextran

EA each
EBL estimated blood loss

EBV Epstein-Barr virus
ECF extracellular fluid
ECG electrocardiogram
ECT electroconvulsive therapy
ED effective dose; emergency department
EDD estimated date of delivery
EEG electroencephalogram
(E)ENT (eye) ear, nose, throat
EKG electrocardiogram
EL elixir
EMG electromyogram
EN enema
eom extraocular movement
EP ectopic pregnancies
ER emergency department; ejection rate
ESP extrasensory perception
ESRD end-stage renal disease
EST electroshock therapy
ET endotracheal; etiology; effective temperature
ETOH alcohol

F Fahrenheit; father; female
FBP femoral blood pressure
FBS fasting blood sugar
f/c/s fever, chills, sweats
FD fatal dose; forceps delivery
FEV forced expiratory volume
FF force fluids; fat free; flat feet; foster father
FFP fresh-frozen plasma
FHR fetal heart rate
fl fluid or full liquid diet
FOB foot of the bed
FP false positive; family practice; frozen plasma
FSH follicle-stimulating hormone
FUO fever of unknown origin
FV fluid volume
fx fracture; family
Fx Hx family history

g gram
GB gallbladder; Guillain-Barré syndrome
GC gonococcus
GH growth hormone
GI gastrointestinal
gm gram
GP general practitioner
gr grain
grav I, II, III, etc. pregnancy one, two, three, etc.
GT gastrostomy tube
GTH gonadotropic hormone
gtt drops
GTT glucose tolerance test
GU genitourinary
GYN gynecology

h hour; height; high; hormone
HA headache; high anxiety
HAV hepatitis A virus
Hb hemoglobin
HB heart block; hemoglobin; house bound
HBV hepatitis B virus
hCG human chorionic gonadotropin
Hct hematocrit
HD heart disease; Hodgkin's disease
HGH human growth hormone
H&H hemoglobin and hematocrit
HIV human immunodeficiency virus (AIDS)
HL hearing loss
HLA human lymphocyte antigen
HO house officer; high oxygen
HOB head of the bed
hr hour
HR heart rate; hospital record
hs at bedtime
HS herpes simplex; house surgeon
HSV herpes simplex virus
HTN hypertension

HVD hypertensive vascular disease
hx history
hypo hypodermic

IC inspiratory capacity; intercostal; intracellular; intracerebral; intracranial
ICP intracranial pressure
ICS intercostal space
ICU intensive care unit
ID infant death; ineffective dose; intradermal
I&D incision and drainage
IDDM insulin-dependent diabetes mellitus
IE immunoelectrophoresis
Ig immunoglobulin
IH infectious hepatitis
IM intramuscular; infectious mononucleosis
IN intranasal
I&O intake and output
IOP intraocular pressure
IP intraperitoneal; interphalangeal
IPPB intermittent positive pressure breathing
irr irregular
IS in situ; intercostal space; interspace
IT inhalation test; intratracheal tube
ITT insulin tolerance test
IUD intrauterine; device
IV intravenous; intravascular
IVP intravenous push
IVPB IV piggyback

JEJ jejunum
JRA juvenile rheumatoid arthritis
JV jugular vein (venous)
JVD jugular vein distention
JVP jugular vein pressure (pulse)

K absolute zero; Kelvin
K^+ potassium

kg kilogram
KJ knee jerk
KUB kidney/ureter/bladder
KVO keep vein open

L liter; left; length; low; lower
LA lactic acid; left arm; left atrial; left atrium
LAD left anterior descending (coronary artery)
LAP left atrial pressure
lat lateral
LBBB left bundle-branch block
LCA left coronary artery
LCH left costal margin
LD lethal dose; left deltoid; living donor
LE lower extremity; left eye
LFD lactose-free diet; least fatal dose
LFT liver function tests
LGH lactogenic hormone
LH luteinizing hormone
LL left leg; left lower; left lung
LLE left lower extremity
LLL left lower lobe
LLQ left lower quadrant
LMP last menstrual period
LOA leave of absence
LOC loss of consciousness; level of consciousness
LOM loss of motion
LP lumbar puncture; low protein
LPN licensed practical nurse
LS lumbar sacral; left side; liver and spleen
LSB left sternal border
LT left; left thigh; long term
LUE left upper extremity
LUL left upper lobe
LUQ left upper quadrant
LV left ventricle; live vaccine
LVH left ventricular hypertrophy

m meter; minim
M murmur; male; marred; minute; month; mother
MA mental age
MAP mean arterial pressure
MD medical doctor; manic depressive; medium dose; muscular dystrophy
ME medical examiner; middle ear
MED minimal effective dose
mEq milliequivalent
mg milligram
Mg magnesium
MG myasthenia gravis
MI myocardial infarction; mitral insufficiency
ml milliliter
ML middle lobe; midline
mm millimeter
MM mucous membrane; malignant melanoma; multiple myeloma
mm^3 cubic millimeter
mm Hg millimeters of mercury
MP mean pressure; menstrual period
MR mental retardation; metabolic rate; mitral reflux
MRI magnetic resonance imaging
MRSA methicillin-resistant *Staphylococcus aureus*
MS multiple sclerosis; mitral stenosis
MSL midsternal line
MSO_4 morphine sulfate
MSW master's degree in social work
MV mitral valve

N nasal; nerve; normal
Na sodium
NAD no appreciable discase
NAS no added salt; no added sugar
NC no casualty; not cultured
ND no disease; normal delivery
NE no effect; not evaluated

NF normal flow; not found
ng nasogastric
NH nursing home
NI no information; not identified
NIDDM non–insulin-dependent diabetes mellitus
NIH National Institutes of Health (Bethesda, Maryland)
NKDA no known drug allergies
noc night
NPN nonprotein nitrogen
NPO nothing by mouth
NR do not repeat; no response; not readable
NS normal saline; nervous system; no sample; not sufficient
NT nasotracheal; not tested
N&V nausea and vomiting

O eye; none; opening; oral
OB obstetrics
OBS organic brain syndrome
OC office call; on call; oral contraceptive
OD overdose
OH occupational history
OM otitis media
OOB out of bed
OP opening pressure; osmotic pressure
OR operating room
ORIF open reduction internal fixation
OS left eye; mouth; oral surgery
OT occupational therapy
OTC over the counter

p after; position; pressure; protein; pulse; pupil
PA physician's assistant; pathology; primary anemia; pulmonary artery
P&A posterior/anterior
Paco$_2$ partial pressure of carbon dioxide (arterial)
Pao$_2$ partial pressure of oxygen (arterial)

Pap Papanicolaou test (smear)
PAR postanesthesia room
pat paroxysmal atrial tachycardia
pc after meal; platelet count; pulmonic closure
PCA patient-controlled analgesia
PCN penicillin
Pco$_2$ partial pressure of carbon dioxide
PCV packed cell volume
PCWP pulmonary capillary wedge pressure
PD postural drainage; papilla diameter; poorly differentiated
PDR *Physician's Desk Reference*
PE physical examination; pleural effusion; pulmonary emboli
PEEP positive end-expiratory pressure
PEG pneumoencephalogram
pe percutaneous endoscopic gastrostomy tube (peg tube)
PERRLA pupils equal, round, reactive to light, and accommodating
PET positron emission tomography
PG pregnant; prostaglandin
pH hydrogen ion concentration
PI present illness; pulmonary infarction
PID pelvic inflammatory disease
PKU phenylketonuria
pm afternoon
PM post mortem
PMH past medical history
PMS premenstrual syndrome
PN percussion note; pneumonia
PO by mouth; postop
Po$_2$ partial pressure of oxygen
poly many
PP partial pressure; pink puffers (emphysema)
PR per rectum; practical remission; peripheral resistance; pulse rate
PRN as needed

PS per second; physical status; *Pseudomonas*
pt patient; pint
PT physical therapy; parathyroid; pneumothorax
PTT partial thromboplastin time
PUD peptic ulcer disease
PV peripheral vascular; peripheral vein
PVC premature ventricular contraction; pulmonary venous congestion
PVD peripheral vascular disease
PUR post void residual

q every; quart
ql as much as desired
qns quantity not sufficient
qs quantity sufficient
QT quiet
QV as much as you like

R right; radiology; rectal; remote; resistance
RA rheumatoid arthritis; renal artery; right arm; right atrium
rad radiation unit; radical; right axis deviation
RAP right atrial pressure
RAS renal artery stenosis
RBBR right bundle-branch block
RBC red blood cell
RCA right coronary artery
RCM right costal margin; red cell mass
RDA recommended daily allowance; right dorsoanterior
RE right eye
REM rapid eye movement
rep repeat
RF rheumatic fever; releasing factor
Rh rhesus factor
RHD rheumatic heart disease
RL right leg (lung)
RLE right lower extremity

RLL right lower lobe
RLQ right lower quadrant
RM radical mastectomy; respiratory movement
RML right middle lobe
RN registered nurse
R/O rule out
ROM range of motion
ROS review of systems
RP refractory period; resting pressure
RPA right pulmonary artery
RR respiratory rate
RRR regular rate and rhythm
RT respiratory therapy; radiation therapy; reaction time
RUA routine urinalysis
RUE right upper extremity
RUL right upper lobe
RUQ right upper quadrant
RV residual volume; respiratory volume
Rx treatment or medications

s without; sacral; salmonella; single; smooth
SA salicylic acid; sarcoma; surface area
SB sternal border; single breath; stillbirth
SBO small bowel obstruction
SC subcutaneous; semiclosed; sickle cell; sugar coated
SD skin dose; septal defect; standard; standard deviation; sudden death
SF scarlet fever; spinal fluid
SG skin graft; specific gravity
SH serum hepatitis; sex hormone
SI sacroiliac; serum iron
SIDS sudden infant death syndrome
sig let it be labeled
SL under the tongue
SLE systemic lupus erythematosus
SM simple mastectomy; systolic murmur

SN suprasternal notch
SO salpingo-oophorectomy
SOB short of breath; shortness of breath
SOBOE short of breath on exertion
SOS if necessary
S/P status post
sp gr specific gravity
SQ subcutaneous; social quotient; square
sr sedimentation rate; sinus rhythm
ss a half; side to side
ST let it stand; straight; subtotal
STAT immediately
STD sexually transmitted disease
STS serologic test for syphilis
SUD sudden unexplained death
SV severe; stroke volume
SVT supraventricular tachycardia
sx symptom; signs
sz schizophrenia

t teaspoon
T temperature; time; temporal; tumor; tablespoon
T_3 triiodothyronine
T_4 tetraiodothyronine
T&A tonsillectomy and adenoidectomy
TAH total abdominal hysterectomy
TB tuberculosis; total base; total body
TBG thyroxin-binding globulin
TBI total body irradiation
tbsp tablespoon
TBW total body water (weight)
T&C type and crossmatch
TCDB turn, cough, and deep breathe
TD therapy (treatment) discontinued
TE tetanus; tooth extracted
tea teaspoon
TF total flow; tubular fluid
TG triglycerides

TIA transient ischemic attack
TIBC total iron-binding capacity
tid three times a day
TKO to keep open
TL time lapse; time limited; total lipids
TLC total lung capacity
TM tympanic membrane
TN total negatives; true negative
TNM tumor, nodes, metastasis
TPN total parenteral nutrition
TPR temperature/pulse/respiration
TS test solution; total solids; triple strength
TSA tumor-specific antigen
TSH thyroid-stimulating hormone
TSI triple-sugar iron
tsp teaspoon
TSP total serum protein
TST triple-sugar iron test
TT thrombin time; total thyroxine
TURP transurethral resection of the prostate
tus cough
TV tidal volume; trial visit
TVC total volume capacity
twe tap water enema
Tx treatment

U unknown; upper; urology
UA urinalysis; uric acid
UA/UC urinalysis with cultures
UD urethral discharge
UE upper extremity
UK unknown; urokinase
U/O urine output
URI upper respiratory infection
USP United States Pharmacopeia
ut dict as directed
UTI urinary tract infection
UV ultraviolet; urinary volume

V vein; vision; voice; volume
VA visual acuity
VB viable birth
VC vital capacity; vena cava
VD venereal disease; vapor density
VDH valvular disease/heart
VDRL Venereal Disease Research Laboratory (test for syphilis)
VF field of vision; ventricular fibrillation
VH vaginal hysterectomy; viral hepatitis
VO verbal order
VP vasopressin; venipuncture; venous pressure
VR vocal resonance; right arm; valve replacement; venous return
VRE vancomycin-resistant *Enterococcus*
VS vital signs; verbal scale
VSD ventricular septal defect
VT tidal volume; ventricular tachycardia
VW vessel wall
VZ varicella-zoster

w watt; water; week; weight; wife
WB weight bearing; whole blood
WBC white blood cell; white blood cell count
w/c wheelchair
WC ward clerk; white blood cell; whooping cough
WD well developed; well differentiated
WL waiting list; workload
WM white male; whole milk
WNL within normal limits
WR Wassermann reactions
WT weight; white
W/V weight/volume

Y year
yd yard
YF yellow fever
YO year(s) old

yr year
ys yellow spot (retina)

UNACCEPTABLE ABBREVIATIONS
(National Pharmacy Association, 2006)

Old Abbreviations	Consider Using
AD	Right ear or R-ear
AS	Left ear or L-ear
AU	Both ears
OD	Right eye or R-eye
OU	Left eye or L-eye
ou	Both eyes
QD (qd)	Each day or daily
QID (qid)	4× each day or 4× daily
QOD (qod)	Every other day
QH (qh)	Every or each hour
QW (qw)	Every or each week
QxH (qxh)	4× an hour
BIW	Twice per week
TIW	Three times per week
MS, MS04 MgSO4	Spell out morphine or magnesium
U	units
IU (iu)	international units
μg	micrograms
X 3d	threex each day or 3× daily
cc	ml
< >	Spell out, less than, greater than
. .. ...	1, 2, 3
⊤ ⊤⊤ ⊤⊤⊤	
♀ ♀♀ ♀♀♀	one, two, three

PREFIXES

a, an absent
ab away from
ad to or toward
aer air
angio blood vessel
ante before
arteri artery
aud ear

bi two
brady slow

cardi heart
cephal head
cerebro brain
chole gallbladder
chondr cartilage
cirrho yellow
co, con with, together
colo colon
contra opposing
cost rib
cran head
crani skull
cyano blue
cysto liquid-filled urinary bladder

dactyl fingers/toes
de down, from
dent (o) teeth
derma skin
dis away, separate
dys bad, difficult

e without
encephala brain
endo within, inside
enter intestines
epi on, over
erythro red
ex, extra outside of

gastr stomach
glycol sugar

hem blood
hemato blood
hemi one half
hepat liver
hyper above beyond
hypo beneath, below

ileo ileum
ili ilium
inter between
intra/intro within

leuko white
lingu tongue
lip fat
litho stone

macro large
mal bad
mega large
melano black
mesi, meso middle
meta change
micro small
mono one
multi many

my muscle
myel bone marrow
myelo spinal cord

neo new, recent
nephr kidney
neuro nervous system

ophthalm eye
osteo bone
ot ear

par near
para beside, near
per through
peri around
phag eat
phleg vein
pneum lung
polio gray
poly many
post after
pre/pro before
proct rectal
psycho the mind

re back
ren kidney
retro back
rhin nose
rhino nose

semi half
splen spleen
spondyl spinal cord
sub below
super above
supra above

tachy fast
tetra four
tri three

uni one

vascular blood vessel
venous vein

Body Fluids

aqua water
chol(e) bile
dacry(o) tears
galact(o) milk
hem(a) blood
hemat(o) blood
hydro water
lacrima tears
mucus secretions from membranes
plasma blood
ptyal(o) saliva
pus liquid inflammation
sangui blood
sanguin(o) very bloody
serum clear portion of blood
urea, uro urine

Body Substances and Chemicals

adip(o) fat
amyl(o) starch
cerumen earwax
collagen connective tissue
ele(o), ole(o) oil
ferrum iron
glyc(o) sugar
hal(o) salt
hyal(o) translucent
lapis stone
lip(o), lipid fat, fatty
lith(o) stone or calculus
mel(i) honey, sugar
natrium sodium
petrous stony hardness
sabum sebaceous gland
sacchar(o) sugar
sal salt

Colors

albus white
chlor(o) green
chrom(o) color
cirrhos orange, yellow
cyan(o) blue
erythr(o) red
leuc(o) white
lutein yellow
melan(o) black
poli(o) gray
rhod(o) red
ruber red
rubor red
xanth(o) yellow

SUFFIXES

ac, al pertaining to
algia pain
ate, ize use, subject

cele protrusion
centesis puncture to remove fluid
cle, cule small
cyte cell

dynia pain

ectomy removal
emesis vomit
emia blood
ent, er, ist person
esis, tion condition

genic origin
gram/graphy written record
graph instrument that records

ia, ism, ity condition
iasis presence of
ible, ile capable
itis inflammation

logy study of

megaly enlargement

ola, ole small
oma tumor
osis, sis abnormal
ostomy opening
ous, tic pertaining to
oxia oxygen

pathy disease
penia deficiency of
pexy, pexis fixation
phagia, phagy eating
phobia fear
plasty surgical shaping
pnea breathing
ptosis prolapse, down

rrhage excessive flow
rrhage, rrhagia suturing
rrhea flow
rrhexis suture

scope examination instrument
scopy examination
stomy surgical opening

tic relating to
tion condition
tome instrument
tomy incision

ule small
ulum small
ulus small
uria urine

SYMBOLS

⚲ standing
⚳ sitting
o- lying
↑ increasing
↓ decreasing
R right
L left
♀ female
♂ male
ʒ dram
℥ ounce
° degree
′ minute
°C Celsius
°F Fahrenheit
® registered trademark
* birth
⊤ death
Θ normal
× times
= equal to
≈ about
ø none or no
→ leading to
@ at
# number
″ seconds
µg microgram
µm micrometer
♂ male
♀ female
+ not definite
ˇ systolic blood pressure
^ diastolic blood pressure

MEDICAL SPECIALISTS

Allergist Treats the body's reactions to unusual sensitivity

Anesthesiologist Provides anesthesia

Cardiac surgeon Surgically treats conditions and diseases of the heart and chest cavity vessels

Cardiologist Treats conditions and diseases of the heart and blood vessels

Dermatologist Treats conditions and diseases of the skin

Endocrinologist Treats conditions and diseases of the endocrine system

Family practitioner Treats clients of all ages with medical methods

Gastroenterologist Treats conditions and diseases of the digestive tract

General practitioner Treats clients of all ages with medical methods

Geneticist Specialist in the study of genetics

Gerontologist Treats conditions and diseases related to the elderly

Gynecologist Treats conditions and diseases of the female reproductive system

Hematologist Treats blood disorders

Intensivist Monitors and treats people in the intensive care unit

Internist Treats nonsurgical conditions and diseases in adults and children

Medical examiner Performs autopsies, analyzes autopsy and pathology evidence related to a crime

Neonatologist Treats conditions and diseases in newborns, particularly premature births

Neurologist Treats conditions and diseases of the brain, spinal cord, and nerves

Neurosurgeon Surgically treats conditions and diseases of the neurologic system

Obstetrician Treats women during pregnancy and postpartum

Oncologist Treats tumors (cancers) with surgical and medical methods

Ophthalmologist Treats conditions and diseases of the eye

Orthopedist Treats conditions and diseases of the muscles and bones

Otolaryngologist Treats conditions and diseases of the ears, nose, and throat

Pathologist Diagnoses conditions and diseases through changes in tissues

Pediatrician Treats conditions and diseases in children

Plastic surgeon Treats or restores structural conditions by corrective surgery

Podiatrist Treats conditions and diseases of the foot

Psychiatrist Treats mental disorders

Pulmonologist Medically treats conditions of the respiratory system

Radiologist Treats conditions and diseases with radiant energy

Rheumatologist Treats conditions and diseases of the muscles and joints

Surgeon Treats conditions and diseases with surgical methods

Thoracic surgeon Surgically treats conditions and diseases of the chest cavity

Urologist Treats conditions and diseases of the urinary and male reproductive systems

MEDICAL ORGANIZATIONS

AAD American Academy of Dermatology
AAI American Academy of Immunologists
AAN American Academy of Neurology
AANS American Association of Neurological Surgery (Surgeons)
AAO American Association of Ophthalmology (Orthodontists)
AAOG American Association of Obstetricians and Gynecologists
AAOO American Academy of Ophthalmology and Otolaryngology
AAOP American Academy of Oral Pathology
AAOS American Academy of Orthopaedic Surgeons
AAP American Academy of Pediatrics (Periodontology); Association of American Physicians
ACFO American College of Foot Orthopedists
ACFS American College of Foot Surgeons
ADA American Dermatological Association; American Diabetes (Dietetic) Association
AES American Epidemiological Society
AGA American Gastroenterological Association
AGS American Gynecological Society
AHA American Heart (Hospital) Association
ALPOS American Laryngological, Philological, and Otological Society
AMA American Medical Association
AMSUS Association of Military Surgeons of the United States
AMWA American Medical Women's (Writer's) Association
ANA American Neurological Association
AOA American Orthopedic (Osteopathic) Association
APA American Podiatry (Psychiatric) (Psychological) Association
AUA American Urological Association

NURSING SPECIALTIES

AD Associate degree nurse
A/NP Adult/nurse practitioner
BS (BSN) Bachelor of science (bachelor of science in nursing)
CCRN Critical care registered nurse
CDE Certified diabetes education
CEN Certified emergency nurse
CNE Certified nurse education
CNM Certified nurse-midwife; clinical nurse manager
CNS Clinical nurse specialist
CRNA Certified registered nurse anesthetist
DN (ND) Doctorate in nursing (nursing doctor)
EdD Doctorate of education
FP-NP Family practice nurse practitioner
G-NP Geriatric nurse practitioner
LPN Licensed practical nurse
LVN Licensed vocational nurse
MEd Master of education
MPH Master of public health
MS (MSN) Master of science (master of science in nursing)
MSNR Master of science in nursing with research
NP Nurse practitioner
NP/C Nurse practitioner/certified
ONS Oncology nurse specialist
PhD Doctor of philosophy
PhDc Doctor of philosophy, candidate
P-NP Pediatric nurse practitioner
RN Registered nurse
RNA Registered nurse anesthetist
RNC Registered nurse certified
TNCC Trauma nurse core course

NURSING ORGANIZATIONS

AAACN American Academy of Ambulatory Care Nursing

AACCN American Association of Critical Care Nurses

AACN American Association of Colleges of Nursing

AAHN American Association for the History of Nursing, Inc.

AALNC American Association of Legal Nurse Consultants

AAMN American Assembly for Men in Nursing

AANA American Association of Nurse Anesthetists; American Association of Nurse Attorneys

AANN American Association of Neuroscience Nurses

AANP American Academy of Nurse Practitioners

AAOH American Association of Occupational Health Nurses, Inc.

AAON American Association of Office Nurses

AASPIN American Association of Spinal Cord Injury Nurses

ABNF Association of Black Nursing Faculty, Inc.

ACCH Association for the Care of Children's Health

ACHNE Association of Community Health Nursing Educators

ACHSA American Correctional Health Services Association

ACNM American College of Nurse Midwives

ACPN Advocates for Child Psychiatric Nursing

ACS American Cancer Society

AHA American Heart Association

AHNA American Holistic Nurses Association

ANA American Nurses Association

AN-Aids Association of Nurses in AIDS Care

ANC Army Nurses Corps

ANF American Nurses Foundation
ANNA American Nephrology Nurses' Association
AONE American Organization of Nurse Executives
AORN Association of Operating Room Nurses
APH American Public Health Association
APIC Association for Practitioners in Infection Control
APON Association of Pediatric Oncology Nurses
ARC American Red Cross
ARN Association of Rehabilitation Nurses
ASORN American Society of Ophthalmic Registered Nurses, Inc.
ASPAN American Society of Post Anesthesia Nurses
ASPRSN American Society of Plastic and Reconstructive Surgical Nurses, Inc.
ATDNF Alpha Tau Delta National Fraternity for Professional Nurses
ATS American Thoracic Society
AUAA American Urological Association Allied, Inc.
AWHONN Association of Women's Health, Obstetric, and Neonatal Nurses
CEP Chi Eta Phi Sorority, Inc.
CGEAN Council on Graduate Education for Administration in Nursing
CGFNS Commission on Graduates of Foreign Nursing Schools
CHA Catholic Health Association of the United States
CNA Canadian Nurses' Association
DANA Drug and Alcohol Nursing Association, Inc.
DDNA Developmental Disabilities Nurses Association
DNA Dermatology Nurses Association
ENA Emergency Nurses Association
FNIF Florence Nightingale International Foundation
FNS Frontier Nursing Service

ICLRN Interagency Council on Library Resources for Nursing
INS Intravenous Nurses Society
NADNA National Association of Directors of Nursing in Long-Term Care
NAHC National Association of Home Care
NAHCR National Association for Health Care Recruitment
NAHN National Association of Hispanic Nurses
NANDA North American Nursing Diagnosis Association
NANN National Association of Neonatal Nurses
NANP National Alliance of Nurse Practitioners
NANPRH National Association of Nurse Practitioners in Reproductive Health
NAON National Association of Orthopaedic Nurses, Inc.
NAPN National Association of Physician Nurses
NAPNAP National Association of Pediatric Nurse Associates and Practitioners
NAPNES National Association for Practical Nurse Education and Service
NASN National Association of School Nurses
NBNA National Black Nurses Association, Inc.
NCCDN National Consortium of Chemical Dependency Nurses
NCF Nurses Christian Fellowship
NCSBON National Council of State Boards of Nursing, Inc.
NEF Nurses Educational Funds, Inc.
NEHW Nurses Environmental Health Watch
NFLPN National Federation of Licensed Practical Nurses, Inc.
NFNA National Flight Nurses Association
NFSNO National Federation of Specialty Nursing Organizations
NGNA National Gerontological Nursing Association
NHPA Nurse Healers Professional Associates

NLN National League for Nursing
NMCHC National Maternal and Child Health Clearinghouse
NNBA National Nurses in Business Association
NNSA National Nurses Society on Addictions
NNSDO National Nursing Staff Development Organization
NOADN National Organization for Associate Degree Nurses
NONPF National Organization of Nurse Practitioner Faculties
NOVA Nurse Organization of Veterans Affairs
NOWWN National Organization of World War Nurses
NSNA National Student Nurses' Association
ONS Oncology Nursing Society
RANCA Retired Army Nurse Corps Association
RNS Respiratory Nursing Society
SERPMHN Society for Education and Research in Psychiatric Mental Health Nursing
SGNA Society of Gastroenterology Nurses and Associates, Inc.
SOHEN Society of Otorhinolaryngology and Head/Neck Nurses
SPN Society of Pediatric Nurses
SRAFN Society of Retired Air Force Nurses, Inc.
SRS Society of Rogerian Scholars
SVN Society for Vascular Nursing
TNS Transcultural Nursing Society
VNAA Visiting Nurse Association of America

BODY REGIONS

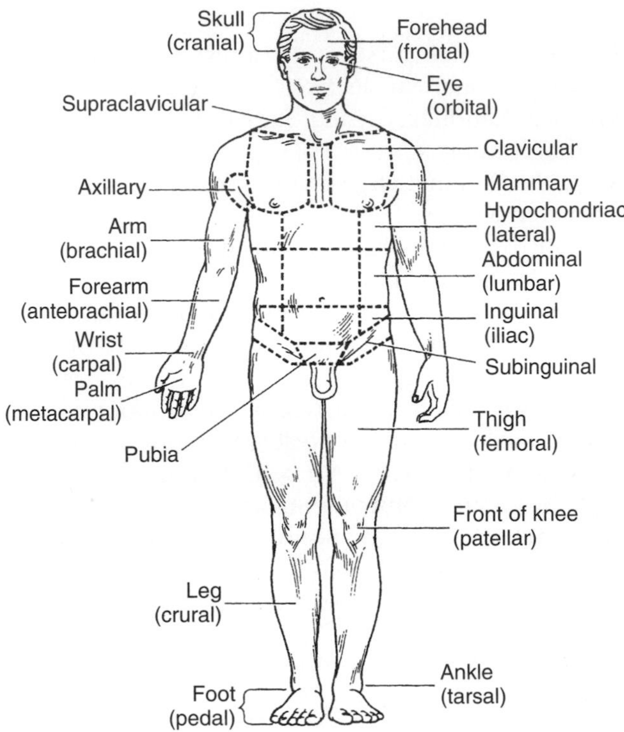

Figure 1-1 Body regions: anterior. (Modified from Austrin MG, Austrin HR: *Learning medical terminology*, ed 9, St. Louis, 1998, Mosby.)

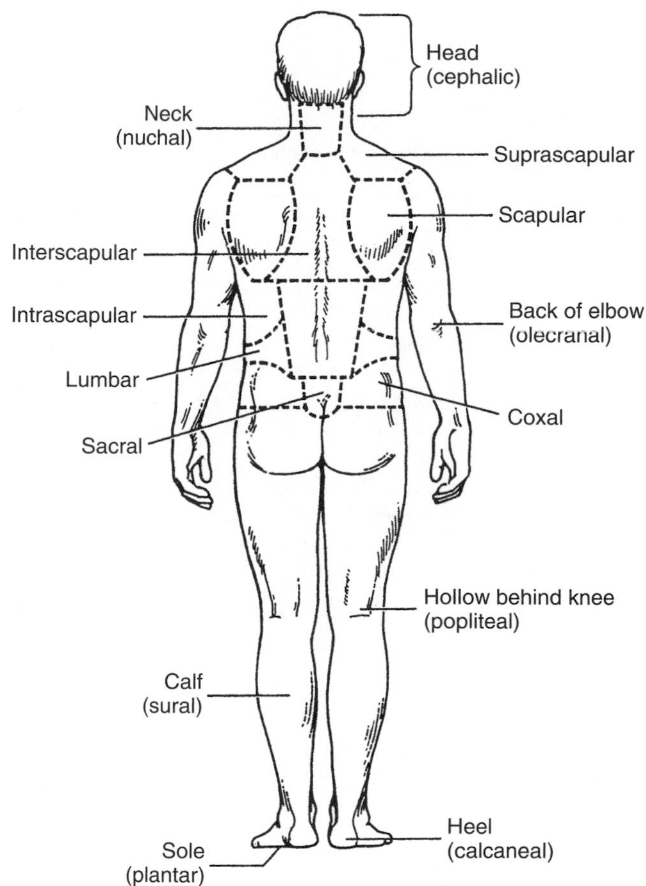

Figure 1-2 Body regions: posterior. (Modified from Austrin MG, Austrin HR: *Learning medical terminology,* ed 9, St. Louis, 1998, Mosby.)

DIRECTIONS AND PLANES

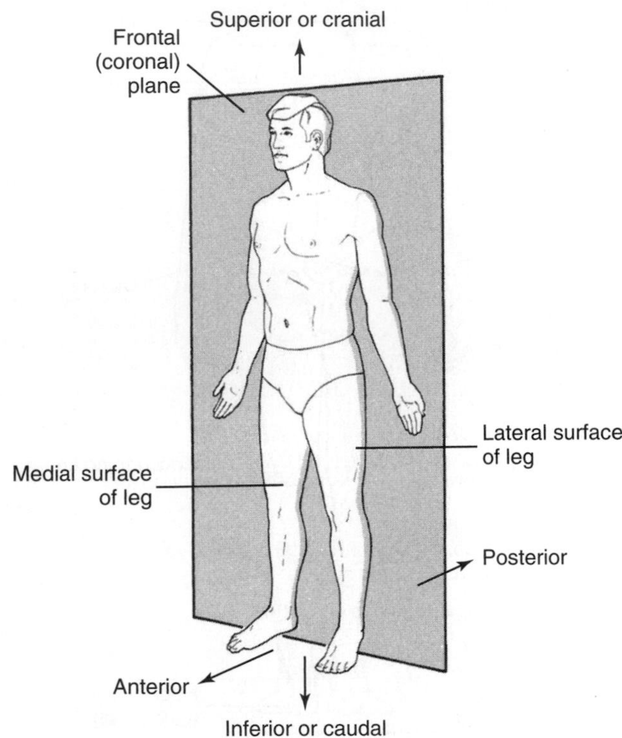

Figure 1-3 Frontal and lateral planes. (Modified from Austrin MG, Austrin HR: *Learning medical terminology*, ed 9, St. Louis, 1998, Mosby.)

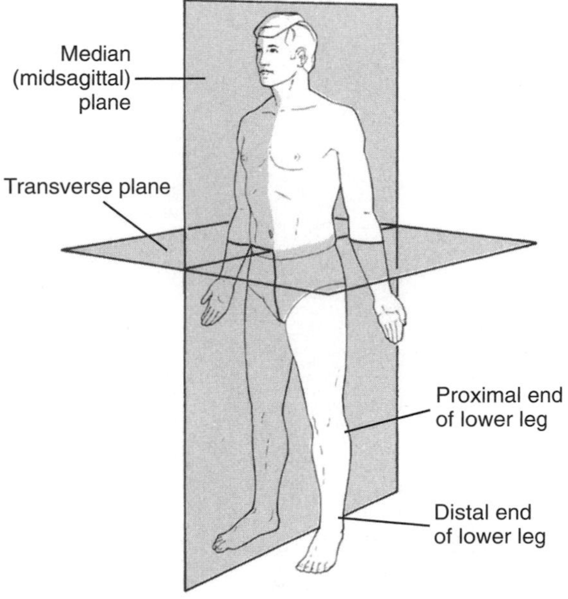

Figure 1-4 Median and transverse planes. (Modified from Austrin MG, Austrin HR: *Learning medical terminology,* ed 9, St. Louis, 1998, Mosby.)

Chapter 2

Medications: Calculations and Administration

For an in-depth study of medications, calculations, and administration, consult the following publications:

Clark JF, Queener SF, Karb VB: *Pharmacologic basis of nursing practice*, ed 6, St. Louis, 1999, Mosby.

Clayton BC, Stock YN: *Basic pharmacology for nurses*, ed 14, St. Louis, 2007, Mosby.

Potter PA, Perry AG: *Fundamentals of nursing*, ed 7, St. Louis, 2008, Mosby.

Skidmore-Roth L: *Mosby's 2008 nursing drug reference*, ed 21, St. Louis, 2008, Mosby.

EQUIVALENT MEASURES

Metric System

To change from a larger to a smaller unit, MULTIPLY the number by 10, 100, etc., or move the decimal point to the RIGHT. To change from a smaller to larger unit, DIVIDE the number by 10, 100, etc., or move the decimal to the LEFT.

Weight

1 kilogram (kg/Kg) = 1000 grams (gm)
1 gram (Gm/gm/g/G) = 1000 milligrams (mg)
1 milligram (mg) = 1000 micrograms (mcg)

Volume

1 liter (L) = 1000 milliliters (mL)
1 deciliter (dL) = 100 milliliters (mL)
1 milliliter (mL) = 1 cubic centimeter (cc)

Length

1 meter (m) = 100 centimeters (cm)
1 meter (m) = 1000 millimeters (mm)
1 centimeter (cm) = 10 millimeters (mm)

Apothecary System

Weight: grains (gr); volume: minims (m), drams (dr), ounces (oz)

Metric-to-Apothecary Conversions

Grams to grains: Multiply grams (gm) by 15
Milligrams to grains: Divide milligrams (mg) by 60

Apothecary-to-Metric Conversions

Grains to grams: Divide grains (gr) by 15
Grains to milligrams: Multiply grains (gr) by 60

Household System

Weight

1 tablespoon (tbsp/T) = 3 teaspoons (tsp/t)
1 cup (c) = 16 tablespoons (tbsp/T)
1 pound (lb) = 16 ounces (oz)

Volume

1 gallon (gal) = 4 quarts (qt)
1 quart (qt) = 2 pints (pt)
1 pint (pt) = 2 cups (c)
1 cup (c) = 8 ounces (oz)
30 cc = 1 ounce (oz)

Kilogram-to-Pound Conversions

Kilograms to pounds: Multiply kilograms (kg) by 2.2

Pounds to kilograms: Divide pounds (lb) by 2.2

Household-Metric Conversions

15 drops (gtt) = 1 mL
1 tsp/t = 5 mL
1 tbsp/T = 15 mL
1 cup/c = 240 mL
1 pint/pt = ≈480 mL
1 quart/qt = ≈960 mL
1 gallon/gal = ≈3785 mL or 4 L

PEDIATRIC BODY SURFACE AREA

$$\text{Child's dose} = \frac{\text{Child's body surface area (BSA) in square meters} \times \text{adult dose}}{1.7}$$

CALCULATING STRENGTH OF A SOLUTION

Solution strength: Desired solution:

$$\frac{X}{100} = \frac{\text{Amount of drug desired}}{\text{Amount of finished solution}}$$

CALCULATING IV DRIP RATES

The *drops per 1 ml* is the number of drops needed to fill a 1-mL syringe.

The *rate* is the number of milliliters per hour.

The *drip rate* is the amount of volume divided by the time needed to infuse.

Following is the equation that can be used to calculate IV drip rates:

$$\frac{\text{Total volume}}{\text{Total time}} = \frac{\text{mL}}{\text{1 minute}} \times \frac{\text{No. of gtt}}{\text{mL}} = \frac{\text{Drops}}{\text{Minute}}$$

Microdrops: A Simple Calculation

10 drops or gtt: mL/hr = gtt/min per micro divided by 6

15 drops or gtt: mL/hr = gtt/min per micro divided by 4

20 drops or gtt: mL/hr = gtt/min per micro divided by 3

60 drops or gtt/mL: mL/hr = gtt/min

DRUG ADMINISTRATION

Routes of Administration

Oral (PO), sublingual (SL), buccal (B), rectal (PR), topical (T), subcutaneous (SC or SQ), intradermal (ID), intramuscular (IM), intravenous (IV), inhalation (IH), transdermal patch (TD), intrathecal (IT), intraosseous (IO), intraperitoneal (IP), intrapleural (IPL), and intraarterial (IA).

Ten Patient Rights

right client
right drug
right dose
right route
right time
right assessment
right documentation
right to know
right evaluation
right to refuse

Types of Drug Preparations

Aerosol spray, capsule (coated), cream (non-greasy), elixir (alcohol), extract (concentrated), gel (clear, semisolid), liniment (oily), lotion, lozenge, ointment (semisolid), paste (thicker than ointment), pills, powder (ground drug), spirit (alcohol), suppository (dissolves at body temperature), syrup (sugar based), tablet (coated), tincture (diluted alcohol), transdermal (absorbed).

Therapeutic Drugs

Palliative gives relief; *example*: pain medications.
Curative cures disease; *example*: antibiotics.
Supportive helps body's functions; *example*: blood pressure medications.
Destructive destroys cells; *example*: chemotherapy.
Restorative returns to health; *example*: vitamins.

Common Allergic Responses

Difficulty breathing, palpitations, skin rashes, nausea, vomiting, pruritus, rhinitis, tearing, wheezing, diarrhea. *Report all allergic responses.*

COMMON DRUG TERMINOLOGY

Absorption The passage of drug molecules into the blood

Abuse A maladaptive pattern of drug usage

Allergic reaction An unpredictable response to a drug

Biotransformation Drug metabolism from active to inactive state

Classification Indicates the effect on a body system

Distribution How a drug is absorbed into the body tissues

Duration Length of time in the body

Excretion The exit of the drug from the body

Form Determines the routes of administration

Genetic difference The makeup by which a person's genetic background may affect the drug's actions in the body

Half-life Time of elimination from body

Idiosyncratic Drugs that are overactive or underactive

Interactions When one drug modifies the actions of another

Medication A substance used in the treatment, cure, relief, or prevention of disease

Onset First response of drug in the body

Peak Highest level of drug in the body

Pharmacokinetics The study of how drugs enter the body, reach their site of action, are metabolized, and exit the body

Physiologic variables The normal difference between men and women and differences in weight may affect the metabolism of a drug

Plateau Concentration of scheduled doses

Side effects Unintended secondary effects
Standards Guidelines for purity and quality of a drug
Therapeutic Beneficial level of drug
Tolerance Low response to a drug
Toxic Not beneficial or lethal level of drug
Trough Lowest level of drug in the body

Drug Dependence

A person may be considered dependent on a drug if he or she possesses at least three of the following qualities over a 12-month period:

- Consumes large doses than intended
- Consumes drug for a longer time period than intended
- Frequent intoxication
- Withdrawal symptoms when away from substance
- Work or social activities are given up to consume more substance
- Continues to use substance despite information or warnings of harm
- Increased time is spent acquiring substances
- Marked tolerance for substance

Modified from American Psychiatric Association: *Diagnostic and statistical manual of mental disorders (DSM-IV)*, rev ed 4, Washington, DC, 1994, The Association.

Drug Actions in Older Adults

Problem	Cause	Intervention
Difficulty swallowing medications	Loss of elasticity in oral mucosa	Rinse mouth before taking pills.
Erosion of esophageal tissues from pills	Delayed esophageal clearance	Position client upright. Crush pill (if possible).
Stomach irritation from medications	Decreased gastric acidity/peristalsis	Drink a full glass of water. Take with food.
Slower drug absorption	Reduced colon muscle tone	Increase fluids. Avoid constipation.
Fragile veins	Reduced skin elasticity	Avoid IV punctures.
Slower drug metabolism	Reduced liver size Reduced hepatic flow	Monitor dosages. Monitor liver effects.
Slower drug excretion	Reduced glomerular filtration	Monitor dosages. Monitor renal effects.

THERAPEUTIC DRUGS THAT REQUIRE SERUM DRUG LEVELS*(†)

Antibiotics

Amikacin (Amikin)
Gentamicin (Garamycin)
Netilmicin (netromycin)
Tobramycin (Nebcin)
Vancomycin (Vancocin)

Anticonvulsants

Carbamazepine (Tegretol)
Phenobarbital
Phenytoin (Dilantin)
Primidone (Mysoline)
Valproic acid

Cardiovascular Drugs

Digoxin (Lanoxin)
Lidocaine (Xylocaine)
Procainamide (Pronestyl)
Quinidine

Respiratory Drug

Theophylline

Antirejection Drug

Cyclosporine

*Specific therapeutic blood levels may vary per facility.
(†)Other drugs may be included depending on the facility.

Syringe Compatibility

	Atropine	Buprenorphine	Butorphanol	Chlorpromazine	Codeine	Diazepam	Dimenhydrinate	Diphenhydramine	Droperidol	Fentanyl	Glycopyrrolate
Arropine			C	C		I	C	C	C	C	C
Buprenorphine											
Butorphanol	C			C		I	I	C	C	C	
Chlorpromazine	C		C			I	I	C	C	C	C
Codeine						I					
Diazepam	I		I	I	I		I	I	I	I	I
Dimenhydrinate	C		I	I		I		C	C	C	I
Diphenhydramine	C		C	C		I	C		C	C	C
Droperidol	C		C	C		I	C	C		C	C
Fentanyl	C		C	C		I	C	C	C		C
Glycopyrrolate	C			C		I	I	C	C	C	
Heparin			I	C		I			I		
Hydroxyzine	C		C	C		I	I	C	C	C	C
Meperidine	C		C	C		I	C	C	C	C	C
Metoclopramide	C		C	C		I	C	C	C	C	
Midazolam	C		C	C			I	C	C	C	C
Morphine	C		C	C		I	C	C	C	C	C
Nalbuphine*	C					I			C		
Pentazocine	C		C	C		I	C	C	C	C	I
Pentobarbital	C		I	I	I	I	I	I	I	I	I
Perphenazine	C		C	C		I	C	C	C	C	
Prochlorperazine	C		C	C		I	I	C	C	C	C
Promazine	C			C		I	I	C	C	C	C
Promethazine	C		C	C		I	I	C	C	C	C
Ranitidine	C			C			C	C		C	C
Scopolamine Hbr	C		C	C		I	C	C	C	C	C
Secobarbital	I		I	I	I	I	I	I	I	I	I
Thiethylperazine			C			I					

Developed by Providence Memorial Hospital, El Paso, Texas.
NOTE: Give within 15 minutes of mixing
C = compatible; I = incompatible; □ = no documented information.
* = compatibility depends on manufacturer, Wyeth and DuPont forms are incompatible.

Syringe Compatibility—cont'd

Heparin	Hydroxyzine	Meperidine	Metoclopramide	Midazolam	Morphine	Nalbuphine	Pentazocine	Pentobarbital	Perphenazine	Prochlorperazine	Promazine	Promethazine	Ranidine	Scopolamine Hbr	Secobarbital	Thiethylperazine
	C	C	C	C	C	C	C	C	C	C	C	C	C	C	I	
	C	C	C	C	C		C	I	C	C		C		C	I	C
C	C	C	C	C	C		C	I	C	C	C	C	C	C	I	
								I							I	
	I	I	I		I	I	I	I	I	I	I	I		I	I	I
	I	C	C	I	C		C	I	C	I	I	I	C	C	I	
	C	C	C	C	C		C	I	C	C	C	C	C	C	I	
I	C	C	C		C	C	C	I	C	C	C	C		C	I	
	C	C	C		C		C	I	C	C	C	C	C	C	I	
	C	C			C		I	I		C	C	C	C	C	I	
		I			I		I					I				
		C	C		C	C	C	I		C	C	C	I	C	I	
I	C		C		I		C	I	C	C	C	C	C	C	I	
	C	C			C		C		C	C	C	C	C	C	I	
	C		C		C	C		I	I	I	C	C	I	C		C
I	C	I	C				C	I	C	C	C	C	C	C	I	
	C							I		C		*	C	C	I	C
I	C	C	C		C			I	C	C	C	C	C	C	I	
	I	I			I	I	I		I	I	I	I		C	I	
		C	C		C		C	I		C		C	C	C	I	I
	C	C	C		C	C	C	I	C		C	C	C	C	I	
	C	C	C		C		C	I		C		C		C	I	
	C	C	C		C	C	C	I	C	C	C		C	C	I	
		C	C	I	C	C	C		C	C		C		C		C
	C	C	C		C	C	C	C	C	C	C	C	C		I	
	I	I	I		I	I	I	I	I	I	I	I		I		I
						C			I				C		I	

From Skidmore-Roth L: *2008 Mosby's nursing drug reference,* ed 21, St. Louis, 2008, Mosby.
Parenteral compatibility occurs when two or more drugs are successfully mixed without liquefaction, deliquescence, or precipitation.

ADMINISTRATION TECHNIQUES

Injection Guide for Needle Size and Volume

	Needle Sizes	Volume Injected (mL)	
		Average	Range
Intradermal	26 or 27 gauge × 3/8 in	0.1	0.001–1.0
Subcutaneous	25–27 gauge × 1/2 to 5/8 in	0.5	0.5–1.5
Intramuscular			
Gluteus medius	20–23 guage × 1 1/2 to 3 in	2–4	1–5
Gluteus minimus	20–23 gauge × 1 1/2 to 3 in	1–4	1–5
Vastus lateralis	22–25 gauge × 5/8 to 1 1/2 in	1–4	1–5
Deltoid	23–25 gauge × 5/8 to 1 in	0.5	0.5–2
Intravenous bolus	18–23 gauge × 1 to 1 1/2 in	1–10	0.5–50 (or more by continuous infusion)

From Clark JB, Queener SF, Karb VB: *Pharmacologic basis of nursing practice*, ed 6, St. Louis, 1999, Mosby.

Flushing Venous Access Devices

Device	Solution/Volume	Frequency
Peripheral capped line	Normal saline (2–5 mL)	Daily 8 hours or after use and before use
Hickman or CVP	Heparinized or normal saline 10 units/mL (5 mL)	Every or after each use
PICC or Cook catheter	Heparinized or normal saline 10 units/mL (5 mL)	Every or after each use
Groshong catheter	Normal saline (10 mL) (20 mL w/viscous med/blood)	Daily week or after each use
Groshong implanted	Normal saline (10 mL)	Daily monthly
Per-Q-Catheter	Heparinized or normal saline 10 units/mL (5 mL)	Every or after each use

Continued

Flushing Venous Access Devices—cont'd

Device	Solution/Volume	Frequency
Gesco catheter	Heparinized or normal saline 10 units/mL (5 mL)	Daily or after each use
Midline-L/Luther Cath (should not use for blood draws)	Heparinized or normal saline 10 units/mL (5 mL)	Daily or after each use
Implanted port (chest)	Huber-type needle Heparinized or normal saline 100 units/mL (5 mL)	Every month or after each use
PAS port (arm)	Heparinized or normal saline 10 units/mL (5 mL) Normal saline (20 mL)	Daily or after each use After blood draws

Flushing policies may vary per facility

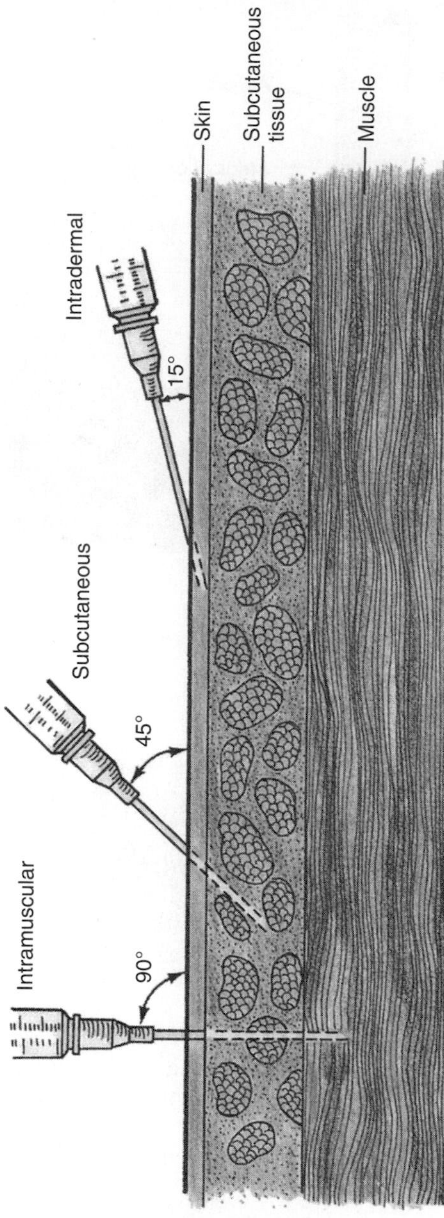

Figure 2-1 Comparison of the angles of insertion of intramuscular, subcutaneous, and intradermal injections. (From Potter PA, Perry AG: *Fundamentals of nursing*, ed 7, St. Louis, 2008, Mosby.)

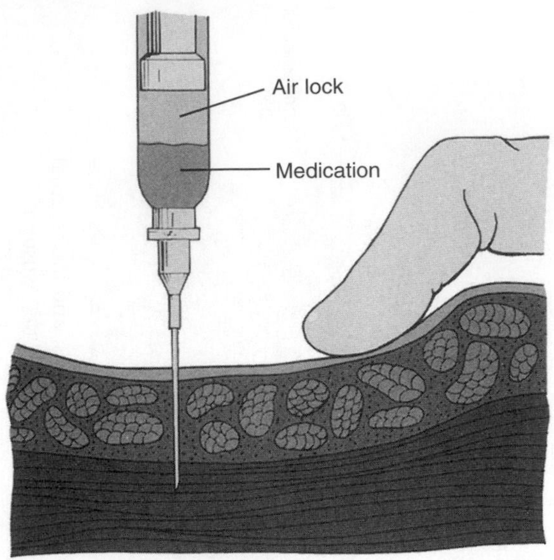

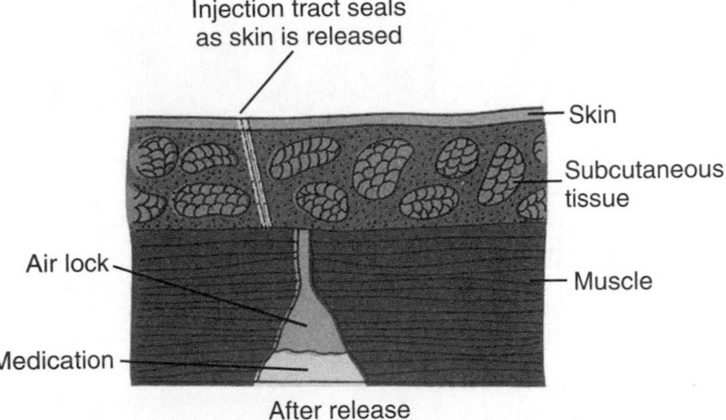

Figure 2-2 **A**, Pull on overlying skin during intramuscular injection moves tissues to prevent later tracking. **B**, Z track left after injection prevents deposit of medication through sensitive tissue. (From Potter PA, Perry AG: *Fundamentals of nursing*, ed 7, St. Louis, 2008, Mosby.)

INJECTION SITES

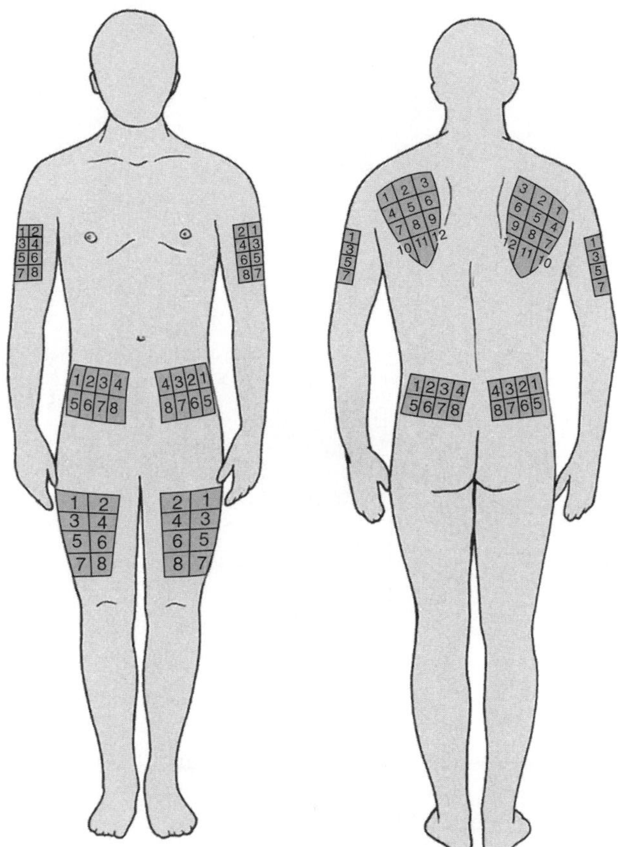

Figure 2-3 Common sites used for subcutaneous injections. (From Potter PA, Perry AG: *Fundamentals of nursing*, ed 7, St. Louis, 2008, Mosby.)

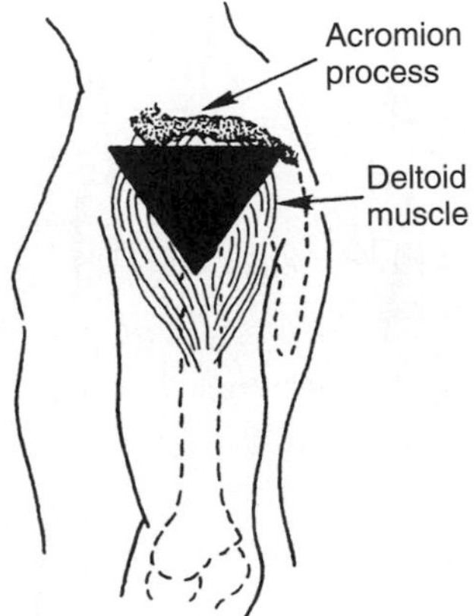

Figure 2-4 Deltoid injections. (From Clark JB, Queener SF, Karb VB: *Pharmacologic basis of nursing practice,* ed 6, St. Louis, 1999, Mosby.)

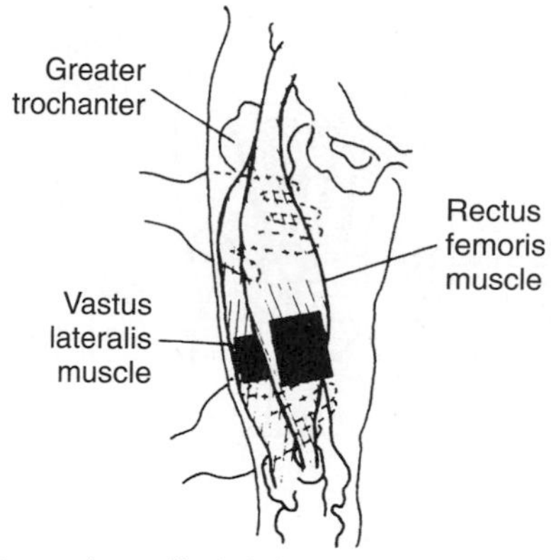

Figure 2-5 Vastus lateralis injections. (From Clark JB, Queener SF, Karb VB: *Pharmacologic basis of nursing practice,* ed 6, St. Louis, 1999, Mosby.)

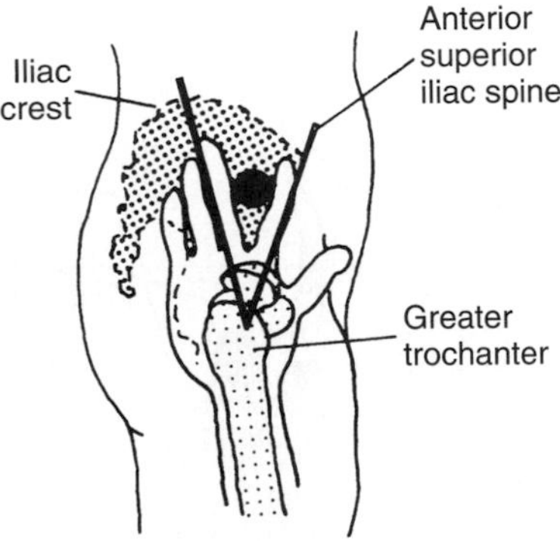

Figure 2-6 Ventrogluteal injections. (From Clark JB, Queener SF, Karb VB: *Pharmacologic basis of nursing practice,* ed 6, St. Louis, 1999, Mosby.)

Chapter 3

Infection Control

For an in-depth study of infection control, consult the following publications:

Hospital Infection Control Practices Advisory Committee, Centers for Disease Control and Prevention: *Guidelines for isolation precautions in hospitals*, Washington, DC, 1996, Public Health Service, US Department of Health and Human Services.

Potter PA, Perry AG: *Fundamentals of nursing*, ed 7, St. Louis, 2008 Mosby.

Universal precautions for prevention of transmission of human immunodeficiency virus, hepatitis B virus, and other bloodborne pathogens in health care settings, *MMWR Morbid Mortal Wkly Rep* 37(Suppl 24): 377, 1988.

BASIC TERMS

Asepsis Prevention of the transfer of microorganisms and pathogens

Chain Path of infection; the components of the infectious disease process

Clean Presence of few microorganisms or pathogens with no visible debris

Colonization Presence of a potentially infectious organism in or on a host but not causing disease

Communicable Ability of a microorganism to spread disease

Contamination Presence of an infectious agent on a surface

Dirty Presence of many microorganisms or pathogens; any soiled item

Disease Alteration of normal tissues, body processes, or functions

Etiology Cause of a disease

Immunity Resistance to a disease associated with the presence of antibodies

Infection Invasion of tissues by a disease-causing microorganism(s)

Medical asepsis Measures that limit pathologic spread of microorganisms

Nosocomial infection A hospital-acquired infection (not present or incubating on admission)

Ports How microorganisms exit and enter a system

Reservoir Storage place for organisms to grow

Source Point that initiates chain of infection

Sterile Absence of all microorganisms

Surgical asepsis Measures to keep pathogenic organisms at a minimum during surgery

Transmission Method by which microorganisms travel from one host to another

Virulence Ability of a microorganism to produce disease

STAGES OF INFECTION

Incubation From initial contact with infectious material to onset of symptoms

Prodrome From nonspecific signs and symptoms to specific signs and symptoms (prodromal)

Illness Presence of specific signs and symptoms

Convalescence During the recovery period, as symptoms subside

THE INFLAMMATORY PROCESS

Stage I

Constriction of blood vessels, dilatation of small vessels, increased vessel permeability; increased leukocytes; swelling and pain. Leukocytes begin to engulf the infection.

Stage II

Exudation with fluids and dead cells.

Serous Clear; part of the blood

Purulent Thick; pus with leukocytes

Sanguineous Bloody

Stage III

Repair of tissues. Examples include:

Regeneration Same tissues

Stroma Connective tissues

Parenchyma Functional part

Fibrous Scar

SUMMARY OF ISOLATION PRECAUTIONS

Handwashing Should be done before and after working with all clients and after removing gloves; immediately if hands become contaminated with blood or other body fluids

Gloves Should be worn whenever contact with body fluids is likely

Mask and/or eye cover Should be worn when splashing of body fluids is likely

Gown Should be worn when soiling of exposed skin or clothing is likely

CPR Should be done with pocket masks or mechanical ventilation, avoiding mouth to mouth

Needles Should not be recapped unless using the one-handed method and *only* if procedure indicates re-capping is needed; needles should have safety guards
CAUTION: *Do not break needles; discard all sharp objects immediately.*

Private rooms Should be used whenever possible

Spills Should be cleaned immediately with bleach and water (one part bleach to nine parts water) for FDA-approved cleaning agent

Specimens Should be collected in leakproof, puncture-resistant container; outside of container must be free of contaminants

Transporting clients Should be kept to a minimum when working with infected clients

TYPES OF ISOLATION PRECAUTIONS

Standard Precautions

- Used to help prevent nosocomial infections.
- Used when working with all clients.
- Replaces the universal precautions and the blood and body precautions.
- Applies to blood, all body fluids, secretions, excretions (except sweat).
- To be used even if blood is not visible.
- Also applies to nonintact skin and mucous membranes.
- Designed to reduce the risk of transmission of microorganisms.

Transmission-Based Precautions

- Used for clients known or suspected to be infected with specific pathogens.
- There are three subgroups of transmission-based precautions.
- Subgroups can be combined for diseases with multiple transmissions routes.
- Subgroups are to be used in addition to standard precautions.

Airborne Precautions

- Used for airborne infectious agents of 5 micrometers or smaller.

Droplet Precautions

- Used for infectious agents larger than 5 micrometers.
- Droplets from the mucous membranes of the nose or mouth.
- Droplets from coughing, sneezing, talking.
- Droplet contracted within 3 feet or less.

Contact Precautions

Contact can be direct or indirect:

- Direct is skin-to-skin contact through touch, turning, bathing.
- Indirect contact is made by touching contaminated items, items within the client's room.

2002 CDC GUIDELINES FOR HAND HYGIENE IN HEALTHCARE SETTINGS

Indications for handwashing and hand antisepsis

A. When hands are visibly dirty or contaminated.
B. Before and after having direct contact with patients.
C. Before donning sterile gloves when inserting a central intravascular catheter.
D. Before inserting indwelling urinary catheters, peripheral vascular catheters, or other invasive devices that do not require a surgical procedure.
E. After contact with a patient's intact skin.
F. After contact with body fluids or excretions, mucous membranes, nonintact skin, and wound dressings if hands are not visibly soiled.
G. If moving from a contaminated-body site to a clean-body site during patient care.
H. After contact with inanimate objects (including medical equipment) in the immediate vicinity of the patient.
I. After removing gloves.
J. Before eating and after using a restroom.

Antimicrobial-impregnated wipes (i.e., towelettes) may be considered as an alternative to washing hands with non-antimicrobial soap and water. They are not as effective as alcohol-based hand rubs or washing hands with an antimicrobial soap and water for reducing bacterial counts on the hands, and they are not a substitute for using an alcohol-based hand rub or antimicrobial soap.

MRSA AND VRE

MRSA methicillin-resistant *Staphylococcus aureus*
VRE vancomycin-resistant *Enterococcus*

These are two of the most difficult infections to treat.

USE **CONTACT PRECAUTIONS** for a skin or body fluid, MRSA, or VRE infection.

USE **DROPLET PRECAUTIONS** for a respiratory MRSA infection and for when MRSA is found in tracheal secretions.

Always wash hands with chlorhexidine gluconate soap before entering and after leaving client's room.

Standard Precautions for MRSA

Masks Necessary if client's respiratory tract is colonized or has an active infection. Must use when suctioning, or when client has a productive cough.

Gowns Necessary if in contact with secretions.

Gloves Necessary for all contact with items that may be contaminated.

Private Room If possible, or with other patients with MRSA and no other infections.

Standard Precautions for VRE

Masks Necessary if contact with secretions is likely.

Gowns Necessary if contact with secretions is likely.

Gloves Necessary for all contact with items that may be contaminated.

Private Room If possible, or with patients who have VRE and no other infections.

COMMON BACTERIA*

Ear *Corynebacterium,* diphetheroids, saprophytes, *Staphylococcus, Streptococcus*

Esophagus/stomach None; usually microorganisms from the mouth or food

Eye *Corynebacterium, Enterobacter, Haemophilus, Moraxella, Neisseria, Staphylococcus, Streptococcus*

Genitalia *Bacteroides, Candida albicans, Corynebacterium, enterococcus, Fusobacterium, Mycobacterium, Mycoplasma, Neisseria, Staphylococcus, Streptococcus*

Ileum (lower) *Bacteroides, Clostridium, Enterobacter, enterococcus, Lactobacillus, Mycobacterium, Staphylococcus*

Ileum (upper) Enterococcus, *Lactobacillus*

Large intestine *Acinetobacter, Actinomyces, Alcaligenes, Bacteroides, Clostridium, Enterobacter,* enterococcus, *Eubacterium, Fusobacterium, Mycobacterium, Peptococcus, Peptostreptococcus*

Mouth *Actinomyces, Bacteroides, Candida albicans, Corynebacterium, Enterobacter, Fusobacterium, Lactobacillus, Peptococcus, Peptostreptococcus, Staphylococcus, Streptococcus, Torulopsis, Veillonella*

Nose *Corynebacterium, Enterobacter, Haemophilus, Moraxella, Neisseria, Staphylococcus, Streptococcus*

Oropharynx *Corynebacterium, Enterobacter, Haemophilus, Staphylococcus, Streptococcus*

Skin *Bacillus, Candida albicans, Corynebacterium,* dermatophytes, *Enterobacter, Peptococcus, Propionibacterium acnes, Staphylococcus, Streptococcus*

*Normal flora found on or in the body.

TUBERCULOSIS

Agent

Mycobacterium tuberculosis*

Bovine TB (Mycobacterium bovis), which is transmitted through cattle and unpasteurized milk

Reservoir

Primarily humans, diseased cattle, badgers, and other small mammals

Mode of Transmission

Spread by respiratory droplets

Direct invasion through mucous membranes

Incubation

4 to 12 weeks

Subsequent risk of pulmonary infection is greatest within the first year

Injections may persist for a lifetime

Prevention

Education regarding the mode of transmission and early diagnosis

Monitoring of groups at risk (people who are HIV positive, recent immigrants, homeless people, people residing in crowded, substandard housing)

Report new cases for public health follow-up

Implement standard precautions and transmission-based airborne precautions immediately with any suspected cases (see p. 61)

Eliminate tuberculosis among dairy cattle

Pasteurize milk

*Some strains are becoming resistant to antibiotics.

OVERVIEW OF COMMON INFECTIOUS DISEASES*†

AIDS

Transmission through blood and body fluids, sexual contact, sharing IV needles, contaminated blood, and from mother to fetus.

Considerations. Education regarding mode of transmission, avoidance of sexual contact with infected persons, use of latex condoms, proper blood screening of all transfusable products, and proper handling of needles and other contaminated material.

Chickenpox/Herpes Zoster Virus (Varicella/Shingles)

Transmission through respiratory droplets or by direct contact with open lesions.

Considerations. Contact isolation, avoid direct contact with lesions, and administration of varicellazoster immune globulin. Caregivers should be chickenpox immune. **New vaccines are available.**

Chlamydia

Transmission through sexual contact.

Considerations. Public education, use of latex condoms.

German Measles (Rubella)

Transmission through respiratory droplets.

Considerations. Education regarding vaccines and prenatal care, avoidance of contact.

*Standard precautions are required for all persons with infectious diseases (see pp. 61–62).
†Check state requirements for reporting infectious diseases.

Gonorrhea

Transmission through vaginal secretions, semen, sexual contact.

Considerations. Public education regarding mode of transmission, use of latex condoms. Some strains are antibiotic resistant.

Hepatitis A and Hepatitis E

Transmission through direct contact with water, food, or feces.

Considerations. Handwashing before touching food, proper water and sewage treatment, reporting of cases, immunoglobulin vaccination when traveling to high-risk areas, proper disposal of contaminants.

Hepatitis B

Transmission through all fluids of an infected source.

Considerations. Hepatitis B vaccination, public education, blood screening, use of gloves when handling secretions, proper sterilization of equipment, reporting of all known cases.

Hepatitis C

Transmission through contaminated blood, plasma, and needles.

Considerations. See Hepatitis B.

Hepatitis D

Hepatitis D can develop only in those individuals who have active Hepatitis B or in those people who are carriers of Hepatitis D.

Measles (Red, Hard, Morbilli, Rubeola)

Transmission through airborne droplets or direct contact with lesions.

Considerations. Public education about vaccine, avoidance of contact with infected persons.

Meningitis (Bacterial)

Transmission through airborne droplets or direct contact.

Considerations. Public education, vaccination, early prophylaxis of exposed contacts.

Mononucleosis

Transmission through saliva.

Considerations. Public education, good hygiene.

Mumps

Transmission through airborne droplets and saliva.

Considerations. Vaccination.

Pneumonia

Transmission through airborne droplets.

Considerations. Vaccination, good hygiene. Some strains are antibiotic resistant.

Polio (Poliomyelitis)

Transmission through oral or fecal contact.

Considerations. Vaccination.

Salmonellosis

Transmission through ingestion of contaminated food.

Considerations. Proper cooking and storage of food, good handwashing before food preparation.

Syphilis

Transmission through sexual contact, direct contact with lesions, and blood transfusions.

Considerations. Public education regarding transmission, prenatal screening, and prenatal follow-up; use of latex condoms, blood screening.

Tetanus (Lockjaw)

Transmission through direct contact of wounds with infected soil or feces.

Considerations. Public education regarding mode of transmission, vaccination.

Tuberculosis

Transmission through airborne droplets; bovine TB through unpasteurized milk.

Considerations. Public education and screening, improvement of overcrowded living conditions, and pasteurization of milk.

Typhoid Fever

Transmission through contaminated water, urine, or feces.

Considerations. Good hygiene, sanitary water, proper sewage care, and vaccinations.

Whooping Cough (Pertussis)
Transmission through airborne droplets and nasal discharge.

Considerations. Vaccination, wearing of masks when near infected clients, reporting of all cases.

FACTS ABOUT INFLUENZA

- Symptoms include fever, headache, dry mouth, fatigue, sore throat, muscle aches.
- Up to 20% of Americans get the flu each year.
- Influenza in conjunction with pneumonia is the sixth leading cause of death in the United States among older adults.
- A person cannot catch influenza from a vaccine.
- Because influenza viruses can change from year to year, an annual influenza shot is needed each fall.
- The best time to receive an influenza vaccine is October through December.
- Influenza vaccine will not protect from other illnesses, such as colds, bronchitis, and the stomach influenza or gastritis.
- Vaccinations can prevent up to 50% of the 140,000 hospitalizations and 80% of the 300,000 deaths that occur each year.
- Influenza can worsen heart and lung diseases and diabetes.
- Influenza can lead to pneunomia.

FACTS ABOUT PNEUMOCOCCAL DISEASE FOR ADULTS

- An infection or inflammation of the lungs.
- In conjunction with influenza it is the seventh leading cause of death in the United States.
- Thirty different causes, including bacterial, viral, fun-gal, mycoplasmas, and chemical.
- *Streptococcus pneumoniae* is the most common cause of bacterial pneumonia. It is one form of pneumonia for which a vaccine is available.
- Half of all pneumonias are believed to be caused by viruses.
- Viral pneumonias may be complicated by an invasion of bacteria with all the typical symptoms of bacterial pneumonia.
- The greatest risk of pneumococcal pneumonia is usually among people who have chronic illnesses of the lung or heart, sickle cell anemia, diabetes, recovering from illness, or those over age 65.
- Prevented by the use of vaccines.
- A person cannot catch pneumococcal diseases from a vaccine.
- Vaccine can be given any time of the year.
- Vaccine can be given at the same time is the influenza vaccine.

*Modified from 2007 American Lung Association

Specimen Collection Techniques

Amount Needed*	Collection Device	Specimen Collection and Transport
Wound Culture		
Only with normal saline	Sterile cotton-tipped swab or syringe	Place sterile test tube or culturette tube on clean paper towel. After swabbing center of wound site, grasp collection tube by holding it with paper towel. Carefully insert swab without touching outside of tube. After washing hands and securing tube's top, transfer labeled tube into bag for transport to laboratory.

Continued

Specimen Collection Techniques—cont'd

Amount Needed*	Collection Device	Specimen Collection and Transport
Blood Culture		
10 mL per culture bottle, from two different venipuncture sites (volume may differ based on collection containers)	Syringes and culture media bottles	Perform venipuncture at two different sites to decrease likelihood of both specimens being contaminated by skin flora. Wash hands. Cleanse area per facility policy. Inject 10 mL of blood into each bottle. Secure tops of bottles, label specimens per facility policy, and send to laboratory.
Stool Culture		
Small amount, approximately the size of a walnut	Clean cup with seal top (not necessary to be sterile) and tongue blade	Using tongue blade, collect needed amount of feces from bedpan. Transfer feces to cup without touching cup's outside surface. Wash hands, and place seal on cup. Label specimen. Transfer specimen cup into clean bag for transport to laboratory.

Urine Culture		
1–5 mL	Syringe and sterile cup	Using syringe to collect specimen if client has Foley catheter. Have client follow procedure to obtain clean-voided specimen if not catheterized. Transfer urine into sterile container by injecting urine from syringe or pouring it from used container. Wash hands and secure top of labeled container. Transfer labeled specimen into clean bag for transport to laboratory.

From Potter PA, Perry AG: *Fundamentals of nursing*, ed 7, St. Louis, 2008, Mosby.
*Agency policies may differ on type of containers, amount of specimen material required, and bagging.

TYPES OF IMMUNITY

Active Antibodies produced in body; long lasting

Natural Antibodies produced during an active infection

Examples: Chickenpox, mumps, measles

Artificial Vaccine of actual antigens

Examples: Mumps measles, rubella (MMR)

Passive Antibodies produced outside the body; short acting

Natural Antibodies passed from mother to child through placenta and breast milk

Artificial Injected immune serum

ANTIBODY FUNCTIONS

IgM First to respond; activates the complement system; stimulates ingestion by macrophage; principal antibody of the blood

IgG Most prevalent antibody; major antibody of the tissues; produced after IgM; only antibody to cross placenta; antitoxin; antiviral

IgA Principal antibody of the GI tract; found in tears, saliva, sweat, breast milk; protects epithelial lining

IgD Only in minute concentrations; function unknown

IgE For allergic reactions

Chapter 4

Basic Nursing Assessments

For an in-depth study of basic nursing assessments, consult the following publications:

AJN/Mosby: *Nursing board's review for the NCLEX-RN examination*, ed 10, St. Louis, 1997, Mosby.

Austrin MG, Austrin HR: *Learning medical terminology*, ed 9, St. Louis, 1998, Mosby.

Lewis SM, Collier IC, Heitkemper MM: *Medical-surgical nursing*, ed 7, St. Louis, 2007, Mosby.

Potter PA, Perry AG: *Fundamentals of nursing*, ed 7, St. Louis, 2008, Mosby.

Weilitz P, Potter PA: *Pocket guide to health assessment*, ed 6, St. Louis, 2006, Mosby.

THE CLIENT INTERVIEW

Demographics

Includes name, address, sex, age, birth date, marital status or significant other, religion, race, education, occupation, hobbies, significant life events.

Health History

Includes history of smoking, heart disease, alcohol or other drug use or abuse, surgeries, injuries, childhood diseases and vaccinations, hypertension, diabetes, arthritis, seizures, cancer, emotional problems, transfusions, drug or food allergies, perception of client's health or illness, lifestyle, hygiene and eating habits, health practices.

Family Medical History

Includes history of heart disease, alcohol or drug use or abuse, diabetes, arthritis, cancer, emotional problems.

Current Situation

Reasons for seeking help or chief complaint; include annual check-up, follow-up care, second opinion, new symptoms, monitoring existing health problem(s).

History of Present Illness

Includes location and quality of symptoms, chronology, aggravating and alleviating factors, associated symptoms, effect on lifestyle, measures used to deal with symptoms, review of body systems.

Medications

Prescribed, occasional use (CPRN), over-the-counter, herbals.

FUNCTIONAL ASSESSMENT

Health Perceptions

General health (good, fair, poor)
Tobacco/alcohol use (how much, how long)
Recreational or prescribed medications (list)
Hygiene practices

Nutrition

Type of diet (list)
Enjoys snacks (yes/no, what type)
Fluid intake (types of fluids)
Fluid restriction (yes/no)
Skin (normal, dry, rash)
Teeth (own, dentures, bridge)
Weight (recent gain or loss)

Respiration/Circulation

Respiratory problems (shortness of breath)
Smoking history
Circulation problems (chest pain, edema, pacemaker)

Elimination

Upper GI (nausea, vomiting, dysphagia, discomfort)
Bowels (frequency, consistency, last bowel movement, ostomy)
Bladder (incontinence, dysuria, urgency, frequency, nocturia, hematuria)

Activity/Exercise

Energy level (high, normal, low)
Usual exercise/activity patterns (recent changes)
Needs assistance with (eating, bathing, dressing)
Requirements (cane, walker, wheelchair, crutches)

Sleep

Problems (falling asleep, early waking, hours per night, napping)
Methods used to facilitate sleep
Feelings on waking (fatigued, refreshed)

Cognitive

Educational level
Learning needs
Communication barriers (list)
Memory loss (yes/no)
Developmental age
Reads English (yes/no)
Other languages (list)

Sensory

Hearing/vision (no problems, impaired, devices)
Pain (yes/no, how managed)

Coping/Stress

Needs (social services, financial counselor)
May need (home care, nursing home)
Coping mechanisms used by client

Self-Perception

How illness/wellness is affecting patient
Body image or self-esteem concerns

Role/Relationships

Significant other or emergency contacts
Primary, secondary, or tertiary roles
Role changes caused by illness/wellness
Role conflicts caused by illness/wellness

Sexuality

Last menstrual period, menopause, breast examination
Testicular examination
How illness may affect sexuality
How hospitalization may affect sexuality
Any questions, needs, or additional concerns

Values/Beliefs

Religious or cultural affiliation
Religious or cultural beliefs concerning health or illness
Holiday or food restrictions while hospitalized
Religious or cultural restrictions on medications or treatments
Religious or cultural rituals needed while hospitalized
Clergy or religious leader requested while hospitalized

CULTURAL ASSESSMENT

Include introductory information, such as:

- Client's name, unit, or room number
- Admission date, admitting diagnosis
- Proposed length of stay

Information about the country can be important:

- What is the cultural or ethnic affiliation?
- In what country was the client born?
- How many years has he or she been in the United States?
- What generation American is the client?

Assess language needs:

- Does the client need an interpreter (what language)?
- Does the client need a communication tool (language board)?
- Could the client use telephone language line (available through most local telephone companies)?

Assess for cultural practices:

- Are there special rituals that may need to be honored?
- Are there special health practices that may need to be honored?
- How will the illness affect cultural practices?
- How will the illness affect cultural rituals?

Assess for cultural supports:

- Which cultural or ethnic supports may help your client?
- To whom does the client turn for help?
- How does the client describe his or her family?
- Who is the client's main source of support?
- Who is the client's main source of hope?

SPIRITUAL ASSESSMENT

Include introductory information, such as:

- Client's name, unit, or room number
- Admission date, admitting diagnosis
- Proposed length of stay
- Religious affiliation
- Local clergy and telephone number

Assess for potential religious supports:

- Minister, priest, rabbi, shaman, emmen, other
- The need for church or prayer services
- The need for confession, communion, religious music
- The need for a Bible, Koran, Bhagavad-Gita, prayer books

Assess for religious practices:

- Are there special rituals that may need to be honored?
- Are there special health practices that may need to be honored?
- Are there special religious dietary needs?
- Is there a special prayer schedule that should be followed?
- Are there special fasting rituals that should be followed?
- How will the illness affect religious practices?
- How will the illness affect religious rituals?

Assess for religious supports:

- Which religious supports may help your client?
- To whom does the client turn for help?
- How does the client describe his or her family?
- Who is the client's main source of support?
- Who is the client's main source of hope?
- Where does your client turn for comfort?
- What gives your client's life meaning?
- Does your client believe that the illness is a punishment?

PHYSICAL ASSESSMENT

Appearance

Stage of development, general health, striking features, height, weight, behavior, posture, communication skills, grooming, hygiene

Skin

Color, consistency, temperature, turgor, integrity, texture, lesions, mucous membranes

Hair

Color, texture, amount, distribution

Nails

Color, texture, shape, size

Neurologic

Pupil reaction, motor and verbal responses, gait, reflexes, neurologic checks

Musculoskeletal

Range of motion, gait, tone, posture

Cardiovascular

Heart rate and rhythm, Homans' sign, peripheral pulses and temperature, edema

Respiratory

Rate, rhythm, depth, effort, quality, expansion, cough, breath sounds, sputum—production, color, and amount—tracheostomy size, nasal patency

Gastrointestinal

Abdominal contour, bowel sounds, nausea, vomiting, ostomy type and care, fecal frequency, consistency, presence of blood

Genitourinary

Urine color; character, amount, odor, ostomy

Classification of Percussion Sounds

Sound	Pitch	Duration	Example
Flat	High	Short	Muscle
Dull	Medium	Medium	Liver, heart
Resonant	Low	Long	Lungs
Hyper-resonant	Lower	Longer	Emphysemic lungs
Tympanic	Lowest	Longest	Stomach, colon

ASSESSMENT TECHNIQUES

Inspection By visual or auditory observation

Auscultation By listening to sounds with a stethoscope

Palpation By touching

Fingertips: Best for texture, moisture, shape

Palmar surface of fingers: Best for vibration

Dorsum of hand: Best for temperature

Percussion By striking the body and assessing the sound

Light percussion: Best for tenderness, density

Sharp percussion: Best for reflexes

TEMPERATURE

Normal Oral Averages

	°C	°F
Infant	36–38	97–100
Child	37	98.6
Adult	37	98.6
Elderly	36	98

Time Required for Reading Glass Thermometer

Oral: 3 to 5 minutes
Axillary: 9 to 10 minutes
Rectal: 2 to 4 minutes

Time Required for Reading Disposable Thermometer

Hold the thermometer in place until the chemically impregnated dots change color (about 45 seconds)

Time Required for Reading Electronic Thermometer

Hold the thermometer in place until the light or auditory signal indicates a reading

Time Required for Reading Tympanic Thermometer

Hold the thermometer in place until the reading is displayed (about 2 seconds)

Distance of Insertion for Rectal Thermometer

Child: 1 inch
Adult: 1 ½ inches

Conversion Used for Fahrenheit

Axillary: Oral minus 1°F
Rectal: Oral plus 1°F

ADVANTAGES AND DISADVANTAGES OF TEMPERATURE MEASUREMENT METHODS

Axilla

Advantages	Disadvantages
Safe, inexpensive, and noninvasive	Takes a long time
Can be used with newborn or unconscious client	Not good for rapid changes

Disposable

Advantages	Disadvantages
Safe	May be less accurate
Noninvasive	More expensive
Comfortable	
Helpful for those in isolations	

Electronic

Advantages	Disadvantages
Rapid measurement, usually 4 seconds	May be less accurate
Ideal for children, unbreakable	Risk of transferring nosocomial infections

Mercury

Advantages	Disadvantages
Accessible to clients at home	Risk of breakage
Inexpensive and easy to store	Risk of mercury exposure

Oral

Advantages	Disadvantages
Comfortable, accurate, easy to obtain	Not recommended for those who have had oral surgery or who have epilepsy
Reflects rapid change in core temperature	

Rectal

Advantages	Disadvantages
Very reliable	May lag behind core temperature during rapid changes
	Should not be used for those with diarrhea or who have had rectal surgery

Skin

Advantages	Disadvantages
Safe, inexpensive, and noninvasive	Lags behind other sites during rapid temperature changes
Can be used on neonates	

Tympanic

Advantages	Disadvantages
Safe, inexpensive, and noninvasive	Cannot be used with hearing aides
Accurate and rapid measurement	Otitis media can distort readings

Special Factors

Circadian rhythm Lower temperatures in morning, higher in afternoon

Hormones Progesterone will raise temperature

Emotions Anxiety will raise temperature

Clinical Signs of Fever

Onset Increased heart rate, increased respirations, pallor, cool skin, cyanosis, chills, decreased sweating, increased temperature

Course Flushed, warm skin, increased heart rate and respiration, increased thirst, mild dehydration, drowsiness, restlessness, decreased appetite, weakness

Abatement Flushed skin, decreased shivering, dehydration, diaphoresis

Fever Patterns

Fungal (infection) Rises slowly and stays high

Intermittent Spikes but falls to normal each day

Persistent Either remains elevated or low grade; often caused by tumors of the central nervous system

Relapsing Febrile for several days, alternating with normal temperatures; often caused by parasites or urinary tract infections

Remittent Spikes and falls, but not to normal; often noted with abscesses, tuberculosis, or influenza viruses

Septic (infection) Wide peak and nadir, often rigors and diaphoresis; often caused by gram-negative organisms

Sustained Same as persistent

THERMAL DISORDERS

Normal Body Temperature: 37° C or 98.6° F

Hypothermia (Stages)

Stage 1 Body temperature drops by 1° C–2° C (1.8°–3.6° F). Shivering occurs. Unable to perform complex tasks with the hands. Blood vessels in the outer extremities contract. Breathing becomes quick and shallow. Goose bumps form to create an insulating layer of air around the body.

Stage 2 Body temperature drops by 2° C–4° C (3.6° F–7.2° F). Shivering becomes violent. Muscle miscoordination becomes apparent. Mild confusion, although the victim may appear alert. Victim becomes pale. Lips, ears, fingers and toes may become blue.

Stage 3 Body temperature drops below approximately 32° C or 90° F. Shivering may stop, difficulty speaking, sluggish thinking, and amnesia appear; inability to use hands and stumbling are usually present. Skin becomes blue and puffy, muscle coordination very poor, walking nearly impossible, and the victim exhibits incoherent/irrational behavior. Pulse and respiration rates decrease, but heart rates (ventricular tachycardia, atrial fibrillation) can occur. Major organs fail.

Treatment: Warm slowly.

Frostbite Damage is caused to skin due to extreme cold. At or below 0° C (32° F), blood vessels close to the skin constrict.

Treatment: Warm slowly.

Hyperthermia Any temperature above normal; severe hyperthermia is indicated by temperatures at or above 42.2° C or 108° F.
Treatment: Replace fluids, watch for chilling.

Heatstroke Temperature above 42.2° C or 108° F
Treatment: Ice to groin and axilla.

Heat cramps Spasms of muscles
Treatment: Replace fluids, watch for chilling.

Temperature Conversions

°F –°C	°F –°C	°F –°C
95.0–35.0	100.2–37.9	105.1–40.6
95.2–35.1	**100.4–38.0**	105.4–40.8
95.4–35.2	100.6–38.1	105.6–40.9
95.5–35.3	100.8–38.2	**105.8–41.0**
95.7–35.4	101.0–38.3	106.0–41.1
95.9–35.5	101.1–38.4	106.2–41.2
96.1–35.6	101.3–38.5	106.3–41.3
96.3–35.7	101.5–38.6	106.5–41.4
96.6–35.9	101.7–38.7	106.7–41.5
96.8–36.0	102.0–38.8	106.9–41.6
97.0–36.1	**102.2–39.0**	107.2–41.8
97.2–36.2	102.4–39.1	107.4–41.9
97.3–36.3	102.6–39.2	**107.6–42.0**
97.5–36.4	102.8–39.3	107.8–42.1
97.7–36.5	103.0–39.4	108.0–42.2
97.9–36.5	103.1–39.5	108.1–42.3
98.2–36.8	103.3–39.6	108.3–42.4
98.4–36.9	103.6–39.8	108.5–42.5
98.6–37.0	103.8–39.9	108.7–42.6
98.8–37.1	**104.0–40.0**	109.0–42.7
99.9–37.2	104.2–40.1	109.2–42.9
99.1–37.3	104.4–40.2	109.4–43.0
99.4–37.3	104.5–40.3	109.6–43.1
99.5–37.5	104.7–40.4	109.8–43.2
100.0–37.8	105.0–40.5	109.9–43.3

To convert to Fahrenheit: $F = (C \times {}^{9}/_{5}) + 32$.
To convert to Celsius: $C = (F - 32) \times {}^{5}/_{9}$.

PULSE

Normal Ranges With Averages

Infant: 90–(140)–160 beats per minute
Child: 80–(100)–120 beats per minute
Adult: Female: 60–(80)–100 beats per minute;
Male: 55–(75)–95 beats per minute

Assessments

Volume/Amplitude of Peripheral Pulses

0 = Absent
1+ = Weak/thready
2+ = Normal
3+ = Bounding

Rhythm

Regular Normal

Regular/irregular Usually regular but occasionally irregular

Bigeminal Skips every other beat (monitor needed for detection)

Pulsus paradoxus (PP), also **paradoxic pulse** and **paradoxical pulse** An exaggeration of the normal variation in the pulse during the inspiratory phase of respiration, in which the pulse becomes weaker as one inhales and stronger as one exhales. It is a sign that is indicative of several conditions including cardiac tamponade and lung diseases (e.g., asthma, COPD).

PULSE POINTS

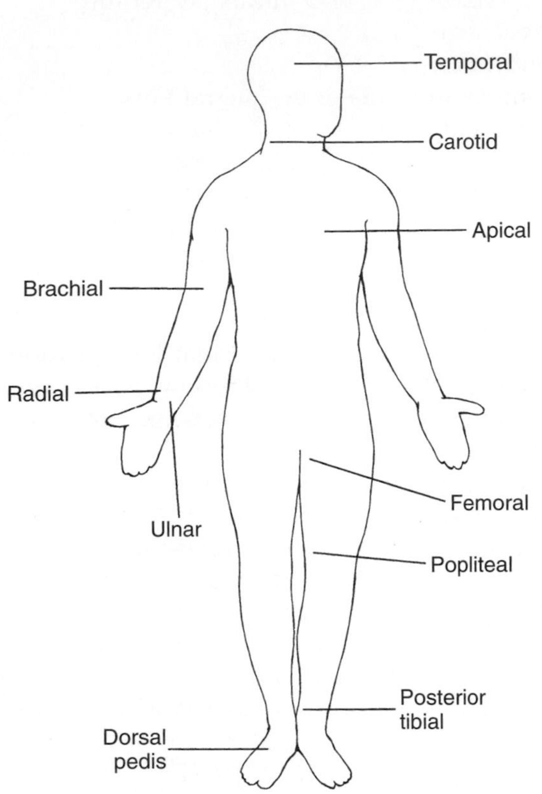

Figure 4-1 Pulse points. (From Potter PA, Perry AG: *Fundamentals of nursing*, ed 7, St. Louis, 2008, Mosby.)

RESPIRATION

Normal Ranges

Infant: 30 to 80 respirations per minute
Child: 20 to 30 respirations per minute
Adult: 15 to 20 respirations per minute

Assessments

Depth: Deep or shallow
Rhythm: Even or uneven
Effort: Ease, quiet, or with great effort
Expansion: Symmetric or asymmetric
Cough: Productive, nonproductive, or absent
Auscultation: Clear, adventitious; crackles, wheezes; diminished, absent, no sounds

Abnormal patterns of breathing

Ataxic respiration Irregularity of breathing, with irregular pauses and increasing periods of apnea. Caused by damage to the medulla oblongata due to strokes or trauma.

Agonal respiration Characterized by shallow, slow, irregular inspirations followed by irregular pauses. They may also be characterized as gasping, labored breathing, accompanied by strange vocalizations. The cause is due to cerebral ischemia, due to extreme hypoxia or even anoxia.

Apneustic respiration Characterized by deep, gasping inspiration with a pause at full inspiration followed by a brief, insufficient release. Caused by damage to the Pons or upper medulla due to strokes or trauma.

Cheyne–Stokes respiration Characterized by periods of breathing with gradually increasing and decreasing tidal volume. Caused by the failure of the respiratory center.

Biot's respiration or **cluster respirations**
Characterized by groups of quick, shallow inspirations followed by regular or irregular periods of apnea. Caused by damage to the medulla oblongata.

BLOOD PRESSURE

Normal Averages (Systolic/Diastolic)

Newborn: 65–90/30–60 mm Hg
Infant: (1 year) 65–125/40–90 mm Hg
(2 years) 75–100/40–90 mm Hg
Child: (4 years) 80–120/45–85 mm Hg
(6 years) 85–115/50–60 mm Hg
Adolescent: (12 years) 95–135/50–70 mm Hg
(16 years) 100–140/50–70 mm Hg
Adult: (18–60 years) 110–140/60–90 mm Hg
(60+ years) 120–140/80–90 mm Hg

Orthostatic/Postural Changes

Take blood pressure and pulse with client lying down. Then have client sit or stand for 1 minute. Retake blood pressure and pulse. Record both sets of numbers. If client is orthostatic, pressure will decrease (20–30 mm Hg) and pulse will increase (5–25 beats per minute) when sitting or standing.
Record and report any orthostasis.

Korotkoff Sounds

Sounds of Blood Pressure

Phase I: Systole (sharp thud)
Phase II: Systole (swishing sound)
Phase III: Systole (low thud or knocking)
Phase IV: Diastole (begins fading)
Phase V: Diastole (silence)

Blood volume Amount of blood in the system

Decreased blood volume Equals decreased pressure, meaning increased need for fluids

Increased blood volume Equals increased pressure, meaning need for fewer fluids

Cardiac output Stroke volume multiplied by heart rate

Diastole Ventricular relaxation

Pulse pressure Systole minus diastole (normal range is 25 to 50)

Systole Ventricular contraction
Viscosity Thickness of the blood
Increased viscosity Equals increased pressure, meaning more work on the heart

The Cuff

Cuff should be 20% wider than the diameter of the limb.

Creating a False High Reading

- Having a cuff that is too narrow
- Having a cuff that is too loose
- Deflating the cuff too slowly
- Having the arm below the heart
- Having the arm unsupported

Creating a False Low High Reading

- Having a cuff that is too wide
- Having a cuff that is too tight
- Deflating the cuff too quickly
- Having the arm above the heart

Creating a False Diastolic Reading

- Deflating the cuff too slowly
- Having a stethoscope that fits poorly in the examiner's ears
- Inflating the cuff too slowly

Creating a False Systolic Reading

- Deflating the cuff too quickly

Height and Weight Conversions

Height

Inches	cm	cm	Inches
1	2.5	1	0.4
2	5.1	2	0.8
4	10.2	3	1.2
6	15.2	4	1.6
8	20.3	5	2.0
10	25.4	6	2.4
20	50.8	8	3.1
30	76.2	10	3.9
40	101.6	20	7.9
50	127.0	30	11.8
60	152.4	40	15.7
70	177.8	50	19.7
80	203.2	60	23.6
90	227.6	70	27.6
100	254.0	80	31.5
150	381.0	90	35.4
200	508.0	100	39.4

From Thompson JM, Bowers AC: *Clinical outlines for health assessment,* ed 4, St. Louis, 1997, Mosby.
1 inch = 2.54 cm; 1 cm = 0.3937 inch.

Continued

Height and Weight Conversions—cont'd

Weight

lb	kg	kg	lb
1	0.5	1	2.2
2	0.9	2	4.4
4	1.8	3	6.6
6	2.7	4	8.8
8	3.6	5	11.0
10	4.5	6	13.2
20	9.1	8	17.6
30	13.6	10	22
40	18.2	20	44
50	22.7	30	66
60	27.3	40	88
70	31.8	50	110
80	36.4	60	132
90	40.9	70	154
100	45.4	80	176
150	66.2	90	198
200	90.8	100	220

1 lb = 0.454 kg; 1 kg = 2.204 lb.

1983 Metropolitan Height and Weight Tables for Adults*

MEN			Small Frame		Medium Frame		Large Frame	
Feet	Inches	cm	Pounds	Kilograms†	Pounds	Kilograms†	Pounds	Kilograms†
5	1	154.9	128–134	58.2–60.9	131–141	59.5–64.1	138–150	62.7–68.2
5	2	157.5	130–136	59.1–61.8	133–143	60.4–65.0	140–153	63.6–69.5
5	3	160.0	132–138	60.0–62.7	135–145	61.4–65.9	142–156	64.5–70.9
5	4	162.6	134–140	60.9–63.6	137–148	62.3–67.2	144–160	65.5–72.7
5	5	165.1	136–142	61.8–64.5	139–151	63.2–68.6	146–164	66.4–74.5
5	6	167.6	138–145	62.7–65.9	142–154	64.5–70.0	149–168	67.7–76.4
5	7	170.2	140–148	63.6–67.2	145–157	65.9–71.4	152–172	69.1–78.2
5	8	172.7	142–151	64.5–68.6	148–160	67.2–72.7	155–176	70.5–80.0
5	9	175.3	144–154	65.5–70.0	151–163	68.6–74.1	158–180	71.8–81.8
5	10	177.8	146–157	66.4–71.4	154–166	70.0–75.3	161–184	73.2–83.6
5	11	180.3	149–160	67.7–72.7	157–170	71.4–77.3	164–188	74.5–85.5
6	0	182.9	152–164	69.1–74.5	160–174	72.7–79.1	168–192	76.4–87.3
6	1	185.4	155–168	70.5–76.4	164–178	74.5–80.9	172–197	78.2–89.5
6	2	188.0	158–172	71.8–78.2	167–182	75.9–82.7	176–202	80.0–91.8
6	3	190.5	162–176	73.6–80.0	171–187	77.7–85.0	181–207	82.3–94.1

Modified from Metropolitan Life Insurance Company, Statistical Bulletin (source of basic data: *1979 Build Study, Society of Actuaries and Association of Life Insurance Medical Directors of America*, 1980), New York, 1983, Metropolitan Life Insurance Company.

Continued

1983 Metropolitan Height and Weight Tables for Adults*—cont'd

WOMEN			Small Frame		Medium Frame		Large Frame	
Feet	Inches	cm	Pounds	Kilograms†	Pounds	Kilograms†	Pounds	Kilograms†
4	9	144.8	102–111	46.4–50.0	109–121	49.5–55.0	118–131	53.6–59.5
4	10	147.3	102–113	46.8–51.4	111–123	50.0–55.9	120–134	54.5–60.9
4	11	149.9	104–115	47.3–52.3	113–126	51.4–57.2	122–137	55.5–62.3
5	0	152.4	106–118	48.2–53.6	115–129	52.3–58.6	125–140	56.8–63.6
5	1	154.9	108–121	49.1–55.0	118–132	53.6–60.0	128–143	58.2–65.0
5	2	157.5	111–124	50.5–56.4	121–135	55.0–61.4	131–147	59.5–66.8
5	3	160.0	114–127	51.8–57.7	124–138	56.4–62.7	134–151	60.9–68.6
5	4	162.6	117–130	53.2–59.0	127–141	57.7–64.1	137–155	62.3–70.5
5	5	165.1	120–133	54.5–60.5	130–144	59.0–65.5	140–159	63.6–72.3
5	6	167.6	123–136	55.9–61.8	133–147	60.5–66.8	143–163	66.0–74.1
5	7	170.2	126–139	57.3–63.2	136–150	61.8–68.2	146–167	66.4–75.9
5	8	172.7	129–142	58.6–64.5	139–153	63.2–69.5	149–170	67.7–77.3
5	9	175.3	132–145	60.0–65.9	142–156	64.6–70.9	152–173	69.1–78.6
5	10	177.8	135–148	61.4–67.3	145–159	65.9–72.3	155–176	70.5–80.0
5	11	180.3	138–151	62.7–73.6	148–162	67.3–73.6	158–179	71.8–81.4

*The weights presented are those associated with the lowest mortality. They are not necessarily the weights at which people are healthiest, perform their jobs optimally, or even look their best. Weights are for persons 25–59 years old (in indoor clothing). Three weight ranges were determined for each sex on each size and attributed to a small, medium, or large frame (in indoor clothing weighing 5 lb for men and 3 lb for women; shoes with 1-inch heels).

†Kilogram ranges determined through direct conversion of pound ranges (# of lb ÷ 2.2 = # of kg).

Chapter 5

Documentation

For an in-depth study of documentation, consult the following publications:

AJN/Mosby: *Nursing board's review for the NCLEX-RN examination*, ed 10, St. Louis, 1997, Mosby.

Austrin MG, Austrin HR: *Learning medical terminology*, ed 9, St. Louis, 1998, Mosby.

Balzer-Riley J: *Communication in nursing: communicating assertively and responsibly in nursing*, ed 6, St. Louis, 2008, Mosby.

Miller MA: *Critical thinking applied to nursing*, St. Louis, 1996, Mosby.

Potter PA, Perry AG: *Fundamentals of nursing*, ed 7, St. Louis, 2008, Mosby.

THE NURSING PROCESS

Assessment Data collection; tools used include client and family interviews, functional areas, physical assessments, and laboratory tests; subjective aspects are those observed by client; objective aspects are those observed by nurse

Analysis Interpretation of collected client data: determination of nursing diagnosis and plan of care; formation of nursing diagnoses

Planning Formation of client's plan of care; client goals are outcomes to be achieved by client

Implementation Nursing interventions; client's plan of care is based on assessments, analysis, and expected outcomes

Evaluation Degree to which client's outcomes have been achieved; revision is an alteration in plan of care when expected outcomes are not achieved

EFFECTIVE DOCUMENTATION

Be factual.
Be accurate.
Be complete.
Be concise.
Be current.
Be organized.

NURSING DIAGNOSES BY FUNCTIONAL AREA

Health Perception

Growth and development, delayed
Health maintenance, ineffective
Health-seeking behavior (specify)
Injury, perioperative positioning: risk for
Injury, risk for

Nutrition

Body temperature, imbalanced, risk for
Fluid volume, deficient
Fluid volume, deficient, risk for
Fluid volume excess
Hyperthermia
Hypothermia
Infant feeding pattern, ineffective
Infection, risk for
Nutrition, imbalanced: high risk for more than body requirements
Nutrition, imbalanced: less than body requirements
Nutrition, imbalanced: more than body requirements
Oral mucous membrane, impaired
Swallowing, impaired
Tissue integrity, impaired

Respiration/Circulation

Airway clearance, ineffective
Aspiration, risk for
Breathing pattern, ineffective
Cardiac output, decreased
Gas exchange, impaired
Tissue perfusion, ineffective (specify type) (renal, cerebral, cardiopulmonary, gastrointestinal, peripheral)

Skin integrity, impaired
Skin integrity, impaired: high risk for
Ventilation, impaired spontaneous
Ventilatory weaning process, dysfunctional

Elimination

Bowel incontinence
Constipation
Constipation, perceived
Diarrhea
Incontinence, functional urinary
Incontinence, reflex urinary
Incontinence, stress urinary
Incontinence, total urinary
Incontinence, urge urinary
Urinary elimination, impaired
Urinary retention

Activity/Exercise

Activity intolerance
Activity intolerance, risk for
Disuse syndrome, risk for
Diversional activity, deficient
Energy field, disturbed
Fatigue
Home maintenance, impaired
Mobility, impaired physical
Peripheral neurovascular dysfunction, risk for
Self-care deficit, bathing/hygiene
Self-care deficit, dressing/grooming
Self-care deficit, feeding
Self-care deficit, toileting

Sleep

Sleep pattern, disturbed

Cognition

Confusion, acute
Confusion, chronic
Knowledge, deficient (specify)
Pain, acute
Pain, chronic
Sensory perception, disturbed (specify) (visual, auditory, kinesthetic, gustatory, tactile, olfactory)
Thought process, disturbed

Coping/Stress

Adjustment, impaired
Anxiety
Community coping, ineffective
Community coping, readiness for enhanced
Coping, defensive
Coping, family: compromised
Coping, family: disabled
Coping, family: readiness for growth
Coping, ineffective individual
Denial, ineffective
Fear
Loneliness, risk for
Management of therapeutic regimen, community ineffective
Management of therapeutic regimen, family ineffective
Management of therapeutic regimen, individual ineffective
Poisoning, risk for
Post-trauma syndrome

Rape-trauma syndrome
Rape-trauma syndrome: compound reaction
Rape-trauma syndrome: silent reaction
Relocation stress syndrome
Self-mutilation, risk for
Suffocation, risk for
Violence, risk for: self-directed or other-directed

Self-Perception
Body image, disturbed
Hopelessness
Personal identity, disturbed
Powerlessness
Self-esteem, chronic low
Self-esteem, risk for situational low
Self-esteem, situational low

Role/Relationships
Breastfeeding, effective
Breastfeeding, ineffective
Breastfeeding, interrupted
Caregiver role strain
Caregiver role strain, risk for
Communication, impaired verbal
Environmental interpretation syndrome: impaired
Family processes, dysfunctional: alcoholism
Family processes, interrupted
Grieving, anticipatory
Grieving, dysfunctional
Infant behavior, disorganized
Infant behavior, disorganized, risk for
Infant behavior organized, readiness for enhanced
Noncompliance (specify)
Parenting, impaired
Parenting, impaired, risk for
Parent/infant/child attachment, impaired, risk for
Parental role conflict
Protection, ineffective

Role performance, ineffective
Social interaction, impaired
Social isolation
Trauma, risk for
Unilateral neglect

Sexuality
Sexual dysfunction
Sexuality patterns, ineffective

Values/Beliefs
Spiritual distress (distress of the human spirit)

NANDA NURSING DIAGNOSES TAXONOMY II

Activity intolerance
Risk for **A**ctivity intolerance
Ineffective **A**irway clearance
Latex **A**llergy response
Risk for latex **A**llergy response
Anxiety
Death **A**nxiety
Risk for **A**spiration
Risk for impaired parent/child **A**ttachment
Autonomic dysreflexia
Risk for **A**utonomic dysreflexia
Risk-prone health **B**ehavior
Disturbed **B**ody image
Risk for imbalanced **B**ody temperature
Bowel incontinence
Effective **B**reastfeeding
Ineffective **B**reastfeeding
Interrupted **B**reastfeeding
Ineffective **B**reathing pattern
Decreased **C**ardiac output
Caregiver role strain
Risk for **C**aregiver role strain
Readiness for enhanced **C**omfort
Impaired verbal **C**ommunication
Readiness for enhanced **C**ommunication
Decisional **C**onflict
Parental role **C**onflict
Acute **C**onfusion
Chronic **C**onfusion
Risk for acute **C**onfusion
Constipation
Perceived **C**onstipation
Risk for **C**onstipation
Contamination
Risk for **C**ontamination
Compromised family **C**oping
Defensive **C**oping

Disabled family **C**oping
Ineffective **C**oping
Ineffective community **C**oping
Readiness for enhanced **C**oping
Readiness for enhanced community **C**oping
Readiness for enhanced family **C**oping
Risk for sudden infant **D**eath syndrome
Readiness for enhanced **D**ecision making
Ineffective **D**enial
Impaired **D**entition
Risk for delayed **D**evelopment
Diarrhea
Risk for compromised human **D**ignity
Moral **D**istress
Risk for **D**isuse syndrome
Deficient **D**iversional activity
Disturbed **E**nergy field
Impaired **E**nvironmental interpretation syndrome
Adult **F**ailure to thrive
Risk for **F**alls
Dysfunctional **F**amily processes: alcoholism
Interrupted **F**amily processes
Readiness for enhanced **F**amily processes
Fatigue
Fear
Readiness for enhanced **F**luid balance
Deficient **F**luid volume
Excess **F**luid volume
Risk for deficient **F**luid volume
Risk for imbalanced **F**luid volume
Impaired **G**as exchange
Risk for unstable blood **G**lucose
Grieving
Complicated **G**rieving
Risk for complicated **G**rieving
Delayed **G**rowth and development
Risk for disproportionate **G**rowth
Ineffective **H**ealth maintenance
Health-seeking behaviors

Impaired **H**ome maintenance
Readiness for enhanced **H**ope
Hopelessness
Hyperthermia
Hypothermia
Disturbed personal **I**dentity
Readiness for enhanced **I**mmunization status
Functional urinary **I**ncontinence
Overflow urinary **I**ncontinence
Reflex urinary **I**ncontinence
Stress urinary **I**ncontinence
Total urinary **I**ncontinence
Urge urinary **I**ncontinence
Risk for urge urinary **I**ncontinence
Disorganized **I**nfant behavior
Risk for disorganized **I**nfant behavior
Readiness for enhanced organized **I**nfant behavior
Ineffective **I**nfant feeding pattern
Risk for **I**nfection
Risk for **I**njury
Risk for perioperative positioning **I**njury
Insomnia
Decreased **I**ntracranial adaptive capacity
Deficient **K**nowledge
Readiness for enhanced **K**nowledge
Sedentary **L**ifestyle
Risk for impaired **L**iver function
Risk for **L**oneliness
Impaired **M**emory
Impaired bed **M**obility
Impaired physical **M**obility
Impaired wheelchair **M**obility
Nausea
Unilateral **N**eglect
Noncompliance
Imbalanced **N**utrition: less than body requirements
Imbalanced **N**utrition: more than body requirements

Risk for imbalanced **N**utrition: more than body requirements
Impaired **O**ral mucous membrane
Acute **P**ain
Chronic **P**ain
Readiness for enhanced **P**arenting
Impaired **P**arenting
Risk for impaired **P**arenting
Risk for **P**eripheral neurovascular dysfunction
Risk for **P**oisoning
Post-trauma syndrome
Risk for **P**ost-trauma syndrome
Readiness for enhanced **P**ower
Powerlessness
Risk for **P**owerlessness
Ineffective **P**rotection
Rape-trauma syndrome
Rape-trauma syndrome: compound reaction
Rape-trauma syndrome: silent reaction
Impaired **R**eligiosity
Readiness for enhanced **R**eligiosity
Risk for impaired **R**eligiosity
Relocation stress syndrome
Risk for **R**elocation stress syndrome
Ineffective **R**ole performance
Readiness for enhanced **S**elf-care
Bathing/hygiene **S**elf-care deficit
Dressing/grooming **S**elf-care deficit
Feeding **S**elf-care deficit
Toileting **S**elf-care deficit
Chronic low **S**elf-esteem
Situational low **S**elf-esteem
Risk for situational low **S**elf-esteem
Self-mutilation
Risk for **S**elf-mutilation
Disturbed **S**ensory perception
Sexual dysfunction
Ineffective **S**exuality pattern

Impaired **S**kin integrity
Risk for impaired **S**kin integrity
Sleep deprivation
Readiness for enhanced **S**leep
Impaired **S**ocial interaction
Social isolation
Chronic **S**orrow
Spiritual distress
Stress overload
Risk for **S**piritual distress
Readiness for enhanced **S**piritual well-being
Stress overload
Risk for **S**uffocation
Risk for **S**uicide
Delayed **S**urgical recovery
Impaired **S**wallowing
Effective **T**herapeutic regimen management
Ineffective **T**herapeutic regimen management
Ineffective community **T**herapeutic regimen management
Ineffective family **T**herapeutic regimen management
Ineffective **T**hermoregulation
Disturbed **T**hought processes
Impaired **T**issue integrity
Ineffective **T**issue perfusion
Impaired **T**ransfer ability
Risk for **T**rauma
Impaired **U**rinary elimination
Readiness for enhanced **U**rinary elimination
Urinary retention
Impaired spontaneous **V**entilation
Dysfunctional **V**entilatory weaning response
Risk for other-directed **V**iolence
Risk for self-directed **V**iolence
Impaired **W**alking
Wandering

Data from North American Nursing Diagnosis Association: *Nursing diagnoses: definitions & classification*, Philadelphia, 2008, The Association.

DEVELOPING A CLIENT'S PLAN OF CARE

The components of the client's plan of care are based on the nursing process, beginning with the client history and assessment. The assessment information is the basis for developing the nursing diagnosis. The client outcomes or intended results are formed to give direction to the nursing interventions. The nursing interventions are the actions needed to achieve the desired client outcomes. The four parts of a care plan are shown on p. 116.

INDIVIDUALIZING CARE PLANS

When a client care plan is developed, the following considerations are needed to individualize the plan to meet each client's needs:

- Age
- Gender
- Level of education
- Developmental level
- General health status (current and before illness)
- Disabilities (physical or mental)
- Strength
- Support systems
- Cultural background
- Spiritual background
- Emotional status

Client's Plan of Care

Nursing Diagnosis		Client Outcome		Nursing Intervention	Evaluation
The Nursing Diagnosis List diagnosis	→	List the goals	→	List the interventions	—
Related to Specific problem	→	Each action should have an outcome	→	Actions per nurse	Can the client accomplish goals?
Secondary to Medical diagnosis	→	Consider the time needed to achieve the goals	→	Actions per client	Did the client accomplish goals?
As Manifested by List the signs/ symptoms	→	Consider individualizing the care plan	→	Individualize interventions	Did symptoms resolve?

CRITICAL PATHWAYS

Critical pathways, part of managed care, incorporate a multidisciplinary approach to client care. When developing a client's plan of care through the use of critical pathways, consider some of the following questions:

Medicine

Which medical treatments will be recommended for the client? How will the medical treatments affect the plan of care and the client's outcomes? How will the prognosis affect the plan of care and the client's outcomes?

Pharmacy

What medications will be prescribed for the client? How will the medications affect the plan of care and the client's outcomes?

Therapy

Will physical or occupational therapy be prescribed for the client? How will physical or occupational therapy affect the plan of care and the client's outcomes?

What kind of discharge planning will the client need? When in the client's course of treatment should discharge planning begin? How will the discharge plans affect the plan of care and the client's outcomes?

Social Work

Will financial, social, or family services be needed for the client? How will these services affect the plan of care and the client's outcomes?

Chaplain

Will emotional or spiritual support be needed for the client? How will this support affect the plan of care and the client's outcomes?

CHARTING

Source-oriented records Include admission sheet, physicians' orders, history, nurses' notes, tests, and reports

Problem-oriented records Include database, problem list, physicians' orders, care plans, and progress notes

Progress Notes

Examples include:

SOAP **S**ubjective data, **O**bjective data, **A**ssessment, **P**lan

SOAPIE **S**ubjective, **O**bjective, **A**ssessment, **P**lan, **I**ntervention, **E**valuation

AIR **A**ssessment, **I**ntervention, **R**esults

Narrative Notes written in paragraph form

Flowsheet Notes written in graph or checklist form

The Client's Chart is a Legal Document (Paper Chart)

- Be complete, concise, legible, and accurate.
- Use ink, sign all charting, cross out errors with a single line, and initial.
- Do not erase or "white out."
- Do not leave spaces.
- Use standard nursing abbreviations and proper medical terminology.
- Include date and time.
- Use proper grammar and accurate spelling.
- Documentation can be called as evidence in a legal action.
- Do not place an incident report in the client's chart.

Electronic Medical Record (EMR)

- Is a legal document and can be called as evidence in a legal action.
- Document using ONLY your username and password.
- Do NOT document using someone else's username.
- Double check to ensure that documentation appears in the correct EMR.
- Use standard abbreviations and proper terminology.
- Use proper grammar and accurate spelling.
- Know the organizational policies for releasing information.
- Follow organizational policy for electronic signatures.
- Follow all organizational confidentiality policy regarding the EMR.

According to *HIPAA* (Health Insurance Portability and Accountability Act), the client owns the information contained within the EMR and has a right to view the originals and to obtain copies under law. Healthcare workers need to know and follow the organizational policies for releasing information to clients.

CHANGE-OF-SHIFT REPORT

Includes:

Client's name, age, room number, and diagnosis

Reason for admission, date, and type of surgery, if applicable

Significant changes during the last 24 hours

Tests and procedures during the last shift

Tests and procedures for the upcoming shift

Important laboratory data, current physical and emotional assessments

Vital signs if abnormal, intake and output, IV fluid status

Activity, discharge planning

Updated changes or effectiveness of care plan on appropriate document

Chapter 6

Integumentary System

For an in-depth study of the integumentary system, consult the following publications:

AJN/Mosby: *Nursing board's review for the NCLEX-RN examination*, ed 10, St. Louis, 1997, Mosby.

Austrin MG, Austrin HR: *Learning medical terminology*, ed 9, St. Louis, 1998, Mosby.

Barkauskas V, Baumann LC: *Health and physical* assessment, ed 3, St. Louis, 2001, Mosby.

Lewis SM, Collier IC, Heitkemper MM: *Medical-surgical nursing*, ed 7, St. Louis, 2007, Mosby.

Patton KT, Thibodeau GA: *Handbook for anatomy and physiology*, St. Louis, 2000, Mosby.

Potter PA, Perry AG: *Fundamentals of nursing*, ed 7, St. Louis, 2008, Mosby.

COMMON INTEGUMENTARY ABNORMALITIES

Type	Characteristics	Assess for
Edema	Fluid accumulation	Trauma, murmur, third heart sound
Diaphoresis	Sweating	Pain, fever, anxiety, insulin reaction
Bromhidrosis	Foul perspiration	Infection, poor hygiene
Hirsutism	Hair growth	Adrenal function
Petechiae	Red/purple spots	Hepatic function, drug reactions
Alopecia	Hair loss	Hypopituitarism, medications, fever, starvation

COMMON SKIN COLOR ABNORMALITIES

Type	Characteristics
Albinism	Decreased pigmentation
Vitiligo	White patches on exposed areas
Mongolian spots	Black and blue spots on back and buttocks
Jaundice	Yellow pigmentation of skin or sclera
Ecchymosis	Black and blue marks; assess for trauma, bleeding time, or hepatic function
Cyanosis	Bluish color of lips, earlobes, or nails; assess lung and heart status

ABNORMALITIES OF THE NAIL BED

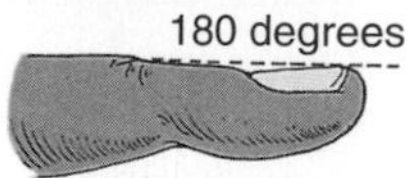

Normal nail: Approximately 160-degree angle between nail plate and nail

180 degrees

Clubbing: Change in angle between nail and nail base (eventually larger than 180 degrees); nail bed softening, with nail flattening; often enlargement of fingertips

Causes: Chronic lack of oxygen: heart or pulmonary disease

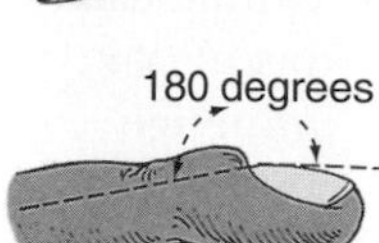

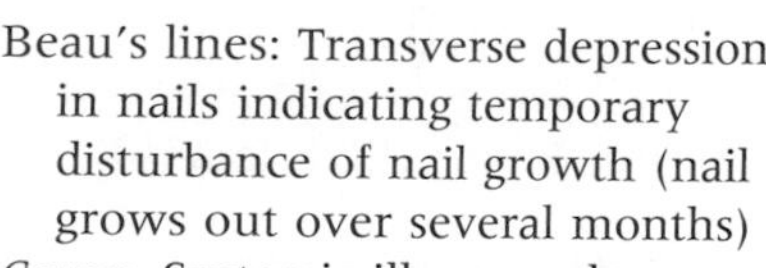

Beau's lines: Transverse depression in nails indicating temporary disturbance of nail growth (nail grows out over several months)

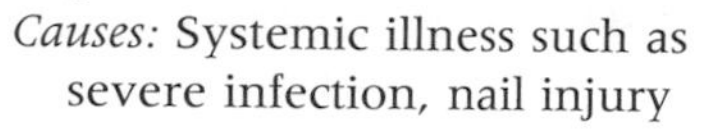

Causes: Systemic illness such as severe infection, nail injury

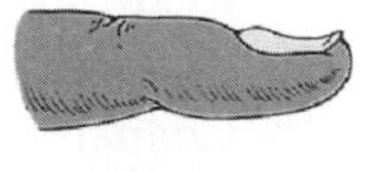

Koilonychia (spoon nail): Concave curves

Causes: Iron deficiency anemia, syphilis, use of strong detergents

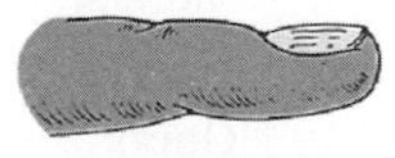

Splinter hemorrhages: Red or brown linear streaks in nail bed

Causes: Minor trauma, subacute bacterial endocarditis, trichinosis

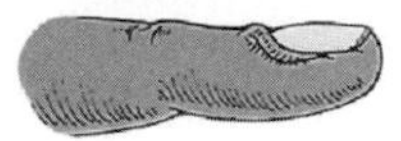

Paronychia: Inflammation of skin at base of nail

Causes: Local infection, trauma

Figure 6-1 Abnormalities of nail bed. (From Potter PA, Perry AG: *Fundamentals of nursing*, ed 7, St. Louis, 2008, Mosby.)

PRIMARY SKIN LESIONS

Type	Definition	Example
Macule	Flat, nonpalpable	Freckle, measles
Papule	Palpable, less than 1 cm diameter	Wart, psoriasis
Vesicle	Palpable, less than 1 cm, with fluid	Blister, chickenpox
Nodule	Hard, less than 1 cm, into dermis	Dermofibroma
Plaque	Palpable or not, greater than 1 cm	Psoriasis, candidiasis
Bulla	Vesicle, greater than 1 cm	Poison oak, impetigo
Tumor	Nodule, greater than 1 cm	Lipoma, fibroma
Pustule	Pus-filled vesicle	Acne
Wheal	Irregular, flat-topped	—
Cyst	Fluid-filled, large	—

SECONDARY SKIN LESIONS

Type	Definition	Example
Scale	Dead epithelium	Psoriasis
Erosion	Absence of epidermis	Chancre
Crust	Dried exudate	Blister
Fissure	Crack in the epidermis	Cracked lips
Ulcer	Necrotic epidermis	Open sore
Scar	Connective tissue	Healing site
Keloid	Overgrowth of scar	—
Lichenification	Thickening of skin	Eczema
Hyperkeratosis	Thickening of skin	Callus

PRESSURE POINTS

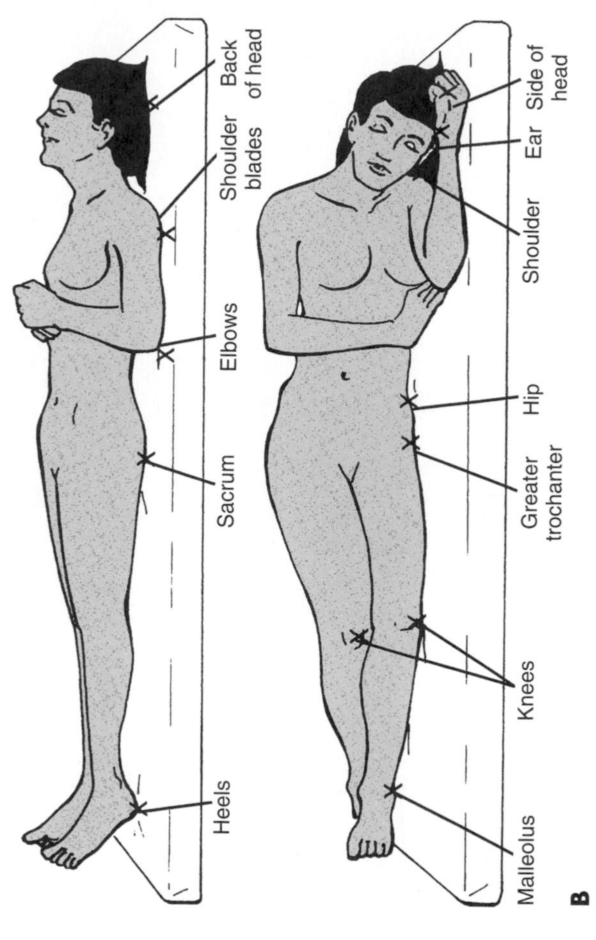

Figure 6-2 Pressure points. **A,** Supine position. **B,** Lateral position. (A-E from Sorrentino SA: *Mosby's essentials for nursing assistants,* ed 3, St. Louis, 2006, Mosby.)

Continued

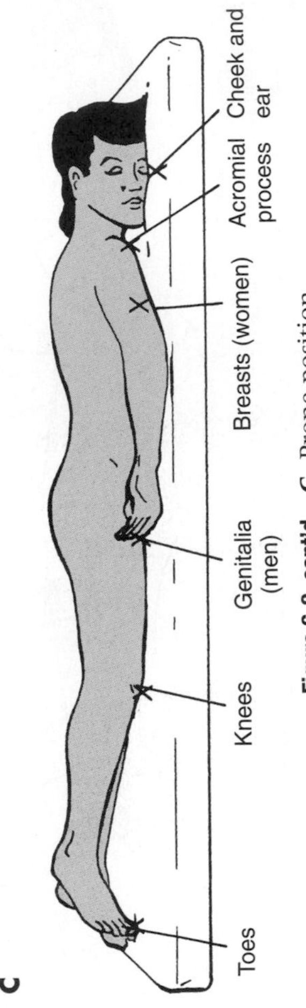

Figure 6-2, cont'd **C,** Prone position.

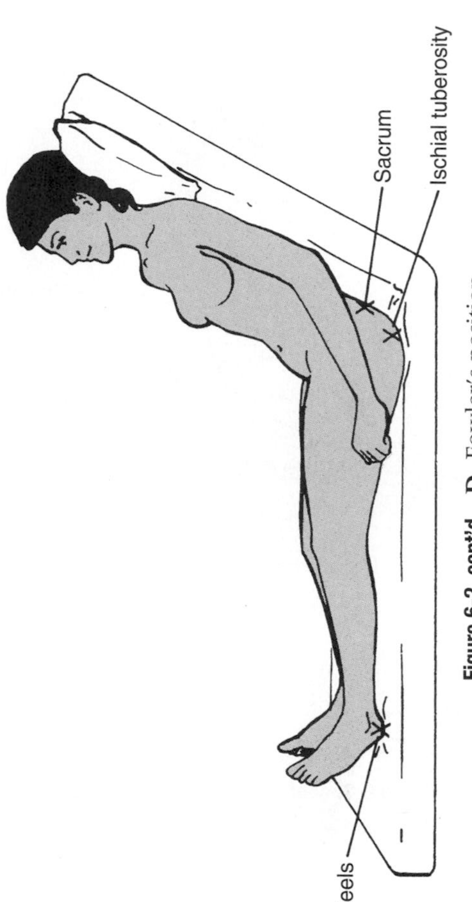

Figure 6-2, cont'd **D,** Fowler's position.

Continued

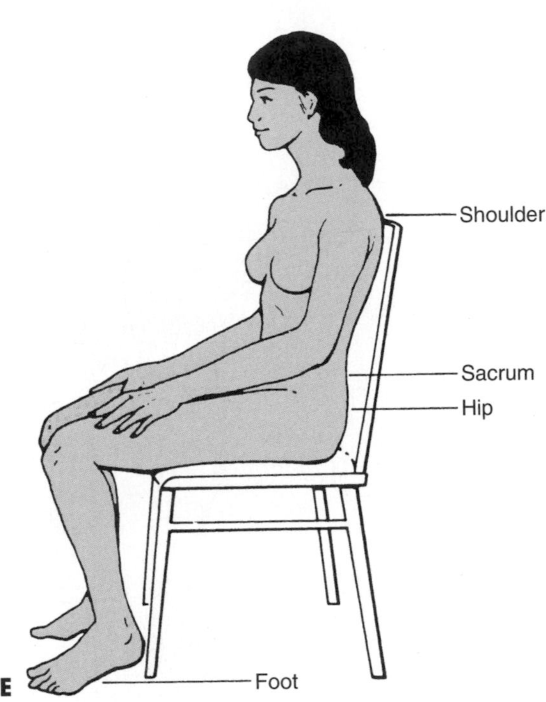

Figure 6-2, cont'd E, Sitting position.

PRESSURE ULCER STAGES

In February 2007, the National Pressure Ulcer Advisory Panel (NPAUP) redefined the stages of pressure ulcers.

Suspected Deep Tissue Injury: Purplish localized area of intact skin or blood-filled blister. The area may be preceded by tissue that is painful, firm, mushy, boggy, warmer, or cooler as compared to adjacent tissue. Deep tissue injury may be difficult to detect in individuals with dark skin tones.

Stage I: Intact with non-blanchable redness of a localized area usually over a bony prominence. Darkly pigmented skin may not have visible blanching; its color may differ from the surrounding area. The area may be painful, firm, soft, warmer, or cooler as compared to adjacent tissue.

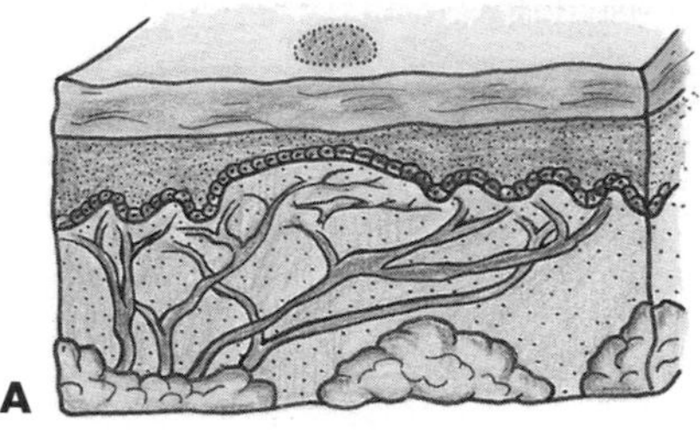

Stage II: Partial thickness loss of dermis presenting as a shallow open ulcer with a red pink wound bed, without slough. May also present as an intact or open/ruptured serum-filled blister. Presents as a shiny or dry shallow ulcer without slough or bruising. This stage should not be used to describe skin tears, tape burns, perineal dermatitus, maceration, or excoriation.

Figure 6-3 Pressure ulcer stages. **A,** Stage I. (Courtesy Laurel Wiersma, RN, MSN, Clinical Nurse Specialist, Barnes Hospital, St. Louis, MO. From Potter PA, Perry AG: *Fundamentals of nursing,* ed 7, St. Louis, 2008, Mosby.)

Continued

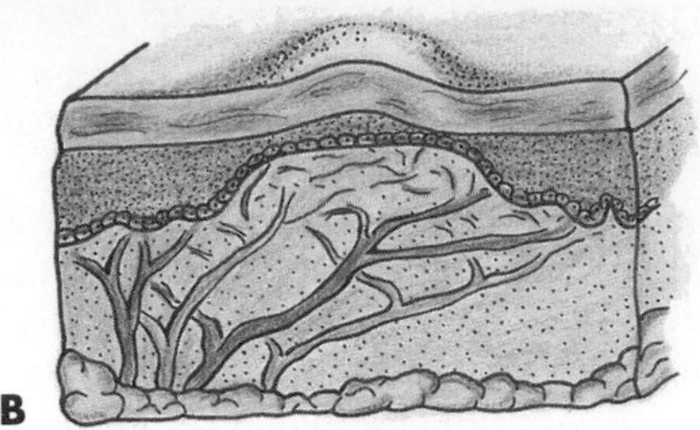

Stage III: Full thickness tissue loss. Subcutaneous fat may be visible, but bone, tendon, or muscle are not exposed. Slough may be present but does not obscure the depth of tissue loss. May include undermining and tunneling.

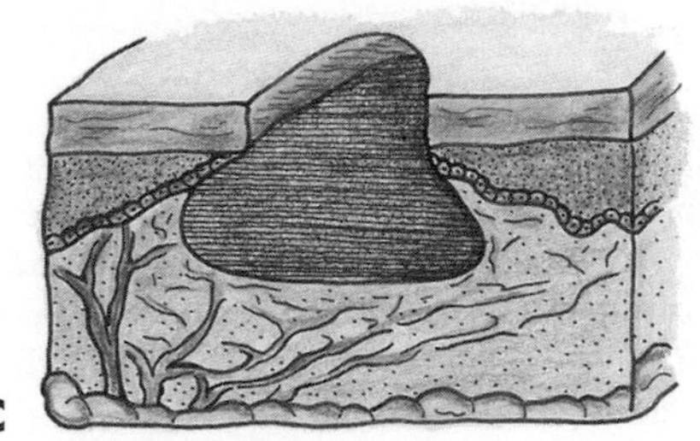

Figure 6-3, cont'd Pressure ulcer stages. **B,** Stage II. **C,** Stage III. (Courtesy Laurel Wiersma, RN, MSN, Clinical Nurse Specialist, Barnes Hospital, St. Louis, MO. From Potter PA, Perry AG: *Fundamentals of nursing,* ed 7, St. Louis, 2008, Mosby.)

Stage IV: Full thickness tissue loss with exposed bone, tendon, or muscle. Slough or eschar may be present on some parts of the wound bed. Often include undermining and tunneling. The depth of a stage IV pressure ulcer varies by anatomical location. Exposed bone/tendon is visible or directly palpable.

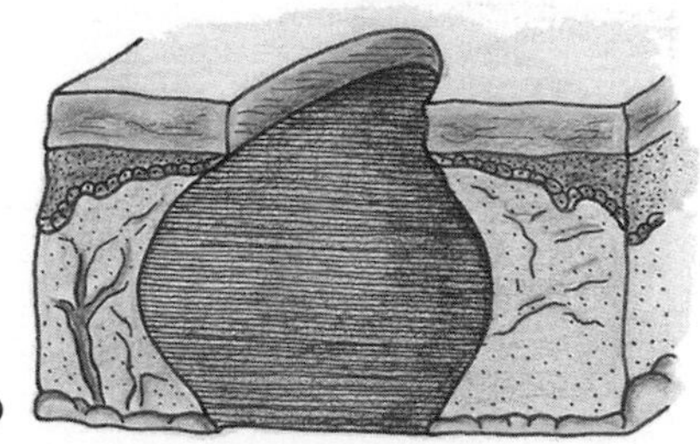

Figure 6-3, cont'd Pressure ulcer stages. **D,** Stage IV. (Courtesy Laurel Wiersma, RN, MSN, Clinical Nurse Specialist, Barnes Hospital, St. Louis, MO. From Potter PA, Perry AG: *Fundamentals of nursing,* ed 7, St. Louis, 2008, Mosby.)

Unstageable: Full thickness tissue loss in which the base of the ulcer is covered by slough (yellow, tan, gray, green, or brown) and/or eschar (tan, brown, or black) in the wound bed. Until enough slough and/or eschar is removed to expose the base of the wound, the true depth, and therefore stage, cannot be determined. Stable (dry, adherent, intact without erythema, or fluctuance) eschar on the heels serves as "the body's natural (biological) cover" and should not be removed.

The Braden Scale for Predicting Pressure Sore Risk

Patient's Name ____________ **Evaluator's Name** ____________ **Date of Assessment** ____________

Sensory Perception Ability to respond meaningfully to pressure-related discomfort	1. Completely limited: Unresponsive (does not moan, flinch, or grasp) to painful stimuli, due to diminished level of consciousness or sedation.	2. Very limited: Responds only to painful stimuli. Cannot communicate discomfort except by moaning or restlessness.	3. Slightly limited: Responds to verbal commands, but cannot always communicate discomfort or need to be turned.	4. No impairment: Responds to verbal commands. Has no sensory impairment that would limit ability to feel or voice pain or discomfort.

	or Limited ability to feel pain over most of body surface.	or Has a sensory impairment that limits the ability to feel pain or discomfort over half of body.	or Has some sensory impairment that limits ability to feel pain or discomfort in one or two extremities.	
Moisture				
Degree to which skin is exposed to moisture	1. Constantly moist: Skin is kept moist almost constantly by perspiration, urine, etc. Dampness is detected every time patient is moved or turned.	2. Very moist: Skin is often, but not always, moist. Linen must be changed at least once a shift.	3. Occasionally moist: Skin is occasionally moist, requiring an extra linen change approximately once a day.	4. Rarely moist: Skin is usually dry; linen requires changing only at routine intervals.

Continued

The Braden Scale for Predicting Pressure Sore Risk—cont'd

Patient's Name ______	**Evaluator's Name** ______		**Date of Assessment** ______	
Activity Degree of physical activity	1. Bedfast: Confined to bed.	2. Chairfast: Ability to walk severely limited or nonexistent. Cannot bear own weight and/or must be assisted into chair or wheelchair.	3. Walks occasionally: Walks occasionally during day, but for very short distances, with or without assistance. Spends majority of shift in bed or chair.	4. Walks frequently: Walks outside the room at least twice a day and is outside of room at least once every 2 hours during waking hours.

Mobility				
Ability to change and control body position	1. Completely immobile: Does not make even slight changes in body or extremity position without assistance.	2. Very limited: Makes occasional changes but unable to make frequent or significant changes independently.	3. Slightly limited: Makes frequent although slight changes in position independently.	4. No limitations: Makes major and frequent body changes on position independently.

Continued

The Braden Scale for Predicting Pressure Sore Risk—cont'd

Patient's Name ____________ **Evaluator's Name** ____________ **Date of Assessment** ____________

Nutrition Usual food intake pattern	1. Very poor: Never eats a complete meal. Rarely eats more than a third of food offered. Eats two servings or less of protein, meat, or dairy products per day. Takes fluids poorly. Does not take a liquid dietary supplement.	2. Probably inadequate: Never eats a complete meal. Rarely eats more than half of food offered. Protein intake includes only three servings of meat or dairy products per day.	3. Adequate: Eats over half of meals. Eats a total of four servings of protein each day. Occasionally will refuse a meal but will take a supplement.	4. Excellent: Eats most of every meal. Usually eats a total of four or more servings of meat and dairy products. Occasionally eats between meals.

		Occasionally will take a dietary supplement	
	or Is NPO and/or maintained on clear liquids or IV lines for more than 5 days.	or Receives less than optimum amount of liquid diet or tube feeding.	or Is on tube feeding or TPN regimen that probably meets most of nutritional needs.

Continued

The Braden Scale for Predicting Pressure Sore Risk—cont'd

Patient's Name ______ Evaluator's Name ______ Date of Assessment ______

Friction and Shear			
	1. Problem: Requires moderate to maximum assistance in moving. Complete lifting without sliding against sheets is impossible. Frequently slides down in bed or chair, requiring frequent repositioning with maximum assistance. Spasticity, contractures, or agitation leads to almost constant friction.	2. Potential problem: Moves feebly or requires minimum assistance. During a move, skin probably slides to some extent against sheets, chair, restraints, or other devices. Maintains relatively good position in chair or bed most of the time but occasionally slides down.	3. No apparent problem: Moves in bed and in chair independently and has sufficient muscle strength to lift up completely during move. Maintains good position in bed or chair at all times.

TOTAL SCORE______

The Mouth			
Structure	**Normal**	**Abnormal**	**Assess for**
Lips	Pinkish	Pallor	Anemia
	Bluish (in black clients)	Pallor	Anemia
	Smooth	Blister	Herpes
	Symmetric	Swelling	Allergic reaction
	Moist	Red, cracked	Vitamin B deficiency
Bucca	Pinkish	Pallor	Anemia, leukoplakia/cancer
	Moist	Blue	Hypoxia
		Dry	Dehydration
Gums	Pinkish	Red, swollen	Phenytoin excess, leukemia, vitamin C deficiency
		Dark lines	Bismuth poisoning

Continued

The Mouth—cont'd

Structure	Normal	Abnormal	Assess for
Periodontium	Pinkish	Red, swollen	Calcium deposits
Saliva	Moderate	Excessive	9th or 10th cranial nerve injury
Tongue	Centered	Not centered	12th cranial nerve damage
	Dark pink	Red, sore	Anemia
	Smooth	Decreased papillae	Riboflavin/niacin deficits
	Medium sized	Vertical fissure	Dehydration
		Oversized	Hypothyroidism
Uvula	Centered	Not centered	Tumor
	Moves	Does not move	9th or 10th cranial nerve damage
Tonsils	Pink	Red	Pharyngitis
		Swollen	Tonsillitis

Chapter 7

Skeletal System

For an in-depth study of the skeletal system, consult the following publications:

AJN/Mosby: *Nursing board's review for the NCLEX-RN examination*, ed 10, St. Louis, 1997, Mosby.

Austrin MG, Austrin HR: *Learning medical terminology*, ed 9, St. Louis, 1998, Mosby.

Lewis SM, Collier IC, Heitkemper MM: *Medical-surgical nursing*, ed 7, St. Louis, 2007, Mosby.

Patton KT, Thibodeau GA: *Handbook for anatomy and physiology*, St. Louis, 2000, Mosby.

Potter PA, Perry AG: *Fundamentals of nursing*, ed 7, St. Louis, 2008, Mosby.

Seidel HM, Benedict GW, Ball JW, Dains JE: *Mosby's guide to physical examination,* ed 6, St. Louis, 2006, Mosby.

SKELETON—ANTERIOR VIEW

1 Cranium
2 Orbit
3 Maxilla
4 Mandible
5 Clavicle
6 Sternum
7 Humerus
8 Xiphoid process
9 Costal cartilage
10 Vertebral column
11 Innominate (hip)
12 Ilium
13 Pubis
14 Ischium
15 Lesser trochanter
16 Ulna
17 Radius
18 Sacrum
19 Greater trochanter
20 Carpals
21 Metacarpals
22 Phalanges
23 Femur
24 Patella
25 Tibia
26 Fibula
27 Tarsals
28 Metatarsals
29 Phalanges

Figure 7-1 Skeleton-anterior view. (Modified from Austrin MG, Austrin HR: *Learning medical terminology,* ed 9, St. Louis, 1998, Mosby.)

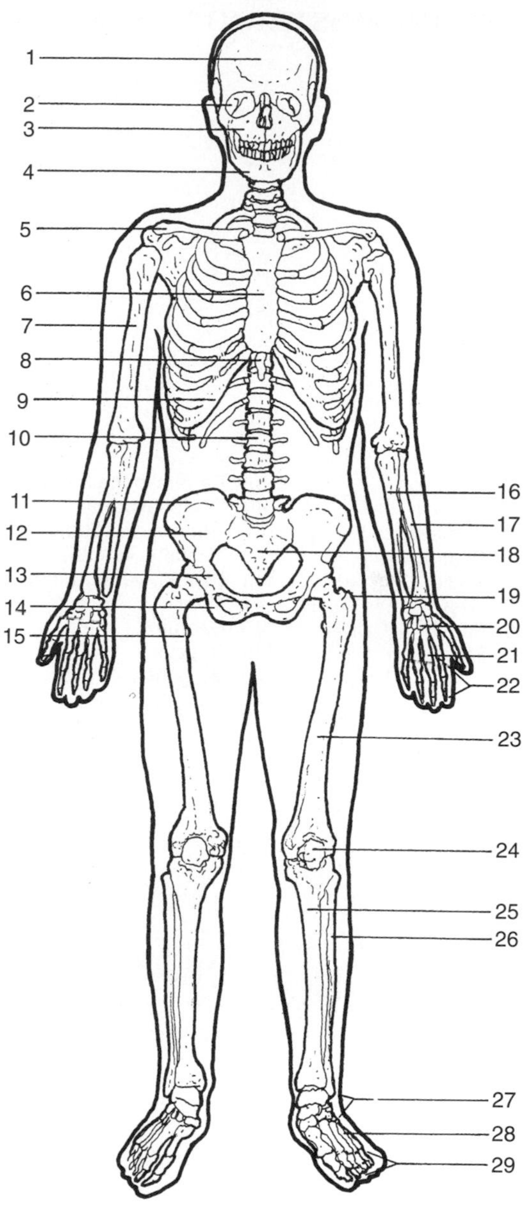
1
2
3
4
5
6
7
8
9
10
11
12
13
14
15
16
17
18
19
20
21
22
23
24
25
26
27
28
29

SKELETON—POSTERIOR VIEW

30 Acromion
31 Scapula
32 Humerus
33 Olecranon
34 Radius
35 Ulna
36 Femur
37 Fibula
38 Tibia
39 Parietal bone
40 Occipital bone
41 Cervical vertebrae (7)
42 Thoracic vertebrae (12)
43 Lumbar vertebrae (5)
44 Ilium
45 Sacrum
46 Coccyx
47 Ischium

Figure 7-2 Skeleton-posterior view. (Modified from Austrin MG, Austrin HR: *Learning medical terminology*, ed 9, St. Louis, 1998, Mosby.)

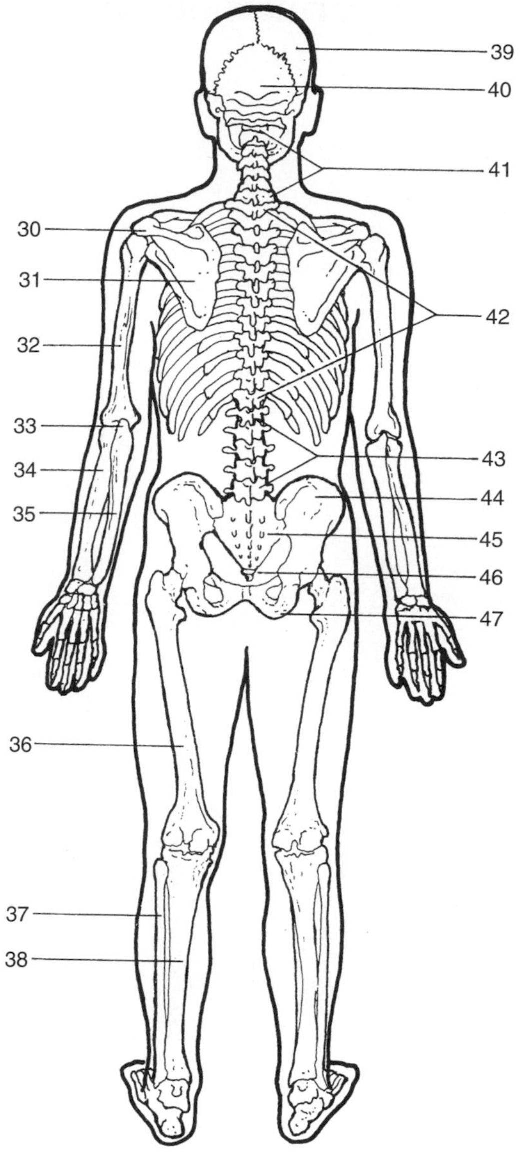
39
40
41
30
31
42
32
33
43
34
44
35
45
46
47
36
37
38

BONES AND SUTURES OF THE SKULL

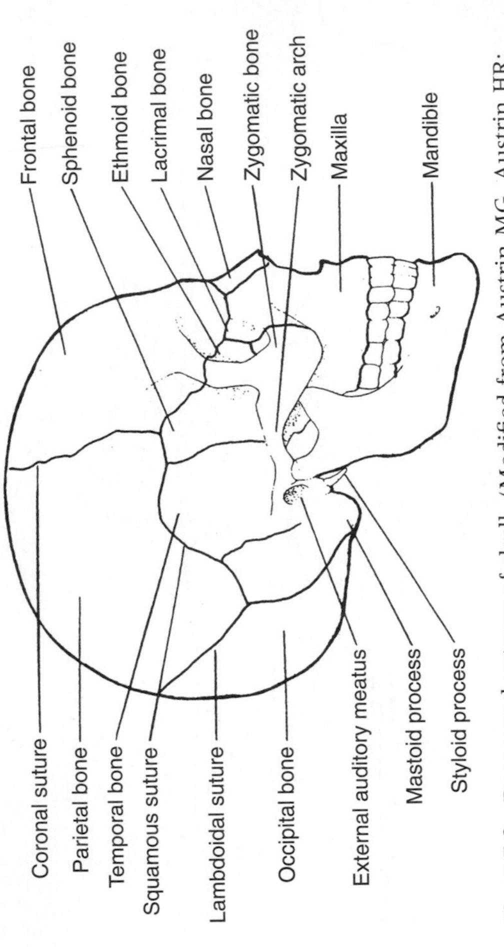

Figure 7-3 Bones and sutures of skull. (Modified from Austrin MG, Austrin HR: *Learning medical terminology*, ed 9, St. Louis, 1998, Mosby.)

TYPES OF FRACTURES

Closed simple Fracture does not break skin

Comminuted Bone is splintered into fragments

Compression Caused by compressive force; common in lumbar vertebrae

Depressed Broken skull bone driven inward

Displaced Fracture produces fragments that become misaligned

Greenstick Fracture in which one side of bone is broken and other side is bent

Impacted telescoped Bone is broken and also wedged into another break

Incomplete Continuity of the bone has not been completely destroyed

Longitudinal Break runs parallel with the bone

Oblique Fracture line runs at a 45-degree angle across the longitudinal axis

Open compound Fracture breaks through skin (can be categorized into grades 1 to 4 depending on severity)

Pathologic A disease process weakens bone structure so that a slight degree of trauma can cause fracture (most common in osteoporosis and cancers of the bone)

Segmental Fracture in two places (also called *double fracture*)

Silver-fork Fracture of lower end of radius

Spiral Break coils around the bone; can be caused by a twisting force

Transverse Fracture breaks across the bone at a 90-degree angle along the longitudinal axis

POSSIBLE COMPLICATIONS FROM FRACTURES

Complication	Early Clinical Signs
Pulmonary embolism	Substernal pain, dyspnea, rapid weak pulse; *may occur without symptoms*
Fat embolism	Mental confusion, restlessness, fever, tachycardia, dyspnea
Gas gangrene	Mental aberration, infection
Tetanus	Tonic twitching, difficulty opening mouth; *may occur without symptoms*
Infection	Pain, redness, swelling
Compartment syndrome	Deep localized pain, numbness, weakness
	Decreased circulation distal to the fracture

TYPES OF TRACTION

Traction is a process in which a steady pull is placed on a part or parts of the body. Traction can be used in reducing a fracture, maintaining a body position, immobilizing a limb, overcoming a muscle spasm, stretching an adhesion, and correcting deformities.

Countertraction A force that pulls against traction

Suspension traction A process to suspend a body part with use of frames, splints, slings, ropes, pulleys, and weights

Skin traction A process of applying wide bands directly to the skin and attaching weights to them; also called Buck's and Russell's

Buck's traction A process of applying a straight pull on the affected extremity; used for muscle spasms and to immobilize a limb

Russell's traction Knee is suspended in a sling to which a rope is attached; allows for some movement and permits flexion of the knee joint; often used with a femur fracture

Skeletal traction A process in which traction is applied directly to the bone. A wire or pin is inserted through the bone distal to the fracture.

Bryant's traction (Bryant's extension) Traction applied to the lower leg with the force pulling vertically, employed especially in fractures of the femur in infants and young children

Dunlop's traction Used on children with certain fractures of the upper arm, when the arm must be kept in a flexed position to prevent problems with the circulation and nerves around the elbow

TYPES OF SYNOVIAL JOINTS

Ball and socket Head of one bone fits into socket of another bone; has greatest range of motion. *Examples:* hip and shoulder

Hinge Convex end of one bone fits into concave end of another bone; movement is on one plane; joints can flex or extend. *Examples:* elbow, knee, ankle, fingers, and toes

Pivot Arch shaped; rotates only. *Examples:* C1 and C2 vertebrae

Saddle Convex bone fits into concave bone; movement is on two planes; joints can flex or extend and abduct or adduct. *Example:* thumb

Gliding Two flat bones move over each other. *Examples:* carpal, tarsal, clavicle, sternum, ribs, vertebrae, fibula, and tibia

Condyloid Oval; circular movement. *Example:* wrist

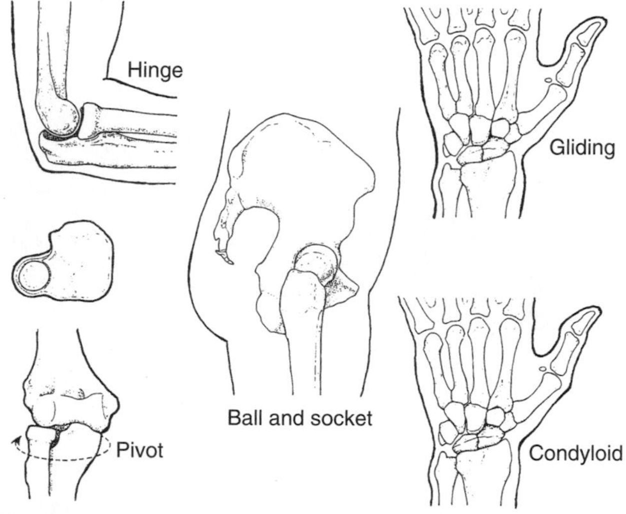

Figure 7-4 Synovial joints. (Modified from Austrin MG, Austrin HR: *Learning medical terminology,* ed 9, St. Louis, 1998, Mosby.)

Chapter 8

Muscular System

For an in-depth study of the muscular system, consult the following publications:

AJN/Mosby: *Nursing board's review for the NCLEX-RN examination*, ed 10, St. Louis, 1997, Mosby.

Austrin MG, Austrin HR: *Learning medical terminology,* ed 9, St. Louis, 1998, Mosby.

Lewis SM, Collier IC, Heitkemper MM: *Medical-surgical nursing*, ed 7, St. Louis, 2007, Mosby.

Patton KI, Thibodeau GA: *Handbook for anatomy and physiology*, St. Louis, 2000, Mosby.

Potter PA, Perry AG: *Fundamentals of nursing*, ed 7, St. Louis, 2008, Mosby.

Seidel HM, Benedict GW, Ball JW, Dains JE: *Mosby's guide to physical examination*, ed 6, St. Louis, 2006, Mosby.

ANTERIOR SUPERFICIAL MUSCLES

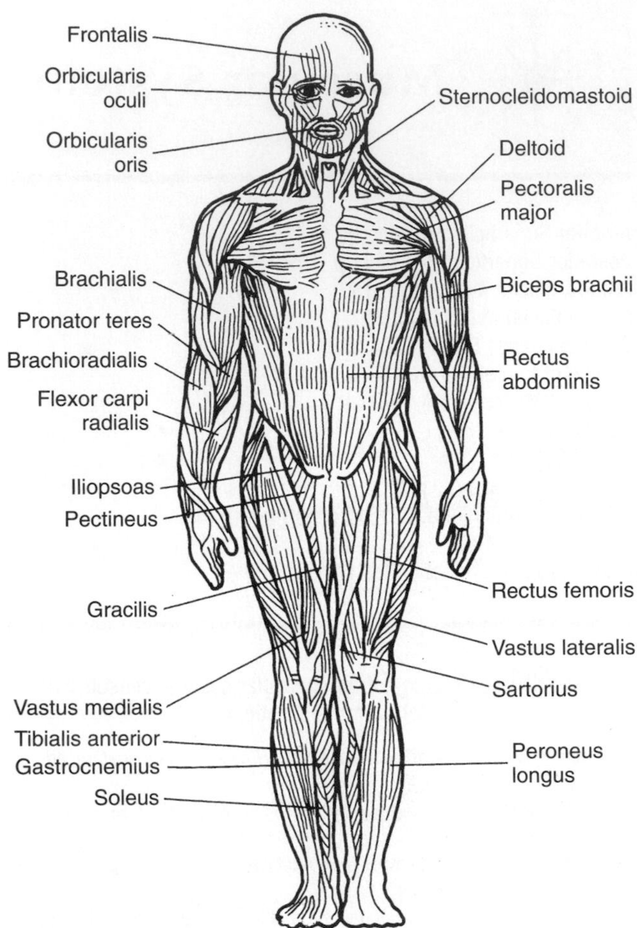

Figure 8-1 Anterior superficial muscles. (Modified from Austrin MG, Austrin HR: *Learning medical terminology,* ed 9, St. Louis, 1998, Mosby.)

POSTERIOR SUPERFICIAL MUSCLES

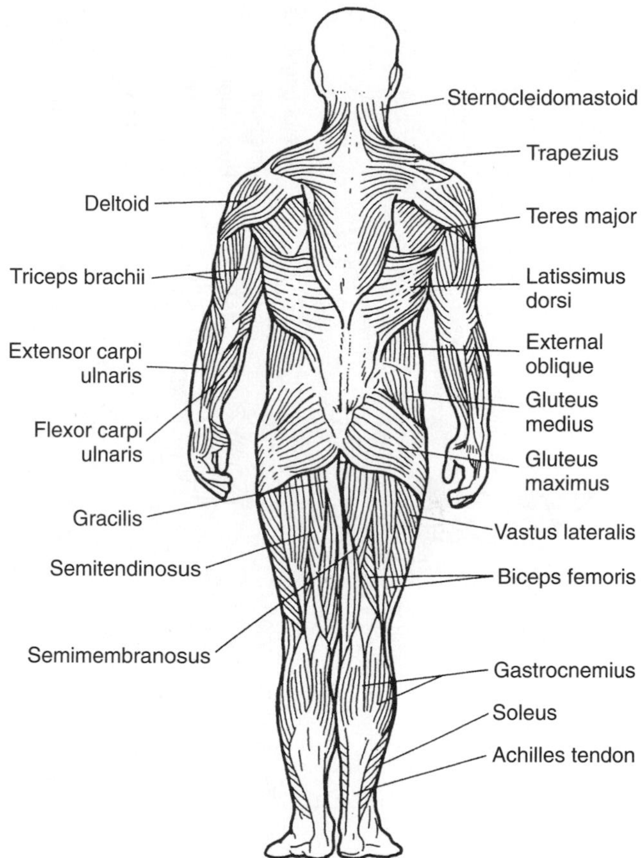

Figure 8-2 Posterior superficial muscles. (Modified from Austrin MG, Austrin HR: *Learning medical terminology,* ed 9, St. Louis, 1998, Mosby.)

ANTERIOR FACIAL MUSCLES

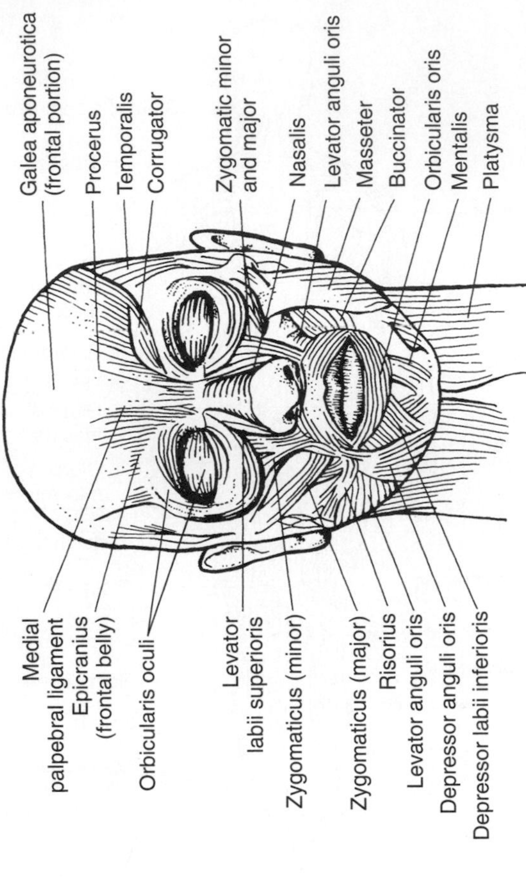

Figure 8-3 Anterior facial muscles. (Modified from Austrin MG, Austrin HR: *Learning medical terminology*, ed 9, St. Louis, 1998, Mosby.)

LATERAL FACIAL MUSCLES

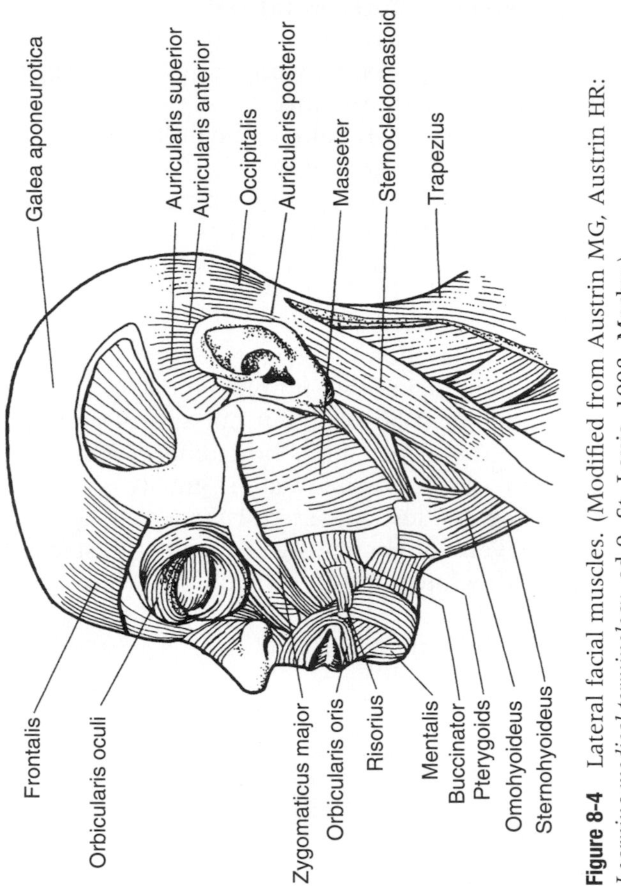

Figure 8-4 Lateral facial muscles. (Modified from Austrin MG, Austrin HR: *Learning medical terminology*, ed 9, St. Louis, 1998, Mosby.)

GRADING MUSCLE STRENGTH

Scale	Percent	Interpretation
5	100%	Normal
4	75	Full movement, but not against resistance
3	50	Normal movement against gravity
2	25	Movement if gravity eliminated
1	10	No movement
0	0	Paralysis

The "0/5 to 5/5" scale

- 0/5: no contraction
- 1/5: muscle flicker, but no movement
- 2/5: movement possible, but not against gravity
  NOTE: test the joint in its horizontal plane
- 3/5: movement possible against gravity
  NOTE: do not test against resistance
- 4/5: movement possible against some resistance
  NOTE: this category can be subdivided into $4^-/5$, 4/5, and $4^+/5$
- 5/5: normal strength

EFFECTS OF IMMOBILITY

Benefits

Decreased need for oxygen
Decreased metabolism and energy use
Reduced pain

Bowel Changes

Constipation caused by decreased peristalsis
Poorer sphincter and abdominal muscle tone

Cardiac Changes

Heart rate increase of one-half beat per day, caused by increased sympathetic activity
Decreased stroke volume and cardiac output caused by increased heart rate
Hypotension caused by vasodilatation, leading to thrombosis or edema

Integumentary Changes

Decreased turgor caused by fluid shifts
Increased decubitus ulcers caused by prolonged pressure
Increased skin atrophy caused by decreased nutrition

Metabolic Changes

Decreased metabolic rate
Increased catabolism (protein breakdown) leading to a negative nitrogen imbalance, which results in poorer healing
Hypoproteinemia leading to fluid shifts and edema

Musculoskeletal Changes

Decreased muscle strength of 20% per week
Decreased physical endurance and muscle mass
Muscle atrophy caused by decreased contractions
Osteoporosis caused by increased calcium extraction

Demineralization begins on second day of immobilization
Increased fractures caused by porous bones
Increased hypercalcemia
Muscle shortening leading to contracture

Respiratory Changes

Less alveoli expansion caused by less sighing
Increased mucus in lungs caused by less ability to clear them
Decreased chest movement restricts lung expansion
Stiff intercostal muscles caused by less stretching
Shallow respirations leading to decreased capacity
Increased secretions caused by supine position of lungs
Less oxygen leading to more carbon dioxide, which results in acidosis
Atelectasis caused by decreased blood flow

Neurosensory Changes

Decreased tactile sensation
Increased restlessness, drowsiness, and irritability
Increased confusion and disorientation caused by hypercalcemia

Urinary Changes

Poor emptying caused by positioning
Urinary stasis leading to more calcium in kidneys, leading to increased renal calculi
Urinary retention and distention caused by poor emptying
Incontinence caused by poor muscle tone
Inability to void caused by overstretching of the bladder
Infection caused by stasis and alkalinity
Urinary reflux caused by stasis, leading to infections

Range of Motion (ROM)

Type	Function	Examples
Flexion	Decrease angle	Bend elbow or knee, chin down, make fist, bend at waist or wrist, lift leg, bend toes
Extension	Increase angle	Straighten elbow or knee, chin straight, hands open, back, fingers, or toes straight
Hyperextension	Straighten joint beyond limits	Head tilted back, fingers pointed up
Abduction	Move away from midline	Legs or arms away from body, fingers spread apart
Adduction	Move toward midline	Legs together, arms at side, fingers together
Rotation	Move around axis	Circle of head, hand, foot, leg, arm, fingers, toes
Eversion	Turn joint outward	Foot or hand pointed away from the body
Inversion	Turn joint inward	Foot or hand pointed toward the body
Pronation	Move joint down	Palm downward, elbow inward
Supination	Move joint up	Palm upward, elbow outward

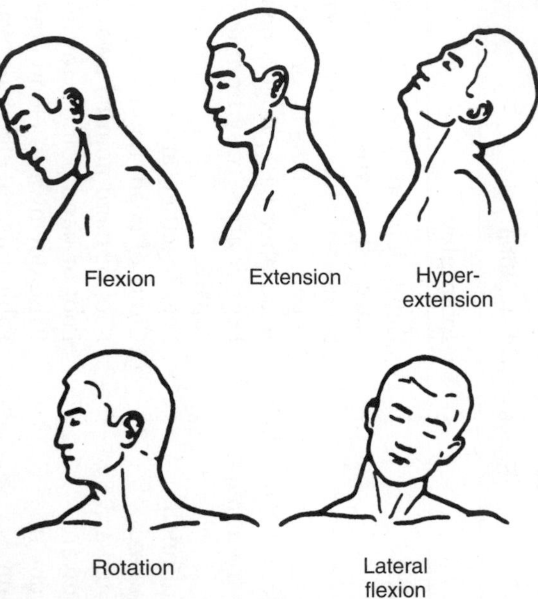

Figure 8-5 Range-of-motion exercises. (From Monahan F et al.: *Phipps' medical-surgical nursing: health and illness perspectives,* ed 8, St. Louis, 2007, Mosby.)

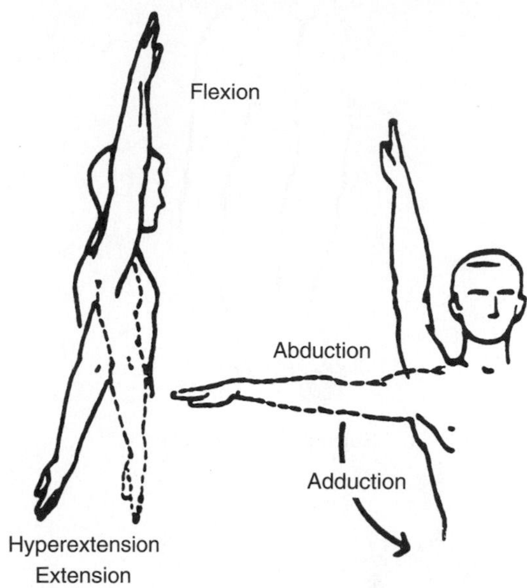

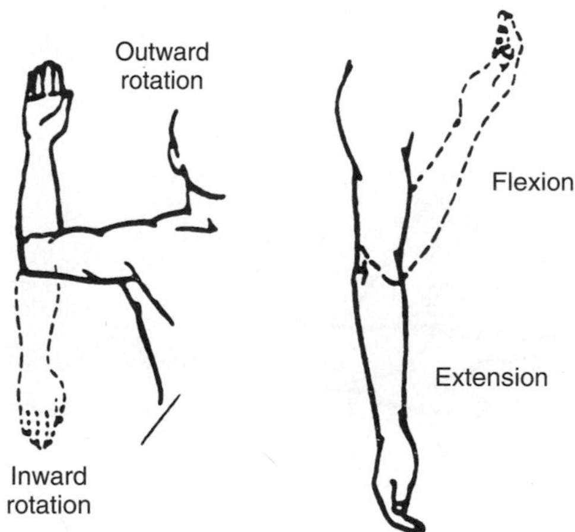

Figure 8-5, cont'd

Continued

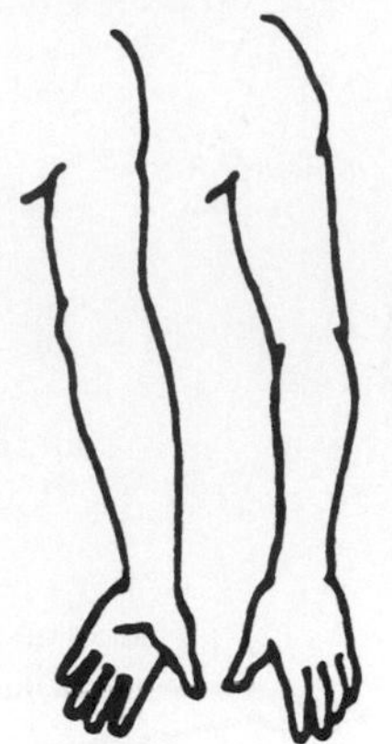

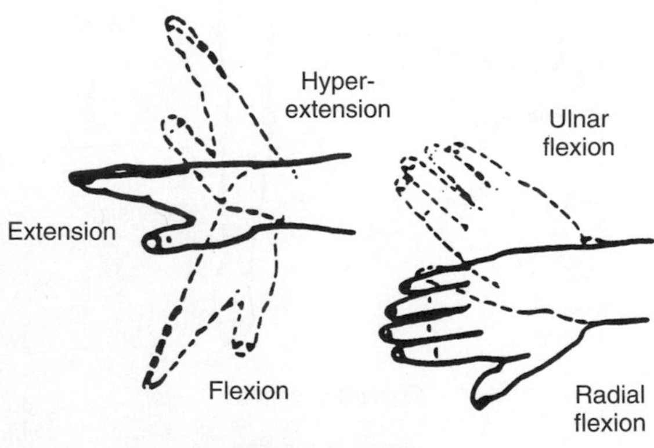

Figure 8-5, cont'd

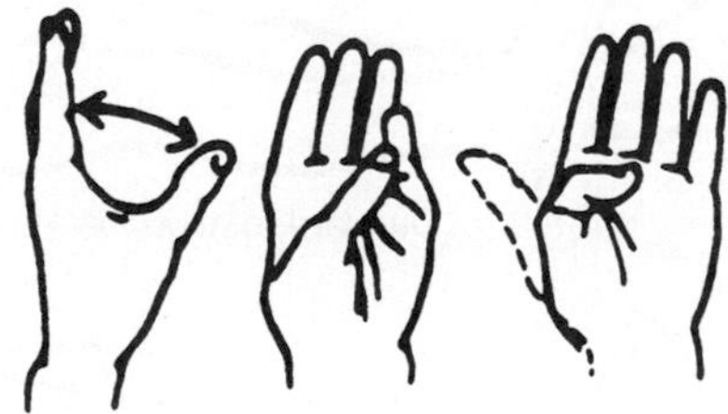

Figure 8-5, cont'd

Continued

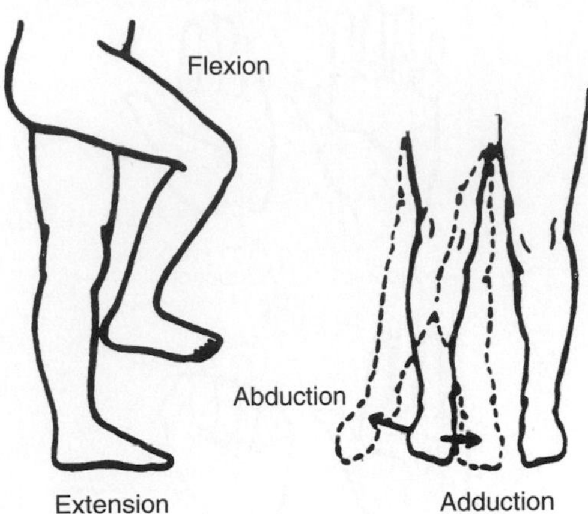

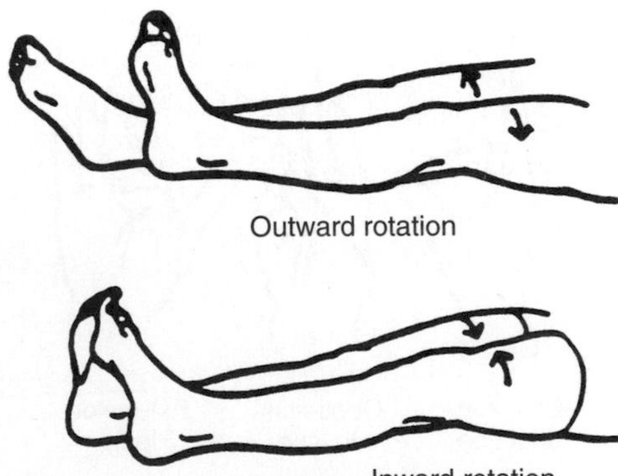

Figure 8-5, cont'd

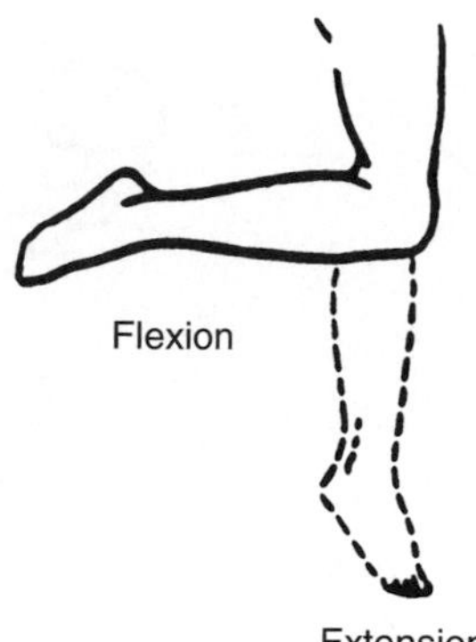

Figure 8-5, cont'd

Continued

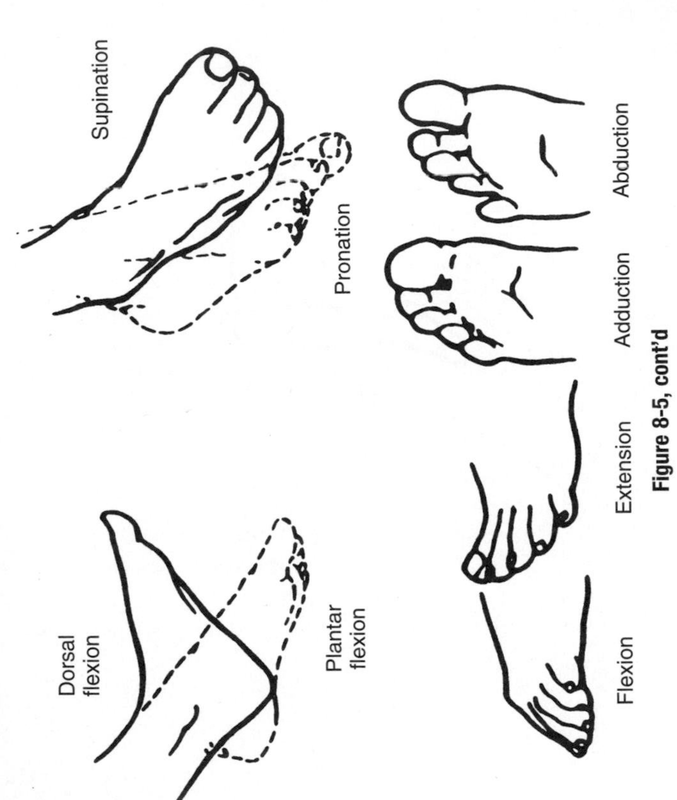

Figure 8-5, cont'd

USE OF HEAT*

Local Effects

Increased skin temperature
Vasodilatation, which increases oxygen and nutrients to area
Increased muscle relaxation
Decreased stiffness and spasm
Increased peristalsis

Indications

Stiffness
Arthritis
Pain

Contraindications

Trauma because of increased bleeding
Edema because of increased fluid retention
Malignant tumors because of increased cell growth
Burns because of increased cell damage
Open wounds because of increased bleeding
Acute areas such as appendix because of possible rupture
Testes because of destruction of sperm
Sensory-impaired clients because of increased chance of burns
Confused clients because of increased chance of injury

*The use of heat may require a physician's order, but may vary per facility policy.

USE OF COLD*

Local Effects

Vasoconstriction, which decreases oxygen to area
Decreased metabolism and thus decreased oxygen needs
Decreased fluid in area and thus decreased swelling
Decreased pain through numbness
Impaired circulation and increased cell death caused by lack of oxygen

Indications

Sprains
Fractures
Swelling
Bleeding

Contraindications

Open wounds because of decreased chance of healing
Impaired circulation because of increased chance of injury
Sensory-impaired clients because of increased chance of injury
Confused clients because of increased chance of injury

*The use of cold may require a physician's order, but may vary per facility policy.

GIVING A MASSAGE

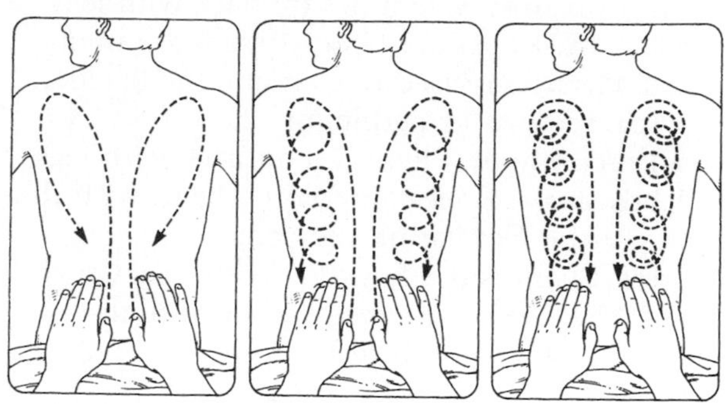

A MASSAGE TECHNIQUE

- Assess if massage is contraindicated.
- Start with the client lying flat or on his or her side.
- Begin with the forehead and work down the body.
- Use a gentle but firm touch.
- Always stroke toward the heart.
- Rub downward on the chest and back.
- Stroke upward on the arms.
- Use a light lotion or oil.

POSITIONING

Dorsal lithotomy Client lies on back with legs well apart. Knees are bent; stirrups are often used. Position is used to examine the bladder, vagina, rectum, or perineum.

Dorsal recumbent Client lies on back with legs slightly apart. Knees are slightly bent, with the soles of the feet flat on the bed.

Fowler's Client is partly sitting with knees slightly bent. The head of the bed can be at semi-Fowler's (45 degrees) or high Fowler's (90 degrees).

Knee-chest Client rests on knees and chest, with head turned to the side. Position is used to examine the rectum or vagina.

Left lateral Client lies on left side, hips closer to the edge of the bed.

Left Sims' Client lies on left side, with right knee bent against the abdomen. Used in rectal examinations and giving enemas.

Prone Client lies on abdomen with arms at sides.

Reverse Trendelenburg Client lies on back with legs together. Bed is straight, with head of bed higher than the foot.

Side lying Client's head is in straight line with spine. Use pillows to support head, arms, and upper leg.

Supine (horizontal recumbent) Client lies on back with legs together and extended.

Trendelenburg Client lies on back with legs together. Bed is straight, with head of bed lower than the foot. Used in pelvic surgery.

Positions for Examination

Position	Areas Assessed	Rationale	Limitations
Sitting	Head and neck, back, posterior thorax and lungs, anterior thorax and lungs, breasts, axillae, heart, vital signs, and upper extremities	Sitting upright provides full expansion of lungs and provides better visualization of symmetry of upper body parts.	Physically weakened client may be unable to sit. Examiner should use supine position with head of bed elevated instead.

From Potter PA, Perry AG: *Fundamentals of nursing*, ed 7, St. Louis, 2008, Mosby.

Continued

Positions for Examination—cont'd

Position	Areas Assessed	Rationale	Limitations
Supine	Head and neck, anterior thorax and lungs, breasts, axillae, heart, abdomen, extremities, pulses	This is the most normally relaxed position. It prevents contracture of abdominal muscles and provides easy access to pulse sites.	If client becomes short of breath easily, examiner may need to raise head of bed.
Dorsal recumbent	Head and neck, anterior thorax and lungs, breasts, axillae, heart	Clients with painful disorders are more comfortable with knees flexed.	Position is not used for abdominal assessment because it promotes contracture of abdominal muscles.

Lithotomy	Female genitalia and genital tract	This position provides maximal exposure of genitalia and facilitates insertion of vaginal speculum.	Lithotomy position is embarrassing and uncomfortable, so examiner minimizes time that client spends in it. Client is kept well draped. Client with severe arthritis or other joint deformity may be unable to assume this position.
Sims'	Rectum and vagina	Flexion of hip and knee improves exposure of rectal area.	Joint deformities may hinder client's ability to bend hip and knee.

Continued

Positions for Examination —cont'd

Position	Areas Assessed	Rationale	Limitations
Prone	Musculoskeletal system	This position is used only to assess extension of hip joint.	This position is intolerable for client with respiratory difficulties.
Knee-chest	Rectum	This position provides maximal exposure of rectal area.	This position is embarrassing and uncomfortable. Clients with arthritis or other joint deformities may be unable to assume this position.

Chapter 9

Nervous System

For an in-depth study of the nervous system, consult the following publications:

Lewis SM, Collier IC, Heitkemper MM: *Medical-surgical nursing*, ed 7, St. Louis, 2007, Mosby.

Potter PA, Perry AG: *Fundamentals of nursing*, ed 7, St. Louis, 2008, Mosby.

STRUCTURES OF THE BRAIN

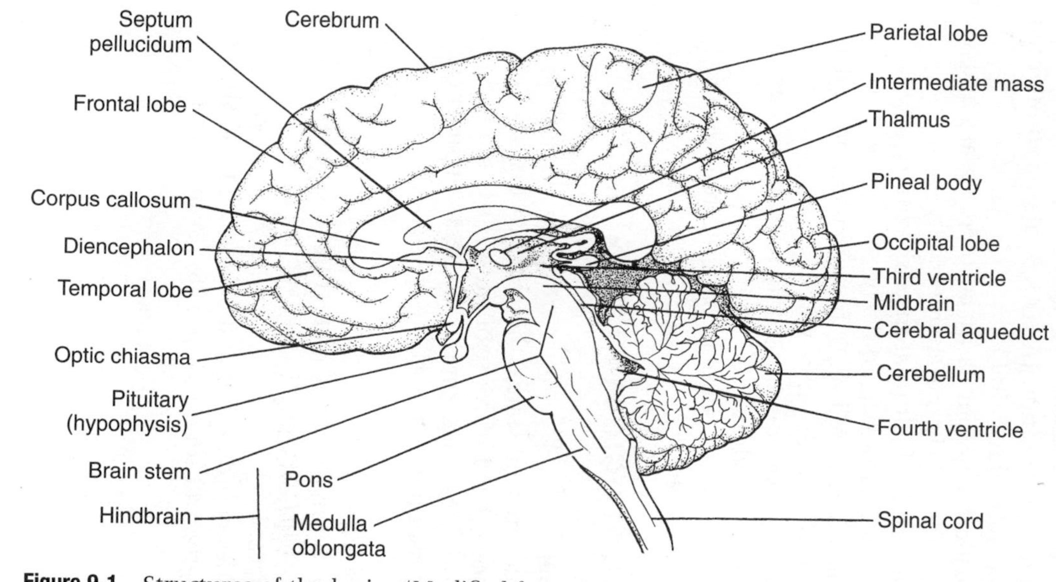

Figure 9-1 Structures of the brain. (Modified from Austrin MG, Austrin HR: *Learning medical terminology*, ed 9, St. Louis, 1998, Mosby.)

LEVELS OF CONSCIOUSNESS

Alert Awake and aware, responds appropriately, begins conversation (A&O × 3: alert and oriented to person, place, time)

Lethargic Sleeps but easily aroused, speaks and responds slowly but appropriately

Obtunded Difficult to arouse, slow to respond, and returns to sleep quickly

Stuporous Aroused only through pain; no verbal response, never fully awake

Semicomatose Responds only to pain but has gag and blink reflexes

Comatose No response to pain; no reflexes or muscle tone

NEUROLOGIC FUNCTION

Cerebral

Includes mental status, thought processes, emotions, level of consciousness, orientation, memory language, appropriateness, intelligence, and developmental age

Cranial Nerves

For a summary of the cranial nerves, see p. 191

Cerebellar

Includes coordination and balance; muscle size, strength, and tone (see p. 158); evaluation of reflexes

Glasgow Coma Scale

		Response
Best Eye Opening Response (Record "C" if eyes closed by swelling)	Spontaneously	4
	To speech	3
	To pain	2
	No response	1
Best Motor Response to Painful Stimuli (Record best upper limb response)	Obeys verbal command	6
	Localizes pain	5
	Flexion-withdrawal	4
	Flexion-abnormal	3
	Extension-abnormal	2
	No response	1
Best Verbal Response (Record "E" if endotracheal tube in place; "T" if tracheostomy tube in place)	Oriented × 3	5
	Conversation confused	4
	Speech inappropriate	3
	Sounds incomprehensible	2
	No response	1

Modified from Thompson JM et al.: *Mosby's clinical nursing*, ed 5, St. Louis, 2002, Mosby.

WARNING SIGNS OF IMPENDING STROKE

- Numbness of face, arm, or leg
- Weakness of face, arm, or leg
- Difficult speaking or understanding
- Sudden decreased or blurred vision
- Loss of balance
- Dizziness when accompanied by any of the above signs

Neurologic Deficits by Location

Location	Possible Deficit	Nursing Interventions
Frontal lobe	Weakness with plegia	Assess function, PT/OT
	Expressive aphasia	Assess for speech therapy
	Focal or grand mal seizures	Educate family on seizures
	Impaired thought, reasoning and memory, emotional or personality changes	Coordinate neuropsychologic evaluation
Temporal lobe	Visual field loss, impaired memory	Assess visual problems
	Temporal lobe seizures	Monitor for seizures
	Receptive aphasia, dysnomia	Assess speech impairment

Parietal lobe	Sensory deficits, impaired joint position, vibration, light touch Impaired left-right discrimination Sensory seizures, visual field loss	Assess level of neglect Refer to PT/OT for assistance Educate family regarding deficits Monitor for seizures
Occipital lobe	Visual hallucinations Seizures	Refer to ophthamologist if needed Monitor for seizures Educate and support family
Cerebellum	Decreased coordination, ataxia Nystagmus, increased headaches Increased intracranial pressure	Assess level of deficit Educate and support client Monitor headaches
Brainstem	Cranial nerve palsies, ataxia Sensory or motor impairment Sudden death	Assess level of deficit Safety precautions Educate and support family

PT, Physical therapy; *OT,* occupational therapy.

SEIZURE TERMINOLOGY

Seizure Abnormal electrical activity in the brain

Epilepsy Recurrent unprovoked seizures

Generalized Tonic-Clonic Seizure Previously called *Grand Mal. Tonic* means stiffening and *Clonic* means rhythmic shaking. There is abnormal electrical activity affecting the whole brain (thus the term "generalized").

Partial Seizure Sometimes confused with *Petit Mal.* Only a part of the brain is affected.

Simple Partial The patient remains alert and is behaving appropriately.

Complex Partial The person is conscious but impaired.

Absence Seizure Previously called *Petit Mal.* This is a generalized seizure *without* shaking.

Post-ictal state The period following a generalized or partial seizure, during which the person usually feels sleepy or confused.

Aura A warning of a seizure. Actually, the aura is an early part of the seizure itself.

Febrile seizures Generally occur in infants and young children; they are most often generalized tonic-clonic seizures. They typically occur in children with a high fever, usually higher than 102°.

Status epilepticus (SE) A state of continuous or frequently reoccurring seizures lasting 30 minutes or more.

CARE OF THE CLIENT WITH SEIZURES

Equipment and Procedures

Bed should be in the lowest position.
Side rails should be *up* and padded.
Oxygen and suction equipment should be nearby.
Indicate "seizure precautions" on plan of care.
Note if client has an aura before seizures.
Use digital thermometers, NOT glass thermometers.
Clients should shower rather than use a tub.
Always transport the client with portable oxygen.
Client with frequent generalized atonic seizures should wear a helmet.

During the Seizure

Call for help, but DO NOT try to restrain the person.
Time the seizure.
STAY WITH THE PERSON.
Help the person to lie down. Place something soft under the head.
Turn the person on his or her side if possible.
Remove glasses and loosen tight clothing.
DO NOT place anything between the teeth.
DO NOT attempt to remove dentures.
Monitor the duration of the seizure and the type of movement.

After the Seizure

Turn the person to one side to allow saliva to drain; suction if needed.
Perform vital signs and neurologic checks as needed.
DO NOT offer food or drink until fully awake.
Reorient the person.
Notify physician *unless* person is being monitored specifically for seizures.
Notify physician *immediately* if seizure occurs without regaining consciousness or if an injury occurs.
Record all observations.

Document the time and length of the seizure and if there was an aura.

Document the sequence of behaviors during the seizures (eye movement and so forth).

Document an injury and what was done about it.

Note what happened with the person just after the seizure (did he or she reorient?).

A CLIENT'S SLEEP HISTORY

- Have the client describe his or her specific problem.
- Have the client describe his or her symptoms and alleviating factors.
- Assess the client's normal sleep pattern.
- Assess the client's normal bedtime rituals.
- Assess for current or recent physical illnesses.
- Assess for current or recent emotional stress.
- Assess for possible sleep disorders.
- Assess the client's current medications and their possible effects on sleep.

SLEEP DISORDERS

Bruxism Tooth grinding during sleep

Insomnia Chronic difficulty with sleep patterns

Initial insomnia Difficulty falling asleep

Intermittent insomnia Difficulty remaining asleep

Terminal insomnia Difficulty going back to sleep

Narcolepsy Difficulty in regulating between sleep and awake states; person may fall asleep without warning

Nocturnal enuresis Bedwetting

Sleep apnea Intermittent periods of cessation of breathing during sleep

Sleep deprivation Decrease in the amount and quality of sleep

Somnambulism Sleepwalking, night terrors, or nightmares

Drugs and Their Adverse Effects on Sleep

Hypnotics

- Interfere with reaching deep sleep stages
- Only temporary increase in quantity of sleep
- May cause "hangover" during day
- Excess drowsiness, confusion, decreased energy
- May worsen sleep apnea in older adults

Diuretics

- Cause nocturia

Antidepressants and Stimulants

- Suppress rapid eye movement (REM) sleep

Alcohol

- Speeds onset of sleep
- Disrupts REM sleep
- Awakens person during night and causes difficulty returning to sleep

Caffeine

- Prevents person from falling asleep
- May cause person to awaken during night

Continued

Drugs and Their Adverse Effects on Sleep—cont'd

Nonbenzodiazepines

- Anxiety and irritability
- Sleep walking, eating, or driving

Digoxin

- Causes nightmares

Beta-Blockers

- Cause nightmares
- Cause insomnia
- Cause awakening from sleep

Valium

- Decreases stages 2 and 4 and REM sleep
- Decreases awakenings

Narcotics (Morphine/Meperidine [Demerol])

- Suppress REM sleep
- If discontinued quickly, can increase risk of cardiac dysrhythmias because of "rebound REM" periods
- Cause increased awakenings and drowsiness

From Potter PA, Perry AG: *Fundamentals of nursing*, ed 7, St Louis, 2008, Mosby.

SEDATION SCALE

S = Sleepy, but easy to arouse
1 = Awake and alert
2 = Slightly drowsy, but easy to arouse
3 = Drowsy, drifts to sleep during conversation
4 = Somnolent, minimal or no response to physical stimulation

Modified from McCaffery M, Pasero C: *Pain: clinical manual*, ed 2, p. 267, St. Louis, 1999, Mosby.

PERIPHERAL NERVES

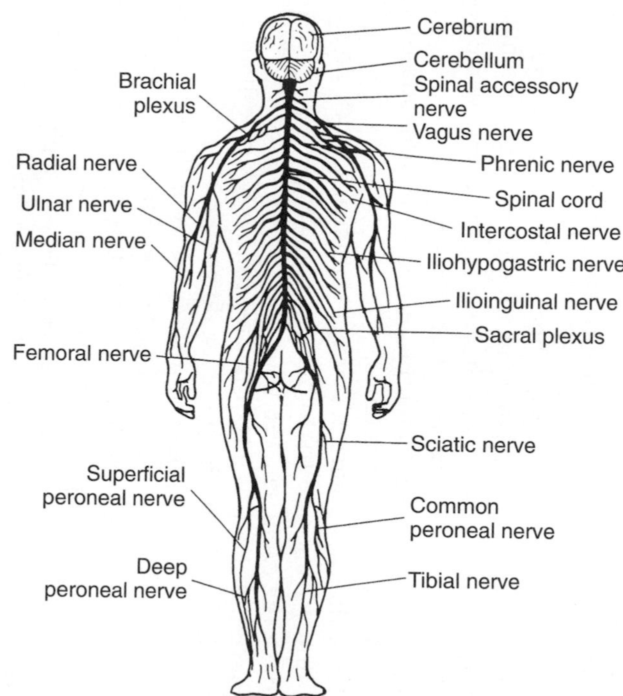

Figure 9-2 Peripheral nervous system, with some cranial nerves. (Modified from Austrin MG, Austrin HR: *Learning medical terminology*, ed 9, St. Louis, 1998, Mosby.)

Assessing Motor Function	
Level of Spinal Cord	**Assessment: Note Response to the Items Below**
C4 to C5	Have the client shrug his or her shoulders against your hands, or apply resistance by pushing downward on the client's shoulders.
C5 to C6	Have the client flex his or her arm at the elbow while you apply resistance by pushing the arm away from the client.
C7	Have the client straighten his or her flexed arm and try to keep it flexed while you apply resistance.
	Have the client pinch his or her thumb and index finger together and hold firmly while you try to pull them apart.
C8 to T1	Have the client squeeze your fingers.
L2 to L4	Have the client lift his or her leg from a lying position while you apply resistance by pushing the leg down.
	Have the client extend his or her leg from the knee-flexed position while you apply resistance to keep the knee flexed.
L5	Have the client dorsiflex his or her feet upward while you apply resistance to the dorsal aspects of the feet.
L5 to S1	Have the client bend at the knee while you apply resistance against the move.
S1	Have the client plantar flex the feet downward while you apply resistance to the plantar aspects of the feet.

Cranial Nerves

Number	Name	Type	Function	Method of Assessment
I	Olfactory	Sensory	Smell	Identify odors
II	Optic	Sensory	Vision	Snellen chart
III	Oculomotor	Motor	Vision	Pupil reaction
IV	Trochlear	Motor	Vision	Vertical vision
		Sensory	Cornea	Blink reflex
V	Trigeminal	Motor	Chewing	Clench teeth
VI	Abducens	Motor	Vision	Lateral vision
VII	Facial	Sensory	Taste	Identify tastes
		Motor	Expression	Smile/frown
VIII	Acoustic	Sensory	Equilibrium	Weber's and Rinne tests
IX	Glossopharyngeal	Sensory	Taste	Identify tastes
		Motor	Swallowing	Gag reflex
X	Vagus	Sensory	Pharynx	Identify tastes
		Motor	Vocal	Voice tones
XI	Accessory	Motor	Shoulders	Shrug shoulders
XII	Hypoglossal	Motor	Tongue	Protruding tongue

Types of Reflexes		
Name	**Elicited by**	**Proper Response**
Babinski	Stroking lateral sole of foot	Great toe fans out
Chaddock	Stroking below lateral malleolus	Great toe fans out
Oppenheim	Stroking tibial surface	Great toe fans out
Gordon	Squeezing calf muscle	Great toe fans out
Hoffmann	Flicking middle finger down	Flexion of the thumb
Ankle clonus	Brisk dorsiflexion of foot with knee flexed	Up and down movement of the foot
Kernig	Straightening leg with thigh muscle flexed	Pain along posterior of thigh
Brudzinski	Flexing chin on chest	Limitations with pain

REFLEX GRADING SCALE

Grade	Symbol	Interpretation
5	5+	Hyperactive (with clonus)
4	4+	Hyperactive (very brisk)
3	3+	Brisk
2	2+	Normal (average)
1	1+	Diminished but present
0	0	Absent

PAIN ASSESSMENT

Gather information about the client's condition in the following areas:

Definition

The words used by the client to describe pain, such as pressure, stabbing, sharp, tingling, dull, heavy, or cold. It is important to use and understand the client's language concerning pain and to believe the client who reports pain.

Onset

When did the pain first begin (date and time)?

Duration

How long does the pain last (persistent, minutes to hours, comes and goes, seconds)? Does the pain occur at the same time each day?

Location

In what area of the body does the pain begin? It may be helpful to have the client point to the exact area if possible. NOTE: A client may say the pain is in the stomach but may point over the lower abdominal area. Also ask if the pain radiates, moves, or goes to a different area of the body. Have the client point to these areas as well.

Severity

How bad is the pain? Or have the client rate the pain. Have a rating scale ready to use and explain your scale. Use the same scale in subsequent assessments. *Examples:* A 0 to 10 scale with 0 being no pain and 10 being the worst pain, or a color scale with blue being no pain and red being the worst pain.

Precipitating Factors

What was the client doing before the pain began (exercise, bending over, work)?

Aggravating Factors

What makes the pain worse?

Alleviating Factors

What makes the pain get better or go away (pain medications, relaxation, rest, music)?

Associated Factors

Nausea or vomiting?
Anger or agitation?
Depression or drowsiness?
Fatigue or sleeplessness?

Observed Behaviors

Agitation or restlessness?
Bracing or fidgeting?
Rubbing or guarding?
Not eating or sleeping?

Vocalizations

Crying or moaning?
Gasping or groaning?
Sighing or noisy breathing?

Facial Expressions

Grimacing or clenched teeth?
Wincing or furrowed brow?
Sadness or eyes closed?
Frightened or tightened lips?

PAIN RATING SCALES

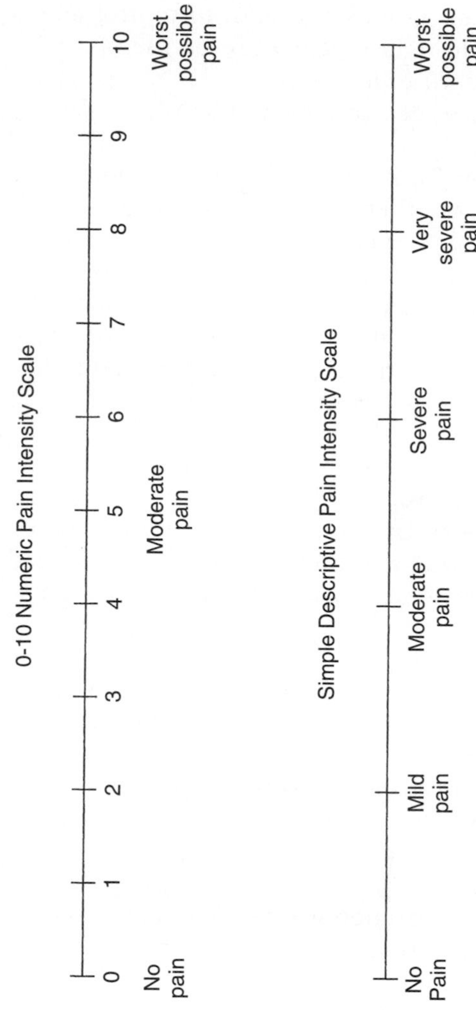

Figure 9-3 Pain rating scales. (Modified from Austrin MG, Austrin HR: *Learning medical terminology*, ed 9, St. Louis, 1998, Mosby.)

NONPHARMACOLOGIC TREATMENTS OF PAIN

Biofeedback Clients can learn to control muscle tension to reduce pain with the use of biofeedback units.

Cold Used to decrease pain or swelling (see p. 170).

Distraction Turning the client's attention to something other than the pain, such as music, visitors, or scenery.

Heat Used to decrease tension (see p. 169).

Imagery Uses the client's imagination to create pleasant mental pictures. These pictures are a form of distraction. This activity is said to be a form of self-hypnosis.

Massage See p. 171.

Menthol Used to increase blood circulation to painful areas.

Nerve blocks Used to block severe, unrelieved pain. A local anesthetic, sometimes combined with cortisone, is injected into or around a nerve.

Positioning See p. 172.

Pressure Used to stimulate blood flow to painful areas. Apply firm but not excess pressure for 10 to 60 seconds.

Range of motion exercises See p. 161.

Relaxation Relieves pain by reducing muscle tension. Music or relaxation tapes may be helpful.

TENS (transcutaneous electric nerve stimulation) A mild electric current is thought to interrupt pain impulses.

Vibration Used to simulate blood flow to painful areas.

CHRONIC NONMALIGNANT PAIN: NURSING CARE GUIDELINES*

Do not argue with the client about whether the client is in pain.

Do not refer to the client as a narcotics addict.

Do not tell the client that he or she will become an addict if he or she continues to receive narcotics.

Do not use a placebo to try to determine if the client has "real" pain.

Be alert to any changes in the client's pain condition or pain regimen.

Recognize the differences between acute and chronic pain.

Avoid sudden withdrawal of narcotics or sedatives from a client with chronic pain.

When analgesics are required, give them orally if possible. (The effects of oral analgesics will generally last longer than IV or IM medications.)

Review analgesics being used for relief of chronic versus acute pain.

Offer pain relief alternatives (See p. 196).

Review the client's support systems and suggest additional ones if appropriate.

Help those living with the client to understand the client's pain management routine.

Assess the client for depression, anxiety, and stress. (Additional stresses may add to the client's overall pain experience.)

Assess suicidal risk.

*Modified from McCaffery M, Beebe A: *Pain clinical manual for nursing practice,* ed 2, St. Louis, 1999, Mosby.

Average Adult Doses for Analgesics

Drug	IM Dose (mg/mL)	Oral Dose (mg)*	Half-Life (hr)	Duration (hr)
Aspirin	—	500–1000	15–30 min	4–6
Acetaminophen	—	500–1000	2–3	4–6
Ibuprofen	—	400–800	1.8–2.5	4–6
Salicylate (e.g., Trilisate)	—	500–1000	1–4	6–12
Naproxen	—	500	2–3	6–8
Indomethacin	—	25–75	4–6	8–12
Ketorolac	30–60	10–20	2–3	6
	15–30	—	2–3	6
Celecox (Celebrex)	—	200–400	8–12	24
Diclofenac (Voltaren)	—	50–200	2–3	4–6
Fenoprofen (Nalfon)	—	200–600	30 min	4–6
Fentanyl	.05–.10	Oralet 5 mcg/kg	8 min	1–2
Nabumetone (Relafen)	—	500–750	22–30	—
Piroxicam (Feldene)	—	10–20	30–60	48–72

Oxycodone with acetaminophen (Percocet)	—	5	2–3	4–6
Propoxyphene (Darvon)	—	32–65	1–2	4–6
Levorphanol	2	2–4	2–4	4–8
Morphine	2–15	10–60	1–3	3–7
Codeine	30–60	15–60	2–4	4–6
Hydromorphone (Dilaudid)	1–4	1–10	2–3	4–5
Meperidine (Demerol)	50–100	50–150	1–2	2–4
Methadone	2.5–10	5–40	1–3	4–6
Tramadol (Ultram)	—	50–100	6–8	3–7

Data from *Drug Facts & Comparisons,* St. Louis, 2002. Facts & Comparisons; *Physician's desk reference,* ed 54, Montvale, NJ, 2000, Medical Economics.

*Oral dose = usual dosage range for single dose.

THE EYE

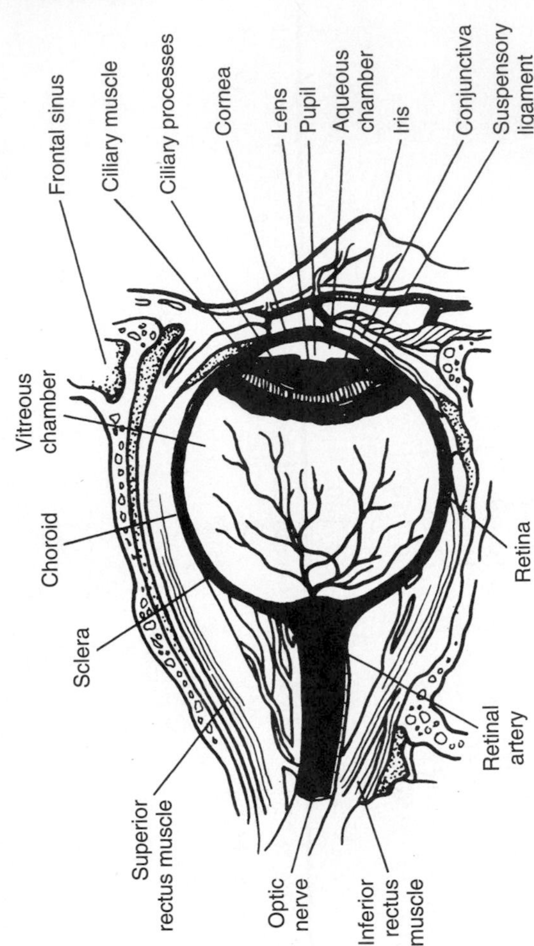

Figure 9-4 Structures of the eye. (Modified from Austrin MG, Austrin HR: *Learning medical terminology*, ed 9, St. Louis, 1998, Mosby.)

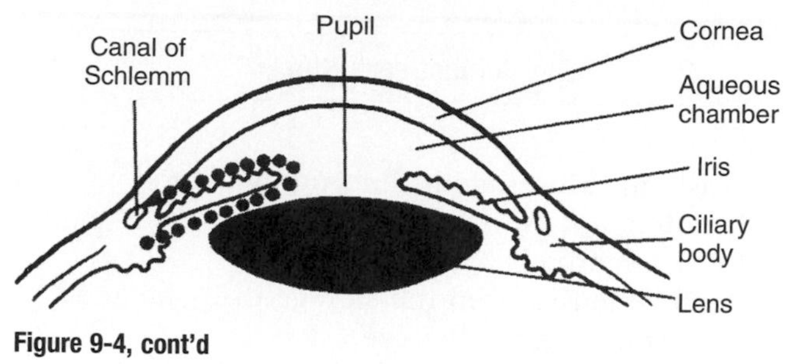

Figure 9-4, cont'd

PUPIL SIZE

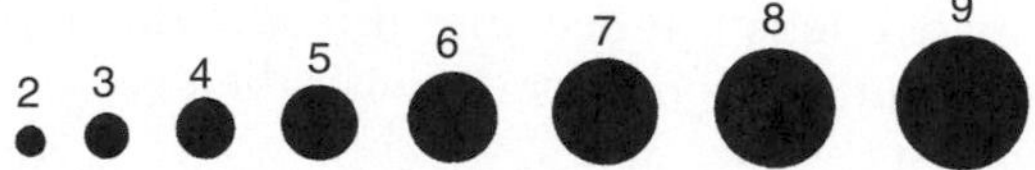

Figure 9-5 Chart showing pupil sizes in millimeters. (From Potter PA, Perry AG: *Fundamentals of nursing*, ed 7, St. Louis, 2008, Mosby.)

Contact Lens Care

Do

- Wash and rinse hands thoroughly before handling a lens.
- Keep fingernails clean and short.
- Remove lenses from the storage case one at a time and place on the eye.
- Start with the same lens (left or right) each time of insertion.
- Use lens placement technique learned from eye specialist.
- Use proper lens care products.
- Wear lenses daily and follow the prescribed wearing schedule.
- Remove a lens if it becomes uncomfortable.
- Keep regular appointments with the eye specialist.
- Remove lenses during sunbathing, showering, or swimming.

Do Not

- Use soaps that contain cream or perfume for cleaning lenses.
- Let fingernails touch lenses.
- Mix up lenses.
- Exceed prescribed wearing time.
- Use saliva to wet lenses.
- Use homemade saline solution or tap water to wet or clean lenses.
- Borrow or mix lens care solution.

From Potter PA, Perry AG: *Fundamentals of nursing*, ed 7, St. Louis, 2008, Mosby.

BRAILLE ALPHABET

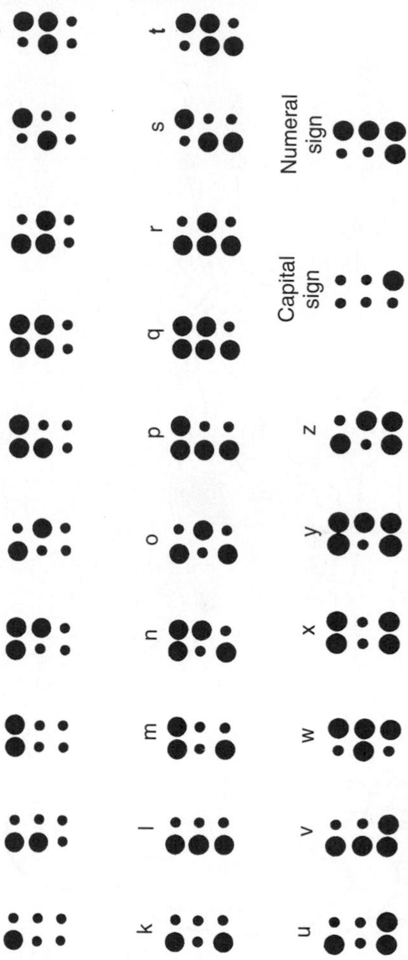

Figure 9-6 Braille alphabet. (From Sorrentino SA: *Mosby's textbook for nursing assistants,* ed 7, St. Louis, 2008, Mosby.)

THE EAR

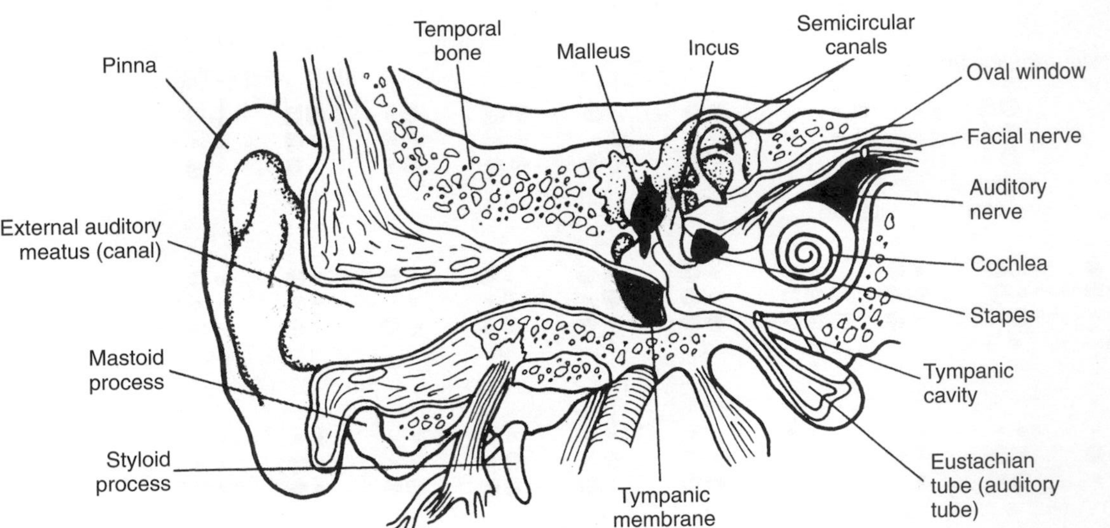

Figure 9-7 Structures of the ear. (From Austrin MG, Austrin HR: *Learning medical terminology*, ed 9, St. Louis, 1998, Mosby.)

Assessing Client's Use of Sensory Aids

Eyeglasses

- Purpose for wearing glasses (e.g., reading distance, or both)
- Methods used to clean glasses
- Presence of symptoms (e.g., blurred vision, photophobia, headaches, irritation)

Contact Lenses

- Type of lens worn
- Frequency and duration of time lenses are worn (including sleep time)
- Presence of symptoms (e.g., burning, excess tearing, redness, irritation, swelling, sensitivity to light)
- Techniques used by the client to clean, store, insert, and remove lenses
- Use of eyedrops or ointments
- Use of emergency identification bracelet or card that warns others to remove client's lenses in case of emergency

Artificial Eye

- Method used to insert and remove eye
- Method for cleaning eye
- Presence of symptoms (e.g., drainage, inflammation, pain involving the orbit)

Hearing Aid

- Type of aid worn
- Methods used to clean aid
- Client's ability to change battery and adjust hearing-aid volume

From Potter PA, Perry AG: *Fundamentals of nursing,* ed 7, St. Louis, 2008, Mosby.

SIGN LANGUAGE ALPHABET

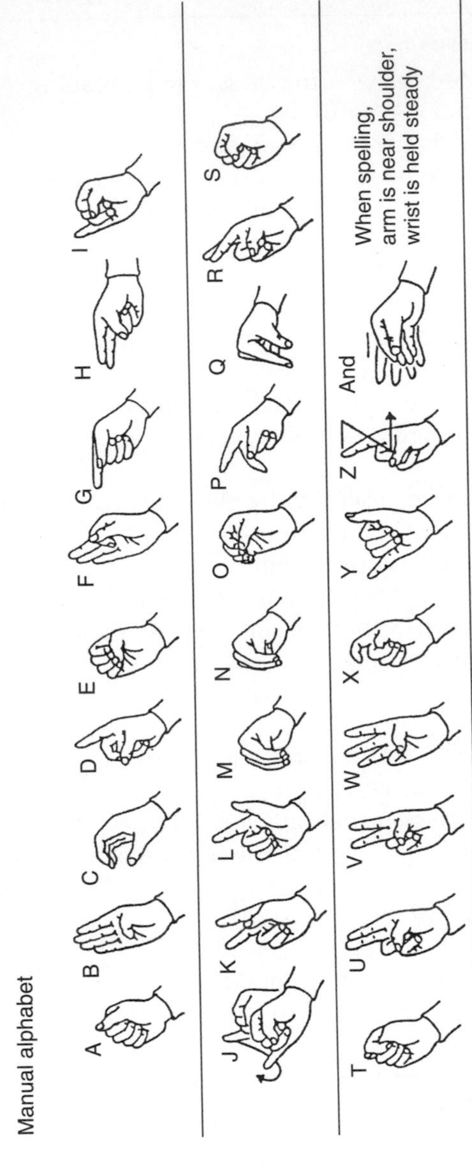

Figure 9-8 Sign language alphabet.

SIGN LANGUAGE NUMBERS

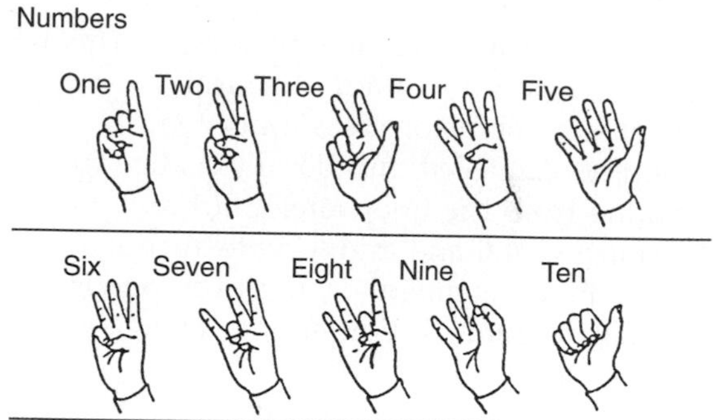

Figure 9-9 Sign language numbers.

TIPS FOR COMMUNICATING WITH OLDER ADULTS

- First, get the person's attention. This will help if the person is hard of hearing.
- Sit face to face. Lip reading may be helpful.
- Appropriate lighting is important. Avoid glare and dimly lit areas.
- Maintain good eye contact. This will help to instill trust.
- Speak slowly and clearly. This will help if the person is hard of hearing.
- Use short simple words and phrases.
- Ask one question at a time. This may help with sensory overload.
- Give the person extra time to answer. This will help if the person is hard of hearing.
- Repeat statements or ideas if needed.
- Rephrase, if needed, but do not change the meaning from the first statement.
- Minimize visual and auditory distractions.
- Do not shout. Remember, not everyone is deaf.
- Summarize points if you are not being understood.
- Expect errors or emotional outbursts in a confused person.
- You may need to restart the conversation.
- You may need to stop the conversation if the person is unable to communicate.

Chapter 10

Circulatory System

For an in-depth study of the circulatory system, consult the following publications:

Austrin MG, Austrin HR: *Learning medical terminology*, ed 9, St. Louis, 1998, Mosby.

Guzzetta CE, Dossey BM: *Cardiovascular nursing: holistic practice*, St. Louis, 1992, Mosby.

Lewis SM, Collier IC, Heitkemper MM: *Medical-surgical nursing*, ed 7, St. Louis, 2007, Mosby.

Potter PA, Perry AG: *Fundamentals of nursing*, ed 7, St. Louis, 2008, Mosby.

PRINCIPAL ARTERIES OF THE BODY

1 Angular
2 Right common carotid
3 Brachiocephalic
4 Arch of aorta
5 Right coronary
6 Left coronary
7 Aorta
8 Celiac
9 Superior mesenteric
10 Common iliac
11 Internal iliac (hypogastric)
12 External iliac
13 Deep medial circumflex femoral
14 Deep femoral
15 Femoral
16 Popliteal
17 Anterior tibial
18 Peroneal
19 Posterior tibial
20 Dorsal pedis
21 Arcuate
22 Dorsal metatarsal
23 Occipital
24 Internal carotid
25 External carotid
26 Left common carotid
27 Subclavian
28 Pulmonary
29 Lateral thoracic
30 Axillary
31 Brachial
32 Splenic
33 Renal
34 Inferior mesenteric
35 Radial
36 Ulnar
37 Deep palmar arch
38 Superficial polmar arch
39 Digital

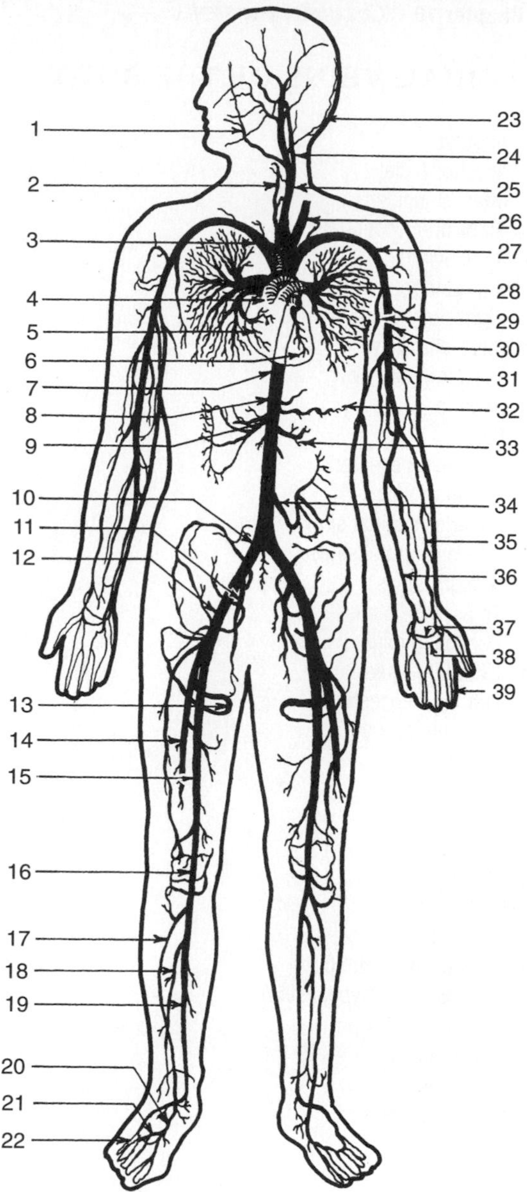

Figure 10-1 Principle arteries of the body. (From Austrin MG, Austrin HR: *Learning medical terminology,* ed 9, St. Louis, 1998, Mosby.)

PRINCIPAL VEINS OF THE BODY

1 Angular
2 Anterior facial
3 Internal jugular
4 Right brachiocephalic
5 Subclavian
6 Superior vena cava
7 Right pulmonary
8 Right coronary
9 Inferior vena cava
10 Hepatic
11 Portal
12 Superior mesenteric
13 Common iliac
14 Superior sagittal sinus
15 Inferior sagittal sinus
16 Straight sinus
17 Transverse sinus
18 Cervical plexus
19 External jugular
20 Left brachiocephalic
21 Left pulmonary
22 Cephalic
23 Axillary
24 Left coronary
25 Basilic
26 Splenic
27 Median basilic
28 Long thoracic
29 Inferior mesenteric
30 Internal iliac (hypogastric)
31 External iliac
32 Volar digital
33 Femoral
34 Great saphenous
35 Popliteal
36 Peroneal
37 Posterior tibial
38 Anterior tibial
39 Dorsal venous arch

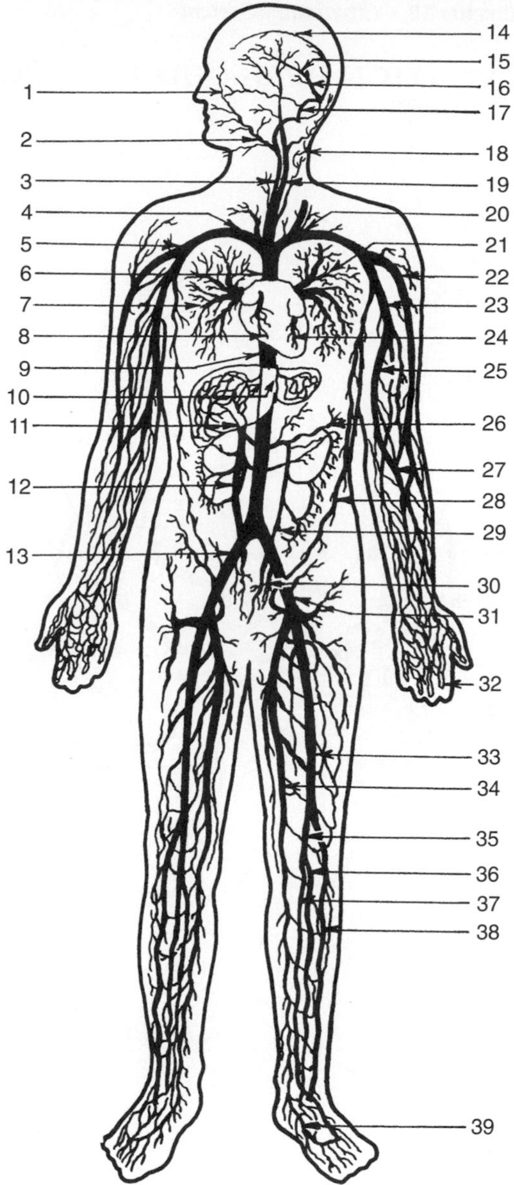

Figure 10-2 Principle veins of the body. (From Austrin MG, Austrin HR: *Learning medical terminology*, ed 9, St. Louis, 1998, Mosby.)

CIRCULATION OF BLOOD THROUGH THE HEART

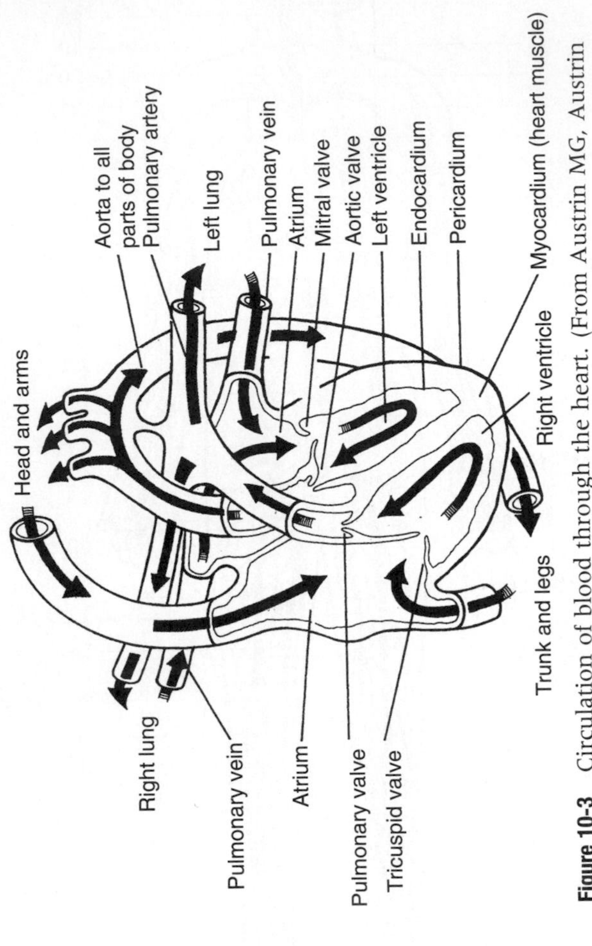

Figure 10-3 Circulation of blood through the heart. (From Austrin MG, Austrin HR: *Learning medical terminology*, ed 9, St. Louis, 1998, Mosby.)

CORONARY ARTERIES

Right Coronary Artery

Right atrium arid anterior right ventricle
Supplies blood to:
- Posterior septum (90%)
- Posterior papillary muscle
- Sinus and atrioventricular (AV) nodes (80%–90%)
- Inferior aspect of left ventricle

Left Coronary Artery

Left anterior descending (LAD)
Supplies blood to:
- Anterior left ventricular wall
- Anterior papillary muscle
- Left ventricular apex
- Anterior interventricular septum
  - Septal branches supply conduction system
  - System bundle of His and bundle branches

Circumflex

Supplies blood to:
- Left atrium
- Posterior surfaces of left ventricle
- Posterior aspect of the septum

BASIC CARDIAC ASSESSMENTS

S_1

First heart sound—heard when the mitral and tricuspid valves close. After ventricles are filled with blood, a dull, low-pitched "lub" is heard. Systole begins when ventricles contract. Systole is shorter than diastole.

S_2

Second heart sound—heard when the aortic and pulmonic values close. After blood goes to aorta and pulmonary artery, a high-pitched, snappy "dub" is heard.

CARDIAC HISTORY

Client History

Heart attacks, rheumatic fever, fevers, hypertension, dizziness, syncope, diabetes, lung or endocrine diseases.

Health Habits

Smoking, alcohol, diet, exercise, stress.

Family History

Coronary disease, strokes, or obesity in parents or grandparents.

Signs and Symptoms

Chest pain, shortness of breath, orthopnea, syncope, hypertension, dyspnea, edema, cough, palpitations, wheezing, need for extra pillow to sleep, fatigue, weakness.

TOPOGRAPHIC AREAS FOR CARDIAC AUSCULTATION

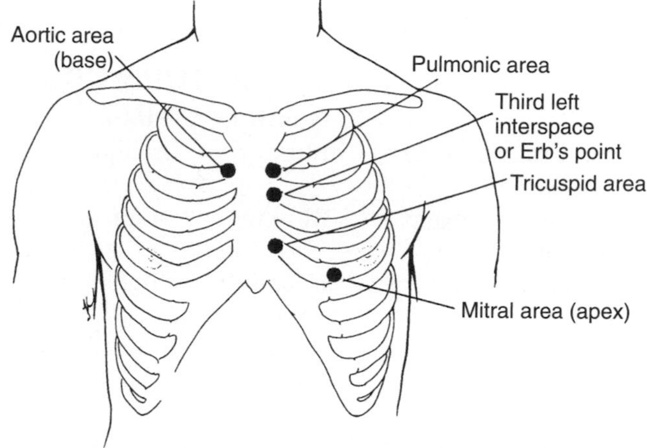

Figure 10-4 Topographic areas for cardiac auscultation. (From Monahan F et al.: *Phipps' medical-surgical nursing: health and illness perspectives,* ed 8, St. Louis, 2007, Mosby.)

ABNORMAL HEART SOUNDS

S_1 Varying intensity with different beats—indicates possible heart blockage

S_2 Increased intensity at aortic valve—indicates possible hypertension

S_3 Increased intensity at pulmonic valve—indicates possible hypertension

Systole Sharp sound—indicates possible deformity

Diastole Presence of S_3 in the elderly—indicates possible heart failure

S_1 S_2 S_3 "Ken tuck ky"

S_4 S_1 S_2 "Ten nes see"

QUALITY AND PITCH OF MURMURS

Type	Quality	Pitch
Aortic and pulmonary stenosis	Harsh	Medium-high
Mitral and tricuspid regurgitation	Blowing	High
Ventricular septal defect	Usually harsh	High
Mitral stenosis	Rumbling	Low
Aortic regurgitation	Blowing	High

MURMUR GRADING SCALE

1 Difficult to hear

2 Faint but recognizable

3 Heard easily with stethoscope

4 Loud, often with a palpable thrill

5 Very loud; associated with a thrill

6 Stethoscope not needed to hear; can be heard with stethoscope 1 inch from chest

Cardiovascular Drugs

Agent	Side Effects	Consideration
Digoxin (Lanoxin) (IV/PO)	Fatigue, headache, anoxia	Monitor rhythm and blood pressure during administration
Digitoxin (PO)	Arrhythmia, nausea, vomiting	Monitor heart rate and blood pressure
Nitroglycerin (IV/PO/buccal/ointment/transdermal)	Headache, hypotension, nausea, vomiting, flushing, arrhythmia	Monitor for arrhythmia
Amrinone (IV)	Arrhythmia, hypotension, thrombocytopenia	Monitor rhythm, blood pressure, and heart rate
Milrinone (IV)	Arrhythmia, hypotension, thrombocytopenia	Monitor rhythm blood pressure, and heart rate
Dobutamine (IV)	Tachycardia, angina, shortness of breath, headache, ventricular ectopy, nausea	Monitor output Monitor rhythm and blood pressure Check peripheral pulses

Continued

Cardiovascular Drugs—cont'd

Agent	Side Effects	Consideration
Dopamine (IV)	Tachycardia, angina, shortness of breath, headache, ventricular ectopy, nausea	Monitor output Monitor rhythm and blood pressure Check peripheral pulses
Epinephrine (IV)	Arrhythmia, hypertension, headache, hyperglycemia, nausea	Monitor output Monitor rhythm and blood pressure Check peripheral pulses
Norepinephrine	Bradycardia, tachycardia, angina, headache, dizziness	Monitor rhythm and blood pressure Have atropine available Monitor fluid balance
Isoproterenol (IV)	Arrhythmia, hypertension, nausea, vomiting, flushing headache	Monitor rhythm and blood pressure Monitor for arrhythmia Monitor fluid balance

ASSESSMENT OF PULSE SITES*

Temporal Found over the **temporal bone,** above and lateral to the eye; easily accessible, used often in children

Apical Best found between the **fourth and fifth intercostals space,** midclavicular line; used to auscultate heart sounds and before the administration of digoxin

Carotid Found on either side of the neck over the **carotid artery;** used to assess circulation during shock or cardiac arrest and when other peripheral pulses are poor

Brachial Found in the **antecubital area** of the arm; used to auscultate blood pressure and to assess circulation of the lower arm

Radial Found on the **thumb side of the forearm** at the wrist; used to assess circulation of the head and peripheral circulation

Ulnar Found at the **wrist on the opposite side of the radius;** used to assess circulation of the hand and in Allen's assessment test

Femoral Found below the **inguinal ligament,** midway between the symphysis pubis and the anterosuperior iliac spine; used to assess circulation of the leg; can be used to assess circulation during shock or cardiac arrest or when other peripheral pulses are poor

Popliteal Found **behind the knee;** used to assess lower leg circulation

Posterior tibial Found on the **inner side of each ankle;** used to assess foot circulation

Dorsalis pedis Found along the **top of the foot** between extension tendons of the great and first toes; used to assess the circulation of the foot

*See Figure 4-1, p. 94.

EDEMA GRADING SCALE

1+ Barely detectable
2+ Indentation of <5 mm
3+ Indentation of 5 to 10 mm
4+ Indentation of >10 mm

PULSE GRADING SCALE

4-Point Scale

0 No pulse
1+ Weak, thready, fading, easily obliterated
2+ Difficult to palpate
3+ Normal
4+ Bounding

3-Point Scale

0 Absent
1+ Weak, thready
2+ Normal
3+ Full, bounding

Tissue Perfusion

Area	Abnormality	Reveals
Skin color	Cyanotic	Decreased venous return
	Pallor	Decreased arterial flow
	Dusky	Decreased arterial flow
Temperature	Cool	Decreased arterial flow
Fluid	Mild edema	Decreased arterial flow
	Great edema	Decreased venous return
Texture	Thin or thick	Decreased venous return and arterial flow
	Shiny	Decreased venous return and arterial flow
Nails	Cyanotic	Decreased arterial flow

Chapter 11

Respiratory System

For an in-depth study of the respiratory system, consult the following publications:

Austrin MG, Austrin HR: *Learning medical terminology*, ed 9, St. Louis, 1998, Mosby.

Guzzetta CE, Dossey BM: *Cardiovascular nursing: holistic practice*, St. Louis, 1992, Mosby.

Lewis SM, Collier IC, Heitkemper MM: *Medical-surgical nursing,* ed 7, St. Louis, 2007, Mosby.

Patton KT, Thibodeau GA: *Handbook of anatomy and physiology,* St. Louis, 2000, Mosby.

Potter PA, Perry AG: *Fundamentals of nursing*, ed 7, St. Louis, 2008, Mosby.

LOWER RESPIRATORY TRACT

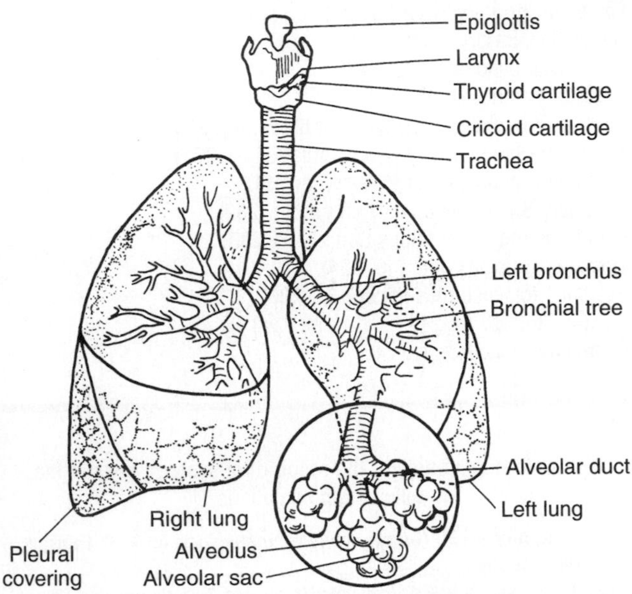

Figure 11-1 Lower respiratory tract. (From Austrin MG, Austrin HR: *Learning medical terminology,* ed 9, St. Louis, 1998, Mosby.)

UPPER RESPIRATORY TRACT

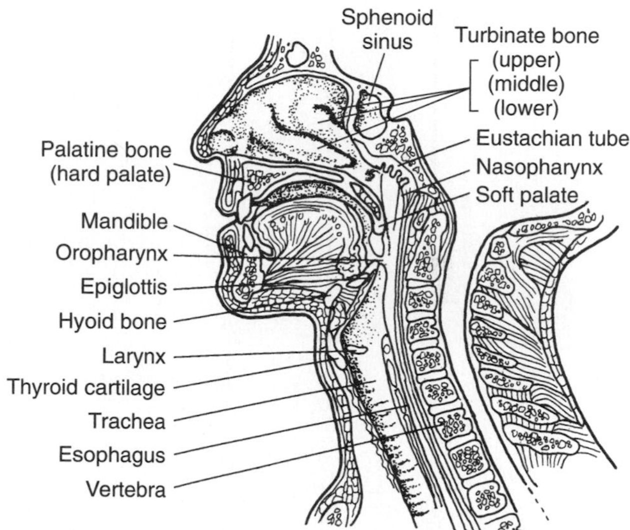

Figure 11-2 Upper respiratory tract. (From Austrin MG, Austrin HR: *Learning medical terminology,* ed 9, St. Louis, 1998, Mosby.)

CHEST WALL LANDMARKS

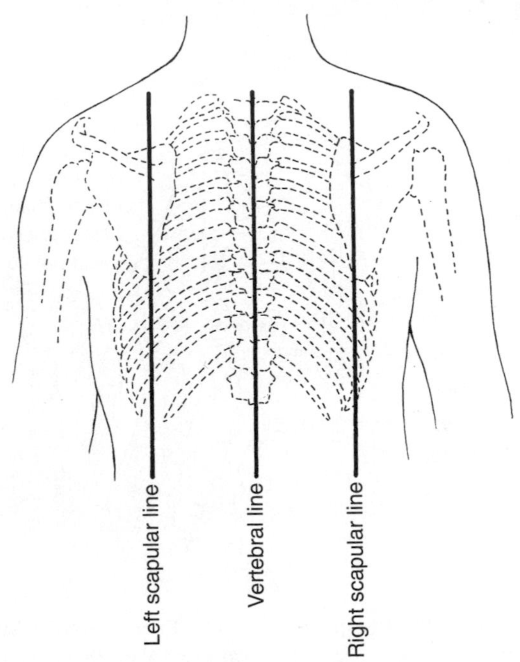

Figure 11-3 Chest wall landmarks. (From Potter PA, Perry AG: *Fundamentals of nursing*, ed 7, St. Louis, 2008, Mosby.)

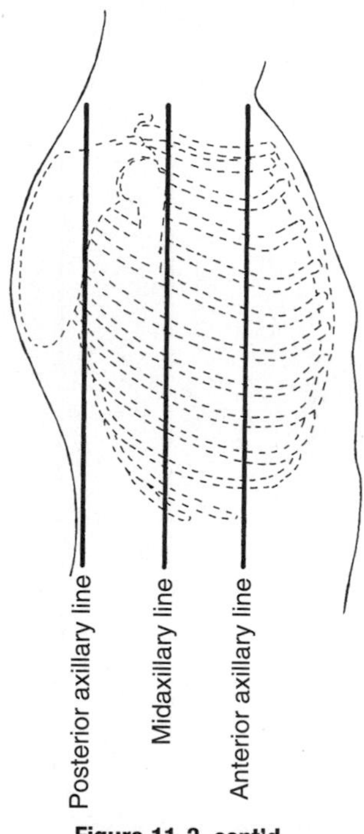

Figure 11-3, cont'd

Continued

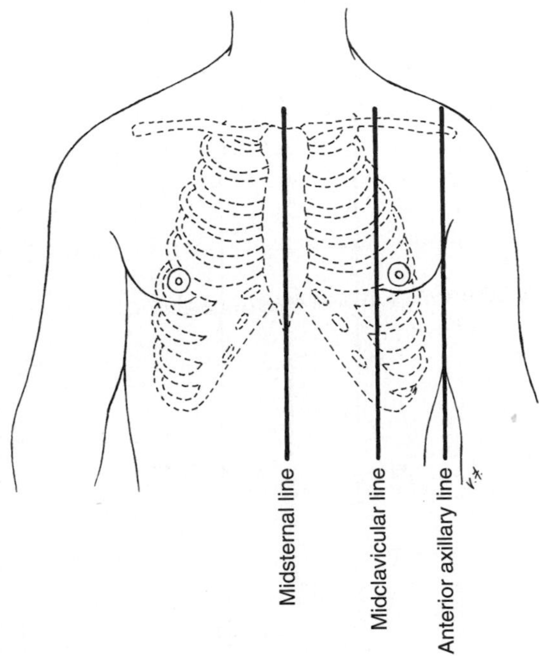

Figure 11-3, cont'd

NORMAL BREATH SOUNDS

Vesicular Soft, low-pitched sighing over bronchiole and alveoli base on inspiration

Bronchial Moderate, high-pitched sound over trachea

Bronchovesicular Moderate sound over first and second intercostal spaces

Tracheal Loudest and highest pitched of normal breath sounds, harsh and tubular

SIGNS AND SYMPTOMS OF HYPERVENTILATION

Tachycardia, chest pain, shortness of breath
Dizziness, lightheadedness, disorientation
Paresthesia, numbness
Tinnitus, blurred vision, tetany

SIGNS AND SYMPTOMS OF HYPOVENTILATION

Dizziness, headache, lethargy
Disorientation, convulsions, coma
Decreased ability to follow instructions
Cardiac arrhythmias, electrolyte imbalance, cardiac arrest

SIGNS AND SYMPTOMS OF HYPOXIA

Restlessness, anxiety, disorientation
Decreased concentration, fatigue
Decreased consciousness, dizziness
Behavioral changes, pallor
Increased pulse and blood pressure
Cardiac arrhythmias, cyanosis, clubbing, dyspnea

Common Abnormalities of the Lung

Type	Characteristics	Assess for
Apnea	Periods of not breathing	Sleep problem, impending death
Bradypnea	<10 breaths per minute	Drug overdose, alcohol overdose
Dyspnea	Difficulty breathing	Low hemoglobin, acidosis
Stridor	High-pitched sounds	Obstruction
Tachypnea	>20 breaths per minute	Anxiety, fever
Hyperpnea	Increased rate and death	Pain, reaction to altitude
Hyperventilation	Acidosis	Increased rate and depth
Cheyne-Stokes breathing	Alternating periods of hyperpnea and apnea	Impending death
Kussmaul respirations	Extreme rate and depth	Diabetic ketoacidosis, renal failure
Asymmetric	Lungs do not expand equally	Fractured ribs, missing lung, pneumothorax

ABNORMAL AND ADVENTITIOUS SOUNDS

Crackles/rales Fine, crackle-like sounds, usually on inspiration

Alveolar High pitched

Bronchial Low pitched

Rhonchi Coarse, harsh, over fluid (usually on expiration)

Wheezes Squeaky, musical on inspiration or expiration

Friction rub Grating sound of pleurae rubbing together, generally on the anterior side

Assessment questions regarding respiratory status may include:

Time pattern

When did the breathing sound start?
How long did it last?
Is there a pattern to the occurrences?

Quality

How would you describe it?

Relieving factors

What makes it better?

Aggravating factors

What makes it worse?

Other

What other symptoms are also present?
Is there any coughing?
Is there any difficulty breathing?

The following tests may be ordered for those clients with abnormal breath sounds:

- Chest X-ray
- Pulmonary function tests
- Blood tests (including an arterial blood gas)
- CT scan of the chest
- Analysis of a sputum sample

COMMON LUNG DISORDERS

Asthma

Signs and Symptoms: Dyspnea, cough, tachypnea.
Listen for: Decreased sounds with wheezes.

Atelectasis

Signs and Symptoms: Tachypnea, cyanosis, use of accessory muscles.
Listen for: Decreased sound with crackles.

Bronchiectasis

Signs and Symptoms: Chronic cough with large amounts of foul-smelling sputum production, coughing up blood, cough worsened by lying on one side, fatigue, shortness of breath worsened by exercise, weight loss, wheezing, paleness, skin discoloration, bluish, breath odor. Clubbing of fingers may be present.
Listen for: Wheezes and crackles.

Bronchitis

Signs and Symptoms: Cough with sputum, sore throat and fever, prolonged expiration.
Listen for: Prolonged expiration, wheezes, crackles.

Cystic fibrosis (CF)

Signs and Symptoms: Recurrent respiratory infections, such as pneumonia or sinusitis, coughing or wheezing, no bowel movements in first 24 to 48 hours of life, stools that are pale or clay-colored, foul-smelling, or that float. Infants may have salty-tasting skin, weight loss, or failure to gain weight normally in childhood, diarrhea, delayed growth, fatigue.
Listen for: Wheezes and crackles.

Emphysema

Signs and Symptoms: Dyspnea, cough with sputum.
Listen for: Wheezes, rhonchi.

Interstitial Lung Disease (ILD)

Signs and Symptoms: Shortness of breath during exercise. When the disease is severe and prolonged, heart failure with swelling of the legs may occur.
Listen for: dry cough without sputum.

Neoplasm

Signs and Symptoms: Cough with sputum, chest pain.
Listen for: Decreased sounds.

Pleural Effusion

Signs and Symptoms: Pain, dyspnea, pallor, fever, cough.
Listen for: Decreased sounds, friction rub.

Pneumonia

Signs and Symptoms: Chills, productive cough, rapid swallow rate.
Listen for: Fine crackles or friction rub.

Pneumothorax

Signs and Symptoms: Pain, dyspnea, cyanosis, tachypnea.
Listen for: Decreased sound on affected side.

Pulmonary Edema

Signs and Symptoms: Tachypnea, cough, cyanosis, orthopnea, use of accessory muscles.
Listen for: Rales, rhonchi, wheezes.

Positions for Postural Drainage

Lung Segment	Position of Client
Adult	
Bilateral	High Fowlcr's

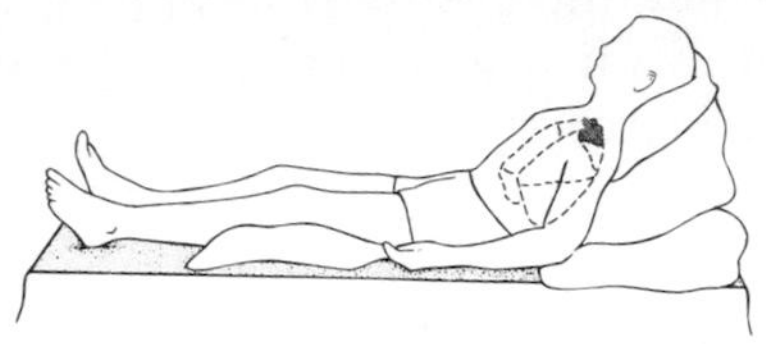

Lung Segment	Position of Client
Apical segments Right upper lobe— anterior segment	Supine with head elevated

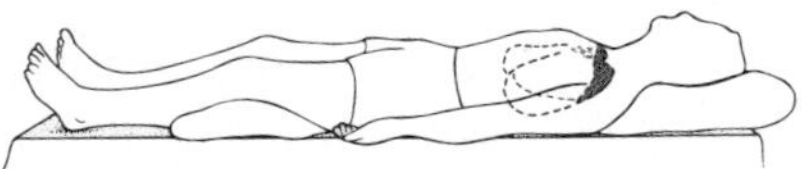

Lung Segment	Position of Client
Left upper lobe— anterior segment	Supine with head elevated

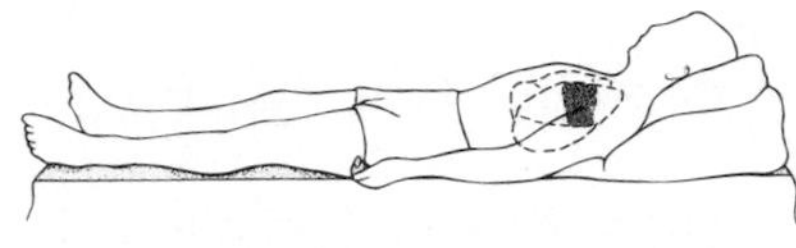

Modified from Potter PA, Perry AG: *Fundamentals of nursing,* ed 7, St. Louis, 2008, Mosby.

Positions for Postural Drainage—cont'd

Lung Segment	Position of Client
Right upper lobe—posterior segment	Side lying with right side of chest elevated on pillows

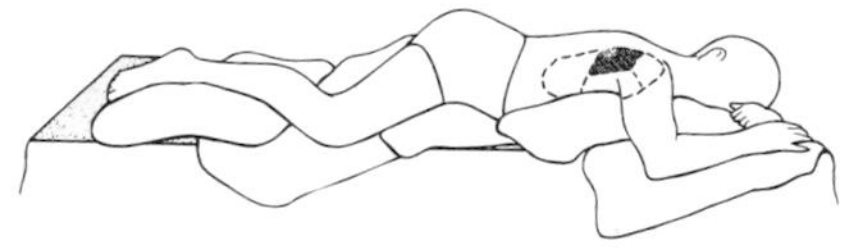

Lung Segment	Position of Client
Left upper lobe—posterior segment	Side lying with left side of chest elevated on pillows

Lung Segment	Position of Client
Right middle lobe—anterior segment	Three-fourths supine position with dependent lung in Trendelenburg position

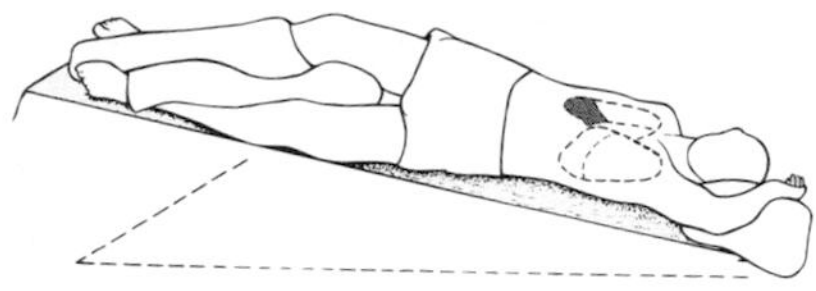

Continued

Positions for Postural Drainage—cont'd

Lung Segment	Position of Client
Right middle lobe—posterior segment	Prone with thorax and abdomen elevated

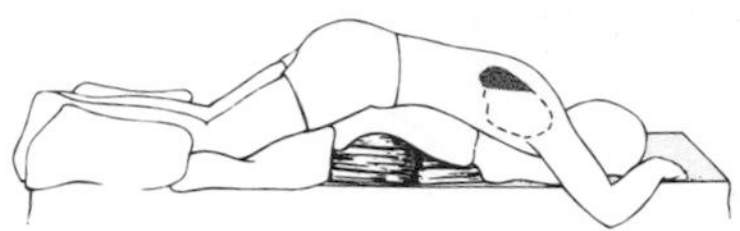

Lung Segment	Position of Client
Both lower lobes—anterior segments	Supine in Trendelenburg position

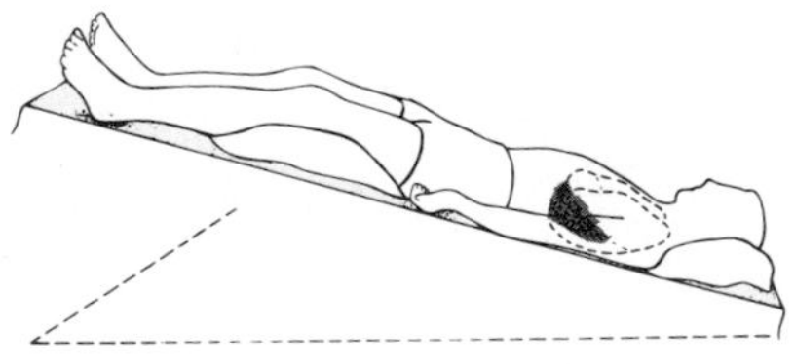

Lung Segment	Position of Client
Left lower lobe—lateral segment	Right side lying in Trendelenburg position

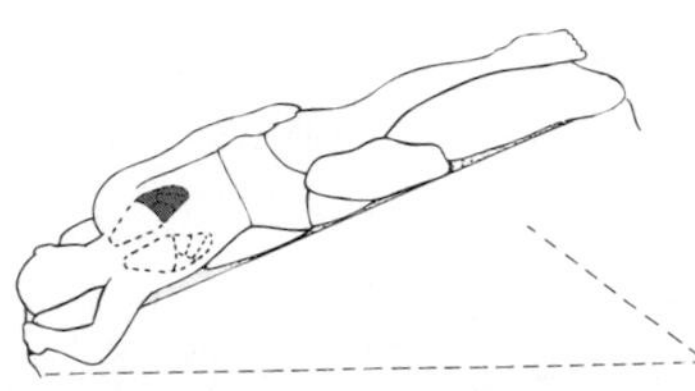

Modified from Potter PA, Perry AG: *Fundamentals of nursing,* ed 7, St. Louis, 2008, Mosby.

Positions for Postural Drainage—cont'd

Lung Segment	Position of Client
Right lower lobe—lateral segment	Left side lying in Trendelenburg position

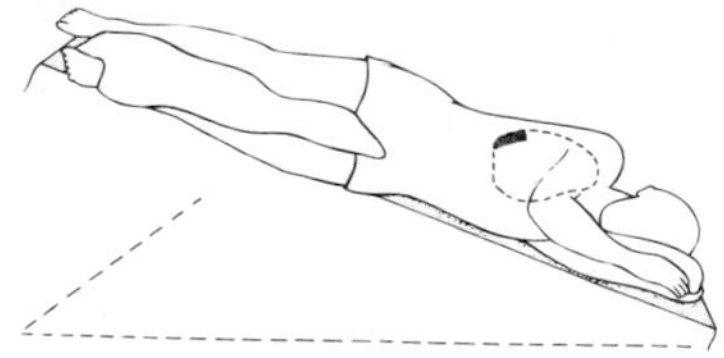

Lung Segment	Position of Client
Right lower lobe—posterior segment	Prone with right side of chest elevated in Trendelenburg position

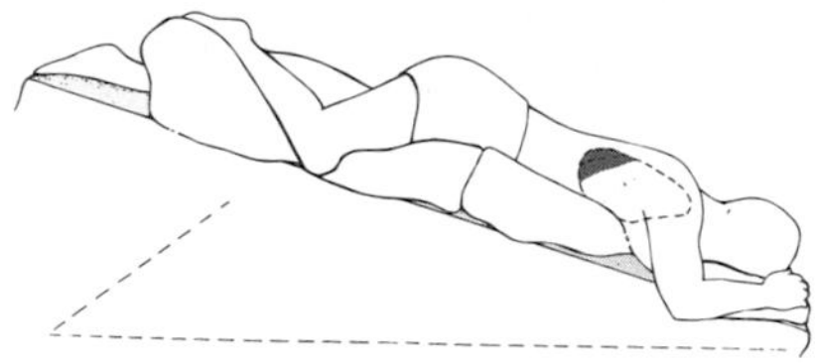

Lung Segment	Position of Client
Both lower lobes—posterior segment	Prone in Trendelenberg position

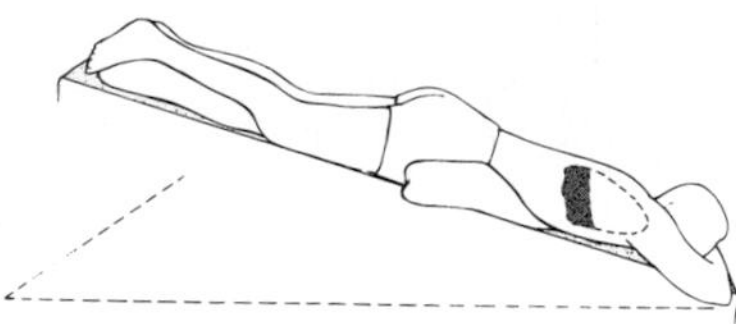

Continued

Positions for Postural Drainage—cont'd

Lung Segment	Position of Client
Child	
Bilateral—apical segments	Sitting on nurse's lap, leaning slightly forward flexed over pillow

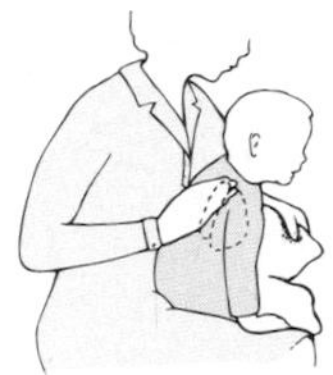

Lung Segment	Position of Client
Bilateral—middle anterior segments	Sitting on nurse's lap, leaning against nurse

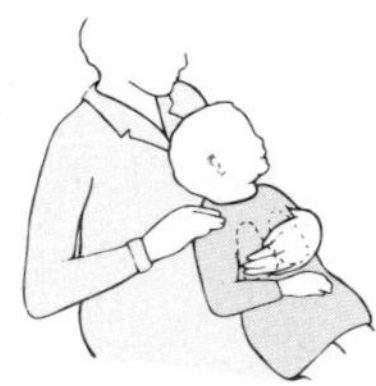

Lung Segment	Position of Client
Bilateral lobes—anterior segments	Lying supine on nurse's lap, back supported with pillow

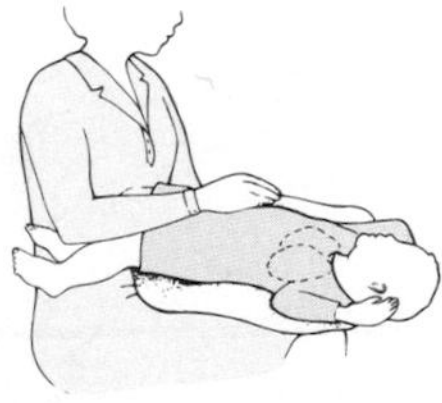

Modified from Potter PA, Perry AG: *Fundamentals of nursing,* ed 7, St. Louis, 2008, Mosby.

OXYGEN THERAPY*

Cannula

1 liter = 24% oxygen
2 liters = 28% oxygen
3 liters = 32% oxygen
4 liters = 36% oxygen
5 liters = 40% oxygen
6 liters = 44% oxygen

If client requires more oxygen than 6 liters, a mask may be needed. Humidification may be added for comfort.

Simple Mask

5–6 liters = 40% oxygen
7–8 liters = 50% oxygen
10 liters = 60% oxygen

Should not be run below 5 liters per minute.

Partial Rebreathing Mask

6–10 liters = up to 80% oxygen

Level of oxygen will depend on client's overall respiratory and health status. *Should not be run below 5 liters per minute. Reservoir bag should never be fully collapsed.*

Nonbreathing Mask

Will deliver 80% to 100% oxygen. *Should not be run below 5 liters per minute. Reservoir bag should never be fully collapsed.*

*Oxygen is a drug, and therefore a physician's order is required for use.

Pulmonary Functions

Name	Description	Average	Considerations
Tidal volume (VT)	Amount of air inhaled or exhaled	5–10 mL/kg	Decreased in older adults and clients with restrictive lung disease
Residual volume (RV)	Amount of air left in lung after deep exhalation	1200 mL	Increased in clients with chronic obstructive pulmonary disease
Functional residual capacity (FRC)	Air left in lung after normal exhalation	2400 mL	Increased in clients with obstructive lung diseases
Vial capacity (VC)	Amount of air exhaled after maximal inhalation	4800 mL	Decreased with pulmonary edema and atelectasis
Total lung capacity (TLC)	Total air in lungs after maximal inhalation	6000 mL	Decreased with restrictive disease Increased with obstructive disease

Chapter 12

Endocrine System

For an in-depth study of the endocrine system, consult the following publications:

AJN/Mosby: *Nursing board's review for the NCLEX-RN examination,* ed 10, St. Louis, 1996, Mosby.

Lewis SM, Collier IC, Heitkemper MM: *Medical-surgical nursing,* ed 7, St. Louis, 2007, Mosby.

Monahan F et al.: *Phipps' medical-surgical nursing: health and illness perspectives*, ed 8, St. Louis, 2007, Mosby.

Potter PA, Perry AG: *Fundamentals of nursing,* ed 7, St. Louis, 2008, Mosby.

ENDOCRINE GLANDS AND ASSOCIATED STRUCTURES

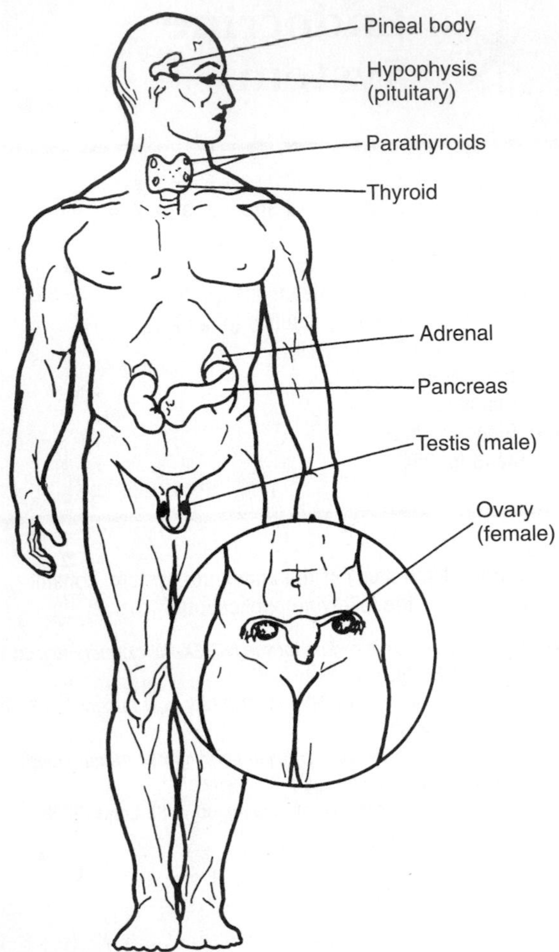

Figure 12-1 Endocrine glands. (From Austrin MG, Austrin HR: *Learning medical terminology*, ed 9, St. Louis, 1998, Mosby.)

DIABETES

Type 1 **Former Names: Juvenile, Insulin Dependent (IDDM)**	**Type 2** **Former Names: Adult-onset, Non-Insulin Dependent (NIDDM)**
Clinical Information	
10% to 15% of diabetic cases	85% to 90% of diabetic cases
Abrupt onset	Gradual onset
Autoimmune islet-cell destruction	Insulin resistance or deficiency
Generally begins before age 40 years but can occur at any age	Generally begins after age 40 years but can occur earlier
Clinical Manifestations	
Weight loss, increased hunger	Fatigue, drowsiness, increased hunger
Excessive thirst, increased urinary frequency	Blurred vision, increased thirst, urinary frequency
Possible ketoacidosis	No ketoacidosis
Prone to ketosis	No ketosis
No endogenous insulin	Has endogenous insulin
Management	
Diet very important	Diet very important
Insulin mandatory	Insulin needed in 25% of cases
Oral hypoglycemic not used	Oral hypoglycemic used in 40% of cases

BLOOD GLUCOSE REACTIONS

Insulin Reaction Hypoglycemia (Glucose Level <60 mg/dL)	**Diabetic Ketoacidosis Hyperglycemia (Glucose Level >250 mg/dL)**
Causes	***Causes***
Too much insulin Skipped or delayed meals Too much exercise	Too little insulin Overeating Emotional stress illness, infection, surgery, heart attack, stroke, pregnancy
Clinical Manifestations	
Early Symptoms	***Early Symptoms***
Sweatiness, shakiness, weakness Headache, dizziness Hunger	Excessive thirst Frequent urination Fatigue, weakness
Late Symptoms	***Late Symptoms***
Numbness of lips/ tongue Difficulty concentrating Mood change/irritability Vision changes, pallor	Abdominal pain, nausea, vomiting General aches, loss of appetite Flushed, dry skin Fruity breath, drowsiness
If Not Treated	***If Not Treated***
Seizures, coma	Labored breathing, coma

TREATMENT FOR BLOOD GLUCOSE REACTIONS

Insulin Reaction Hypoglycemia (Glucose Level <60 mg/dL)	**Diabetic Ketoacidosis Hyperglycemia (Glucose Level >250 mg/dL)**
Do the Following:	
Give the client *one* of the below:	Alert physician
10 to 15 g glucose or 2 glucose tablets	Monitor blood sugar
5 pieces of candy or 4 oz juice	Test urine for ketones
1 mg IM glucagon	Provide IV hydration per physician's orders
Repeat any *one* of the above in 15 minutes if needed	Provide potassium replacements
Document reaction	*Give insulin per physician's order*
Inform physician	Document actions

RECOMMENDATIONS FOR MIXING INSULINS

Mixing insulins requires care and skill to avoid inaccurate dosage and possible contamination. Always be sure to have another nurse double check as you mix the insulins.

When mixing insulin, if one is cloudy, the clear insulin is drawn up first, and the cloudy one second.

If giving any cloudy insulin such as NPH, roll the vial between your hands to mix. DO NOT SHAKE. Shaking will cause air bubbles that will displace insulin and cause inaccurate dosing.

Remember: when mixing insulin, if one is cloudy, it gets drawn up second, but the air is inserted into it first.

If in doubt, start over. Never allow insulins to mix in the vials. If this happens, discard and get fresh vials.

Never administer medications you did not prepare to dispense yourself.

When mixing short- and long-acting insulins in the same syringe, first draw up the short-acting insulin (regular insulin, which is clear) and then the long-acting insulin (which is cloudy).

- Clients whose blood sugar levels are well controlled on a mixed-insulin dose should maintain their individual routine.
- Insulin should not be mixed with other medications.
- Insulin should not be diluted unless approved by the prescribing physician.
- Rapid-acting insulins that are mixed with NPH or ultralente insulins should be injected 15

Modified from American Diabetes Association: Clinical practice recommendations for insulin administration, *Diabetes Care* 20(suppl 1): 46s, 2006.

minutes before a meal to promote consistent absorption of insulin.

- Short-acting and lente insulins should not be mixed unless the client's blood sugar level is currently under control with this mixture.

REACTION PREVENTION TIPS

Insulin Reaction	**Diabetic Ketoacidsis**
Eat meals at same time each day	Follow prescribed eating schedule
If meals are delayed: For 1 hour: Drink 4 oz fruit juice For more than 2 hours: Eat 4 oz protein	Know factors that can raise blood sugar Avoid stress and overwork
Take correct insulin as scheduled	Take correct insulin as scheduled
Wear diabetic identification	Wear diabetic identification
Check blood sugar as needed	On sick days: *Do not stop insulin*
Carry quick-acting sugar at all times	Check urine for ketones every 12 hours Monitor blood glucose every 2 to 4 hours Maintain good fluid intake Alert physician if glucose is >240 mg/dL

General Client and Family Information

With an increase in activity, never omit insulin.

Before vacations, call physician to see whether insulin dose needs adjusting.

Know insulin peaks and how body reacts to insulin highs and lows.

Inform family and friends of possible reactions and how to treat them.

Hypoglycemic Agents*

Types	Peak (hr)	Duration (hr)
Oral agents		
Chlorpropamide (Diabinese)*	1	24–60
Tolbutamide (Orinase)*	5–8	6–12
Tolazamide (Tolinase)*	4–6	12–24
Glipizide (Glucotrol)†	1–3	10–24
Glyburide (DiaBeta, Micronase, Glynase)†	2–8	24
Acarbose (Precose) [Alpha Inhibitors]	1	14–24
Acetohexamide (Dymelor)*	1.3–8	12–24
Glirnepirde (Amary)	2–3	24
Metformin (Glucophage)[Biquanides]	1–3	9–17
Miglitol (Glyset) [Alpha Inhibitors]	2–3	24
Nateglinide (Starlix) [Meglitinides]	0–1	2–3
Repaglinide (Prandin) [Meglitinides]	60–90 min	<4

*First generation agents
†Second generation agents

Type	Name	Color	Onset	Peak	Duration (hr)
Rapid-acting	Humalog (insulin lispro)	Clear	5–10 minutes	30–90 minutes	3–5
	NovoLog (insulin aspart)	Clear	5–10 minutes	40–50 minutes	3–5
Short-acting	Humulin-R (insulin regular)	Clear	30 minutes	1–2 hours	4–6
Intermediate-acting	Humulin-N (insulin NPH)	Cloudy	1–2 hours	4–6 hours	8–24
	Novolin-L (insulin lente)	Cloudy	1–3 hours	6–15 hours	10–24
Long-acting	Humulin-U (insulin ultralente)	Cloudy	4–6 hours	8–30 hours	24–36
	Lantus (insulin glargine)	Clear	Within a few minutes	Adsorbed into the blood slowly so that there is no time of greatest effect	24

ADRENAL GLANDS

Cushing's Syndrome Hyperfunction	**Addison's Disease Hypofunction**
Clinical Manifestations	
Excessive cortisol production	Inadequate cortisol production
Increased ACTH from pituitary	Insufficient ACTH from pituitary
Increased protein catabolism	Flaccid muscles/paralysis
Muscle wasting and fragile skin	Muscle weakness and anorexia
Osteoporosis and compression fractures	Nausea/vomiting and diarrhea
Bruises easily/poor healing	Abdominal pain
Obesity/moon face/ buffalo hump	Weight loss
Hyperglycemia and worsening of diabetes	Frequent hypoglycemia
Decreased immunity	Decreased cardiac output
Sodium and water retention	Hyponatremia and hypo-osmolality
Edema/hypertension	Hypotension and arrhythmias
Hypokalemia/hypochloremia	Hyperkalemia
Renal calculi hypercalcemia	Hypercalcemia
Irritability	Lethargy
Anxiety	Depression

PITUITARY GLAND*

Hyperpituitarism

Clinical Information. This disorder is generally caused by tumors, which lead to an increase in hormone levels. The most common hormones involved are the following:

GH Growth hormone, which causes gigantism

ACTH Adrenocorticotropic hormone (corticotropin), which causes Cushing's disease

TSH Thyroid-stimulating hormone, which causes hyperthyroidism

LH Luteinizing hormone

FSH Follicle-stimulating hormone

Hypopituitarism

Clinical Information. This disorder is usually caused by tumors, necrosis, or glandular dysfunction, leading to a decrease in hormone levels. The most common problems associated with hypopituitarism are:

Dwarfism Caused by a decreased growth hormone

Hypophysectomy The removal or destruction of pituitary gland

Postpartum necrosis Caused by hypotension after delivery

Functional disorders Caused by starvation or anemia

*Specific problems, signs, and symptoms will depend on the hormone involved.

THYROID GLAND

Hyperthyroidism	Hypothyroidism
Clinical Manifestations	
Increased body metabolism	Decreased body metabolism
Nervousness/restlessness	Lethargy and headaches
Short attention span	Memory deficit
Tachycardia (>100 beats/min; bounding heard sounds)	Bradycardia (<60 beats/min; weak heart sounds)
Increased blood pressure	Decreased blood pressure
Reduced vital capacity	Lowered respiratory rate
Skin warm, moist, and smooth	Skin cool, dry, and rough
Hair fine, nails soft	Hair coarse, nails brittle
Weakness and fatigue	Weakness and fatigue
Demineralization of bones	Stiff joints
Hypercalcemia	Mild proteinuria
Brisk reflexes	Decreased reflexes
Increased appetite/weight loss	Decreased appetite/weight gain
Muscle wasting	Muscular stiffness
Diabetes worsens	Diabetic clients need less insulin
Increased stools	Constipation
Increased libido	Decreased libido
Decreased fertility	Decreased fertility
Higher body temperature	Lower body temperature

Chapter 13

Digestive System

For in-depth study of the digestive system, consult the following publications:

AJN/Mosby: *Nursing boards review for the NCLEX-RN examination*, ed 10, St. Louis, 1997, Mosby.

Lewis SM, Collier IC, Heitkemper MM: *Medical-surgical nursing*, ed 7, St. Louis, 2007, Mosby.

Monahan F et al.: *Phipps' medical-surgical nursing: health and illness perspectives*, ed 8, St. Louis, 2007, Mosby.

Nix S: *Williams' basic nutrition and diet therapy*, ed 13, St. Louis, 2008, Mosby.

Potter PA, Perry AG: *Fundamentals of nursing*, ed 7, St. Louis, 2008, Mosby.

DIGESTIVE SYSTEM AND ASSOCIATED STRUCTURES

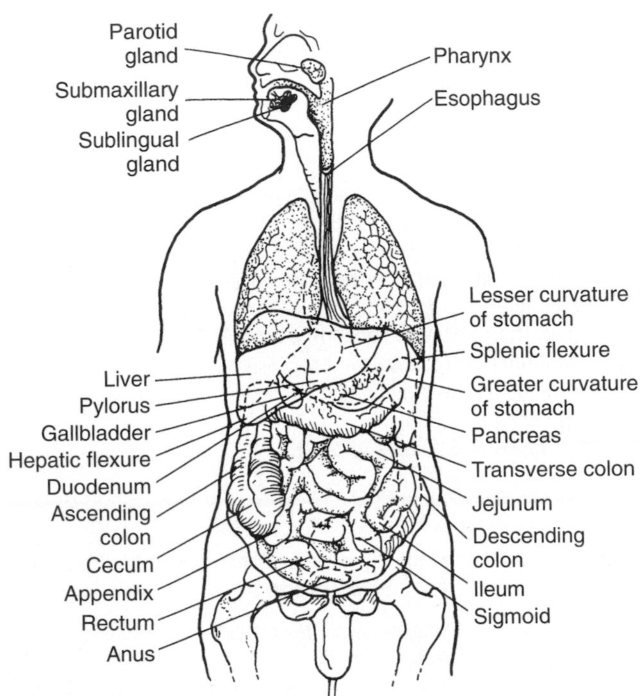

Figure 13-1 Digestive system and associated structures. (From Austrin MG, Austrin HR: *Learning medical terminology*, ed 9, St. Louis, 1998, Mosby.)

Types of Diets

Type	Description	Client Complaint
Regular	Has all essentials, no restrictions	No special diet needed
Clear liquid	Broth, tea, clear soda, strained juices, gelatin	Recovery from surgery or very ill
Full liquid	Clear liquids plus milk products, eggs	Transition from clear to regular diet
Soft	Soft consistency and mild spice	Difficulty swallowing
Mechanical soft	Regular diet but chopped or ground	Difficulty chewing
Bland	No spicy food	Ulcers or colitis
Low residue	No bulky food, apples, or nuts	Rectal disease
High calorie	High protein, vitamin, and fat	Malnourished
Low calorie	Decreased fat, no whole milk, cream eggs, complex carbohydrates	Obese

Continued

Types of Diets—cont'd

Type	Description	Client Complaint
Diabetic	Balance of protein, carbohydrates, fat	Insulin-food imbalance
High protein	Meat, fish, milk, cheese, poultry, eggs	Tissue repair, underweight
Low fat	Little butter, cream, whole milk, or eggs	Gallbladder, liver, or heart disease
Low cholesterol	Little meat or cheese	Need to decrease fat intake
Low sodium	No salt added during cooking	Heart or renal disease
Salt free	No salt	Heart or renal disease
Tube feeding	Formulas or liquid food	Oral surgery, oral or esophageal cancers, inability to eat or swallow

Types of Nutrients

Type	**Function**	**Food Sources**
Carbohydrate	Energy, body temperature	*Simple:* sugars, fruits, nuts *Complex:* grains, potatoes milk
Protein	Tissue growth, tissue repair	Meat, fish, eggs, milk, poultry, beans, peas, nuts
Fat	Energy and repair, carries vitamins A and D	Animal fat, meat, nuts, milk, fish, poultry
Water	Carries nutrients, regulates body processes, lubricates joints	Liquids, most fruits and vegetables

Minerals		
Type	**Function**	**Food Sources**
Calcium	Renews bones and teeth, regulates heart and nerves	Milk, green vegetables, cheese, salmon, legumes
Phosphorus	Renews bones and teeth, maintains nerve function	Cheese, oats, meat, milk, fish, poultry, nuts
Iron	Renews hemoglobin	Meat, eggs, liver, flour, yellow or green vegetables
Iodine	Regulates thyroid	Table salt, seafood
Magnesium	Component of enzymes	Grains, green vegetables
Sodium	Maintains water balance, nerve function	Salt, cured meats
Potassium	Maintains nerve function	Meat, milk, vegetables
Chloride	Formation of gastric juices	Salt
Zinc	Component of enzymes	Meat, seafood

Vitamins

Type	Function	Food Sources
A (retinol)	Helps eyes, skin, hair; fights infection	Yellow fruits and vegetables, liver, kidneys, fish
B_1 (thiamine)	Maintains nerves, aids carbohydrate function	Bread, cereal, beans, peas, pork, liver, eggs, milk
B_2 (riboflavin)	Maintains skin, mouth, nerve functions	Milk, cheese, eggs, cereal, dark green vegetables
B_3 (niacin)	Oxidation of proteins and carbohydrates	Meat, fish, poultry, eggs, nuts, bread, cereal
B_{12}	Aids muscles, nerves, heart, metabolism	Organ meats, milk
C (ascorbic acid)	Maintains integrity of cells, repairs tissue	Citrus fruits, tomatoes, green vegetables, potatoes
D	Enables body to use calcium and phosphorus	Milk, margarine, fish, liver, eggs
F	Antioxidant	Peanuts, vegetable oils
K	Aids in blood clotting	Green leafy vegetables

CALORIC INCREASE NEEDED FOR SELECT INJURY FACTORS

Injury	% Caloric Increase
Minor surgery	10
Mild infection	20
Moderate infection	40
Severe infection	60
Congestive heart failure	30
Cancer therapy	30
Pulmonary disease	30
Wound healing	20–60
Long bone tracture	30–50

Modified from Kobriger Presents. www.kobriger.com

TWO TYPES OF MALNUTRITION

Marasmus

Caused by decreased caloric intake

- Takes months to years to develop
- Individuals appear thin, malnourished
- Weight loss present
- Serum albumin and transferrin levels normal
- Mortality rate low, unless from underlying disease

Kwashiorkor

Caused by decreased protein intake or stress

- Can be due to trauma or infection
- Takes only weeks to develop
- Individuals appear normal, well nourished
- Weight loss may be minimal or masked by edema
- Serum albumin and transferrin levels decreased
- Mortality rate high due to decreased wound healing
- High risk of infection

Modified from Kobriger Presents. www.kobriger.com

COMPARING PEPTIC ULCERS

Gastric Ulcers	Duodenal Ulcers
Located in the antrum of stomach	Located in the first 1 to 2 cm of the duodenum
Generally occurs in people aged 45 to 70 years	Generally occurs in people aged 40 to 60 years
Most common ulcer in people >65 years old	Most common ulcer in people <65 years old
More common in women	More common in men
Higher mortality rate than duodenal ulcers	Lower mortality rate than gastric ulcers
Less common than duodenal ulcers	Four times more prevalent than gastric ulcers
Risk factors are stress, drugs, alcohol, smoking, and gastritis	Risk factors are chronic obstructive pulmonary disease, alcohol, cirrhosis, pancreatitis, smoking, renal failure, stress
Pain occurs 1 to 2 hours after eating	Pain occurs after eating and at night
Pain felt high in epigastrium	Pain in midepigastric area
Pain may be described as heartburn	Pain is described in the back
Pain relieved by food or liquids	Pain relieved by milk or antacids
May cause weight loss	May cause weight gain
High recurrence rate	Recurs seasonally (spring/fall)
Risk of malignancy	Rarely malignant
High risk of hemorrhage	High risk of perforation

ALTERED BOWEL ELIMINATION PATTERNS

Constipation

Presence of large quantity of dry, hard feces that is difficult to expel; frequency of bowel movements is not a factor.

Causes. Reabsorption of too much water in the lower bowel as a result of medication such as narcotics, ignoring the urge to defecate, immobility, chronic laxative abuse, low fluid intake, low fiber intake, aging, postoperative conditions, or pregnancy.

Remedies. Increase fluids, fiber cereals, fruits and vegetables, exercise, and avoid cheese.

Impaction

Hard, dry stool embedded in rectal folds; may have liquid stool passing around impaction.

Causes. Poor bowel habits, immobility, inadequate food or fluids, or barium in rectum.

Remedies. Digitally remove impaction, increase fluids and fiber, increase exercise, and institute bowel program.

Diarrhea

Expulsion of fecal matter that contains too much water.

Causes. Infection, anxiety, stress, medications, too many laxatives at one time, or food or drug allergies or reactions.

Remedies. Add bulk or fiber to diet, maintain fluids and electrolytes, eat smaller amounts of food at one time, add cheese or bananas to diet, and rest after eating.

Incontinence

Inability to hold feces in rectum because of impairment of sphincter control.
Causes. Surgery, cancer, radiation treatment of rectum, paralysis, or aging.
Remedies. Bowel training, regular meal times, regular elimination patterns.

Abdominal Distention

Tympanites, or enlargement of the abdomen with gas or air as a result of excessive swallowing of air, eating gas-producing foods, or an inability to expel gas.
Causes. Constipation, fecal impaction, or postoperative conditions.
Remedies. Rectal tube can be used to expel air; increase ambulation, and change position in bed.

Obstruction

Occurs when the lumen of the bowel narrows or closes completely.
Causes. External compression can be caused by tumor; internal narrowing can be caused by impacted feces.
Remedies. Remove impaction or tumor.

Ileus (Paralytic Ileus)

Occurs when the bowel has decreased motility.
Causes. Surgery, long-term narcotic use, or complete obstruction.
Remedies. Medical intervention for physical obstructions. Specific action will depend on the cause of the ileus.

Fecal Characteristics

Characteristic	Normal	Abnormal	Assess for
Color	Brown	Clay/white	Bile obstruction
		Black/tarry	Upper GI bleeding, iron
		Red	Lower GI bleeding, beets
		Pale	Malabsorption of fat
		Green	Infection
Consistency	Moist	Hard	Constipation, dehydration
	Formed	Loose	Diet, diarrhea, medications
		Watery	Infection
		Liquid	Impaction
Odor	Aromatic	Pungent	Infection, blood
Frequency	1–2 times per day	5 times per day	Infection, diet
	Once every 3 days	Once every 6 days	Constipation, activity, medications
Shape	Cylindric	Narrow, "ribbon-like"	Obstruction

FOODS AND THEIR EFFECT ON FECAL OUTPUT

To thicken stool, a person should eat:
Bananas, rice, bread, potatoes
Creamy peanut butter, applesauce
Cheese, yogurt, pasta, pretzels
Tapioca, marshmallows

To loosen stool, a person should eat:
Chocolate, raw fruits and vegetables
Spiced foods, greasy or fried foods
Prunes, grapes, leafy green vegetables

To decrease gas, a person should avoid:
Beans, beer, sodas
Cucumbers, cabbage, onions, spinach
Brussels sprouts, broccoli, cauliflower
Most dairy products, corn, radishes

TYPES OF CATHARTICS

Bulk-forming Increases fluids and bulk in the intestines, which stimulates peristalsis. An increase in fluid is needed.
Example: Metamucil

Emollient Softens and delays drying of stool.
Example: Liquid petrolatum

Irritant Stimulates peristalsis by irritating bowel mucosa and decreasing water absorption.
Example: Castor oil

Moistening (stool softeners) Increase water in the bowel.
Example: Colace

Saline When salt is in the bowel, the water will remain in the bowel as well. (Avoid use in clients with impaired renal function.)
Example: Milk of magnesia (MOM), Epsom salts

Suppository Stimulates bowel and softens stool.

ANTIDIARRHEAL MEDICATIONS

Absorbent Absorbs gas

Astringent Shrinks inflamed tissues

Demulcent Coats and protects bowel

TYPES OF ENEMAS

Carminative Used to expel flatus.

Cleansing Stimulates peristalsis; irritates bowel by distention. (Use 1 liter of fluid; have client hold it as long as possible.)

Colonic irrigation Used to expel flatus.

Hypertonic Phosphates irritate bowel and draw fluid into bowel through osmosis (90 to 120 mL—hold 10 to 15 minutes).

Hypotonic Tap water (1 liter—hold 15 minutes). Avoid with cardiac clients.

Medicated Contains a therapeutic agent (e.g., Kayexalate to treat high potassium levels).

Retention Oil given to soften stool (hold for 1 hour).

Saline Draws fluid into the bowel (9 mL of sodium to 1 liter of water—hold 15 minutes).

Soapsuds Irritates and distends bowel (5 mL of soap to 1 liter of water—hold 15 minutes). Use only castile soaps.

COMMON TYPES OF OSTOMIES*

Ileostomy

Effluent. A continuous discharge that is soft and wet. The output is somewhat odorous and contains intestinal enzymes that are irritating to peristomal skin.

Skin Barrier Option. Highly desirable for peristomal skin protection.

Pouch Option. Pouch necessary at all times.

Type of Pouch. Drainable or closed-end for specific needs.

Need for Irrigation. None.

*Illustrations on pp. 269–274 are from *The professional's guide to ostomy patients*. Used with permission of Convatec, a Bristol-Myers Squibb Co. Text discussion of common types of ostomies is also based on the preceding source.

Transverse Colostomy

Effluent. Usually semiliquid or very soft. Occasionally, transverse colostomy discharge is firm. Output is usually malodorous and can irritate peristomal skin. Double-barreled colostomies have two openings. Loop colostomies have one opening, but two tracks—the active (proximal), which discharges fecal matter, and the inactive (distal), which discharges mucus.
Skin Barrier Option. Highly desirable for peristomal skin protection.
Pouch Option. Pouch necessary at all times.
Type of Pouch. Drainable or closed-end for specific needs.
Need for Irrigation. None.

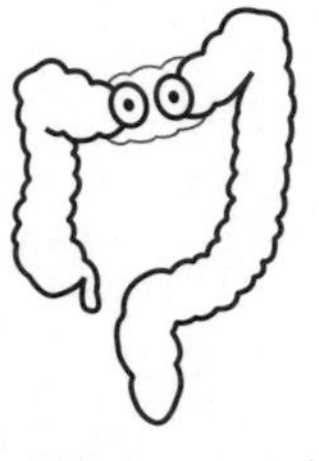

Double-barreled colostomy

Loop colostomy

Descending Colostomy/Sigmoid Colostomy

Effluent. Semisolid from descending colostomy. Firm from sigmoid colostomy. On discharge, there is an odor. Discharge is irritating if left in contact with skin around stoma. Frequency of output is unpredictable and varies with each person.

Skin Barrier Option. May be used for peristomal skin protection if pouch is worn.

Pouch Option. Pouch should be worn if person does not irrigate.

Type of Pouch. Drainable, closed-end, or stoma cap.

Need for Irrigation. Yes, as instructed by enterostomal (ET) nurse or physician.

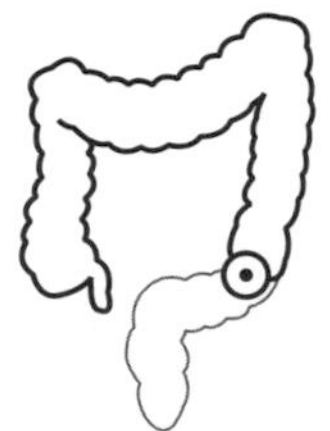

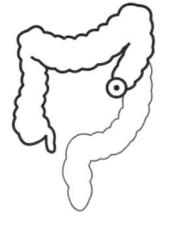

Descending colostomy   Sigmoid colostomy

Urinary Diversion (Ileal Loop, Ileal, or Colonic Conduit)

Effluent. Urine only. Output is constant. Mucus is expelled with urine. Mild odor unless there is a urinary tract infection. Urine is irritating when in contact with skin. Segment of ileum or colon is used to construct stoma.
Skin Barrier Option. Highly desirable for peristomal skin protection.
Pouch Option. Pouch necessary at all times.
Type of Pouch. Drainable pouch with spout.
Need for Irrigation. None.

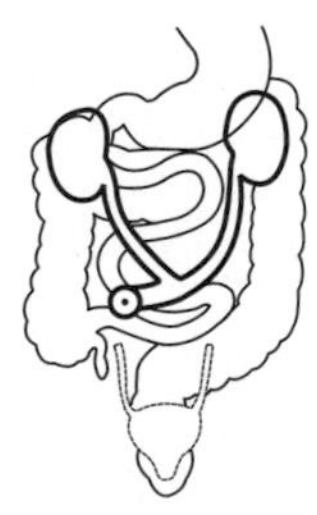

Continent Ileostomy

Effluent. Fluid bowel secretions are collected in a reservoir surgically constructed out of the lower part of the small intestine. Gas and feces are emptied via a surgically created leak-free nipple valve through which a catheter is inserted into the reservoir. For maximum efficiency and comfort, reservoir is usually emptied four or five times daily. Daily schedule for catheterization should be recommended by enterostomal (ET) nurse or physician.

Skin Barrier Option. None. An absorbent pad will provide peristomal skin protection.

Pouch Option. None—but catheter should be available at all times.

Type of Pouch. None. A drainable pouch can be applied if there is leakage of stool between intubations.

Need for Irrigation. Occasionally to liquefy thick fecal matter, the pouch can be irrigated with 1 to 1½ oz of saline or water. Specific care should be clarified by enterostomal (ET) nurse or physician.

Continent Urostomy

Effluent. Urine is maintained in a surgically constructed ileal pouch until emptied by means of a catheter inserted into the stoma. Uses two nipple valves—one to prevent the reflux of urine from backing up into the kidneys, the other to keep urine in the pouch until eliminated. Pouch is drained approximately four times daily. Daily schedule for pouch catheterization should be recommended by ET nurse or physician.

Skin Barrier Option. None. An absorbent pad will provide peristomal skin protection.

Pouch Option. None—but a catheter should be available at all times.

Type of Pouch. None. A urostomy pouch can be applied if there is leakage of urine between intubations.

Need for Irrigation. Irrigate daily with 1 to $1\frac{1}{2}$ oz of saline solution and repeat several times as needed until the returns are clear. Specific care should be clarified by ET nurse or physician.

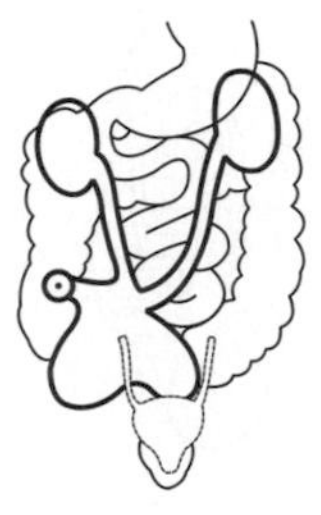

Chapter 14

Urinary System

For an in-depth study of the urinary system, consult the following publications:

AJN/Mosby: *Nursing board's review for the NCLEX-RN examination*, ed 10, St. Louis, 1997, Mosby.

Austrin MG, Austrin HR: *Learning medical terminology*, ed 9, St. Louis, 1998.

Monahan F et al.: *Phipps' medical-surgical nursing: health and illness perspectives*, ed 8, St. Louis, 2007, Mosby.

Patton KT, Thibodeau GA: *Handbook of anatomy and physiology*, St. Louis, 2000, Mosby.

Potter PA, Perry AG: *Fundamentals of nursing*, ed 7, St. Louis, 2008, Mosby.

ORGANS OF THE URINARY SYSTEM

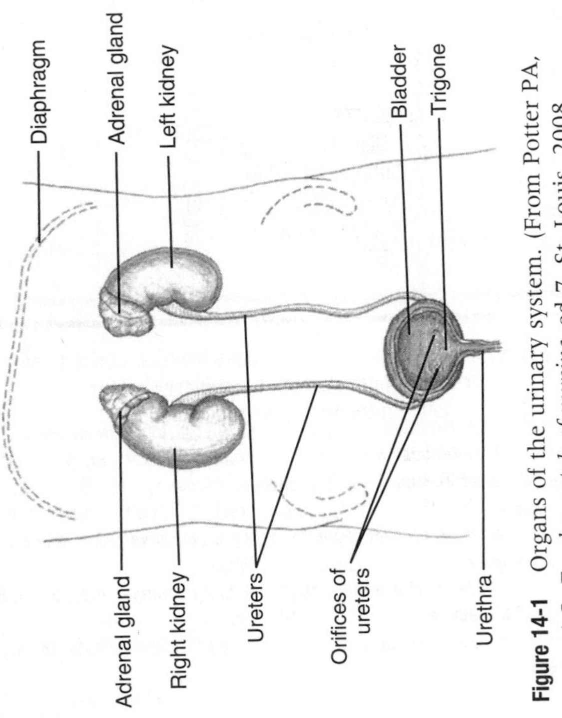

Figure 14-1 Organs of the urinary system. (From Potter PA, Perry AG: *Fundamentals of nursing*, ed 7, St. Louis, 2008, Mosby.)

Altered Urinary Patterns

Pattern	Description	Assess for
Anuria	No urination	Renal failure, dehydration, obstruction
Dysuria	Painful urination	Infection, injury, frequency, blood
Frequency	Voiding small amounts	Infection, injury, pregnancy, stress, intake
Incontinence	Difficulty with control	Infection, injury, distended bladder
Nocturia	Urinating at night	Infection, injury, pregnancy, stress, intake
Oliguria	Little urination	Infection, injury, BUN, dehydration, kidney, disease
Polyuria	Increased urination	Infection, injury, alcohol, diabetes, caffeine, diuretics, increased thirst, dehydration
Retention	Holding on to urine	Infection, injury, pain, distended bladder, medications, restlessness, surgical, complications
	No urination	
Residual	Urine remaining in bladder after voiding	Infection, distention, pain, injury
Urgency	Urgent and immediate need to void	Infection

Urinary Incontinence			
Type	**Description**	**Causes**	**Symptoms**
Function	Involuntary and unpredictable with intact urinary and nervous systems	Changes in environment or cognitive deficits	Urge to void that causes loss of urine
Reflex	Involuntary and occurring at predictable intervals	Anesthesia, medications, spinal cord dysfunction	Lack of urge to void
Stress	Intra-abdominal pressure causes leakage	Coughing, laughing, obesity, pregnancy, weak muscles	Urgency and frequency
Urge	Involuntary passage of urine with strong urgency	Small bladder capacity, bladder irritation, alcohol, caffeine	Bladder spasms, urgency and frequency
Total	Uncontrolled and continuous loss of urine	Neuropathy, trauma, fistula between bladder and vagina	Constant flow, nocturia Unaware of incontinence

Urine Characteristics

Characteristics	Normal	Abnormal	Asses for
Amount in 24 hours	1200 mL	<1200 mL	Renal failure
	1500 mL	>1500 mL	Fluid intake
Color	Straw	Amber	Dehydration, fluid intake
		Light straw	Overhydration
		Orange	Medications
		Red	Blood, injury, medications
Consistency	Clear	Cloudy, thick	Infection
Odor	Faint	Offensive	Infection, medications
Sterile	Yes	Organisms	Infection, poor hygiene
pH	4.5	<4.5	Infection
	8.0	>8.0	Diabetes, starvation, dehydration
Specific gravity	1.010	<1.010	Diabetes insipidus, kidney failure
	1.025	>1.025	Diabetes, underhydration
Glucose	None	Present	Diabetes
Ketones	None	Present	Diabetes, starvation, vomiting
Blood	None	Present	Tumors, injury, kidney disease

MEDICATIONS THAT MAY DISCOLOR URINE

Dark Yellow

- Vitamin B_2

Orange

- Sulfonamide
- Phenazopyridine HCl (Pyridium)
- Warfarin (Coumadin)

Pink or Red

- Thorazine
- Ex-Lax
- Phenytoin (Dilantin)

Green or Blue

- Amitriptyline
- Methylene blue
- Triamterene (Dyrenium)

Brown or Black

- Iron
- Levodopa
- Nitrofurantoin
- Metronidazole (Flagyl)

REASONS FOR URINARY CATHETERS

Intermittent

- Relieve bladder distention
- Obtain a sterile specimen
- Assessment of residual urine
- Long-term management of spinal cord clients

Short-Term Indwelling

- After surgery
- Prevention of urethral obstruction
- Measurement of output in bedridden clients
- Bladder irrigation

Long-Term Indwelling

- Severe urinary retention
- Avoidance of skin rashes or infections

TYPES AND SIZES OF URINARY CATHETERS

Type	Size
Single lumen	8F to 18F (French*)
Double lumen	
With inflated balloon	8F to 10F with 3-mL balloon 12F to 30F with 5- to 30-mL balloon
Common male sizes	16F to 18F
Common female sizes	12F to 16F

Triple lumen is used for continuous bladder irrigation. Coudé-tip catheter is used for men with an enlarged prostate gland.

PREVENTING URINARY CATHETER INFECTIONS

- Use good handwashing techniques before handling.
- Avoid raising the drainage bag above the bladder.
- Allow urine to drain freely into bag.
- Perform good perineal care on client.
- Secure catheter per procedure.
- Empty drainage bag at least every 8 hours.
- Avoid kinking the tubing.
- Clean spigot thoroughly before and after use.
- Avoid dragging drainage bag on the floor.

*The larger the number, the larger the size.

TIMED URINE TESTS

Quanititative albumin (24 hours) Determines albumin lost in urine as a result of kidney disease, hypertension, or heart failure

Amino acid (24 hours) Determines presence of congenital kidney disease

Amylase (2, 12, and 24 hours) Determines presence of disease of the pancreas

Chloride (24 hours) Determines loss of chloride in cardiac patients on low-salt or no-salt diets

Concentration and dilution Determines presence of diseases of the kidney tubules

Creatinine clearance (12 and 24 hours) Determines the ability of the kidney to clear creatinine

Estriol (24 hours) Measures this hormone in women with high-risk pregnancies caused by diabetes

Glucose tolerance (12 and 24 hours) Determines malfunctions of the liver and pancreas

17-Hydroxycorticosteroid (24 hours) Determines functioning ability of the adrenal cortex

Urinalysis (random times) Determines levels of bacteria, WBC, RBC, pH, specific gravity, protein, and bilirubin

Urine culture (random times) Determines the amount and type of bacteria in the urine

Urine sensitivity (random times) Determines the antibiotics to which the microorganisms will be sensitive or resistant

Urobilinogen (random times) Determines presence of obstruction of the biliary tract

Chapter 15

Reproductive System

For an in-depth study of the reproductive system, consult the following publications:

AJN/Mosby: *Nursing board's review for the NCLEX-RN examination*, ed 10, St. Louis, 1996, Mosby.

Austrin MG, Austrin HR: *Learning medical terminology*, ed 9, St. Louis, 1998, Mosby.

Lewis SM, Collier IC, Heitkemper MM: *Medical-surgical nursing*, ed 7, St. Louis, 2007, Mosby.

Patton KT, Thibodeau GA: *Handbook of anatomy and physiology*, St. Louis, 2000, Mosby.

Potter PA, Perry AG: *Fundamentals of nursing*, ed 7, St. Louis, 2008, Mosby.

MALE STRUCTURES

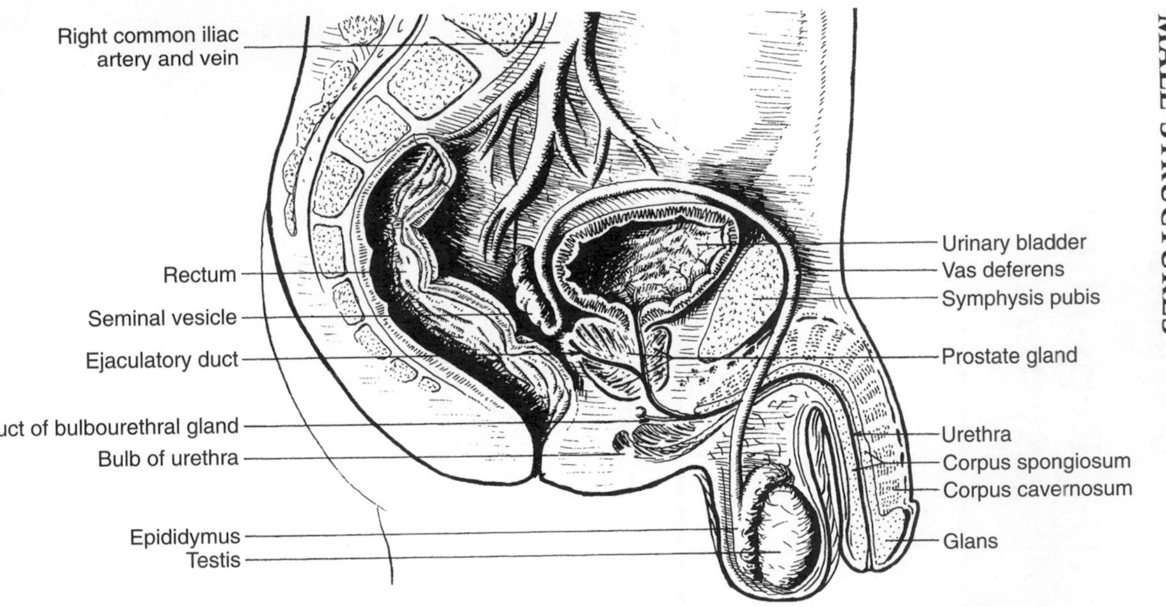

Figure 15-1 Male genitourinary system. (From Austrin MG, Austrin HR: *Learning medical terminology*, ed 9, St. Louis, 1998, Mosby.)

FEMALE STRUCTURES

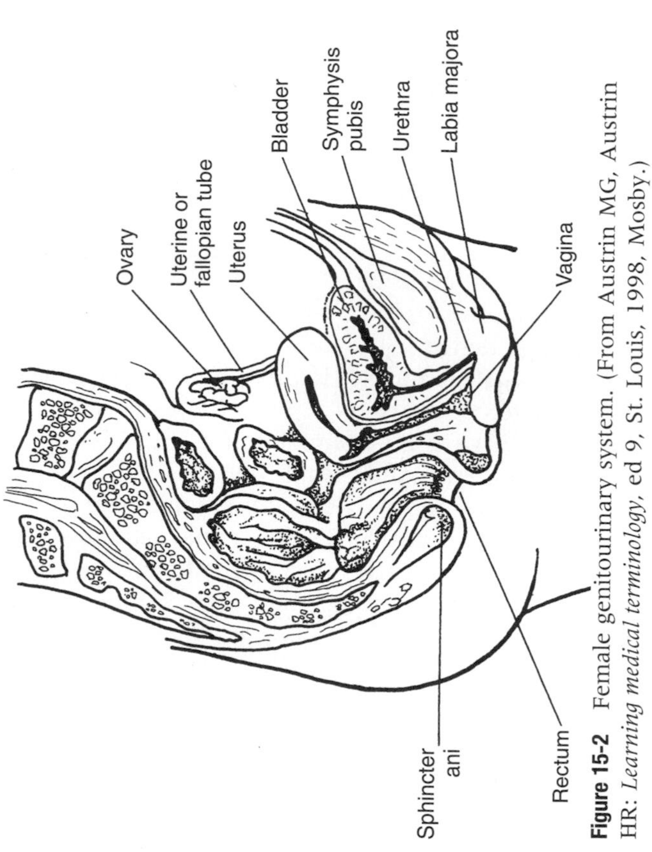

Figure 15-2 Female genitourinary system. (From Austrin MG, Austrin HR: *Learning medical terminology*, ed 9, St. Louis, 1998, Mosby.)

ASSESSING SEXUAL HISTORY

Include the following information:

Male

Practice of testicular examinations
Last prostate examination and results
Knowledge of deficit
Concerns or difficulty with sexual activities
Body image concerns
Concerns regarding the effect of treatment on future sexual activities
Attitudes regarding sex

Female

Last menstrual cycle
Onset of menopause
Knowledge deficit
Number of pregnancies, children, and miscarriages
Body image concerns
Practice of breast self-examination
Last mammogram and results
Last Pap smear and pelvic examination and results
Any concerns or difficulty with sexual activities
Concerns regarding the effect of treatment on future sexual activities
Attitudes regarding sex

MEDICATIONS THAT AFFECT SEXUAL PERFORMANCE*

Medications That Affect Sexual Performance

Neurologic Drugs

Anticonvulsants Lethargy, weight changes, menstrual changes

Antidepressants Blurred vision, confusion, loss of libido, failure to reach orgasm, and erectile problems

Hallucinogens Muscle spasms, loss of coordination, aggressive behavior, catatonic syndrome

Tranquilizers Drowsiness, confusion, and decreased desire

Cardiac Drugs

Antiarrhythmic Dizziness, headaches, weakness, fatigue, sexual dysfunction

Antianginal Headache, light-headedness, nausea, vomiting, or weakness

Antihypertensives Loss of libido, weakness

Diuretics Dizziness, headaches, weakness

Endocrine Drugs

Corticosteroids Mood changing, menstrual changes, headaches, weakness

Hypoglycemics Dizziness, drowsiness, heartburn, nausea, constipation, frequent urination

Gastrointestinal Drugs

Cimetidine Impotence, dizziness, nausea

Ranitidine Impotence, decrease libido

*Consult a drug reference book for more information on specific drugs and their side effects.

Common Male Reproductive Disorders

Disorder	Description	Assess for
Hydrocele	Collection of fluid in testes	Pain, swelling
Spermatocele	Cystic mass of the epididymis	Pain, swelling
Varicocele	Dilation of spermatic vein	Pain, swelling
Torsion of spermatic cord	Kinking of cord	Sexual dysfunction
Cancer	Testicular cancer	Enlarged testes, lump
	Penile cancer	Growths, fatigue, weight loss, dysfunction
	Prostate cancer	Urinary dysfunction
Urethritis	Inflammation of urethra	Urgency, frequency, burning with urination
Prostatitis	Inflammation of prostate	Pain, fever, dysuria, urethral drainage
Epididymitis	Inflammation of epididymis	Scrotal pain, edema
Benign prostatic hypertrophy	Enlarged prostate	Dysuria, pain

Common Female Reproductive Disorders

Disorder	Description	Assess for
Uterine prolapse	Displacement of uterus	Dysmenorrhea, backache, pelvic pain
Cystocele	Bladder herniation into vagina	Backache, stress, incontinence
Rectocele	Rectum herniation into vagina	Constipation, hemorrhoids
Ovarian cyst	Enlarged ovaries	Menstrual changes, abdominal swelling
Endometriosis	Seeding of endometrial cells into pelvis	Pain, infertility, menstrual changes
Cervical polyps	Benign tumor	Bleeding between periods and with intercourse, increased cervical mucosa
Cancer	Cervical cancer	Spotting, pain
	Uterine cancer	Pain, abdominal fullness, postmenopausal bleeding
	Ovarian cancer	Ascites, fatigue, weight loss, abdominal fullness

Sexually Transmitted Diseases*

Organism	Diseases	Symptoms	Treatment
Bacteria	Gonorrhea, chancroid, granuloma	Purulent discharge	Penicillin
Spirochete	Syphilis	Stage 1: chancre Stage 2: body rash Stage 3: tumors, nerve damage, cardiac damage	Penicillin
Chlamydia	Nongonococcal urethritis, cervicitis, epididymitis, pelvic inflammatory disease	Purulent drainage, fever, chills, pain, and vomiting	Antibiotics
Virus	Herpes, cytomegalovirus (HPV)	Vesicles	Acyclovir
	AIDS	Pulmonary infections	Antibiotics, supportive care
Protozoa	Trichomoniasis	Itching, greenish discharge	Vinegar
Yeast	Candidiasis	Itching, white, cheesy discharge	Nystatin, miconazole

*Sexually transmitted diseases are any disorders that can be transmitted from one person to another during sexual contact.

Chapter 16

Tests and Procedures

For an in-depth study of tests and procedures, consult the following publications:

AJN/Mosby: *Nursing board's review for the NCLEX-RN examination*, ed 10, St. Louis, 1996, Mosby.

Austrin MG, Austrin HR: *Learning medical terminology*, ed 9, St. Louis, 1998, Mosby.

Lewis SM, Collier IC, Heitkemper MM: *Medical-surgical nursing*, ed 7, St. Louis, 2007, Mosby.

Myers JL: *Quick medication administration reference*, ed 3, St. Louis, 1998, Mosby.

Pagana KD, Pagana TJ: *Mosby's diagnostic and laboratory test reference*, ed 8, St. Louis, 2007, Mosby.

Potter PA, Perry AG: *Fundamentals of nursing*, ed 7, St. Louis, 2008, Mosby.

LABORATORY VALUES*

Complete Blood Cell Count

Red blood cells (RBC)	Males: 4.25–6.1 × 10 mL Females: 3.6–5.4 × 10 mL
White blood cells (WBC)	4,000–10,000 mm^3
Neutrophils	Adult: 48–73% Child: 30–60%
Lymphocytes	Adult: 18–48% Child: 25–50%
Monocytes	0–9%
Eosinophil	0–5%
Basophil	0–2%
Hemoglobin (Hgb)	Males: 13–18 g/dL Females: 12–16 g/dL
Hematocrit (Hct)	Males: 40–54% Females: 37–47%

Coagulation

Platelet	130,000–400,000 mL
Prothrombin time (PT)	10–14 sec
Partial thromboplastin time (PTT)	30–45 sec
Thrombin time (TT)	Control ±5 sec
Fibrinogen split products (FSP)	Negative reaction at >1:4 dilution
Iron/ferritin (Fe) (deficiency)	0–20 ng/mL
Reticulocyte count	0.5–1.5% of RBC

*Averages may vary per facitity.

Blood Chemistry

Sodium (Na^+)	135–145 mEq/L
Potassium (K^+)	3.5–5.5 mEq/L
Chloride (Cl^-)	95–112 mEq/L
Anion gap	4–14 mEq/L
Carbon dioxide (CO_2)	24–32 mEq/L
Blood urea nitrogen (BUN)	7–25 mg/dL
Creatinine (Cr)	0.7–1.3 mg/dL (males) 0.6–1.2 mg/dL (females)
Glucose	70–110 mg/dL
Calcium (Ca^{++})	8.5–10.5 mg/dL
Magnesium (Mg)	1.3–2.1 mg/dL
Phosphorus	2.5–4.5 mg/dL
Osmolality	275–295 mOsm/kg

Hepatic Enzymes

AST	0–42 U/L
ALT	0–48 U/L
Alkaline phosphatase	Adult: 20–125 U/L Child: 40–400 U/L
Bilirubin: Direct	0–0.2 mg/dL
Bilirubin: Total	0–1.2 mg/lb
Amylase	50–150 U/L
Lipase	0–110 U/L

Urine Electrolytes

Sodium (Na^+)	40–220 mEq/L
Potassium (K^+)	25–125 mEq/L
Chloride (Cl^-)	110–250 mEq/L

Lipids

Cholesterol	120–240 mg/dL
Low density lipoprotein (LDL)	62–130 mg/dL
High density lipoprotein (HDL)	35–135 mg/dL
Triglycerides	0–200 mg/dL
Cholesterol/LDL ratio	1:6 1:4.5

Thyroid

T4—Thyroxine	4–12 ug/dL
T3 Uptake	27–47%
TSH	0.5–6 milU/L

Cardiac Enzymes

Creatine phosphokinade (CK) Levels rise 4 to 8 hours after an acute MI, peaking at 16 to 30 hours and returning to baseline within 4 days (25–200 U/L; 32–150 U/L)

CK-MB CK isoenzyme Increases 6 to 10 hours after an acute MI, peaks in 24 hours, and remains elevated for up to 72 hours

<12 IU/L if total CK is <400 IU/L

<3.5% of total CK if total CK is >400 IU/L

Lactate dehydrogenase (LDH) Increases 2 to 5 days after an MI; the elevation can last 10 days (140–280 U/L)

Acid-Base Imbalances

Clinical Manifestations	
Acidosis	**Alkalosis**
Respiratory Manifestations	
Causes	
Carbonic excess, pneumonia, hyperventilation, obesity	Carbonic deficit, anxiety, fear, hyperventilation, anemia, asthma
Signs and Symptoms	
Confusion/CNS depression	Unconsciousness (late sign)
Laboratory Values	
pH 7.25 (low) $Paco_2$ 60 mm Hg (high) Bicarbonate normal $Paco_2$ 60 mm Hg (acute) Pao_2 80 mm Hg (chronic)	pH 7.52 (high) $Paco_2$ 31 mm Hg (low) Bicarbonate normal Pao_2 90 mm Hg (high)
Metabolic Manifestations	
Causes	
Bicarbonate deficit, ketoacidosis, starvation, shock, diarrhea, renal failure	Bicarbonate excess, Cushing's syndrome, hypokalemia, hypercalcemia, excessive vomiting, diuretics
Signs and Symptoms	
Weakness, disorientation, coma	Respiratory depression, tetany, mental dullness

Continued

Acid-Base Imbalances—cont'd

Clinical Manifestations

Acidosis	Alkalosis
Laboratory Values	
pH <7.35	pH >7.45
Urine pH <6	Urine pH >7
$Paco_2$ normal	$Paco_2$ normal
K^+ >5	K^+ <3.5
Bicarbonate <21 mEq/L	Bicarbonate >28 mEq/L

ARTERIAL BLOOD GASES

Acid-base balance (pH) Measures hydrogen concentration (7.35–7.45)

Oxygenation (PaO_2) Measures partial pressure of dissolved oxygen in the blood (80–100 mm Hg)

Saturation (SO_2) Measures percentage of oxygen to hemoglobin (95–98%)

Ventilation ($PaCO_2$) Measures partial pressure of carbon dioxide (38–45 mm Hg)

Nursing Interventions

Preparation Cleanse the area over the artery per organizational policy. Collect an arterial blood gas (ABG) per organizational policy.

Post-ABG The sample will need to go to the laboratory immediately. Some facilities may require an advance call to the laboratory before an ABG test specimen can be sent.

ELECTROLYTE IMBALANCES

Clinical Manifestations

Hyponatremia (less than 135 mEq/L)

Signs and Symptoms Fatigue, abdominal cramps, diarrhea, weakness, hypotension, cool, clammy skin.

Causes Overhydration, kidney disease, diarrhea, syndrome of inappropriate antidiuretic hormone secretion (SIADH).

Hypernatremia (greater than 145 mEq/L)

Signs and Symptoms Thirst, dry, sticky mucous membranes, dry tongue and skin, flushed skin, increased body temperature.

Causes Dehydration, starvation.

Hypokalemia (less than 3.5 mEq/L)

Signs and Symptoms Weakness, fatigue, anorexia, abdominal distention, arrhythmias, decreased bowel sounds.

Causes Diarrhea, diuretics, alkalosis, polyuria.

Hyperkalemia (greater than 5 mEq/L)

Signs and Symptoms Anxiety, arrhythmias, increased bowel sounds.

Causes Burns, renal failure, dehydration, acidosis.

Hypocalcemia (less than 8.3 mEq/L)

Signs and Symptoms Abdominal cramps, tingling, muscle spasms, convulsions; assess magnesium level.

Causes Parathyroid dysfunction, vitamin D deficiency, pancreatitis.

Hypercalcemia (greater than 10 mEq/L)

Signs and Symptoms Deep bone pain, nausea, vomiting, constipation; assess magnesium level.

Causes Parathyroid tumor, bone cancer/ metastasis, osteoporosis.

Hypomagnesemia (less than 1.3 mEq/L)

Signs and Symptoms Tremors, muscle cramps, tachycardia, hypertension, confusion; assess calcium level.

Causes Parathyroid dysfunction, cancer, chemotherapy, polyuria.

Hypermagnesemia (greater than 2.5 mEq/L)

Signs and Symptoms Lethargy, respiratory difficulty, coma; assess calcium level.

Causes Parathyroid dysfunction, renal failure.

Hypochloremia (or Hypochloraemia) (less than 96 mEq/L)

Signs and Symptoms: Fatigue, weakness, dizziness.

Causes: Loss of fluid, severe vomiting or diarrhea, prolonged diuretic or laxative use.

Hyperchloremia (or Hyperchloraemia) (greater than 108 mEq/L)

Signs and Symptoms: Thirst, dry mucous membranes, tongue, and skin.

Causes: High sodium level, kidney failure, diabetes insipidus, diabetic coma.

Hypophosphatemia (less than 2.2 mEq/L)

Signs and Symptoms: Nausea, bone and joint pain, constipation.

Causes: Post stomach surgery, lack of vitamin D, high calcium levels, kidney damage, several endocrine disorders

Hyperphosphatemia (greater than 4.8 mEq/L)

Signs and Symptoms: Abdominal cramps, numbness and tingling.

Causes: Excess dairy intake, increased vitamin D, low calcium levels, kidney failure, tumor lysis syndrome.

FLUID VOLUME IMBALANCES

Fluid Volume Deficit (Hypovolemia)

Signs and Symptoms Hypotension, weight loss, decreased tearing or saliva, dry skin or mouth, oliguria, increased pulse or respirations, increased specific gravity of urine, increased serum sodium levels.
Causes Dehydration, insufficient fluid intake, diuretics, sweating or polyuria, excessive tube feedings leading to diarrhea.

Fluid Volume Excess (Hypervolemia)

Signs and Symptoms Edema, puffy face or eyelids, ascites, rales or wheezes in lungs, bounding pulse, hypertension, sudden weight gain, decreased serum sodium levels.
Causes Overhydration, renal failure, congestive heart failure.

Common Fluid Volumes*

Small glass of water: 200 mL
Small bowl of soup: 180 mL
Water pitcher: 1 liter
Ice cream: 120 mL
Juice: 120 mL
Teapot: 240 mL
Gelatin: 120 mL
Medium cup: 30 mL

Common IV Solutions

Normal saline: 0.9% saline (NS)
5% Dextrose in water (D_5W)
5% Dextrose in 0.9% saline (D_5NS)
5% Dextrose in 0.45% saline (D_5 ½NS)
Lactated Ringer's (NaCl, K^+, Ca^{++}, lactic acid)

*Volumes may vary per institution.

Drugs Affecting Hemostasis

Medication	Drug Class	Peak Time	Duration	Half-Life
Alteplase	Thrombolytic	5–10 min	2–3 hr	5 min
Anistreplase	Thrombolytic	45 min	4–6 hr	70–120 min
Aspirin	Antiplatelet	15 min–2 hr	4–6 hr	15–30 min
Dalteparin	Anticoagulant	3–5 hr	12 hr	3.5 hr
Dipyridamole	Antiplatelet	75 min (PO)	3–4 hr	10 hr
		6.5 min (IV)	30 min	10 hr
Enoxaparin	Anticoagulant	3–5 hr	12 hr	4.5 hr
Heparin	Anticoagulant	2–4 hr (SQ)	8–12 hr	1–2 hr
		5–10 (min) (IM)	2–6 hr	1–2 hr
Ibuprofen	NSAID/antiplatelet	1–2 hr	4–6 hr	1.8–2 hr

Continued

Drugs Affecting Hemostasis—cont'd

Medication	Drug Class	Peak Time	Duration	Half-Life
Ketorolac	NSAID/antiplatelet	30–60 min (PO)	4–6 hr	2–8 hr
		30–90 min (IM)	4–8 hr	5–6 hr
Pentoxifylline	Antiplatelet	1–4 hr	Unknown	0.8–1.6 hr
Plavix	Antiplatelet	1 hr	Unknown	8 hr
Reteplase	Thrombolytic	5–10 min	Unknown	13–16 min
Streptokinase	Thrombolytic	30–60 min	4–12 hr	23 min
Sulfinpyrazone	Antiplatelet	1–2 hr	4–6 hr	4 hr
Ticlopidine	Antiplatelet	2 hr	14–21 days	12.6 hr single dose 4–5 days multidose
Urokinase	Thrombolytic	End of infusion	12 hr	20 min
Warfarin	Anticoagulant	0.5–3 days	2–5 days	0.5–3 days

Data from *Drug Facts & Comparisons*, St. Louis, 2002, Facts & Comparisons; *Physicians' desk reference*, ed 54, Montvale, NJ, 2000, Medical Economics.

DIAGNOSTIC TESTS

Angiography Records cardiac pressures, function, and output (Client may need special postprocedure vital signs taken.)

Antinuclear antibody (ANA) A group of antibodies used to diagnose lupus (SLE)

Arterial blood gases Measurements of arterial blood pH, PO_2, $PaCO_2$, and bicarbonate (Blood sample needs to be kept on ice.)

Arteriography Radiographic examination with injections of dye used to locate occlusions (Client may need special postprocedure vital signs taken.)

Arthrography Radiographic examination of the bones

Arthroscopy Procedure that allows examination of the joint

Barium study Radiographic examination to locate polyps, tumors, or other colon problems (Barium needs to be removed after procedure.)

Barium swallow Detects esophageal narrowing, varices, strictures, or tumors (Barium needs to be removed after procedure.)

Biopsy Removal of specific tissue (Assess client for pain after procedure.)

Blood tests See section on laboratory values for normal values

Bone densitometry Test to determine bone mineral content and density; used to diagnose osteoporosis

Bone marrow biopsy Examination of a piece of tissue from bone marrow (Assess client for pain after procedure.)

Bone scan Radioisotope used to locate tumors or other bone disorders (Client must be able to lie flat.)

Brain scan Radioisotope used to locate tumors, strokes, or seizure disorders (Client must be able to lie flat.)

Bronchoscopy Inspection of the larynx, trachea, and bronchi with flexible scope (Client may need sedation.)

Cardiac catheterization Uses dye to visualize the heart's arteries (Client may need special postprocedure vital signs taken.)

Chest X-ray (radiograph) Used to look for pneumonia, cancer, and other diseases of the lung

Cholangiography Radiographic examination of the biliary ducts

Cholecystography Radiographic examination of the gallbladder

Colonoscopy Uses flexible scope to view colon (Client may need to be sedated.)

Colposcopy Examination of the cervix and vagina

Computed tomography (CT) scan Three-dimensional radiography (Client must be able to lie flat.)

Culdoscopy Flexible tube used to view pelvic organs

Culture and sensitivity Determines source and type of bacteria

Cystoscopy Direct visualization of bladder with cystoscope

Dilatation and curettage Dilatation of the cervix followed by endometrial cleansing (done in surgery)

Doppler Ultrasound used to show venous or arterial patency

Echocardiography Ultrasound that records structure and functions of the heart

Electrocardiography Records electrical impulses generated by the heart

Electroencephalography Records electrical activity of the brain (Client should be resting.)

Electromyography Records electrical activity of the muscles

Endoscopy Inspection of upper GI tract with flexible scope (Client may need to be sedated.)

Endoscopic retrograde cholangiopancreatography (ERCP) Radiographic examination of the gallbladder and pancreas

Exercise stress test Recording of the heart rate, activity, and blood pressure while the body is at work

Fluoroscopy Radiographic examination with picture displayed on television monitor

GI series Radiographic examination using barium to locate ulcers (Barium must be removed after procedure.)

Glucose tolerance test (GTT) Determines ability to tolerate an oral glucose load; used to establish diabetes

Hemoccult Detects blood in stool, emesis, and elsewhere

Holter monitor Checks and records irregular heart rates and rhythms (generally over a 24-hour period)

Intravenous pyelography (IVP) Radiographic examination of the kidneys after dye injection

KUB Radiographic examination of the kidneys, ureter, and bladder

Laparoscopy Abdominal examination with a flexible scope

Lumbar puncture Sampling of spinal fluid, often called a spinal tap (can be done bedside)

Magnetic resonance imaging (MRI) Three-dimensional radiograph similar to CT scan

Mammography Radiographic examination of the breast

Myelography Injection of dye into subarachnoid space to view brain and spinal cord

Oximetry Method to monitor arterial blood saturation

Pap smear Detects cervical cancer

Proctoscopy Inspection of lower colon with flexible scope (Client may need to be sedated.)

Pulmonary function test (PFT) Measures lung capacity and volume to detect problems

Pyelography Radiographic examination of kidneys

Sigmoidoscopy Inspection of lower colon with flexible scope (Client may need to be sedated.)

Small bowel follow-through (SBFT) Done in addition to a GI series

Spinal tap See lumbar puncture

Thallium Radionuclear dye used to assess heart functions

Titer A blood test to determine the presence of antibodies

Tuberculin skin test Test for tuberculosis using tuberculin purified protein derivative (PPD)

Ultrasound Reflection of sound waves

Urine tests See Chapter 14

Venography Radiographic examination used to locate a thrombus in a vein

Chapter 17

Surgical Nursing Care

For an in-depth study of surgical nursing care, consult the following publications:

Beare PG, Myers JL: *Adult health nursing,* ed 3, St. Louis, 1988, Mosby.

Lewis SM, Collier IC, Heitkemper MM: *Medical-surgical nursing,* ed 7, St. Louis, 2007, Mosby.

Meeker MH: *Alexander's care of the patient in surgery,* ed 13, St. Louis, 2007, Mosby.

Potter PA, Perry AG: *Fundamentals of nursing,* ed 7, St. Louis, 2008, Mosby.

NURSING CARE BEFORE SURGERY

Teaching

Include the following information:

Smoking or drinking restrictions before surgery
Dietary or fluid restrictions before surgery
Review of surgical procedure
Postoperative deep breathing, positioning, and range of motion exercises
Postoperative pain and pain relief measures available
Postoperative activity or dietary restrictions
Postoperative dressing procedures
Review of drains, nasogastric, catheter, and IV lines that may be inserted during surgery

History

Include the following information:

Chief complaint or reason for surgery
Prior surgeries and responses or impressions
Drug allergies
Physical limitations such as vision or hearing problems, limps, or paralysis
History of smoking and drinking
Last drink or food intake
Medications and the last time taken
Nonprescription or recreational drug use and when taken last
History of strokes, heart attacks, seizures, diabetes, and thyroid or adrenal disease
Concerns, questions, or special requests
Significant other and where they can be reached after surgery

Checklist

Include the following information:

Signed consent form in front of the chart

List of clothes and valuables and their placement in a safe place

Record of vital signs and last time voided

List of prostheses such as dentures and limbs removed

List of preoperative medications and when administered

Review of preoperative laboratory values and tests

Preoperative surgical scrubbing (Figures 17-1 and 17-2)

Review of Body Systems

Note any problems, including the following:

Cardiac Arrhythmia, edema, cyanosis, chest pain, hypertension, murmur, heart rate, blood pressure

Respiratory Cough, shortness of breath, dyspnea, wheezing, orthopnea, orthostasis, diminished sounds, rate, depth

Neurologic Headaches, dizziness, ringing in ears, gait, reflexes, muscle strength, emotions

Gastrointestinal Nausea, vomiting, weight gain or loss, ulcers, Crohn's disease or ulcerative colitis, devices

Genitourinary Urgency, frequency, retention, urinary tract infections, need for Foley catheter or other devices

Skin Bruising, open sores, rashes, signs of infection, general condition

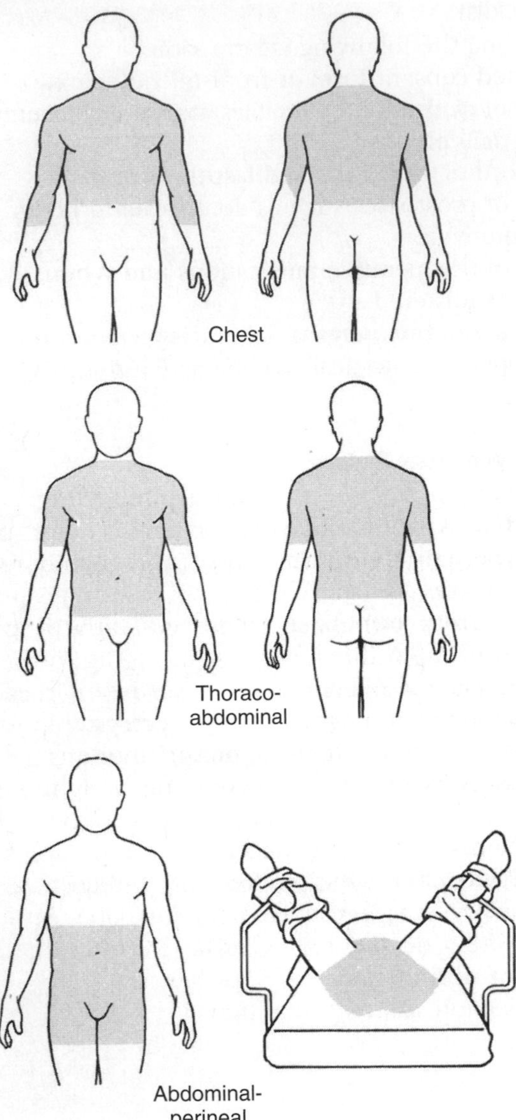

Figure 17-1 Surgical skin preparations.

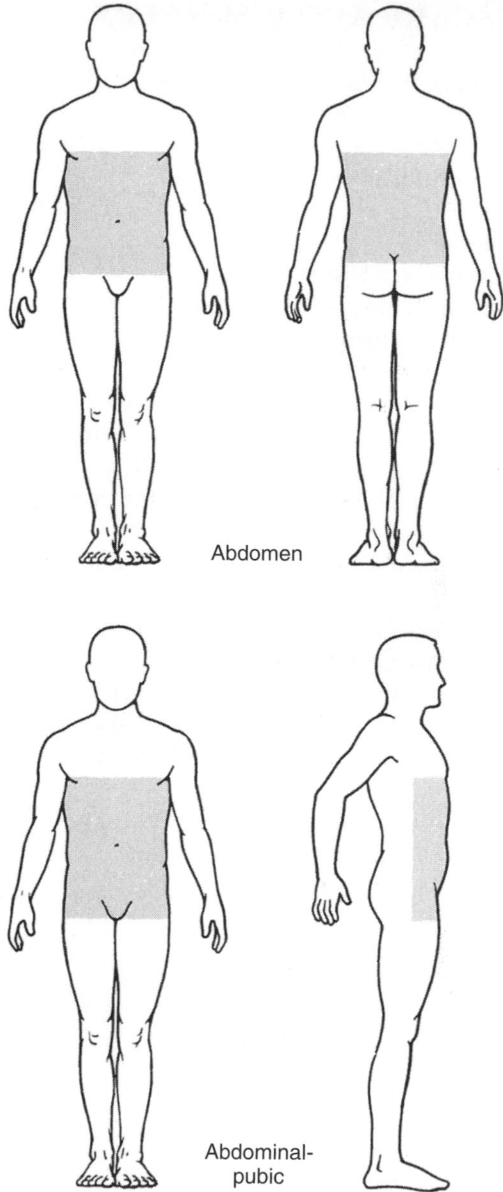

Figure 17-2 Surgical skin preparations.

NURSING CARE AFTER SURGERY

Objectives

Provide a safe environment for the client.
Monitor the client's condition.
Recognize potential complications.
Prevent complications.

Information Needed*

Type of surgery and anesthetic
Findings and results of the surgery
Any complications during the surgery
Transfusions given during surgery
Current respiratory condition of the client
Current cardiac and circulatory condition of the client
Types and number of incisions, drains, tubes, and IV lines
Current vital signs and when they need to be taken next
Current laboratory values and when specimens need to be drawn next
Dressing location, condition, and changes (the first change is generally done by the surgeon)
Neurologic status and need for future neurologic checks
Time, frequency, and route of administration of pain medications
Additional postoperative orders
Notify any family or significant others waiting for the client

*Can be found in the chart.

CARE OF BODY SYSTEMS AFTER SURGERY

Cardiac

Possibility of hemorrhage, shock, embolism, thrombosis.

Monitor blood pressure, heart rate, rhythm, quality.

Check for Homans' sign, leg tenderness, leg edema.

Check capillary refill, hemorrhage, shock, pedal pulses.

Pulmonary

Possibility of obstruction, atelectasis, pneumonia.

Turn client every 1 to 2 hours unless contraindicated.

Have client cough and deep breathe using pillows to splint incisions every 1 to 2 hours.

Assess lungs for rales, rhonchi, or wheezes.

Check oxygen saturation per policy protocol and/or with each check of vital signs.

Perform oral or deep suction as needed.

Have client use incentive spirometer as ordered every 1 to 2 hours.

Use humidification to ease breathing and chest therapy if ordered.

Ensure adequate hydration to help thin secretions and postural drainage to drain secretions.

Assess for adequate pain relief to help breathing.

Neurologic

Perform neurologic and reflex checks as needed.

Assess orientation, level of consciousness, and pain control as needed.

Assess for restlessness, fatigue, and anxiety.

Explain the need for the procedure to the client.

Genitourinary

Assess for adequate fluid intake and output and for bladder distention.

Assess the need for and care of Foley catheter or need for straight catheterization.

Gastrointestinal

Assess bowel sounds for possible ileus (indicated by no sounds).

Assess for nausea, vomiting, distended abdomen, and gas pains.

Skin

Assess wound for drainage and signs of infection.

Assess for skin breakdown.

TYPES OF DRESSINGS

Name	Uses
Absorbent	Drains wound (increases evaporation)
Antiseptic	Prevents infection
Dry	With wound with little or no drainage
Hot/moist	Promotes wound healing by second or third intention; increases blood supply to wound
Occlusive	Prevents invasion of bacteria
Protective	Protects wound from injury
Wet to damp	Dressing removed before wound dries
Wet to dry	With open wound that has necrotic tissue; wound with greatest drainage
Wet to wet	With wound that needs to be kept very moist

COMMON SURGICAL PROCEDURES*

Anastomosis Creation of a passage between two vessels

Angiectomy/angioplasty Removal/repair of a vessel

Aortotomy Incision into the aorta

Arteriectomy/arterioplasty Removal/repair of an artery

Arthrectomy/arthroplasty Removal/repair of a joint

Atriotomy Incision into an atrium of heart

Biopsy Incision to remove a tissue sample

Bronchotomy/bronchoplasty Incision into repair of bronchus

Cholecystectomy Removal of the gallbladder

Choledochectomy Removal of a portion of the common bile duct

Colectomy Partial removal of the colon

Coronary artery bypass graft (CABG) A large vein from the body is removed and sutured to either side of an obstructed coronary artery

Craniectomy/cranioplasty Removal/repair of a portion of the skull

Cystectomy/cystoplasty Removal/repair of the bladder

Dermabrasion Surgical removal of epidermis or a portion of the dermis

Embolization Suturing or sealing of a vessel

Esophagectomy/esophagoplasty Removal/repair of the esophagus

Fasciectomy/fascioplasty Removal/repair of the fascia

Gastrectomy/gastroplasty Removal/repair of the stomach

*Refer to sections on prefixes and suffixes to build surgical vocabulary.

Graft Surgical replacement of tissue, skin, or muscle

Hysterectomy Removal of the uterus

Laminectomy Removal of the posterior arch of a vertebra

Laryngectomy/laryngoplasty Removal/repair of the larynx

Lymphangiectomy/lymphangioplasty Removal/repair of a lymph vessel

Mastectomy/mastopexy Removal/reduction of a breast

Myectomy/myoplasty Removal/repair of an ovary

Nephrectomy Removal of a kidney

Oophorectomy/oophoroplasty Removal/repair of a testicle

Orchiectomy/orchioplasty Removal/repair of a testicle

Osteoclasis Reconstruction of a fractured bone

Percutaneous transluminal coronary angioplasty (PTCA) A balloon procedure used to push an obstruction against a vessel wall to allow blood to flow through

Pericardiectomy Removal of the pericardium

Phlebectomy/phleboplasty Removal/repair of a vein

Pneumonectomy Removal of a lung

Radical mastectomy Removal of a breast, pectorals, lymph nodes, and skin

Rhinoplasty Plastic repair of the nose

Splenotomy/splenorrhapy Incision into/repair of the spleen

Thoracoplasty Removal of a rib to allow collapse of the lungs

Valvulotomy/valvuloplasty Incision into/repair of a valve

RED BLOOD CELL TRANSFUSIONS

Typing Selecting the ABO blood type and Rh antigen factor of a person's blood (other antigens can also affect transfusion compatibility)

Cross-matching Mixing the recipient's serum with the donor's red blood cells in a saline solution; if no agglutination occurs, the blood may be safely given

Blood Type	Can Generally Donate to	Can Generally Receive From
A–	A–, A+	A–, O–
B–	B–, B+	B–, O–
AB–	AB–, AB+	AB–, A–, B–, O–
A+	A+	A+, A–, O+, O–
B+	B+	B+, B–, O+, O–
AB+	AB+	All blood types
O–	All blood types	O–
O+	O+, A+, B+, AB+	O+, O–

Before Administering Blood to a Client

Check facility's policy on infusing blood products.

Check the client's ID band for proper identification.

Check the client's blood type and Rh antigen.

Get the blood from blood bank only when ready to infuse.

Compare the client's blood type with the type of blood to be infused.

Two people should check and co-sign blood.

Start infusion of blood with normal saline solution.

Administer blood at a slower rate for the first 15 minutes. Blood should be infused within 4 hours.

Use appropriate blood tubing and needles (may vary per facility).

Document action on appropriate flow sheets (may vary per facility).

Instruct client to report *any* discomfort (blood reactions).

Special vital signs are needed (may vary per facility).

Some facilities may medicate the client with acetaminophen or diphenhydramine (Benadryl) before infusion.

Blood Reactions

Possible reactions include difficulty breathing, wheezing, tachypnea, fever, tachycardia, change in blood pressure, chest pain, disorientation, rash, or hives. *If a reaction begins, stop the infusion*. Begin a normal saline flush to keep the IV line open and administer prescribed antihistamines. Notify a physician, recheck blood, retype, and cross-match. *Do not* discard the blood—the laboratory may want to analyze it for the cause of the reaction. The physician may require a urine sample from the client.

BLOOD TRANSFUSION ALTERNATIVES

Considerations for clients who may refuse blood transfusions based on cultural or religious reasons.

Volume Expanders

Crystalloid—Ringer's lactate, normal saline, hypertonic saline
Colloids—Dextran, gelatin, hetastarch
Perfluorochemicals—Fluosol DA-20

Hemostatic Agents for Bleeding/Clotting Problems

Topical—Avitence, Gelfoam, Oxycel, Surgicel
Injectable—Desmopressin, tranexamic acid, ε-aminocaproic acid, vitamin K

Techniques and Agents for Managing Anemia

Oxygen support
Maintain intravascular volume
Nutritional support
Iron
Dextran (Imferon)
Folic acid
Vitamin B_{12}
Erythropoietin
Granulocyte colony-stimulating factor (GCSF)
Perfluorocarbon solutions

Techniques to Limit Blood Loss During Surgery

Hypotensive anesthesia
Induced hypothermia
Intraoperative blood salvage
Intraoperative or hypervolemia hemodilution
Reduce blood flow to skin
Mechanical occlusion of bleeding vessels
Meticulous hemostasis

Techniques That Can Limit Blood Sampling

Transcutaneous pulse oximeter
Pulse oximeter
Pediatric microsampling
Planning ahead with multiple tests per sample

Techniques to Locate and Arrest Internal Bleeding

Electrocautery
Laser surgery
Argon beam coagulator
Endoscope
Gamma knife radiosurgery
Embolization

Chapter 18

Client Safety

For an in-depth study of client safety, consult the following publications:

Lueckenotte AB: *Pocket guide to gerontologic assessment*, ed 3, St. Louis, 1998, Mosby.

Potter PA, Perry AG: *Fundamentals of nursing*, ed 7, St. Louis, 2008, Mosby.

ADMISSION SAFETY

When a client is admitted to the hospital or nursing home, it is important that the client is aware of all equipment located in his or her room. This can prevent accidents and make the stay in the hospital or nursing home safer. Point out the following items on admission: call light or bell, room lights, bathroom, bathroom lights, nurses' station, side rails, and room number.

Make sure that all equipment is working properly.

ONGOING SAFETY

To ensure ongoing safety, take the following precautions:

Clear the client's room of excess debris.

No furniture should be blocking the doorway to the client's room.

Immediately clean up any water or other liquid spills on the floor.

Do not leave needles or other sharp items near the client.

Remove unmarked bottles and syringes from client's room.

Label all IV and central lines, and nasogastric, gastrostomy, and jejunostomy tubes.

Check all electrical equipment for proper functioning and condition.

Double check all medications before giving them to the client, referring to the ten client rights.

Double check the client ID bracelet before giving medications, performing any procedures, and transferring the client to another department for tests, another unit, surgery, or therapy appointments.

SPECIAL CLIENT SITUATIONS

Hospitalized clients with the following problems may require additional safety measures:

Alcohol Withdrawal

Signs and Symptoms. Confusion, sweating, pallor, palpitations, hypotension, seizures, coma. Protocols may vary by facility.

Withdrawal protocols may include seizure precautions, keeping the side rails up and padded, taking vital signs frequently (every 30 to 60 minutes or per hospital protocol), and close observation. Provide a safe environment. Perform neurologic, memory, or orientation checks. Document any withdrawal activity and actions taken.

Bleeding/Hemorrhage

Locate the source of the bleeding. Apply direct pressure with a clean drape. Call for assistance but stay with the client. Assess for early signs of shock such as change in sensorium and later signs of shock such as hypotension, pale skin, and a rapid, weak pulse.

Prevention. Closely supervise confused or heavily medicated clients and clients just returning from surgery. Make sure surgical dressings are secure. Encourage clients to call for assistance if bleeding begins. Document any bleeding and actions taken.

Choking

Follow standard Heimlich maneuver guidelines.

Prevention. Closely supervise confused or heavily medicated clients. Make sure clients are sitting up or are placed in high Fowler's position when eating. Encourage the use of the call lights. Assess the client's ability to chew and swallow. Order a diet appropriate to the client's eating ability. Document any choking situations and actions taken.

Drug Reactions

Assess for difficulty breathing, wheezing. tearing, palpitations, skin rash, pruritus, nausea or vomiting, rhinitis, diarrhea, and a change in mood or mental status. *These are general drug reactions, not the side effects of specific drugs. Immediately report all drug reactions.*

Prevention. Closely supervise confused or heavily medicated clients, or those clients who are taking medications for the first time. Encourage the use of the call lights should any of the signs of a drug reaction occur. *Know your client's drug allergies.* Document all drug reactions and actions taken.

Syncope and Common Causes

Neurologic Vertebrobasilar TIAs, subclavian steal syndrome, hydrocephalus

Metabolic Hypoxia, hyperventilation, hypoglycemia

Cardiac Orthostatic hypotension, vasovagal reaction or syncope

Vasomotor Obstructive lesions, arrhythmias

Assess for: Dizziness, light-headedness, visual blurring or any visual or hearing changes, weakness, apprehension, nausea, sweating, blood pressure and pulse.

Prevention or Intervention. *Stay with the client.* Help client sit or lower to chair, bed or floor. Protect patient's head at ALL times. *Call for help.* Elevate legs, assess vital signs, use ammonia (if needed), help client sit up slowly when client is ready, document per organizational policy.

THE CONFUSED CLIENT

Assess for the source of the confusion. Possible sources include age, medications, disease, and infection. The confused client may be at risk for falls.

Falls

Assess for the client's ability to ambulate, environment, mental status, medications.
Prevention. Closely supervise confused or heavily medicated clients, encourage the use of call lights or the use of night lights, raise side rails, post sign alerting others of the possibility of falls, lock wheelchair, use gait belts, encourage client to use grab bars or side rails, avoid water/liquid spills, and use nonskid footwear.

Falls Assessment checklist

One or more of the following items can place a person at risk for falls:

___ Over 70 years old	___ Weak
___ Hearing or visual loss	___ Urinary frequency
___ Disoriented/confused	___ Agitated
___ History of falls	___ Uses cane or walker
___ Does not speak or understand English	___ Psychotropic drug use
___ Diuretic use	___ Cardiac drug use
___ Electrolyte imbalance	___ Hypotensive
___ Cardiac disease	___ Neurologic disease
___ Recent MI	___ Peripheral vascular disease
___ Uncontrolled diabetes	___ Recent CVA

Restraints

When to Use

- To prevent injury
- To restrict movement
- To immobilize a body part
- To prevent harm to self or others

Restraints should be used only when all other methods of keeping a client safe have been tried.

Types of Restraints

Jackets/vests, belts, mittens, wrist or ankle, crib net, elbow.

Guidelines

- Obtain physician's order and follow facility protocol.
- Explain purpose to client; check circulation every 30 minutes.
- Release temporarily (once per hour).
- Provide range of motion.
- Document need and examination schedule.
- Report problems and tolerance; provide emotional support.

Never secure restraints to the side rails or the nonstationary portion of the main frame of the bed.

Complications

- Skin breakdown (pad bony areas)
- Nerve damage (do not overtighten, release often)
- Circulatory impairment (check for problems often, provide range of motion)
- Death (from inadequate or improper use)

Prevention

- Keep the side rails up when you are not with the client.
- Monitor vital signs and the client's drug doses and levels.
- Monitor the client's electrolytes and neurologic status.
- Reorient client to place and time as needed.
- Place call light in easy reach.
- Attend closely to personal care needs.
- Encourage family, friends, and clergy to visit often.

Comparison of Delirium and Dementia

Feature	Delirium	Dementia
Onset	Rapid, often at night	Usually insidious
Duration	Hours to weeks	Months to years
Course	Fluctuates over 24 hr Worse at night Lucid intervals	Relatively stable
Awareness	Always impaired	Usually normal
Alertness	Fluctuates	Usually normal
Orientation	Impaired; often will mistake people or places	May be intact May confabulate
Memory	Recent and immediate memory impaired	Recent and remote memory impaired
Thinking	Slow, accelerated, or dreamlike	Poor in abstraction Impoverished
Perception	Often misperceptions	Becomes absent
Sleep cycle	Disrupted at night Drowsiness during day	Fragmented sleep
Physical	Often sick	Often well at first

COMMON PSYCHIATRIC DISORDERS

Alcoholic psychosis A confused, disoriented state after intoxication

Anorexia nervosa An eating disorder; loss of appetite for food not explainable by disease

Anxiety disorder No mechanisms to block varying degrees of anxiety

Bulimia Disorder in which vomiting is self-induced after eating large amount of food

Conversion disorder Sensory or motor impairment in the absence of organic cause

Depression Feeling of hopelessness or sadness or loss of interest

Dissociative disorder Person escapes stress through memory or identity changes

Korsakoff's syndrome Delirium/hallucinations often caused by chronic alcohol use

Mania Characterized by a state of extreme excitement

Manic-depressive Mood swing of very high to very low

Paranoia Delusions of persecution or of grandeur

Personality disorder Repetitive, irresponsible, and manipulative behaviors

Phobia A morbid fear or anxiety about an item or a place

Psychosis Loss of reality

Psychosomatic Person is limited in coping skills, which produces physical effects

Schizophrenia Profoundly withdrawn from reality, often with bizarre behaviors

COMMON PSYCHIATRIC TESTS

Beck Depression Inventory Self-report measure of feelings and attitudes

Brief Psychiatric Rating Scale Standardized rating scale for person over 18 years old

Rorschach Test Ten ink blots used to analyze thought processes

Thematic Apperception Test Unstructured set of pictures for which the client makes up stories; to uncover conflict or to reveal needs

Wechsler Adult Intelligence Scale Verbal and cognitive test

TREATMENT METHODS

Antipsychotic drugs Antipsychotics and tranquilizers

Antidepressant drugs Tricyclics and monoamine oxidase (MAO) inhibitors

Antianxiety drugs Minor tranquilizers or propanediols and benzodiazepines

Behavior modification Rewards given to modify behavior

Behavior therapy Aversion therapy to modify behavior

Cognitive therapy Patient examines his or her own beliefs and attitudes

Electroconvulsive therapy Shock therapy given to the brain to induce a seizure

Insulin therapy Places client in coma; to treat schizophrenics

Prefrontal lobotomy Frontal lobes of the brain are separated

Psychoanalytic therapy Therapy to gain insight into the origins of the condition

Psychotherapies Group therapy of psychiatric disorders

EMERGENCIES

Fire Safety

RACE—Rescue clients, **A**lert others/pull **A**larm, **C**ontain fire, **E**xtinguish fire. Know the facility's emergency telephone number. Know your location. Speak clearly. Know the facility's fire drill and evacuation plan. Close windows and doors. Turn off oxygen supply. All extinguishers are labeled A, B, C, or D according to the types of fires they are meant to extinguish. Some extinguishers can be used for more than one type of fire and will be labeled with more than one letter. The types of fires the letters correspond to are:

A: Paper or wood
B: Liquid or gas
C: Electrical
D: Combustible metal

Any of the following emergencies may require CPR.

Heart Attack

Signs and Symptoms. Chest pain; shortness of breath; dyspnea; a squeezing, crushing, or heavy feeling in the chest; lightheadedness; pain in left arm or in the jaw; nausea.
Intervention. Calm the client and turn on the call light. Begin oxygen at 2 liters if nearby. Remain calm and stay with the client until help arrives. Document symptoms and actions taken.

Pulmonary Embolism

Signs and Symptoms. Chest pain, shortness of breath, dyspnea, cyanosis, and possible death.
Causes. Immobility, deep vein thrombosis.
Intervention. Calm client and turn on the call light. Begin oxygen at 2 liters if nearby. Remain calm and stay with the client until help arrives. Document symptoms and actions taken.

Prevention. Elevate legs, use antiembolism stockings, dorsiflexion of foot, perform range of motion exercises, check Homans' sign, perform coughing and deep breathing exercise, and administer low dosages of heparin as prescribed while client is hospitalized. Do not massage lower legs.

Cardiac Arrest

Remain calm and turn on the call light. Begin CPR (follow standard guidelines) until more experienced staff arrives and takes over. Clear furniture from the room and ask family to move to waiting area. (Some facilities will allow family to watch CPR activity.)

Seizures

Sign and Symptoms

Grand mal Total body stiffness, staring, jerking muscles

Petit mal Daydreaming, staring

Causes. Neurologic disease, cancer, head injury, fever, or pregnancy-induced hypertension.

Interventions. Remain calm and turn on the call light. Ensure the client's safety, lower the bed, and raise side rails. Stay with the client, time the seizure, and make sure the client does not hit his or her head. Document seizure activity and actions taken.

Shock

Signs and Symptoms

Mild/early Warm, flushed skin, changes in orientation, widening pulse pressure

Moderate/mild Cool, clammy, pale skin, hypotension, narrowing pulse pressure, sweating, pallor, rapid pulse, decrease in urinary output

Severe/late All the symptoms of moderate/mild shock plus irregular pulse, oliguria, shallow, rapid breathing, obtunded, or comatose

Causes. Hemorrhage, infection, or hypovolemia.

Intervention. Monitor vital signs, assess orientation, and keep the client warm. Record all symptoms and vital signs.

Chapter 19

Care of the Dying

For an in-depth study of death and dying, bereavement, and cultural and religious rituals, consult the following publications:

Elkin MK, Perry AG, Potter PA: *Nursing intervention and clinical skills*, ed 4, St. Louis, 2008, Mosby.

Giger JN, Davidhizar RE: *Transcultural nursing: assessment and intervention*, ed 5, St. Louis, 2008, Mosby.

Husted GL, Husted JH: *Ethical decision making in nursing*, ed 2, St. Louis, 1995, Mosby.

Kübler-Ross E: *On death and dying*, New York, 1969, Collier Books.

Kübler-Ross E: *Questions and answers on death and dying*, New York, 1974, Collier Books.

STAGES OF DYING AND GRIEF

Denial

- Client or family may refuse to accept the situation.
- Client or family may not believe the diagnosis.
- Client or family may be seeking second and third opinions.
- Client or family may claim that the tests were wrong.
- Client or family may claim that the tests were mixed up with those of someone else.
- Client may sleep more or be overly talkative or cheerful.

Anger

- Client or family may be hostile.
- Client or family may have excessive demands.
- Client may be withdrawn cold, or unemotional.
- Feelings may include envy, resentment, or rage.
- Client may be angry at family for being well.
- Client may be uncooperative or manipulative.
- **This may be the time that clients are the hardest to care for but the time when they need us the most!**

Bargaining

- Client or family may promise to improve or change habits such as quit smoking, eat less, exercise more.
- Bargaining may be intertwined with feelings of guilt.
- Bargains are often with the physicians or with God.

Depression
- Client or family may speak of the upcoming loss.
- Client or family may cry or weep often.
- Client or family may want to be alone.

Acceptance
- Client may exhibit a decreased interest in the surroundings.
- Client may not want visitors during this time.
- Do not confuse acceptance with depression.
- There seems to be a calmness or peace about the client.

INTERACTING WITH THE DYING CLIENT AND THE FAMILY

Interventions should be based on the stage of dying and grief.

Denial

This stage is used as a coping or protective function and should not be viewed as a bad quality. It can be a time when a client or family can gather their thoughts, feelings, and strengths.

You should:

- Listen, listen, listen (remember, they may talk a lot).
- Get a sense of what they are worried about.
- Be honest with communications.
- Not give the client false hope.
- Not argue with the client or family.

Anger

This is often directed at caregivers; ensure that caregivers will not stop caring.

You should:

- Not take anger personally.
- Help family not to take anger personally.
- Visit the client often and answer call lights promptly.
- Assist the family with much-needed breaks.

Bargaining

Because many of the bargains may be with a divine power, the period may pass unnoticed.

You should:

- Offer frequent chances for the client or family to talk.
- Offer visits from clergy or other supports.

Depression

Some clients or families may not have a good outlet for their depression.

You should:

- Not force cheerful or important conversation.
- Allow the client or family to voice concerns.
- Offer visits from clergy.
- Offer cultural or religious supports.

Acceptance

Client may want to be alone and families may feel rejected.

You should:

- Encourage family to come often but for brief visits.
- Offer visits from clergy.
- Offer cultural or religious supports.

NURSING INTERVENTIONS WITH IMPENDING DEATH

Personal Care

- Good mouth care: keep mouth moist; do not use lemon swabs.
- Skin care: use lotions, massage, good lip care.
- Artificial tears, if eyes are open.
- Adequate pain control with medications, massage, positioning.
- Suctioning if there are increased secretions to ease breathing.
- Clean and straighten linens often.
- Change position of client as needed to promote comfort.
- Provide adequate hydration.

Recognize Special Needs

- Encourage visits by clergy.
- Assess for the need for Last Rites, Holy Communion, or other ceremonies.
- Allow for religious music, holy books, and other supports.
- Allow time for the family or friends to pray.
- Encourage cultural or religious rituals or practices.

Prepare the Family

- Describe the physical changes that may be taking place as death approaches.
- Allow the family as much time as possible with the dying client.
- Offer the family opportunities for cultural or religious rituals.
- Keep family updated as to the time of approaching death.
- Be honest when telling the family about the impending death.
- Allow for sleep and hygiene needs of the family or friends.
- Allow family or friends time to voice fears or concerns.
- Allow the family time for questions.
- Allow the family time for tears.

RELIGIOUS DEATH RITUALS

Buddhism Belief in reincarnation; Last Rites and chanting at the bedside are encouraged.

Confucianism Belief in reincarnation; burning incense and flowers are laid at the bedside to assist the spirit on its journey.

Eastern and Russian Orthodox Last Rites must be conducted while the patient is still conscious.

Hindu Patient may wish to be placed on the floor to be closer to the earth in death. Family is encouraged to wash and prepare the body. Chapters 2, 8, and 25 of the *Bhagavad-gita* and the holy book are read.

Jehovah's Witness There are no special death rites; however, church elders may assist the family with final arrangements.

Judaism (Conservative/Orthodox) The body is washed by the burial society and wrapped in white linen. No embalming or flowers are used. A cantor will assist the rabbi in the funeral. Burial should be done within 24 hours and should not be done on the Sabbath.

Judaism (Reform/Liberal) No restrictions on the time or day of removal or burial.

Lutheran May accept Holy Communion, and Last Rites are optional.

Methodist and Baptist May wish to invite religious clergy to be near at the time of death.

Mormon Anointing of the sick and Communion are encouraged. Church elder may assist the family with arrangements. The body is washed by the relief society. If the person has been "through the temple," the person is dressed in white with a green apron.

Muslim Chapter 36 of the *Qu'ran* is read to the patient. The family will encourage the patient to recite, "There is no god but Allah and Mohammed is a messenger of Allah" before dying. The family will assist in washing the body and wrapping it in a white cloth.

Shinto All jewelry is to be removed and the body is washed and dressed in a white kimono.

Taoism The family may wish to have a priest at the bedside at the time of death.

Roman Catholic Anointing of the sick and Holy Communion is encouraged. A rosary service the evening before the funeral is often done.

RELIGIOUS PRAYERS

Jewish Prayer on Behalf of the Sick

May God who blessed those who came before us in history and in life, heal ________ who is ill. May the Holy One have mercy upon ________; O Lord, reduce the pain and bind the wounds. Give skill to those who help in healing. And speedily restore ________ to perfect health, both spiritual and physical. Amen.

A Prayer for Quiet Confidence

The Very Reverend John Wallace Suter, Fourth Dean of Washington National Cathedral 1928, *Book of Common Prayer.*

O God of peace, who hast taught us that in returning and rest we shall be saved, in quietness and confidence shall be our strength:

By the might of our Spirit lift us, we pray Thee, to Thy presence, where we may be still and know that Thou art God.

Through Jesus Christ our Lord, Amen.

A Litany for Preserving the Inner Self and the Earth

The Reverend Frederick Quinn, Chair of the Environment Committee of the Commission on Peace of the Diocese of Washington Cathedral.

Lord of the universe, you placed the earth in our trust; help us to preserve it wisely. Help us to cherish ourselves upon this earth in all its mystery. Treasure its fragile beauty and honor its diversity; help us to turn from paths of selfishness and destruction; let all creation reflect God's wonder and all creatures, in their own voices, sing God's praise.

Muslim Prayer of Healing

(The Holy *Qu´ran,* Chapter II: 153–157)
O ye who believe! Seek help with patient perseverance and prayer; for God is with those who patiently persevere. And say not of those who are slain in the way nay, they are living, though ye perceive it not. Be sure we shall test you with something of fear and hunger, some loss in goods or lives or the fruits of your toil, but give glad tidings to those who patiently persevere. Who say, when afflicted with calamity: "To God we belong, and to Him is our return." They are those on whom descend blessings from God, and mercy, and they are the ones that receive guidance.

A Hindu Prayer for Healing the Body and Spirit

May the Supreme Lord of the Universe nourish the body so that I may have only auspicious words, that I may see only good things, that I may see the divinity in all things and everywhere experience the many forms of the One Supreme God: that all people on earth may be blessed.

LEGAL CONSIDERATIONS

Coroner's case Those deaths in which the county coroner must be made aware: deaths such as homicides, suicides, and suspicious or accidental deaths.

Death certificate The legal document that identifies the date, time, and cause(s) of death.

Documentation The date and time of death, along with the health care workers' final activities, should be noted in the client's chart.

Do not resuscitate Because these words may have different meanings for different people, it should be clearly documented what the meaning is for each client. Health care facilities will want to make sure that the wishes of the person and family are being carried out completely and correctly.

Establishing the time of death Absence of response to external stimuli, heart rate, respiration, and pupillary reflexes.

Final disposition Final destination for the body. The hospital or county morgue or funeral home is generally the final disposition of the body.

Life-sustaining procedure Any medical procedure that in the judgment of the physician would only prolong the dying process.

Living will A document that informs the physician that in the event of a terminal illness or injury the person wishes to have life-sustaining procedures stopped or withheld.

Organ donations The law requires all hospitals that receive Medicare dollars to ask for organ donations on death.

Persistent vegetative state A condition of irreversible cessation of all functions of the cerebral cortex that results in a complete chronic and irreversible cessation of all cognitive functions. This condition must be documented by two physicians.

Postmortem/autopsy An examination conducted to determine the exact cause of death.

Power of attorney for health care A legal document in which a person specifies another person to make his or her medical decisions in the event the person cannot.

Pronouncement Certification as to the time of death. In most states, only a physician is responsible for this procedure.

CARE OF THE BODY IMMEDIATELY AFTER DEATH

If the family is *not* present at the time of death:

- Assess for any special religious, cultural, or family instructions.
- Review the facility's policies and procedure for preparation.
- Assess for any legal limitations in preparing the body.
- Wear gloves when preparing the body.
- The body should be placed flat, arms and legs straight.
- The eyes and mouth should be closed.
- Remove all IV lines, NG tubes, Foley catheters, etc.
- Clean away any excretions/secretions.
- Dress the body in a clean gown, if possible.
- Remove all excess equipment and trash from room.
- Set personal items (dentures/glasses) near the client.
- Pack up all other personal items.
- Document your work in the client's chart and wait for family.

If the family *is* present at the time of death:

- Allow family time to be with their loved one.
- Ask family if there are any religious or cultural rituals that need to be honored.
- Ask family for time to prepare the body.
- Allow family to assist with the body if they wish.
- Allow family as much time as possible with the loved one.
- Assist the family in packing up the belongings.
- Assist the family with any paperwork.
- Allow family to call nonpresent family members, if needed.

- Support the family in deciding on a funeral home or other arrangements.
- After the family has gone, prepare the body for removal per the facility's protocol.
- Document your work in the client's chart.

General Guidelines for Autopsies, Burial Versus Cremation, and Organ Donations

	Accepts Autopsies	Burial vs Cremation	May Donate Organs
Agnostic	Yes	Both	Yes
Amish	Yes	Burial	Reluctant
Arab	Discouraged	Burial	Reluctant
Atheist	Yes	Both	Yes
Baha'i	Yes	Burial	Yes
Buddhist	Yes	Cremation	Yes
Cambodian	Yes	Both	Yes
Catholic (Orthodox)	Reluctant	Burial	Reluctant
Catholic (Roman)	Yes	Both	Yes
Chinese	Yes	Both	Yes
Christian	Yes	Both	Yes
Christian Scientist	Reluctant	Both	Reluctant
Eastern Orthodox	Reluctant	Burial	Yes

Filipino	Yes	Both	Yes
Gypsy	Reluctant	Burial	Reluctant
Hindu	Reluctant	Both	Yes
Hispanic	Yes	Both	Yes
Hmong	Yes	Both	Yes
Islamic	Reluctant	Burial	Reluctant
Japanese	Yes	Both	Yes
Jehovah's Witness	Reluctant	Both	Reluctant
Judaism (Hasidim)	Reluctant	Burial	Reluctant
Judaism (Orthodox)	Reluctant	Burial	Reluctant
Judaism (Reform)	Yes	Both	Yes
Korean	Yes	Both	Reluctant
Laotian	Yes	Both	Yes
Mennonite	Yes	Both	Yes

Continued

General Guidelines for Autopsies, Burial Versus Cremation, and Organ Donations—cont'd

	Accepts Autopsies	Burial vs Cremation	May Donate Organs
Mormon	Yes	Burial	Yes
Native American	Reluctant	Both	Reluctant
Quaker	Yes	Cremation	Yes
Russian Orthodox	Yes	Both	Yes
Seventh Day Adventist	Reluctant	Both	Yes
Shinto	No	Both	No
Sikhism	Reluctant	Stillborn: Burial All others: Cremated	Yes
Taoist	Yes	Both	Yes
Thai	Yes	Both	Yes
Vietnamese	Yes	Cremation	Yes

MULTIORGAN PROCUREMENT

Organs and Tissues That Can Be Donated

Organs. Heart, lungs, liver, pancreas, kidneys, intestines.

Bones/Soft Tissues. Humerus, ribs, iliac crest, vertebrae, femur, tibia, fibula, tendons, ligaments, fascia lata.

Other Tissues. Eyes, heart valves, skin, saphenous vein.

Consent Hierarchy	Potential Donors
1. Signed donor card	1. Victims of cerebral trauma
2. Spouse	2. Trauma victims
3. Adult son or daughter	3. Some drug overdoses
4. Either parent	4. Primary brain tumors
5. Adult brother or sister	5. Anoxic brain damage
6. Grandparent	6. Cerebral or subarachnoid bleeds
7. Legal guardian	

Special Notes Regarding Procurement

Procuring an organ(s) is a surgical procedure that takes place in the operating room under sterile conditions.

When applicable, after the procurement, prosthetic replacement and proper suturing are completed to restore the body to its natural appearance.

Donating organs should not interfere with funeral arrangements or with the desire to have an open-casket funeral.

There is no cost to the donating family for the procurement or transplant procedure.

Appendix

English-to-Spanish Translation Guide: Key Medical Questions

The following is a guide to help you complete the history and examination of Spanish-speaking patients. The first sets of questions are introductory and general ones used at the beginning of the examination. Questions for pain assessment follow. The rest is arranged by body system. Each system's section contains basic vocabulary, questions used for history taking, and instructions that would facilitate examination. The intent of this guide is to offer an array of questions and phrases from which the examiner can choose.

Hints for Pronunciation of Spanish Words

1. *h* is silent.
2. *j* is pronounced as *h*.
3. *ll* is pronounced as a *y* sound.
4. *r* is pronounced with a trilled sound, and *rr* is trilled even more.
5. *v* is pronounced with a *b* sound.
6. *i* and a *y* by itself is pronounced with a long *e* sound.
7. *qu* is pronounced as a *k* sound; *cu* is pronounced as a *qu* sound.

8. *e* is pronounced with a long *a* sound.
9. Accent marks over the vowel indicate the syllable that is to be stressed.

Introductory

I am ______.	Soy ______.
What is your name?	¿Cómo se llama usted?
I would like to examine you now.	Quisiera examinarlo(a) ahora.

General

How do you feel?	¿Cómo se siente?
Good	Bien
Bad	Mal
Do you feel better today?	¿Se siente mejor hoy?
Where do you work? (What is your profession or job?) (What do you do?)	¿Dónde trabaja? (¿Cuál es su profesión o trabajo?) (¿Qué hace usted?)
Are you allergic to anything?	¿Tiene usted algerias?
Medications, foods, insect bites?	¿Medicinas, alimentos, picaduras de insectos?
Do you take any medications?	¿Toma usted algunas medicinas?
Do you have any drug allergies?	¿Es usted alérgico (a) algún médicamento?
Do you have a history of	¿Padece usted enfermedad
heart disease?	del corazón?
diabetes?	del diabetes?
epilepsy?	la epilepsia?
bronchitis?	de bronquitis?
emphysema?	de enfisema?
asthma?	de asma?

From Seidel HM and others: *Mosby's guide to physical examination,* ed 6, St Louis, 2006, Mosby.

Pain

Have you any pain?	¿Tiene dolor?
Where is the pain?	¿Dónde está el dolor?
Do you have any pain here?	¿Tiene usted dolor aqui?
How severe is the pain?	¿Qué tan fuerte es el dolor?
Mild, moderate, sharp, or severe?	¿Ligero, moderado, agudo, severo?
What were you doing when the pain started?	¿Qué haciá usted cuando le comenzó el dolor?
Havc you ever had this pain before?	¿Ha tenido este dolor antes? (¿Ha sido siempre así?)
Do you have a pain in your side?	¿Tiene usted dolor en el costado?
Is it worse now?	¿Está peor ahora?
Does it still pain you?	¿Le duele todavía?
Did you feel much pain at the time?	¿Sintió mucho dolor entonces?
Show me where.	Muéstreme dónde.
Does it hurt when I press here?	¿Le duele cuando aprieto aquí?

Head

Vocabulary

Head	La cabeza
Face	La cara

History

How does your head feel?	¿Cómo siente la cabeza?

Have you any pain in the head?	¿Le duele la cabeza?
Do you have headaches?	¿Tiene usted dolores de cabeza?
Do you have migraines?	¿Tiene usted migrañas?
What causes the headaches?	¿Qué le causa los dolores de cabeza?

Examination

Lift up your head.	Levante la cabeza.

Eyes

Vocabulary

Eye	El ojo

History

Have you had pain in your eyes?	¿Ha tenido dolor en los ojos?
Do you wear glasses?	¿Usa usted anteojos/gafas/lentes/espejuelos?
Do you wear contact lenses?	¿Usa usted lentes de contacto?
Can you see clearly? Better at a distance?	¿Puede ver claramente? ¿Mejor a cierta distancia?
Do you sometimes see things double?	¿Ve las cosas doble algunas veces?
Do you see things through a mist?	¿Ve las cosas nubladas?
Were you exposed to anything that could have injured your eye?	¿Fue expuesto a cualquier cosa que pudiera haberle dañado el ojo?
Do your eyes water much?	¿Le lagrimean mucho los ojos?

Examination

Look up.	Mire para arriba.
Look down.	Mire para abajo.
Look toward your nose.	Mírese la nariz.
Look at me.	Míreme.
Tell me what number it is.	Digame qué número es ésta.
Tell me what letter it is.	Digame qué lera es éste.

Ears/Nose/Throat

Vocabulary

Ears	Los oídos
Eardrum	El tímpano
Laryngitis	La laringitis
Lip	El labio
Mouth	La boca
Nose	La nariz
Tongue	La lengua

History

Do you have any hearing problems?	¿Tiene usted problemas de oir?
Do you use a hearing aid?	¿Usa usted un audífono?
Do you have ringing in the ears?	¿Le zumban los oídos?
Do you have allergies?	¿Tiene alergias?
Do you use dentures?	¿Usa usted dentadura postiza?
Do you have any loose teeth, removable bridges, or any prosthesis?	¿Tiene dientes flojos, dientes postizos, o cualquier prostesis?
Do you have a cold?	¿Tiene usted un resfriado/resfrío?

Do you have sore throats frequently?	¿Le duele la garganta con frecuencia?
Have you ever had a strep throat?	¿Ha tenido alguna vez infección de la garganta?

Examination

Open your mouth.	Abra la boca.
I want to take a throat culture. This will not hurt.	Quiero hacer un cultivo de la garganta. Esto no le va a doler.

Cardiovascular

Vocabulary

Heart	El corazón
Heart attack	El ataque al corazón
Heart disease	La enfermedad del corazón
Heart murmur	El soplo del corazón
High blood pressure	Presión alta

History

Have you ever had any chest pain? Where?	¿Ha tenido alguna vez dolor de pecho? ¿Dónde?
Do you notice any irregularity of heart beat or any palpitations?	¿Nota cualquier latido o palpitación irregular?
Do you get short of breath? When?	¿Tiene usted problemas con la respiracion? ¿Cuándo?
Do you take medicine for your heart? How often?	¿Toma medicina para el corazón? ¿Con qué frecuencia?
Do you know if you have high blood pressure?	¿Sabe usted si tiene la presión alta?

Is there a history of hypertension in your family?	¿En su familia se encuentron varias personas con presión alta?
Are any of your limbs swollen?	¿Están hinchados algunos de sus miembros?
Hands, feet, legs?	¿Manos, pies, piernas?
How long have they been swollen like this?	¿Desde cuándo están hinchados así? (¿Qué tanto tiempo tiene usted con esta inchason?)

Examination

Let me feel your pulse.	Déjeme tomarle el pulso.
I am going to take your blood pressure now.	Le voy a tomar la presión ahora.

Respiratory

Vocabulary

Chest	El pecho
Lungs	Los pulmones

History

Do you smoke?	¿Fuma usted?
How many packs a day?	¿Cuántos paquetes al día?
Have you any difficulty in breathing?	¿Tiene dificultad al respirar?
How long have you been coughing?	¿Desde cuándo tiene tos?
Do you cough up phlegm?	¿Al toser, escupe usted flema(s)?
What is the color of your expectorations?	¿Cuándo usted escupe, qué color es?
Do you cough up blood?	¿Al toser, arroja usted sangre?
Do you wheeze?	¿Le silba a usted el pecho?

Examination

Take a deep breath.	Respìre profundo.
Breathe normally.	Respìre normalmente.
Cough.	Tosa.
Cough again.	Tosa otra vez.

Gastrointestinal

Vocabulary

Abdomen	El abdomen
Intestines/bowels	Los intestinos/las entrañas
Liver	El hígado
Nausea	Náusea
Gastric ulcer	La úlcera gástrica
Stomach	El estomago, la panza, la barriga
Stomachache	El dolor de estómago

History

What foods disagree with you?	¿Qué alimentos le caen mal?
Do you get heartburn?	¿Suele tener ardor en el pecho?
Do you have indigestion often?	¿Tiene indigestión con frecuencia?
Are you going to vomit?	¿Va a vomitar (arrojar)?
Do you have blood in your vomit?	¿Tiene usted vómitos con sangre?
Do you have abdominal pain?	¿Tiene dolor en el abdomen?
How are your stools?	¿Cómo son sus defecaciones?
Are they regular?	¿Son regulares?
Have you noticed their color?	¿Se ha fijado en el color?
Are you constipated?	¿Está estreñido?
Do you have diarrhea?	¿Tiene diarrea?

Genitourinary

Vocabulary

Genitals	Los genitales
Kidney	El riñón
Penis	El pene, el miembro
Urine	La orina

History

Have you any difficulty urinating?	¿Tiene dificultad en orinar?
Do you urinate involuntarily?	¿Orina sin querer?
Do you have a urethral discharge?	¿Tiene descho de la uretra?
Do you have burning with urination?	¿Tiene ardor al orinar?

Musculoskeletal

Vocabulary

Ankle	El tobillo
Arm	El brazo
Back	La espalda
Bones	Los huesos
Elbow	El codo
Finger	El dedo
Foot	El pie
Fracture	La fractura
Hand	La mano
Hip	La cadera
Knee	La rodilla
Leg	La pierna
Muscles	Los músculos
Rib	La costilla
Shoulder	El hombro
Thigh	El muslo

History

Did you fall and how did you fall?	¿Se cayó, y cómo se cayó?
How did this happen? How long ago?	¿Cómo sucedío esto? ¿Cuánto tiempo hace?

Examination

Raise your arm.	Levante el brazo.
Raise it more.	Más alto.
Now the other.	Ahora el otro.
Stand up and walk.	Parese y camine.
Straighten your leg.	Enderece la pierna.
Bend your knee.	Doble la rodilla.
Push	Empuje
Pull	Jale
Up	Arriba
Down	Abajo
In/out	Adentro/afuera
Rest	Descanse
Kneel	Arrodíllese

Neurologic

Vocabulary

Brain	El cerebro
Dizziness	El vértigo, el mareo
Epilepsy	La epilepsia
Fainting spell	El desmayo
Unconscious	La insensibilidad (inconsiente)

History

Have you ever had a head injury?	¿Ha tenido alguna vez daño a la cabeza?
Do you have convulsions?	¿Tiene convulsiones?
Do you have tingling sensations?	¿Tiene hormigueos?

Do you have numbness in your hands, arms, or feet?	¿Siente entumecidos las manos, los brazos, o los pies?
Have you ever lost consciousness? For how long?	¿Perdió alguna vez el sentido? (inconsiente) ¿Por cuánto tiempo?
How often does this happen?	¿Con qué frecuencia ocurre esto?

Examination

Squeeze my hand.	Apriete mi mano.
Can you not do it better than that?	¿No puede hacerlo más fuerte?
Turn on your left/right side.	Voltéese al lado izquierdo/al lado derecho.
Roll over and sit up over the edge of the bed.	Voltéese y siéntese sobre el borde del la cama.
Stand up slowly. Put your weight only on your right/left foot.	Párese despacio. Ponga peso sólo en el pie derecho/izquierdo.
Take a step to the side.	Dé un paso al lado.
Turn to your left/right.	Doble a la izquierda/derecha.
Is this hot or cold?	¿Está frío o caliente esto?
Am I sticking you with the point or the head of the pin?	¿Le estoy pinchando con la cabeza del alfiler?

Endocrine/Reproductive

Vocabulary

Uterus	El útero, la matríz
Vagina	La vagina

History

Have you had any problems with your thyroid?	¿Ha tenido alguna vez problemas con tiroides?
Have you noticed any significant weight gain or loss?	¿Ha notado pérdida o aumento de peso?
What is your usual weight?	¿Cuál es su peso usual?
How is your appetite?	¿Qué tal su apetito?

Women:

How old were you when your periods started?	¿Cuántos años tenía cuando tuvo la primera regla?
How many days between periods?	¿Cuántos días entre las reglas?
When was your last menstrual period?	¿Cuándo fue su última regla?
Have you ever been pregnant?	¿Ha estado embarazada?
How many children do you have?	¿Cuántos hijos tiene?
When was your last Pap smear?	¿Cuándo fue su última prueba de Papanicolado?
Would you like information on birth control methods?	¿Quiere usted información sobre los métodos del control de la natalidad?
Do you have a vaginal discharge?	¿Tiene descho vaginales?

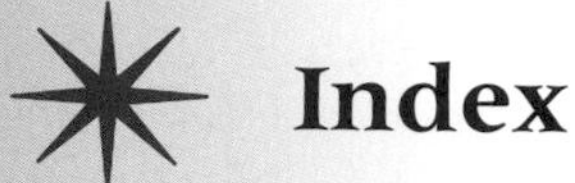

Index

f indicates illustrations

U

LOOK-ALIKE AND SOUND-ALIKE MEDICATIONS

A Common Cause for Medication Errors

Accupril	Accutane
Accupril	Monopril
acetohexamide	acetazolamide
Allegra	Viagra
Alora	Aldara
alprazolam	lorazepam
Ansaid	Asacol
Asacol	Os-Cal
asparaginase	pegaspargase
Bumex	Buprenex
Bumex	Permax
Calan	Colace
Cardene	Cardizem
carvedilol	captopril
carvedilol	carteolol
cefazolin	cefprozil
Cefol	Cefzil
Cefotan	Ceftin
codeine	Cardene
codeine	iodine
codeine	Lodine
cyclobenzaprine	cyproheptadine
cyclophosphamide	cyclosporine
Cytosar-U	Cytovene
Cytotec	Cytoxan
Darvon	Diovan
Demerol	Desyrel
Denavir	indinavir
diazepam	lorazepam
Diovan	Zyban
doxorubicin	daunorubicin
doxorubicin	idarubicin
Elavil	Oruvail
Elavil	Plavix